D1178422

THE SAXOPHONE WINTER

"One of the great charms of fiction has always been its ability to recreate the world of the author's youth as he shared it with his contemporaries, 'etherealized by distance,' as Hawthorne put it so well. If successful, such recreations send a message to readers who weren't there, either because of geography or time, of what it was like to be a human being in that particular place and at that particular time. The moving, poetic and beautifully realistic *Saxophone Winter* by Robert Harlow does all that with an intensity achieved by the masters of that most humane of musical instruments in its title."—*Josef Škvorecký*

"In *The Saxophone Winter,* Robert Harlow gives us a most appealing young protagonist, a convincing portrait of an isolated B.C. town, and a moving account of growing up at a time when the world is preparing for war. The most remarkable and enjoyable thing about this book may be Harlow's strong affection for his memorable characters—an affection I was happy to share." —*Jack Hodgins*

NOVELS BY ROBERT HARLOW:

ROYAL MURDOCH

A GIFT OF ECHOES

SCANN

MAKING ARRANGEMENTS

PAUL NOLAN

FELICE: A TRAVELOGUE

THE SAXOPHONE WINTER

ROBERT HARLOW

Douglas & McIntyre
Vancouver/Toronto

88 89 90 91 92 5 4 3 2 1

Douglas & McIntyre Ltd.
1615 Venables Street
Vancouver, British Columbia
V5L 2H1

Canadian Cataloguing in Publication Data

Harlow, Robert, 1923–
The saxophone winter

ISBN 0-88894-589-2

I. Title.
PS8515.A74S3 1988 C813'.54 C88-091064-X
PR9199.3.H37S3 1988

All the characters, events and places in *The Saxophone Winter* are entirely fictional. Any resemblance they may bear to real persons, experiences and locations is illusory.

Cover illustration by Jeff Burgess
Cover and series design by Barbara Hodgson
Typeset by The Typeworks
Printed and bound in Canada by D. W. Friesen & Sons Ltd.

For Susan (especially) and Tom Main
who knew what to do and how to do it.
And
For Salamander

CHAPTER ONE

1

THE HIGH SCHOOL BURNED IN THE LATE COLD FALL OF 1938. During that day in early December, the crispness that had been in the air for weeks became, by noon, plain cold; by four o'clock, when the sun lay chilled and dying on the horizon, the blue steel sky tightened down harder and harder so that it pressed frigid air hurtfully against the exposed skin of anyone who walked the streets of Long River. The town lay five degrees south of the arctic flatlands where the really cold weather formed and drifted south along the valleys between the ranges of mountains that upend the land in Central British Columbia.

At six, when the thermometer outside his parents' kitchen door registered twenty-five below, Christopher Waterton must have been among the first to see smoke rise straight into the clear dark sky. He'd been sitting at his homework desk in front of the bedroom window and had just finished a picture of a saxophone for art class—"Draw something useful," Blenkin had said—when he looked up. He hadn't been sure what was burning until he put on his outdoor clothes and ran a hundred yards down York Street. From there he could see the old squat bell tower on top of the high school; the smoke from the fire made it look like a chimney.

As he ran he heard the fire siren begin a low stiff growl downtown at the fire station. The growl became an undulating scream, and then he knew that the big 1914 LaFrance fire truck, with its ladders and hoses, was beginning to move at twenty miles an hour up Manchester, along Fourth Avenue and down Liverpool Street to where the school stood burning.

The school had six rooms. His own grade nine room was on the west side at the south end. Its windows were already lit by fire that flared up from the furnace room in the basement. The grade ten room had no flames in it that he could see. The fire appeared to be in the wide hallway that ran between the north and south stairs where assembly was held whenever the 180 students were addressed by Principal Grandison.

Christopher stood and watched. His school was burning. Schools didn't burn. It was as if a teacher or a father had made a mistake, lost control. It was happening and no one could shout at it and make it stop. It was *there* and fierce; it made him want to laugh, but he also wanted to see the fight between it and the firemen.

When the truck arrived, he ran toward it. There was already a crowd: one hundred, maybe two hundred. The air above the slanted shingle roof was dancing as if it were summer. Before the hoses were working the bell tower tipped and disappeared into the fire below. The flames stood straight in the air, and the water the firemen aimed at them fell back, cascaded down the slant of the hot roof, slid across the windows and froze. Christopher watched the brown-stained shingled building become an ice palace.

The violence of the fire inside the school was masked by the shell around it, but still it made the crowd silently excited. Christopher felt it too. When he tried to swallow, the muscles in his throat caught and heaved.

He saw Smith and Callaghan and then the Bells arrive and begin to run around the school; they cheered the fire and booed the firemen. The police had come on foot from their homes. They didn't need their uniforms. Everyone knew who they were. Billy MacLean, the youngest of them, caught Johnny Bell by the arm and told him he'd kick his butt up between his shoulder blades if he didn't stop asking the chief if he could get him a drink of water. The teachers came one at a time; they stood looking pale and sick about what was happening. Miss Lee, the English teacher, stood near Christopher and kept saying out loud to herself, "Fire is the worst." Then Mr. Grandison—Evil-eye Grandison, whose left eye had been shot out in the Battle of Vimy Ridge in the Great War—arrived and stared at everybody as if his good eye were glass too. He'd been principal since 1925. He paced, looked at the fire, then at the ground. Then he spoke at anyone nearby.

"We'll find who did it," he said. "It wasn't spontaneous combustion, that's certain." His voice was colder than the air. "Where's John Purvis?" he asked. "Someone should talk to him."

Why Purvis? He'd quit school two years ago. Christopher looked for him in the crowd, but he was probably at the rink helping Howard Streeter make ice. Howard would think making ice was more important than seeing a fire.

"Young Waterton," Mr. Grandison said to Christopher. "Is your father here?"

"I don't know sir, I came. . . ."

"Never mind. There he is," he said and walked ten paces, saying as he went, "Will the School Board meet tonight after they put this out? I'll need some direction about what to do."

"We'll see."

Christopher didn't need to hear his father's voice to know what he said. It was the reply he always gave to a request.

"I'll get the key to the elementary school and we can meet there. Most of the Board's here." Mr. Grandison gestured around with his hand as if he might be summoning them.

Christopher moved closer and looked at his father's face. It was never easy to see what he was thinking. He said, "I know what to do and when to do it."

The school was nearly burned, and now Evil-eye had no place to play Hitler. He was going to be only an ordinary person soon. Christopher watched Grandison see him again and then turn away once more. Christopher, who had turned fourteen in September, had been three months in grade nine. He was junior again, after grade eight, where his class had run the elementary school playground.

"If you're a bunch of rowdies, you'll be treated as such," Evil-eye had told them on their first day. They knew the speech he'd give. Half the parents in town could remember his first assembly and could tell their children what to expect. But the change that had been the hard one for Christopher was not going to high school, it was that old Mr. Charles Abling had died, after nineteen years as Chairman of the School Board. Now his father was Chairman and that was as bad as having a preacher for a father.

Flames rose thick into the black air. Christopher turned and moved quickly away from Evil-eye and his father. He heard a rumble; timbers cracked fast down a bass scale and then there was a sound like a giant drum being hit hard by something wet. The roof collapsed inward. Then the windows along the near side exploded: glass and ice floated for a long moment in the air. He stood still and watched. The firemen and their helpers ran backwards across the ice they had made with the spray from their hoses.

"Okay, that's it," the chief yelled. "We got a chance." He charged toward the north entrance. His men followed behind streams of freezing water.

Christopher stood watching the shattered ice palace. It no longer gave off a steady light but flickered a bruised red. The walls were still standing, but he wondered about the floors in the rooms, and whether his homeroom desk was burned along with the books he'd left in it. His nose was cold and beginning to run. He took his mitt off and wiped his nose with the back of his hand. Then he sneezed and felt in his mackinaw pocket for a handkerchief. A scribbler was there, rolled up; it was the one he'd had on his desk when he'd first seen the smoke, but he couldn't remember putting it in his pocket. He looked and saw that the drawing of a saxophone was in it, protected from wrinkling between its pages. He blew his nose through his fingers onto the snow as he'd seen men do and put the drawing back into the scribbler so it wouldn't be ruined. The saxophone was near-perfect. He'd stared so long at Gabe Sommerville's horn when Gabe played Saturdays at the Royal Ballroom that he knew where every pad and key was and how the curves of the instrument went. Blenkin might not accept that a saxophone was useful, but Christopher wanted him to like the idea. Blenkin taught P.E., as well as Art and Junior Business, and there was no turning around in town without running into him. Clarence Blenkin was everywhere: basketball, hockey, skiing, even church.

Christopher's mother called him Poor Clarence, as if that were his name. His father and two brothers were dentists at the coast. "Poor Clarence wound up in Long River making eleven hundred a year. No wonder he has a temper." And his father had said, "There are a lot of us who wound up in Long River, and there are men with families making a damned sight less."

As he watched the flames die, he saw Fielder arrive. His friend wore mackinaw pants, boots, two sweaters, a long scarf and a cap with earflaps, but with its bill torn off. "What IS this?" he shouted. "My God, I almost missed it."

"Where've you been?"

"My mother is having her baby. Right this very damned moment. How d'you like that?"

"You said not till after Christmas."

"My parents are so stupid they can't even count up to nine."

"Tell me. Get it over with."

"This is way more important. The doc sent the old man home to wait, so I skipped."

"Big holiday coming up. Look, no school."

"They'll save this wreck, Waterton. You watch. Your old man'll see to that just to spite me."

"The roof's gone, and the windows are blown. What's there to save?"

"My neck if we don't have Christmas exams." Fielder put his arm across Christopher's shoulders. "Ran all the way," he said. "Let's see that."

"What?"

He took the scribbler and let it fall open. "Cheater. Doing homework. What's this?"

"A saxophone, idiot."

"Who drew it for you?"

"I did. Give it, give it."

"No. Let me see. Who's it for? Blenkin?"

Christopher reached and snatched the book. The drawing fell out. "Fielder, I'll plough you." He bent down. Fielder pushed him face-first into the snow. He rolled over with the drawing carefully clutched in one mitt. Fielder danced above him as if he were waiting for an opponent to get up and fight again. Christopher got to his knees and put the picture of the saxophone safe between the pages of the scribbler. He watched Fielder along the edge of his vision and saw that he was looking at the fire now. He shoved his shoulder into Fielder's gut and watched him trip back and go down. He ran then, not away but only somewhere else to keep the game interesting. Fielder didn't follow. He liked best to lead and, most of the time, Christopher let him. They were close. People asked them: Are you brothers, twins maybe? In the years since his father had gotten his job here and they'd moved from Victoria, Christopher had had only one steady friend. "For when you need one," his mother had said. Which was right. He went with the Bells and Cameron for hockey and bobsledding in the winter and swimming in the summer. Skiing he did by himself. Fielder was someone he could argue, fight, and play games with; be crazy with. He walked backward, half waiting for Fielder, half staring at the smoking fire, and ran into someone shorter than he was who didn't make a sound.

He turned his head to see if he should say sorry. It was Emily Gordon. She always appeared as if she weren't sure which way to look, so in the end she stared into your eyes and then away and then back again. Her older sister, Pat, was in his grade nine class. She had a voice like a machine gun and a faster brain. He said sorry to the quiet Gordon and moved on toward the south side of the school where his father was now talking with Mr. Butterworth, and Mr. Kroll who owned the pharmacy. They were talking about having a school board meeting tomorrow noon. "Will we get a new school?" Christopher asked his father.

"We'll see." He glanced at the building. It was solid ice. "I'll get the chief to show me around when it's finally out."

"Wait till morning," Mr. Kroll said.

His father nodded, but Christopher knew he would stay here and see through the school tonight. "Can I come with you?"

"Go tell your mother I'll be a while," he said.

He wasn't unfriendly. It was simply that future moments interested him more than right now. "It's always fun when I get to be next on the list." Christopher remembered when his mother had said that: at dinner on her birthday, while his father had got up to go to the basement to bring back the easel he'd made for her—one she could adjust either to sit or to stand at.

He didn't answer his father. He was cold and wanted to go home anyway. The innards of the school were smouldering; the hoses were freezing out the last of the blaze. The crowd was leaving. He looked for Fielder, but he was probably gone too. He'd come to the fire without permission, and there was his sister to sit with if his father wanted to go back to the hospital to see the baby.

He turned once more toward the school. Now it looked half-destroyed instead of burned—as if an airplane had crashed through its roof. The ice on its sides was black. The spotlight from the fire truck and the glow from the street lights made peculiar shadows. He backed up the slant of the hill on the southwest side of the building, and the changing perspective made a different picture. The school was not totally burned, only gutted. His father would find a way to rebuild it. When he got home, he'd sit in the living room thinking it out while he pretended to read *Popular Mechanics* or a spring seed catalogue.

He thought about having to redraw the saxophone for Blenkin. He looked at his thick-mitted hand and saw that the scribbler wasn't there, but his fingers still thought they held it. He looked at his other hand. That mitt didn't have hold of it either. He felt stupid standing and clutching at nothing. He could produce another drawing, even better than the last one, in less than an hour. But the scribbler had his math in it.

Then he saw in the dimness Emily Gordon walk toward him. She held the scribbler and drawing in her gloved hands. She had on boots and heavy blue ski pants and a red ski jacket with a hood that peaked above her face.

"Thanks," he said, and took the scribbler from her.

She pointed to the drawing. "What's this all about?"

He laughed, surprised and then awkward. She switched her weight from one foot to the other and then back again, more excited than nervous, and she drew her breath in over a laugh of her own that he'd not heard before.

"It's a saxophone." He took the drawing from her.

"I know." She moved, a little hunch-shouldered, like an athlete, and as if she were starting to leave.

"It's for Art," he said. "Blenkin."

"It looks very good."

"It is." He knew that for once he wasn't boasting.

"I don't think I've seen a real saxophone, ever."

"Gabe Sommerville plays one at the Royal on Saturdays."

"You go there? Your mum and dad let you?"

He shook his head. "Not really. After the early show on Saturdays I go there and watch for a while."

She backed a step or two away and began to turn toward her part of town. Then she stopped and faced York Street where he lived. "I forgot. I'm supposed to eat with my grandmother tonight."

"I should wait for my dad," he said. The lie cut him off from his real feelings: he wanted Emily to tell him again that she liked the saxophone. "What time is it?" He looked at her to keep her from moving away.

"Seven, half past?" She shrugged. Gran'll keep something hot for me."

"I have to do the drawing over now," he told her, and let that be the reason to leave his father behind. He thought there would be words to say to her, but after ten steps he knew there weren't any in his head. He held the scribbler carefully so that it fell open, and put the drawing inside it. The cold was getting to him. He shivered.

"Don't throw it away," Emily said.

"I do a lot of them." Then there were the words his feelings wanted. "It's the only thing I can draw. I'm stupid at Art."

"No you're not. It's awfully good."

"Three-and-a-half out of ten is my top mark." He laughed and they bumped in the dark on York Street. A bump, not a touch, but it made him remember Marjorie when he'd been five. They'd touched, hugged and kissed, and her mother had been very angry. His own mother had laughed.

Halfway up the hill, she said, "Do you want one? A saxophone?"

"Wouldn't do much good if I did."

"*Do* you?"

"Yes." Under her grandmother's streetlight he stopped and exposed the drawing again. "It's a curved piece of pipe," he said, and he knew he was sounding like his father. "See those? They're the pads and keys to make the notes. If they're all up it's a high note."

"What's that?" She pointed.

He traced the line he'd drawn just above the long curved surface of the saxophone's neck. It ended at a final small pad near the mouthpiece. "Gabe says it's the octave key. You work it with your thumb and when it's off its hole it makes everything eight notes higher.

"You blow in there?"

"Yes, it has a reed on it that makes the sound." He looked at Emily. She was standing square on the sidewalk, feet apart, her arms by her sides and her head back so she could see past the hair that had come out from under her fur-trimmed hood. He held the drawing out to her. "Do you want it?" She took it, and he rolled the scribbler up in his hand.

"Thanks," she said, and smiled at him.

"I could make you another if that's too wrecked."

She shook her head. "This is fine."

Her Grandmother McLeod shouted from the fog made by her open front door. "Emily, is that you? Who're you with?"

"Christopher."

"Christopher who?"

"Waterton."

"Well, is he coming in, dear, or what? Aren't you cold?"

"We've been to the fire at the school, Gran."

"And I've been on the phone for an hour with people giving me the news. Now come in and eat, both of you."

"I can't, Mrs. McLeod," Christopher said, and backed away. "I'm due home." He waved to Emily and began to run up York Street. Then, having escaped Mrs. McLeod, he turned and saw Emily still on her grandmother's porch. She was brushing the snow off her feet with a broom. He stood in the middle of the street and watched for her to look around at him, but she opened the door, went in and closed it behind her. He began to walk up the hill, but his mind wouldn't let her go.

She was only in grade eight.

She was lucky to have a grandmother to visit.

Emily's eyes didn't blink when she looked straight at him. He'd only seen her with Pat, her sister, and when Pat was around nobody looked at anyone else.

Emily hadn't really asked for the drawing. He'd shoved it at her, but she'd accepted it. If she took it home, Pat would see it, and ask Emily, "What're you doing with that creep?"

Nothing, Pat, nothing. I just gave your baby sister a drawing.

He began to run again.

His house had white clapboard siding and a green shingled roof that looked as if it rose up higher than it should. They rented it for thirty dollars a month. That was the only information about family finances that he knew. His parents never mentioned money, except to say that there wasn't any. But there was some. They lived on York Street. Not the best, but good. No street was rich anymore. They rented, but his father kept the house as if he owned it. Last summer, during a week of July evenings, Christopher had helped him paint the posts, stringers, and 612 white pickets that surrounded the house. And while they painted there was a question he wanted to ask, but the right moment was too hard to find. His father worked quick and silent at anything he did.

They went at it steadily. After a while it stopped being a marathon and became a test. Could he stick it out? Just work like his father until it was done, not complaining and seeing that what was happening was more than a job: it was a step toward becoming a man, someone who didn't ask for help, pulled a lot more than his own weight and did everything as well as it could be done. He hadn't failed the test, but he didn't expect he'd be told he'd passed. When they had finished the last picket and post, his father had stood up and looked at him and then down the stretch of fence along the back of the lot.

"If it was my place I'd put another coat of paint on it."

"You've given the landlord too much already."

"I live here. He doesn't." His father looked as if he might turn away, but he didn't. He hesitated, then pointed toward the fence beside the garage where their eight-year-old blue Chev was housed. "I guess you remember," he said.

"What?"

"The picket I ripped off from there and whaled you with for ruining Dan Carter's corn—you and the Bells."

"It was a stupid thing to do—the only corn anybody ever grew this far north."

"My hand on your bare rump would've been enough."

It wasn't an apology. It was a statement. It said that in all fairness he now thought the picket had been too much punishment.

"We were rotten kids."

"I don't think so."

Now, suddenly it had become an easier memory. Almost funny. Himself running around in a circle being held by his father and the picket hurting and scaring him. He laughed. His father smiled. The time for the question had arrived.

Nervous, Christopher said, "Will you give me something?"

"You mean pay you for this?"

"No. I want something for Christmas."

His father smiled again and stooped to put the lid on a paint can. "I think Christmas is a way of getting something for no work at all."

"I only want one present.

"One?"

"Just one. A saxophone."

"Those things cost money."

"I'll help save up."

"Like you did for your bike?"

"I was only eight then."

"What would you do with one?"

"Learn to play it."

"Don't you think it'd be better to learn something useful?"

He couldn't turn away now, or plead. Because he'd asked, and now there was no more to say, he waited, awkward. After a moment his father said, "A man gets the big things for himself." He picked up their brushes and the paint cans. "You did a fine job here. It's good to see you growing up."

"Thank you," Christopher said, and had wished, not for the saxophone, but that there might be some hope. In July that had been good enough.

He saw that his mother was still in the kitchen. They'd eaten at five, as they always did, almost as soon as his father got home. Christopher opened the door, curious. It was nighttime and she was baking: not always a good sign. Sarah was helping. She was cracking walnuts into a bowl, which was the kind of job she liked to do. She was big for seven years old. In another year or two he thought that maybe she could mow the lawn. He took his jacket off.

"Dad said he'd be along in a while."

"I didn't go," his mother said. "Was it awful?"

"No, what do you mean?"

She was baking because the fire had made her nervous. "Is it gone altogether?"

"No." He sat down on the high stool his father had made for the kitchen. "It's still standing. It's a big block of ice."

"I suppose," she said. "When I was eight our whole town burned.

We had to be taken away on a train. That was in 1908. I can still feel the waves of heat when we ran to the station."

He'd heard the story. He said, "Fielder was there. His mother's having the baby."

She turned from her batter. "Tonight? Poor Pamela. A month early. Everything about that baby has been unplanned."

"Fielder said his parents just can't count to nine."

She laughed then, and looked a little surprised. He liked that. "Fielder's fourteen," he told her, "his sister's seven. Same as me and Sarah. So, where's your new baby?"

She looked at Sarah. The colour in her cheeks darkened. "This is my baby."

"Some baby. Hold her on your lap and she'd break your legs." He laughed now, too, and reached over to pat Sarah on the head.

"I don't like you," his sister said.

"Yes you do."

She threw a walnut at him. He got up from the stool. The heat from the kitchen stove was too much; he found it hard to breathe. He went to his bedroom and put his math scribbler with the rest of his homework on his desk. He'd had the desk since he was eleven and he'd grown enough since then so that it wasn't comfortable to sit at. No school, no homework; but, still, he wanted to do the drawing of the saxophone over again. He picked up another piece of Blenkin's precious drawing paper, a ruler and a pencil, and went through the kitchen to the dining room. It was cool there. His mind held the curves of the horn so clear that it was as if he were tracing them onto the paper. Gradually it took shape—not a bent pipe anymore, but an instrument.

Miss Lee was a bit nuts at the fire tonight. He'd never heard her talk to herself before. He liked her. She said extra things in class that weren't in the books they were studying. One thing was that somewhere, sometime, people had thought they could draw a picture of what they wanted—a kind of future for themselves. They'd worship it or pray to it, and whatever they'd drawn was supposed to come true. What he was drawing looked good enough to worship.

He turned on the big Stromberg Carlson radio in the living room. It was nearly twelve years old, but it had ten tubes and could pull in stations from all over the continent. Long River was north and high up—a good place for radio signals to arrive on the bounce from great distances. When the tubes were warmed up, he twisted the dial until he heard dance music. At nine o'clock, stations in the United States began broadcasting from the ballrooms where the big bands played. For a year now, he'd listened until he knew all the leaders and what their orchestras sounded like. Ted Weems was at the Trianon in Chicago, Freddie Martin was at the Coconut Grove in Los Angeles, Glen Gray was at the Casa Loma in Toronto, and the big swing bands—Harry James, Benny Goodman, Artie Shaw, Glen Miller, Tommy and Jimmy Dorsey—all came to the Palladium in Hollywood. It was like travelling in dreams: you don't go, you're just there. The band that came on now was Glen Cunningham's from the Bal Tabern in San Francisco. It had a good saxophone player whose sound leapt up out of the music the band was playing.

He sat at the dining room table, and the saxophone in front of him grew more complex, and the one on the radio made him stop drawing when it soloed again. There was no one playing it: it was huge and golden, and it made music by itself. He closed his eyes and got close to it, held it, and it began to play for him. The people danced, and when it was over the people stood still in the middle of the ballroom and applauded. The more he held it, the better he knew how to play it, and one night the horn didn't have to play by itself anymore. He had become as good a musician as the man in Cunningham's band.

He put the pencil down and looked up. His mother was standing at the door to the kitchen. She had flour on one cheek and her apron needed to be pitched into the laundry basket. The music on the radio was "Deep Purple," and it featured a trombone.

"Can I see?"

He gave the drawing to her. She did watercolour paintings, good ones. "I'm no artist," he told her. "I must've taken after Dad."

"Oh, I hope so," she said, and laughed.

He was surprised. "Why?"

"Because he knows so many other things." She sat opposite him at the table, and Sarah came out from the kitchen and leaned against her mother, a pout on her face. "You always talk to Chris," she said. Her mother paid her some attention. "How many more walnuts do you have left to crack for the icing?"

"Five," Sarah said.

"Bring them and you can do them here."

He saw his mother turn in her deliberate way and look at him again. "It's a good drawing, almost too good for you." She smiled. "It shouts out how strong you feel about it."

The band on the radio was playing its theme song. The saxophone was at the heart of it, and he was afraid the words he might say to her would make her try to argue him out of wanting a horn, but he said them anyway: "It's three weeks to Christmas."

She nodded and looked away.

"Is there a chance I'll get one?"

"You wouldn't really want to know, would you?"

"Yes."

"Can't you wait a little until you're older?"

"You got paints when you were five years old."

"You got skis when we came here. And we bought you your new ones to jump with for your birthday."

"And I use them. I'll use the horn too."

"Why aren't we talking about the fire?"

"Because you hate fires, so don't change the subject."

Her eyes were as near black as they could get, and if he didn't know better he might have thought the way they reflected light meant they had tears in them. His mother wasn't a crier. "Life isn't paints and saxophones," she said.

"What is it, then?"

"I don't know, but what I do know is when you want to do something and it's just not for you, the hurt is no fun. No fun at all."

He reached across the table and took the drawing away from her. "I want a try at it. Gabe said he'd teach me."

"I know. But what is he? Lucky to be a clerk in a store. And he got that Pritchard girl in trouble and had to marry her. He drinks, he's twenty-three years old, and look at him."

"He's a nice guy."

"Not for a fourteen-year-old to be hanging around."

"I already do. I see him." He got up from the table, because he didn't want to talk about it anymore. "I've got sixteen dollars saved up. Can I give it to Dad to help buy it?"

"Why don't you ask him yourself?"

"All that would happen is I'd get told how there's no money left in the world and everyone's starving—"

"Well, they are. Would you like to have Christmas at the Isonovichs'?"

"Isonovich was at the fire. He had better clothes on than Fielder."

"Relief and handouts, Christopher. It's no way to have to live."

"Last year in grade one Sonia Isonovich never had ski pants," Sarah said. "She came to school in *dresses*, and Miss Goodman held her on her lap until she got warm." Sarah cracked the shell of her last walnut. "And then she died."

"Sonia died from diphtheria," he said, too loud, "not from no ski pants."

"One probably caused the other," his mother said. "These aren't good days at all."

The way she said them, the words sounded as if they'd come from the Bible, and they settled like cold stones in his gut. "But you can still paint," he told her, and switched off the radio. The silence made him angry. She did paint. All the time. She was up there in the attic, with its windows on the north slope of the roof, and she had her easel there and canvas and pieces of board and paper and paints. In the summer she sketched outside. His father never complained. He thought she was beautiful and he loved her. Fielder's parents shouted at each other anytime, anywhere. Some guys had fathers who'd skipped out, and the Isonovichs were rich compared to them. His father hugged his mother. She let him, and always kissed him back whenever he came home, before he sat in his chair to read, or go down to the basement to build something.

He came in now, through the back door. Boots in the closet, mackinaw, scarf, hat all hung up. Slippers on. Sarah went to be hugged by him, and she wanted to be held by the hands so she could flip over backward and land on her feet. Christopher went through the dining room to the kitchen door and listened to them talk. The school wasn't a total loss, but it was a wreck. The first thing to do was get a roof on it and the windows back in so the central hall could be rebuilt. The damage to the rooms was mostly from water and smoke and, he said, "from firemen running around hosing and axing everything in sight. They don't open doors, they break them down." With only ten days to the Christmas holidays, he was going to recommend to the School Board that it extend the holiday and get a contractor to clean up and repair the building by mid-January if possible.

"Who?" his mother asked.

His father shrugged. "Brant. I'd like that. He hasn't had a real job in over a year."

"Mayor Courtney will want Sanderson to have it."

"Maybe. We'll see. Brant's a good man."

"Courtney won't like it."

"Courtney's the Mayor. I'm the Board Chairman and this is my business."

"The very new Board Chairman," she said, and shook her head. "The stories about that man—deals, women. . . ."

"The man is new, the chair is old," he said.

The big difference between them was that he never bothered with side issues in an argument. Christopher saw his father look at him. "You'll have extra time to ski, Chris."

He spoke without thinking. "I'd rather be playing a saxophone." He said it and then was afraid, embarrassed too, because his father looked at him as if he were retarded.

"The boy has a one-track mind."

"I'm not going to say any more about it." He went through the kitchen, past his mother, father, and Sarah and into his room. "Good night," he said, and closed the door. He sat in the dark on his bed. In August, even in November, Christmas had been a long time away. He had talked to Gabe and had gone to see him at the radio, record, and music store where he worked. They had asked Mr. English about secondhand instruments. He'd said he could have one shipped from Vancouver. "Tell my dad," he'd said.

"Does he want one?" Mr. English asked, teasing.

"It's for Christmas."

It was a small town and sales of musical instruments—except for ten dollar guitars and violins—were scarce enough that he was sure Mr. English had told his father.

He wanted it over with. It felt as if he'd stopped his life by hoping. One way or another, on Christmas morning time was going to start up again. But he wanted a saxophone. Any kind, tenor, alto—or an old C-Melody that they didn't even make anymore.

He undressed and went to bed without turning the light on and tried to stop his mind from hoping and making pictures of Christmas morning. With the horn. Without it. Wanting something that big when times were bad was an embarrassment. People would laugh if he talked about it. Gabe, Fielder, and now Emily were the only ones who knew.

Emily had asked direct questions (Do you want one? *Do* you?) and he'd wanted to say yes to her. He liked the way she'd made him give her an answer. Her hair under the streetlight had a gold colour in it. He hadn't remembered it that way from other times he'd seen her in her grandmother's yard or downtown.

He'd liked giving Emily the drawing. Except she was in elementary school. Her sister Pat was the most popular girl in his class. Nobody voted for anybody else for anything—except Fielder, who always nominated Monica Lewis for everything, because once she'd told on him for breaking a window when they were all in grade eight. He still wanted revenge.

Christopher knew Fielder didn't mind staying after school with Miss

Lee, who supervised detentions. She wasn't like the other teachers; her slip often showed, and the seams of her stockings were always halfway around toward the front of her legs. Everybody liked her, even Fielder. "She's been to Ethiopia," he'd said. "Went on a boat in 1934 when she was only nineteen." Which made her twenty-four now, and still she didn't know how to dress herself. But she'd been to the far side of Africa. She'd sat on the desk beside Fielder during a detention, and they'd talked about it. People liked Fielder. By himself, he was a serious person.

Christopher put his hands behind his head and stared up into the darkness. Miss Lee's eyes were dark and her hair darker. Emily's eyes were hazel; the real word for them was eager—but not for attention. Her eyes said she wanted to cheer for you. "Do you want one? A saxophone? *Do* you?" Times were tough and you should only want what you needed. She hadn't cared that the horn was too much. "What's that?" she'd asked.

"It's the octave key. It makes everything eight notes higher."

He wanted to know where she'd put his drawing when she got home. He didn't want her to hide it. He was back under the streetlight with her. When old Mrs. McLeod had asked him in, what if he'd said yes? What if. What if he got what he wanted for Christmas. What if he became Junior Ski Jumping Champion, and what if. . . . What if. . . what?

Emily was only in grade eight. He dug the pillow out from under his head and held it across his chest. It felt good. The thickness of it was like his mackinaw and Emily's red jacket between them when they'd bumped. Bumped. He kept the pillow close to him and held on. Her eyes and her voice were real.

2

The town had grown up so that it had two centres. Uptown there were the school grounds and the residential streets. Downtown clustered around the civic hall, which stood in a little park, and the streets—all named after British cities—connected downtown with uptown. The river came in from the west and curved south so that it held the whole community in the crook of its arm. At the southwest was a range of a half-dozen hills called the Castles because they stood as if separate from each other, although they weren't. The smaller five hills were good for downhill skiing; the central and tallest hill had a ninety-foot trestle on top of it, used by the men who jumped on Sundays for a ten dollar prize, winner take all. Halfway down the hill's left-hand side there was another jump built into the slope which was called the boy's jump, and at the bottom of the hill, was a meadow that ran all the way into town and stopped at the skating rink. Long River was very compact, miniature. Its population was maybe four thousand, and without the highway, railroad, cement plant, and the lumber mills further west along the river, where it seldom flooded, there would be no reason for its existence. The plant and the mills worked short shifts now, when they worked at all.

Christopher's father was General Foreman under Harrison Dodd, the Municipal Engineer, whose department looked after the powerhouse, the water system, the roads, the streetlights, and the sidewalks. It wasn't the job he should have had, but it was a good one in 1938. Fielder's father had a two-ton truck, only it was owned by the Royal Bank. The Bells' father worked for the township, and Isonovich's dad, who had never been able to learn English, only worked in the winter during emergencies and in the summer when repairs were done on the streets or ballast was needed along the railway line.

Emily's father was Dr. Gordon, the dentist. There was another dentist named McKillop, who was young, but not many went to him. He demanded payment in advance for his services. At Junior Chamber of Commerce meetings he sometimes made speeches that always included how much it had cost him to go through Dental College—seven years of training—and he also usually told them that you don't apply for the job of dentist. You gave up a significant fraction of your life to become one, and so the fees he earned should be equally significant. He had some supporters among people who hoped sometime to charge significant fees for their services too, but mostly people tolerated him and waited to see when he would leave. Dr. Gordon, on the other hand, often took a hundred pound sack of turnips in exchange for an extraction or a filling.

There was one Negro, who cut hair, and one Jew, who ran a clothing store, and perhaps fifty Chinese in town. The Indians (from the Carrier Tribe) stood very quietly on the edges of the sidewalks downtown. The women wore purple headscarves, beaded moccasins, and solid black dresses; the men wore mackinaw pants and workshirts, but they also had moccasins on their feet. They appeared to be thinking deeply or listening hard. They sold birchbark baskets and moccasin slippers and gloves made out of deerskin. Christopher's mother bought the slippers and wore them around the house, even though they smelled of the smoke that had cured the skins. She said they were beautiful works of art.

When he walked from his house on York Street to downtown, Christopher had to pass first the half-burned high school and the two-storey elementary school. When he and Fielder headed down from Fielder's place over on Sheffield to go skating, they often wanted to go into the school and look around, but they didn't dare. Evil-eye Grandison came by every hour, as if it were his duty to guard the place from vandals. He made his staff attend meetings morning and afternoon in Mr. Littler's office at the elementary school, until Christopher's father suggested he ease up and let them off to go skiing or home to the coast for the holidays. Evil-eye walked with his head cocked to his blind side, and his good eye saw everything.

The School Board had met twice during the day after the fire and, at the dinner table, the talk—which made meals worth sitting down to—was usually about the fire and often about Grandison.

"He wanted to have the kids report to the elementary school and pick up work to do at home and then hand in at the end of the day."

"The poor man is obsessed," his mother said.

"With what?" his father asked.

"Suffering, I think. What did you do?"

"Put it to a vote. It was touch and go."

"You could have told them that acts of God should be treated as such."

"What are you saying, Laura?"

"That when God does something rotten we always get holidays."

"Like right after He made the world?"

"Well, yes, there's always Sunday, of course."

They weren't being absolutely serious, but they weren't laughing as they usually did. There was a pressure on them both, a new kind that he hadn't seen before. It had been a long time since a contract this big had been put out to tender. Mayor Courtney believed in what his father called crony-ism.

The pressure had begun when his father called for tenders. Mayor Courtney phoned at breakfast time. Christopher answered, because when it rang then it was usually Fielder. The breathing at the other end of the line had been like a soft stutter. Then: "That you, Peter Waterton?"

When his father took the phone, he simply listened until the mayor was done, and then he said, "I don't want to talk about this over the phone, Mr. Mayor. I can come to your office." He looked at his watch while Courtney talked again. "No," his father said. "I believe this is municipal business, and I don't think we should do it at your hotel." When he put down the phone, he turned and looked at his family.

Christopher hadn't liked what he saw in his eyes. "He's mad at you, isn't he?"

His mother said, "He's angry you didn't consult."

"I made tomorrow the day tenders are to be in."

"Forty-eight hours? Can a contractor move that fast?"

"I could if I wanted the job." He looked away. "We have to get the kids back to school."

"Are you going to see him?"

"Of course. But as Board Chairman in his office. I'll see we have a witness to whatever ranting he wants to do."

"I suppose Charles Abling and the old Board would have consulted first."

"Charlie saw nothing wrong with going to the Grand every morning and carving up whatever there is to carve up in this town."

"Jobs are scarce, Peter," his mother said.

And his father told her, grinning, "They can't fire the General Foreman for something the Chairman of the School Board has done."

He and Fielder walked on past the school with their skates slung over their shoulders. The outdoor rink opened during the holidays at 2:30 and closed down at 5:30 and then opened again from 7:00 to 10:00. Howard Streeter, who was old enough to have grey hair, ran it with the help of some rink rats who got free skate time and sometimes a little money for scraping the ice and shovelling snow off it after a storm. Howard seldom left his ticket booth and candy shop, which was between the women's and the men's dressing rooms, except to kick someone out. He wore laced rubber hightop boots with his pants tucked down into them. He didn't just point the way when he told someone to leave, he kicked them and kept on kicking them until they were out the door. His rubber boots did double duty. They weren't so hard-toed that they did any real damage to those they came in contact with, and they kept his feet dry when he was out on the rink with the hose making ice.

Fielder never did anything unless he could do it well. He could shoot marbles, play basketball, play lacrosse, and skate. He didn't have skis and his mother sent him by bus to his grandparents at the coast in the summers, so Christopher had never seen him swim or dive. The rink was crowded. Fielder never just entered a room; he plunged in, especially into a room full of people bigger than he was. The rink was a place where those who had quit school and didn't have a job hung out. All of them were over sixteen; some were over twenty. It was a long day for them. They had to come early to sweep the ice, shovel snow, sweep the floors, build fires, and then reserve a place on the benches that were nailed to the walls on both sides of the dressing room.

It was important to follow Fielder's natural example at the rink. The rats sat around looking as if they were just going to go to sleep, but if someone came in hesitant and alone, one of them would ask, "What d'you think you're doing? Hey look what's here. Didn't you hear? No York Street snots allowed in today, especially you." Everything stopped then—no skates were laced or tightened, people heading out the door onto the rink turned to watch, everybody on the benches sat up, and Howard Streeter pretended not to notice.

The rat couldn't throw you out. Your nickel was already paid. But you didn't say that and spoil his fun. You sat down near the door and took your boots off and stuffed them under the bench where ten other pairs were. There was silence, which was part of it.

"Going to take a hint, kid?"

One word in reply was an excuse to get worse than you were already going to get. And there was no appeal. Howard's reply was always, "Go tell your mommy." And there was no hurry; it kept on happening whether something was done or not. The worst thing they could do was shove you down the hole in the outhouse attached to the far end of the dressing room. Not all the way down, but close enough to make you think you were going to wind up in ten feet of shit at the bottom.

The idea was to take it. Say you did do something in retaliation and somehow won—only a fantasy, because no one ever did win—say you called the police or your parents, you'd be decked after that every time you came around a corner, or worse. Stories in *Chums Annual*, or *Triumph*, or *The American Boy* where the little guy stood up to the bully and won were stupid. In real life there wasn't an end to the story; it kept right on happening. There were two ways out: one was to put your head down and wait until they were through with you, and the other was to grow big enough to join them. Or not.

Fielder sat down and began to put on his skates. No one picked on him. It was a kind of class thing, or maybe it had to do with being powerful in a certain way. The Police Chief's kid got it the worst. The Magistrate had four boys and they travelled together.

Christopher sat beside Fielder and unlaced his boots. John Purvis was there on the bench down at the back of the room. He coughed and got up and came over. He was nearly eighteen now. He'd quit school when he was still fifteen, but not because he was dull. He never gave a reason.

"I got four from Paraguay." He reached into his jacket pocket. "I ordered a bunch on approval. Look. Twenty-five cents."

The stamps had yellows and purples and bright blues and reds on them. "You gonna get them?"

"The old man's away again."

Christopher nodded. John's father's second wife looked like a hen with glasses on and didn't want to fix meals for him, let alone give him money for his stamp collection. She had married John's widowed father, who was a commercial traveller, and had her own children since. Sometimes she locked the doors on John, and Howard let him stay and keep the fire going all night so he could sleep on the bench nearest it.

Purvis had a face like a rising moon. It was big—big eyes, mouth, teeth—and its skin was yellow with a tinge of orange. Somewhere in the Purvis family there was Indian blood.

Now he said to Purvis, "I've never bought a Paraguay."

"Do you like these? Four for two-bits is a bargain."

"We could buy two each?"

"I'm broke."

"I could lend you. I've been saving."

Purvis got up. "No thanks. They don't have to go back until December 27th." He coughed and laughed at the same time. "Maybe I'll get a dollar out of the old man when he goes on his Christmas drunk."

"Hope so. Those are good ones. Are you skating?"

"No. I'm making ice for Howard at the supper break."

Fielder got up. "Going to skate or collect stamps?"

"Both."

"The joint closes at 5:30."

"Go then, go."

He stood up and looked out onto the ice. There were maybe a hundred people there, going around and around to the waltz music Howard played through a loudspeaker connected to his gramophone. Outside, a fence surrounded the rink. The boards were grey, weathered, twelve feet tall. Fielder was already warmed up and flying. Backward, forward, quick loops and on to full speed again, dodging between people and bouncing off the boards. It was good exercise for hockey, and it was a game: seeing how fast he could go before Flynn, Howard's rat on the ice, whistled him off.

Christopher left the gate and began to skate stiffly down the boards, and then out into the middle where the ice was nearly clear of people. He rode his skates hard and got them comfortable on his feet. Fielder went by. He chased him, caught him, gave him a hip and sent him into the boards. Fielder came back, grabbed him, and they tripped and fell. People swerved and skated around them. They lay dead on the ice. Callaghan jumped them, and then Christopher looked up and saw Emily swerve away, unsteady on her skates, and hold onto the boards. Flynn's whistle sounded. Christopher jumped up and stood beside Emily. Flynn ushered Fielder off the ice and signalled for Christopher to follow. He took Emily's arm and held her up. "Come on," he said. "Flynn won't touch me if I'm helping you."

She laughed. "I'm not very good at skating." Her face was red. He held her left hand in his left and put his arm around her, because that was the thing to do, and they moved off, not quite in time with the music. He hadn't skated with a girl before, let alone put his arm around one, except when Miss Garrett was invited by Blenkin to come to P.E. to teach them ballroom dancing. Last time, he'd got Monica Lewis to waltz with.

Every now and then she tripped, but he managed to hold her up until she was able to skate again. They were beginning to laugh, and Emily was more relaxed. Flynn appeared in front of them, skating backward. "I told you to get off."

"Come on, I'm not bothering anybody."

"I put Fielder off." He looked righteous. "Got to be fair." He was the oldest of the rats, and on the ice he sounded like a schoolteacher.

Emily pulled away and stopped at the gate to the women's dressing room. "Thanks," she said.

"I'll be back," he told her.

"Not until the next change," Flynn said.

Christopher went inside and saw that Fielder was pitching pennies with Smith. Obviously, he was winning, because Smith wanted to go double or nothing. Fielder nodded and pitched to within an inch of the wall. "Emily Gordon?" he said, while Smith was getting set to pitch.

"We're friends," Christopher said, not sure where the words or the easy tone of voice came from.

"Since when?"

He decided on the truth. "Since the fire."

"I was at the fire."

"Afterward."

Smith pitched. His one-cent piece hit the wall and then it spun in a circle and fell closer than Fielder's.

"Does that count?" Fielder said, too loud.
"Tricky," Smith said. "Come on, gimme."
Fielder gave him four cents and sat down on the bench.
The music stopped, the whistle sounded out on the ice, the people reversed and skated the other way to a new waltz. Christopher got up and went outside. The sun was far gone. In a few minutes the lights would be turned on. He looked up. The clouds over the river were thickening. It might snow. He hoped so. The hills out at the Castles needed another foot or two to make for really good jumping.
He wanted to see Emily again. Saying they were friends in front of Fielder and Smith had released a new feeling in him. He skated hard to hold the emotion down until he saw her in the crowd with Dody Wentworth. They were skating slow and easy. Emily's ankles were strong; her skates stood straight on the ice. He cut in front and faced them while he skated backwards. "You just never tried very hard before," he said to Emily. She looked pleased, and he watched her eyes watch him as she skated to the music.
"Were you skating with him?" Dody asked.
"Until he got kicked off."
"Kicked off?" She made it sound as if he'd won a prize. Emily wanted to skate with him. He could see it in her eyes. She glanced at Dody, and Dody's face grinned. "What is this, huh? Who do I get to skate with?"
"Be on the other side," Emily said.
He turned and skated forward again. Emily was on his right and Dody, laughing so hard she was sliding around instead of skating, held onto his left arm. It was hard going, awkward. Dody never got in step and kept giving him the hip as if they were playing hockey. Emily stood straight on her skates and went stiffly forward. In the middle, he was off balance. People were beginning to look. The lights came on and their shadows flickered around them as they moved along the ice. Dody got control of herself, and then she saw Trudy Olson skating alone. "Bye, you two," she said in a loud voice, pronouncing them gossip, and left to tell Trudy about it. He didn't mind. Fielder and Smith knew. Dody and now Trudy knew.
He looked at Emily, and she said, "Dody's a nut."
He skated with her, his gut-muscles tight and his breath short. It began to snow. The flakes were dry and powdery. By the time they'd gone around twice more the rink was white; there was snow in her hair and, when she looked up at him, he could see it sparkling on her eyelashes. He put his arm around her and said, "Let's see how fast you can skate."

She nodded. "And then I have to go."

He sped up gradually, and she skated with him until the first corner, then she coasted around it. On the next straightaway she couldn't keep up; she collapsed and hung on so that he stopped skating and they coasted until they came to a halt at the women's dressing room.

"Thanks," she said.

"This is the third time—" he stopped, awkward.

"For what?"

"Parting," he said, and had to laugh. "I mean, you never say good-bye. Just thanks."

She frowned.

"Are you going home alone?"

"With Dody."

He did a perfect circle on his skates and wound up in front of her again. "Well, see you."

"Walk with us," she said. Her voice had a low note that made it soft at the edges.

He did the circle again. People had to get out of his way and, as he went past her going into the loop, he told her Yes, and he didn't see her going into the dressing room because he was hit and knocked down by a pair who were waltzing. Flynn blew his whistle. "That's it for you. Off, get the hell off."

"Quit picking on me," he shouted.

Flynn looked at him, surprised. "Kid, do what I say or I'll break your damned arm." But there was a small smile on his face.

Christopher laughed, and ran on the points of his skates at Flynn, dodged him and headed for the gate. It felt as if suddenly everyone was saying Yes.

Half the rink was getting ready to leave. He got down on his knees and felt under the bench where he'd left his boots. Smith and Callaghan were sitting there. "Move," he said, and found them. "Where's Fielder?" Smith pointed. He looked around; Fielder was eating a chocolate bar. "You win?"

Fielder nodded, and Smith said, "There's something stupid about double or nothing. Ineluctably, aromatically stupid." His act was big words. He found them in his dictionary and used them any which way.

"It's okay when you win," Fielder told him.

"Punch him out," Callaghan said.

Fielder began to move. Callaghan and Smith stood up, and Smith grabbed at the chocolate bar before Fielder could get to the door.

Christopher wedged himself between them and put an elbow in

Smith's chest. Fielder shoved Callaghan out of the way.

"Outside," Howard shouted from the candy counter. "And watch that hot stove." He sounded like everybody's parents.

They stopped shoving, and Fielder escaped through the door to the rink. Christopher went after him. When they were on the ice, he said, "I'm going with Emily."

Flynn was there. "What did I tell you, Waterton?"

"I'm going. I'm going." He still had his boots in his hands to show him. To Fielder, he said, "Want to come? Dody Wentworth's with her."

Fielder looked at him. "What's going on?"

"Nothing. She invited me."

"Emily did?"

"And Dody's with her. Come on."

Fielder skated in a circle. "I can't figure you, Waterton. They're in grade eight, eh? Bloody cradle-snatcher."

"Are you coming?"

"No."

"All you have to do is walk with her."

Fielder skated away. It was snowing hard. Howard would close the rink soon. He had a cowbell he rang that meant time was up. Christopher skated back to the door and went in. Smith and Callaghan were gone. He knew what was going to happen now, and it made him wish he hadn't asked Fielder to come. He'd go with them all right, but it would be in his own time and they'd be kept waiting. He changed into his boots and dunked his skates in the tin tub of hot water on top of the stove to get them clean. The door opened a dozen times, and then finally Fielder came in.

"Too late," Christopher told him.

"Don't give me that, Waterton."

"Are you coming?"

"Maybe."

"They're waiting." He could see Dody standing near the entrance of the women's dressing room.

"Where's my boots?"

"How am I supposed to know?"

"We came in together."

"They're beside where mine were." Christopher pointed, then bent over and fished them out.

Fielder sat down and took his skates off. Now Emily was at the women's entrance too.

"Dody Wentworth," Fielder said. "The things you do for a friend."
"Hurry up. They'll leave."
"Why don't I walk with Emily and you go with Dody?"
"Come on, Fielder."
"Keep you out of mischief."
Christopher tied the laces of his skates together and hung them over his shoulder.
He waved at Emily and held up one finger to show they'd be right there.
They moved together to the main exit door. Dody's eyes were big and she was quiet, as if that were protection—like a rabbit in the snow. Emily stood solid as she always did. "Fielder's coming too," he said. He opened the door, and Fielder went out first.
"You open doors real good," he said.
Dody laughed and caught up with him. She was no more than an inch taller than Emily, but she was loose at the hips and the shoulders. Gangly. She stood beside Fielder, looked up at him and then turned to Emily with her eyes wide open and her hand over her mouth. Emily didn't react. She looked away from her and up into Christopher's face. Then she smiled, confused a little by Dody and Fielder. It was a serious thing she'd done and the smile trusted that he wasn't just funny like Fielder was being. They began to walk, and her mitt, wedged between his elbow and his ribs, was a sensation he'd not felt before.
"Well, good night," Fielder said, and walked fast away from them. Dody loved the joke. She chased and caught up with him. Christopher watched her, and moved with Emily along the short cleared pathway from the door to the street. He felt tense; Emily was holding his arm, but Fielder was liable to do anything for a laugh.
He did. He saw Dody coming and put his foot out and, when she tripped over it, he pretended to catch her, but instead of a catch it was a push and she landed in the snowbank at the edge of the roadway. She grunted. It was a sound Fielder hadn't expected, and it stopped him. He turned and went to her. She sat up, and Christopher saw the pain in her face, but she laughed. "My skate," she said, and laughed again. Fielder leaned over and offered her his hand. She grabbed it and pulled herself up. He let go and she fell back into the snow. "Oh, Fielder, stop it." She crawled out of the drift and ran after him down the street. Christopher and Emily saw them after that only at a distance. When they passed Dody's place on Stratford Street, Dody had gone in and Fielder was not there.

Their boots crunched hollow on the boards of the wooden sidewalk in front of the row of houses where Dody and Emily lived. On the other side of the street was bush and jackpine. This was the southern edge of town. There were definite borders to Long River. It didn't fade out into houses scattered here and there. It quit all of a sudden, as if it were a bundle of objects—houses, fences, people—with a rope around them. Emily's house was the last one on Stratford Street. It sat on an extra large plot of land, and there were tall trees that had been left standing so that it had the appearance of being a special place and not just an address where people lived. The house was long and low. "It rambles," Christopher's mother had said about it, and then she'd added, "All the others in town are boxes where people are packed away."

Inside the yard, Emily leaned with her back against the cedar tree nearest to the street. It sheltered her from the snow. Christopher was glad it was dark, because he had to stay close so he could see her. Without thinking whether he should or not, he took his mitt off and pushed her hair away from where it had fallen down over one eye. It shocked him, what he was doing. It was as if she were there to be touched and for him to make her hair go in a different way, feel the skin on her forehead. It embarrassed him. He took his hand away, but the hair fell back over her eye and he reached again to shove it under her red toque. She stood quietly, with her lips parted a little, and her eyes wide, which gave her the look of someone who was just about to say yes. In his mind the word was Emily. He wanted to say it, make its three sounds come out of his mouth as part of this touching her. It hurt that he couldn't make himself do it. He watched her. She was watching him too, and he could sense her thinking something private of her own. Suddenly too much was happening. And it was too new—except that pushing her hair up under her toque had come after she'd taken his arm outside the rink, and that had come after they'd skated; and those things were connected back to where they'd bumped—fallen against each other—on the way to her grandmother's after the fire. He stood with his hand on her cheek, stiff and awkward and not moving. Her hands were behind her back against the tree, and she was waiting. At the fire, she had brought his scribbler and drawing to him. She had skated with him and had invited him to walk her home. Whatever might happen between them next, she wanted him to start it. But now he wanted too many new things all at once. It made him silent.

He took his hand away and put it back in his mitt. Beyond her was the house. There were lights on all through it. Dinner time.

Her quiet voice said, "I was thinking about you yesterday."

"Were you? Where? In there?" He pointed, wanting to know, wanting to picture it.

"At the dining room table."

"Eating?" He laughed at his own foolishness.

"No. I was trying to copy your saxophone drawing." She made a soft sound that was more breath than laugh. "I couldn't do it. It's too hard."

"Can't you draw either?"

"Sometimes," she said. "Tilly the Toiler dolls with flouncy dresses."

He waited, wanting to know now what she thought about him, but she didn't say any more. "Come on," he said. "What did you think about me?"

"I thought, it's Christmas in five days and Christopher will have his saxophone."

"I wish you were in charge of the world."

"You'll get one," she said. "Wait and see."

"It's all I do."

Behind them boots crunched on the sidewalk.

"Are saxophones heavy? I was thinking they'd be hard to hold."

"There's a strap with a hook on it. You put it around your neck."

The crunch came closer and didn't stop until he looked around and saw Pat ten feet from them. She halted, boots together like a soldier and the rest of her at attention. Emily said nothing. Chistopher told her hello.

"Gloryowski, little sister, for a minute I thought it was a boy, but it's only Waterton."

"Christopher was at the rink," Emily said.

"Go home, Waterton, she's barely thirteen years old."

He wanted to tell Pat that not even a girl had walked her home. Instead, he moved closer to Emily and grinned at Pat.

"Terrible taste, Emily."

Emily laughed at her sister. "Go on in. It's your turn to set the table anyway."

He had never seen Pat close up anywhere but at school. It was a surprise that she wasn't any different at home. She waved her mitted hands in the air, as if she were on stage. "How long has this been going on?"

"It's none of your business, Patty."

"Next thing you'll invite him in, and then it'll be my business."

"Go inside," Emily said.

Pat didn't move.

He felt Emily take his hand, and they walked together out to the street. "Phone me if you want," she said. Then she went back and walked beside her sister to the house. He didn't hear either of them speak, but at the door, while Pat used the broom to sweep her boots, Emily turned and when she saw him staring back at her, she waved. Then she swept her boots and went inside the house.

3

On Christmas morning there was nothing under the tree for him. There were routines about Christmas that were strictly followed each December. The tree was hunted out and cut on the 17th: a balsam fir, the softest, fullest, prettiest, and most fragrant of all the evergreens, according to his father. It was set up against the west windows in the living room, after the chesterfield had been moved. On Christmas Eve, and when dinner was done that evening, his mother—and lately Sarah—brought the decorations down from the cupboard in her studio upstairs. There were first of all the lights to put on, and then the thick ropes of paper and long strands of gold tinsel, before the baubles were threaded and hung on the branches. Finally, the white angel was made to stand at attention at the top of the tree. The result was always perfection.

Sarah whined from the first moment and progressed to tears by the time the baubles were being hung. Where someone else worked was where the fun was. "No, let me," she shouted at whoever was reaching the highest or stretching to hang a silver ball at the back of the tree: "I want to, I want to." She had waited too long, the promise of the ceremony was too great and, feeling nothing of what she expected, yet wanting the joy to be real because her daddy by all his actions had promised it, she thought the thrill was up or down or around behind the tree, and she cried because she was not there, and felt nothing but cheated. They jollied her, teased her, held her up to where she wanted to be, and finally it was finished. The lights in the room were turned off and the tree lights switched on.

"We're very lucky," his father always said, his voice more anxious than thankful.

On the 22nd, Christopher had phoned Emily, and she'd said to come over, her parents were shopping. He'd run there, and then had felt awkward because he'd arrived so quickly. "Here comes handsome," Pat shouted. She'd been throwing icicles at the tree. Emily had been sitting watching her. "Don't you do it all together?" he'd asked, without thinking.

Emily said, "Do you?"

"Yes, on Christmas Eve."

"That sounds nice," Pat said, through her nose.

"We just leave the stuff around and put it on when we feel like it," Emily said.

"Gives it a certain charm, Gooseberry," Pat told him, and pitched a handful of icicles at the top of the tree. "We go in for charm around here."

There had been presents under the Gordon tree too, boxes to be hefted and rattled, packages to be squeezed and guessed at. But what if they guessed right? At his place, the gifts were put beneath the tree on Christmas Eve, first by Sarah when she went to bed, then by him, and finally by his parents.

This morning, as on every other Christmas, the living room was closed off. No one was allowed to peek until after breakfast—always cornmeal porridge with real cream, and one Japanese orange—until his mother pleaded that it was time. His father opened the door and they all saw the boxes and packages, and an unwrapped toy or two for Sarah hanging from the branches. Presents from everyone to everyone, and more boxes in red and white or holly-patterned paper from relatives across the country.

"I don't believe it," his mother said. "I never do."

"We're crazy," his father answered. "There's enough money spent under that tree to feed us half the year."

The wait had turned breakfast to sand in his mouth. He decided to say nothing and be nonchalant. If he got it, fine; if he didn't—his gut shrivelled.

His father distributed the presents to Sarah, his mother, Sarah again. To himself. Tools: he always got tools for his workshop, just as his mother got useful things. Sarah got dolls and doll clothes, and real clothes. It was all very natural, except what he'd asked for was not there. Then his father noticed it too and got up from his crouch under the tree. "Well," he said, "you're getting too old for presents." Then he reached and held a balsam frond up to reveal a saxophone—gold-coloured, about a foot long, with a stubby cork mouthpiece and a stubbier bell. He handed it to Christopher. It was a kazoo. "The best we could do, I'm afraid. You didn't want anything else."

He felt himself retreating, going away. The kazoo in his hand said, Who do you think you are?

Do what you have to, and don't admit nothing, Purvis had told him once at the rink. He looked at the kazoo. "Thanks," he said, and put it to his lips. He forced the sound in his throat that was necessary to make the kazoo's noise, and tried to look up at them, but he couldn't. His head was down now, and it wouldn't come up.

"Can I see? Can I see?" Sarah's voice worried that it might be something special. Her ruined little face came up close to his. "Can I, Chris?"

He was seated far back in the easy chair, tense while he had waited, and it felt as he got up that he was caught by something that didn't want to let go. The moment hurt: yes or no, but not this. He stood, finally, and what he first saw was his father, still standing by the tree with the remains of Christmas all about his feet. He was smiling with his mouth drawn slightly down at the corners. Then he saw his mother. Her eyes were watching something she didn't like. His own face felt stiff, too, as if it had been hit and the pain hadn't yet begun.

"Christopher?" Sarah said.

And then his mother's voice broke out. "Oh, Peter, what a terrible idea this has been." She stood up too. They were all standing now, and her eyes were empty when she looked at his father. "Go get it." It was not an order or a plea, just talk. His father's face kept on smiling. The corners of it were now bent brightly up, but when he looked at his wife the joke finally died. He turned quickly and went into the master bedroom. His feet came up off the floor in a peculiar way, as if not all the muscles in his legs were working. The closet door opened, shut; he reappeared carrying a black case. His face was controlled again, but his eyes were full of what he had to say. "Here." He handed the black case over. "Eighty-five dollars. Everybody helped. Aunt Ethel—" his voice tensed up— "sent fifty cents. I hope you'll be grateful enough to write and thank her, and everybody else."

"Open it, dear," his mother said.

He didn't want to. *A man gets the big things for himself.*

She took it from him, put it on the floor and opened the lid. He could see it was an alto saxophone—silver-satin finish—not new, but quite beautiful. "Is it what you wanted, Chris?"

He nodded and knelt by his mother in front of the case. He wanted to look at his father and tell him he was sorry for having asked. Now that the horn was here, there was no joy in it, only resentment, as if *he* had been the strong one and *they* had been forced to obey. There was in his head the wild picture of him giving the case back to his father so Christmas could happen over again, but he felt shut off from him, from the horn and from himself.

"Why?" he heard himself say.

"I wanted it to be a bigger surprise." His father's voice was awkwardly hearty.

He felt very young suddenly, and he didn't want to look up into his face and see that there was no truth in it.

"We talked to Gabe Sommerville," his mother said, controlled. "He told us that this kind—" she touched the alto— "would be easier for you to handle—to begin with."

"It's the one," he said to her. "Jimmy Dorsey plays this kind and so does Charlie Barnett and Johnny Hodges."

"You know a lot about it."

He nodded, and put a finger on the bell. The finish was like the finest sand. He wanted it to touch him back. "Gabe has records at his place."

"He told us you'd learned to read music."

"A little. Not all the keys yet."

"You don't need them all to start with."

He looked at her. Her eyes were absolutely black, and she looked as if there had always been a child behind her face who had suddenly taken over. He could see his father, too, now, standing near them with Sarah in his arms. She was whispering in his ear, and he said, "No, mommy's not mad at anyone," and he sounded relieved to say it.

"Thank you," Christopher said to them both.

"Well, come on," his father said. "Show us what you know about it. Can you put the thing together?"

He'd never held one before. Gabe hadn't offered. But he'd seen what had to be done and remembered to pick it up by the bell. It was a Conn. Gabe's tenor sax was a big golden King. Conn was good too. He put the neck-strap over his head and hooked the horn to it. Next came the neck, then the mouthpiece and its ligature. There was one reed. He picked it up and looked at it.

"Gabe said a soft one would be best at the beginning," his mother said quietly as if she were tending a wound.

He put it in his mouth and stood up. The weight was awkward. The instrument swung against his ribs, and the mouthpiece hit him on the cheek. He looked at his father and saw him beginning already to figure how best to hold it, to blow into it, to play it. He held the bell to steady it. "Can I go into my room and play, fool around with it?"

"I'll bring the case," his mother said.

He let her close it and walk down the hallway and into his room with the case held around its middle by both her arms. He opened the curtains on the window to let some natural light into the room and turned to face her. "This was too much, wasn't it?"

She shook her head. "No. He loves you. He really does. But everything's so awful—" she gestured, took in the whole world with it—"out there."

"He's got a good job."

"Yes, and that makes him more anxious than if he didn't."

"Eighty-five dollars is a lot of money."

"Of course it is." She laughed then. "But we do have a monster family. It's a present from all of them."

"Did Aunt Ethel really send fifty cents?"

"Yes, instead of her usual handkerchief."

"They probably think I'm nuts."

"Well, aren't you?" She laughed once more, and then stopped, uncertain. "It's hard to give a grown-up present to—" she stopped again—"someone who's not grown up."

"Come on," his father called from the living room. "There's more Christmas out here." There was something uncertain in his voice too.

He said to his mother, "Should I go back with you?"

"No. There's just more little things for Sarah. We'll see to it."

He watched her go, blue mules on her feet, a present she didn't need, black curly hair and, in between, a thick body, not quite a rectangle. It was her smile and maybe her eyes that made his father think she was beautiful.

He pulled the chair out from his desk and sat on it, carefully, the reed still lodged in his mouth between his teeth and his cheek. There were six mother-of-pearl keys on the horn. He put his right hand on the bottom three and his left up on the others, and worked them as if he were playing a scale. They made a noise: pock. Pock pock pock pock pock. Up and down. He'd seen how Gabe had put his reed on the mouthpiece. It wasn't easy. The ligature had to be square-on or the reed slipped to one side. He didn't know exactly where the tip of it should be either.

He put his lips around the mouthpiece and blew. Nothing happened. He blew harder. A sound burst out of it, exactly like the kazoo, and it made his bottom lip feel as if it had pins and needles in it. "Muscles," Gabe had said. In the cheeks. He put only his top three fingers on the keys and blew. The noise sounded better, as if somewhere behind it there might be a note. He put his teeth on the top of the mouthpiece and rested the reed on his lower lip. The sound was better. In half an hour he had a sore lip and three notes: G, A, and B. Nothing else worked.

Then Fielder phoned.

"Get your bloody great saxophone, Waterton?"

"Yes, it's—lovely." He laughed for the first time about it. "What'd you get?"

"Skates and a stick."

In the background he could hear the new baby crying. It sounded through the phone like a wet foghorn. "What'd your new sister get?"

"What a kid, eh? If she don't shut up soon—pow. Get me out of here. Let's go skating."

"What about Christmas dinner?"

"Seven o'clock, after the kid's asleep. Ridiculous."

"Why?"

"The old man's into the Corby's already. By dinner time he'll be gone for good. How's yours?"

"My what?"

"Old man."

"He doesn't drink."

"Saves his money and buys you saxophones."

"The whole family did. They all chipped in, coast-to-coast. It's the only present I got."

"How much?"

"Eighty-five."

Fielder was quiet for a moment. "Waterton, if we're lucky that's what my old man clears in a month."

He was holding his horn. It rested comfortably under his arm now. "I asked for it, Fielder. Like you asked for skates."

"Sure. Ten ninety-five, and a buck-and-a-quarter for the stick."

"Didn't you get anything else?"

"Socks and underwear. And a new hat, which I'm never ever going to wear. It's red, for God's sake. No, *pink*."

"On you it'll look natural, Fielder."

"I'm coming over."

"I want to phone Gabe Sommerville."

"What for?"

"Lessons. He helped pick out the horn for my family to buy."

"I'll be there," Fielder said, and hung up.

He put the saxophone into its case and left the lid open so he could see it lying there, softly silver, with a few worn spots—one especially near the octave key where the brass showed through. Someone else, or maybe two or three other people, had owned it before him. Where had it played? A ballroom, a nightclub, a hotel dining room? He lay on his bed beside it and touched the keys, all of them, from the big B-flat on the bell to the high F just below where the neck fitted onto the body of the instrument. They made small mechanical noises, and the pads near the top were wet from his having blown so long into it. He thought of a tune in his head, Gabe's favourite on his tenor: "Smoke Gets in Your Eyes." He always stood up at the microphone when he played it and made the melody dive and climb like a big bird. And then at the change of key in the middle part, he blew loud and built it until the main melody came up again and then he let it go soft. The real ballroom dancers held onto each other and swooped across the floor, twirled, reversed, and swayed. But Gabe played every kind of music—tango, rhumba, old-fashioned two-step, waltz, schottische, even a minuet if they wanted it, and always some good fast jazz for the jitterbugs who came dressed for it: the guys in open shirts and slacks and the girls in blouses and full skirts, no stockings and white silk underpants, because when they got going their skirts rose like umbrellas in the wind. "The Sheik of Araby," the Duke's "Caravan," "Bye-Bye Blues," Charlie Barnett's up-tempo "Cherokee." Gabe copied choruses from the records he owned and played them with his eyes closed. Buster Brady's drums and Jim Collins' piano backed him and soloed too. But the best moments were when Gabe's tenor and Marty Franklin's trumpet chased each other and the music got wild. "Sometimes," Gabe told him, and he had laughed, "we don't know what the hell we're doing up there. Just blowing in the same key is all." There'd been nobody in town to teach or show them the correct way to do things. They just listened and figured. "I was fed up with teachers anyway when I got this horn. The square root of the distance to the damned moon. The capital of Argentina is Philadelphia, Napoleon died on his elbow." He'd tapped his horn. "I was ready for this monster here. You got to tame it for yourself."

The phone rang. He went to get it, expecting Fielder again to say he was trapped behind enemy lines and had to pack in wood or shovel snow. Emily had never phoned before. Her voice made his stomach feel as if it were being attacked by something soft. She said Hello, and all he could do was laugh.

"You got it, didn't you?" she said.

"Yes, you were right."

"You said I should be in charge of the world. Am I?"

"I guess you are." The feeling in his stomach was even softer, and stronger. "You did a good job." He wanted to see her, but Fielder was coming and he hadn't phoned Gabe.

"I got skates," she said.

"So did Fielder. He'll be here in a minute."

"I'm going to skate better now. My old ones were too small."

"You're good enough."

"No I'm not. We could skate if the rink was open." She laughed. "Christmas should only be half a day."

"Fielder and I'll probably go to the slough. He has a new stick."

"That means there'll be a hockey game."

"It's big enough down there for just skating too. Bring Dody and we can meet."

"If we can. But I want to see your saxophone."

"I can't take it skating."

"Tomorrow's Boxing Day and we have open house."

"Maybe the next day."

"Can you play it?"

"I've got three notes on it."

"So by the time I see you, you'll have nine."

"Maybe," he said. "If Gabe can give me a lesson before then." The back door opened and closed. Fielder never knocked, and he always had to be sent back outside to sweep the snow off his boots. "Fielder's here," he said to Emily. "Brush your feet," he shouted, and into the phone, he said, "See you later."

"I want to go," Emily said. "I tried them on and they feel really good."

"Make your mother let you go."

"Pat got nothing but clothes—practical clothes. Is she ever mad."

"What did she want?"

Fielder was back inside the kitchen door.

"She's already got skates and skis and a bike. Maybe a colouring book and a doll? I think sometimes she doesn't want to grow up."

He laughed. "You're a brat sister."

"I know, but so is she sometimes."

"Bring Dody."

"I'll try."

"Thanks for phoning." He meant it. It was the first time.

"I waited for you, and when you didn't phone I thought your sax hadn't come."

"I would've killed myself."

"No you wouldn't."

"Maybe. Hey, bring your skates and we'll meet you there."

They said goodbye and Fielder asked who he was talking to, but he was already leading the way to the bedroom to show off his horn. Fielder hardly knew what a saxophone was. He looked at it and then reached out and picked it up. Christopher grabbed it from him. "Fragile."

"What good is it then? Bleat, bleat. Can you go skating?"

"Come on, Fielder, who do you think you are?" He began to laugh at that, and sat down on the bed.

His mother appeared in the doorway.

"Merry Christmas," Fielder said.

"Merry Christmas, Donald."

"Donald," Christopher said. That was always funny. He laughed harder.

Fielder said, "Your son is being merry."

"Yes, I see."

"That—thing," Fielder said, "has made him crazy."

Christopher stopped himself from laughing and put the horn away. When the lid was down, he looked for a place to put it.

"On the shelf in the closet," his mother said.

He looked at her. They were both hiding it from Sarah.

"Going out?" she asked.

"Skating. Fielder's got new skates."

"How nice. Let me see." She looked at them admiringly. "I thought we'd eat at four. Is the rink open?"

"We're going to the slough," Fielder said, and followed her into the kitchen.

Christopher dressed for the cold outside and when he joined them, Fielder headed out the door in a hurry to skate.

"Where's Dad?"

"Playing Snakes and Ladders with Sarah."

"Can I thank him?"

She was peeling potatoes. She turned from the sink and her eyes laughed at him. "You're such a fool sometimes. Of course you can. He needs to be thanked." She faced the sink again. "For everything, all the things he gives us."

He went through to the living room and stood at the door. He was sitting on the floor in front of the tree with Sarah, who was throwing the dice. She watched them fall and said, "Five." She looked up at her father for confirmation. He nodded and, while she moved her counter and landed happy at the bottom of a ladder, he looked up.

"Thanks for the best present I ever got," Christopher said.

"I'm glad you like it." He picked up the dice.

"It's perfect."

"Makes an awful noise." He rolled them.

"I'll do it when you're at work."

His father looked surprised, and appeared for a moment as if he should protest, but then he let it go.

"I'm going skating with Fielder," Christopher said, awkward.

"Your mother doesn't need any help?"

"I'll ask." He turned away and passed his mother on the way out. The turkey was beginning to roast in the oven. The first odours of cooked meat and dressing were in the kitchen, and they made him hungry. "Can I have an orange?"

She nodded. "Take one for Fielder, too."

It was crisp outside. The new snow was dry and, as they went down York Street, it made soft protests underfoot. The oranges were cold against their teeth, and the air was frigid too, but there was a pleasant sun above the southern horizon. The houses they passed were decorated with evergreen boughs, and a few had been able to afford lights. Windows had wreaths of holly in them. There were some kids with new toboggans on the road, and there were others with skis they were trying out. People didn't care if times were tough; they knew what Christmas should be and found the money to make it how they remembered. In the still air they could hear a car with a broken chain slapping against its fender as it went east and faded from their hearing.

"If I ever get a job," Fielder said, "first thing I do is get a car."

Christopher thought he might get a gold-plated horn. People waved to them and shouted Merry Christmas.

"Not a bad place to live," Christopher said.

"On Christmas."

"You want to leave?"

"God, who doesn't? I'd leave right now." Fielder wiped his nose with the back of his mitt. "Three more years."

"Three-and-a-half."

"You sound like my mother," he said. "If it's good she can tell you exactly how far away it is, and if it's bloody doom she tells you to the minute how close it is."

"Doom," Christopher said. "Doom." He laughed.

"What's the joke, idiot?"

"Doom. It's a great word. It says what it means. Doom."

"You're bonkers."

"Doom." He dodged Fielder's stick. "Cut it out, Fielder. My old man says if Hitler keeps it up like he's going now there'll be a war soon. That'll make you think about it."

"What?"

"Doom, stupid."

"No." Fielder looked up into the blue. "They can't have a war yet. I'm not old enough to go."

"Eighteen. Same thing: three-and-a-half years."

"They let you in at seventeen."

"Boy soldiers. That's the army."

"I want the air force," Fielder said.

"Then you got to be eighteen."

"My old man went when he was seventeen."

They headed along First Avenue and then down toward the river on the London Street Extension, which was a one-track road that went past shacks where old bachelors like the gravedigger, Mike Spinney, lived. It bordered Chong's pig farm, and wound up at the edge of the slough, which didn't have a name. The river backed up in here during high water in June and in other seasons it was fed by rain in summer and by melted snow in the spring. It was long and narrow and ran for maybe a thousand yards along the northern edge of town. For most of the year it was a stinking mess, brown and a sick green, but in winter it was solid black ice under a fresh covering of snow. The snow never stayed long. It blew off into the marshes down by the railway track, or it was scraped off by practising hockey players. Now, it wasn't crowded, but a pick-up game was going on at the east end, and the rest of it was being used by a few speed skaters, or couples out teaching their young how to stand up on their new skates.

Christopher knew one thing for sure about himself: he wasn't a great athlete. Skiing, maybe, but basketball, softball, soccer, and especially hockey just made him, in the end, unsure of himself. He was never at the centre of them, always playing back or at the edges. Fielder was the live centre of every team he played on, and now he put on his new skates, grabbed his stick, and headed into the scrub game. Some of the players were adult, and none were as young as he was, but that didn't bother him. He skated up and down the ice, and when the puck came loose he got it on his stick and headed for the goal, suddenly a new member of the team heading west.

Christopher skated in close and watched for an opening on the eastbound team.

"Come on, get with it," someone shouted, and shoved the puck at him.

He went forward. Fielder met him with a body check, but he passed before he went down. A hand was held out to him. He took it and looked up. Gabe Sommerville said, grinning, "Get your horn, man?"

"You know I did," Christopher said, and laughed. "What're you doing here?"

"Irene's over there with the kid."

"Whose side are you on?"

"I'm against you."

"Can we talk then?"

"Sure." Gabe skated out of the game. "That's a nice alto they got you. You like it?"

"Yeah, it's great, but it's not gold like your tenor."

"You're damned lucky to have it at all."

"I put the reed on and got a sound out of it, but that's all."

"How were you holding your mouth?"

Christopher took his mitt off and put two fingers between his lips as if they were the mouthpiece. He blew and was suddenly embarrassed.

"Okay, but not the lip over the bottom teeth—just up stiff against the reed."

"I made some awful sounds."

"Come over. I want to see it again."

"When, Gabe?"

"Tonight, after dinner. We'll have a session when the kid's in bed.

"What will—"

"Irene say? Hello and how are you. Be there at seven-thirty."

In the game, he began slowly, skated up and down with the mob of them. Now there were probably nine or ten on each team. He wanted the time to go fast. He began to skate hard, ran into the middle of the play, bunted and dodged and didn't mind a stick in the ribs or a hip that bounced him off the ice and into the bank of snow that edged the rink. His ankles were tired now and his skates slanted down toward the ice.

He gave up the game, skated to the edge of the slough, sat down on the low bank, loosened his skates and took them off so he could massage his ankle, especially his right one, which was the weakest. When he put his skates back on the sun had begun to move on down toward the horizon. He looked around at it to see if it was time to go home for dinner and saw Emily coming toward him. Dody was with her, but she only said, "Hey, is that Fielder?" and went out onto the ice near the game to watch him.

Emily had on a heavy brown turtle neck and a green scarf that reached down to the belt of her ski pants. Her toque was green, too. She stood close and smiled down at him. "I'm really happy about your horn."

"I'm glad you could come," he told her. "Did you have to wait for Dody?"

She shook her head. "I just said to her that Fielder was here."

"She's nuts."

"So's he," she said, and crouched beside where he was sitting. He turned in the snow so that he was facing her. He reached out and put his arms around her waist and leaned against her. He felt her arms go around his shoulders and press him closer. There were people changing their skates near them, and another couple were coming down the roadway toward them. He stopped holding her. "They'll see us."

She didn't answer; instead, she sat beside him on the low bank. The stories he had thought up or had dreamed of, he forgot now. This had happened. He couldn't think what to say. Finally he asked, "Don't you want to put your skates on?"

She nodded. "Where are your boots?"

"Just along there."

"I want to put mine with them."

He showed her the snowless place under the bank, and felt as if everything he thought and did now was in slow motion. He sat watching her. In his head it was summer almost nine years ago in Victoria, and he floated up the street to Marjorie's house. It had a very tall hedge around it. In the garden at the back there was a gazebo. Marjorie's mother served them orangeade and sugar cookies at the table. Marjorie's front teeth were loose. Four of them, and one was so nearly ready to drop that she could push it straight out with her tongue. They left the table, as they always did, and sat at the back of the small screened-in teahouse. Marjorie made the tooth stick out between her lips, a little white point. He poked at it gently with his finger. She shook her head and laughed. The next time she showed him her tooth between her lips, he leaned close to touch it with his tongue. Down through his body he felt touched himself. He put his tongue out again, this time forcing it between her lips, and then he wanted to be closer. She did too. He pressed hard against her, pushed his tongue farther into her mouth and held her with his arms and hands. She pressed and hugged him back. The feeling in him became fierce. He wanted only to be here. The sharp point of her tooth was no longer between them, and she reached with her thumb and forefinger between their faces and took it from the tip of her tongue. She didn't laugh; instead she smiled and put her tongue out again; it tasted of blood, hers and his own. He closed his eyes. Then Marjorie's mother was there suddenly, and she had been angry enough to hit him. He remembered her eyes as she did it. They were like a dog's when it barked at a stranger. "Your mother must know. Oh, yes, your mother is going to know about this." He had to run home. There was nowhere else to go; when he got there his mother was at the door, and he stood on the porch and said, "I didn't mean to." He meant that he hadn't known what it was they'd done. His mother laughed. "She spanked me," he said, almost crying. And his mother said, "What an adventure my little man has had." The memory ended there. Marjorie's family moved during the summer to another town. He never saw or heard of her again.

Emily got up and glided out onto the ice, and he could see that the new skates were a help to her. He skated beside her and watched how she dug in and pushed forward better than she had at the rink. She smiled across at him and reached out her hand. They skated down along the length of the slough's lazy S until they reached its end where reeds stuck up through the ice and willows stood frozen stiff on the shore. They hadn't spoken, and didn't talk now that they had stopped and faced each other. There was no space between them. He put his arms around her and held her as hard as he could, but it wasn't close enough. He bent his head down toward hers. She watched, and he saw her waiting quietly on the other side of the little distance that separated their eyes. He forgot that he had never really kissed anyone. Their mouths were cold when they touched. He pressed closer. In a while their lips went soft and warmer. Neither of them was breathing. He drew away as if he were surfacing and they took deep breaths and kissed again. This was the beginning he'd been waiting for. He put his mouth close to her ear and said her name.

CHAPTER TWO

1

He hadn't known he would change or, if he did change, how he would handle it. Emily, his horn, the skis he'd got for his birthday were new, and they'd forced shifts inside of him that others couldn't see. It was like watching someone else in a mirror in a darkened room: there were outlines and a shape, but nothing else was absolutely distinct.

Now, mirrors fascinated him. Here at home there was a mirror in the dining room, a long rectangle with a picture of Venice in a square at one end, and one of Delft in Holland at the other. On the back of the door in his parents' room there was a full-length mirror set in a smooth rounded frame that was enameled grey. He could see all of himself in it if he stood back at the side of their bed. And finally there was the bathroom mirror, flecked always with soap, in a white frame, above a white basin which had been cracked when a large bottle of mouthwash had fallen into it.

In the dining room mirror he saw himself passing by—head, shoulders, and chest—a moving picture. He couldn't often see himself in the full-length mirror because it belonged to his parents, but when there was no one home he could go into the bedroom and see what that mirror had to show him. The bathroom mirror, on the other side of a locked door, he could see into as often and nearly as long as he wanted, but it showed him only his face—his eyes, ears, hair, teeth, tongue, skin and, if he breathed out against it, and then sharply in, he could smell the odours on his breath.

The images in those three mirrors were bright and clear, and he could easily sense himself watching another person who was also himself, but neither the watcher nor the watched could tell him why Emily always wanted to be with him as much as he wanted to be with her. Nor about the saxophone—why, through saying and asking and picturing it, drawing it over and over again, it had arrived first as a kazoo and then as the real thing and had changed what once he'd known about his father, and had confirmed what he'd known for a year about Gabe. The skis either meant nothing or a lot. They were an extension of his old life: he'd skied since he was five and had jumped since he was ten.

A mirror had always been something to stand in front of to comb his hair or brush his teeth. What was beneath the hair was never questioned, and what surrounded the teeth he thought was probably ugly. "You're pleasant to look at, but nothing extraordinary," his mother had said. "Don't break your arm patting yourself on the back." Also, "Close your mouth or your brains'll leak out." Or, "Don't be so grim; that frown'll drop on your foot and break it." Those things were supposed to be jokes. If nothing could ever work out in these hard times, then nothing should be taken seriously. Why then did he feel serious? Beyond the image, there in the mirror, nothing else was reflected.

This was a new time. A new year. 1939. Until now there had been only seasons: winter, summer: school, holidays. Years had numbers, like dogs had names. Now 1939 marked a time that he knew he would remember, because things were beginning to happen to him as a person, separate from his family, different from what was happening to Fielder, Smith, Callaghan, the Bells, and Cameron.

Beginning to trade stamps with Purvis, who was nearly four years older, had been something that had happened separate from everyone else. Purvis wasn't just friendly, he was a friend. Gabe Sommerville had also been a surprise. One Friday night he'd cut through the alley behind the Royal Ballroom after the movie at the Regent Theatre. Gabe had been by the back door warming up before his band began to play for the dance. The gold horn he was blowing was suddenly bigger than the man playing it, and the sound stuck in his head and vibrated in his gut. He'd walked in the door and watched Gabe, as if that would tell him how to play.

"Is it hard?" He'd been surprised how blunt the question sounded.

"What?"

"Making it work—your saxophone."

"No harder than any other horn. Maybe easier than a piano." This one reply made him know that unlike a lot of people's answers Gabe's were serious.

"It sounds great." He couldn't think of what else to say. Awkward, he began to go, and then he'd turned again, and said, "I guess they're expensive."

Gabe nodded and blew a run of maybe a dozen notes.

"How much? A hundred?"

"I paid a hundred and ten for this." Gabe's voice was matter-of-fact, like his father when he was talking about building a kite or a raft or a bobsled. Gabe held the saxophone up. "It's a King. I got it from a man who used to play around Toronto."

"Why'd he sell it?"

"Lost three fingers working the edger at the mill. He told me that when he took the job he hadn't eaten in three days."

"Poor guy."

"Times are tough." Gabe turned toward the bandstand. "You want to come in and listen?"

He'd gotten home at 2 A.M. It was the first time he'd seen his mother cry. He never knew whether it was because she was angrier than she'd ever been, or because she was afraid he'd been in an accident.

It had been an accident. He'd walked down that back alley and had had an accident, and it was then that he'd started to glimpse some kind of a mirror in a new room with only a little light in it, where whoever he was becoming had begun to form.

It occurred to him now that it had been accident after accident that had led him to Gabe and his horn. The first one had been his mother and father making love and having a baby. No, it had been a bigger accident than that. His mother had told him that she'd lost a baby four months after she and his father were married. And he'd been born eleven months after that, a time, because of the miscarriage, that wasn't his. It had been a time that had belonged to another human being—his brother's. The next baby would have been someone different. Not him. Not Sarah. Had that boy lived, even the accident of Sarah might never have happened.

But he'd been born. Himself. The end of a long line of accidents that went back to the first man and woman. And his father had by chance got a job in Long River, himself an accident, as was his mother. He was like neither of them (another set of accidents: genes, Miss Garrett said, combine at random to make a person). His father was chunky, with shoulders heavy enough to give him a hunched look, and he had eyes that he was somehow able to hide behind. His mother was heavier than she should be, but not shapeless. She had black eyes and long hair she sometimes plaited and sometimes coiled. Those two had their own life together, built around interruptions by their children. "Children come with marriage," his mother had said, "and they shouldn't be a surprise." He was an expected accident. How peculiar now to have been *theirs*.

"Only once, just once I want to choose some damned thing," Fielder had said to him.

Maybe there wasn't much choice. But what he knew now was that accidents were happening to him, separately, because the shape he sometimes saw in the dim mirror was formed enough to have them. In this tall mirror in his parents' room he was Christopher. In the dark one inside his head, who was he? What is my real name? What am I here to do? He held his hands up and saw the bones in them. With his finger, he pulled his cheek away from his teeth so he could see in the mirror back down the double line of incisors and molars clenched in a dead smile. His skull—he felt it—and the bones at the top of his spine, ribs, the long bones of his arms and legs: a skeleton. No accident.

Miss Garrett said that the skeletal framework of homo sapiens had changed very little in the last fifty thousand years. She used words like "amazingly," to try to make everyone enthusiastic.

He was nearly grown and was within an inch of his father's height. There, at least, they were the same and, if their skeletons were once accidents, they weren't that now; there was a similarity in their bones. But that was all. Last year he'd had pneumonia. Dr. Royce had spent a long time listening with his stethoscope and holding his hand over and near the centre of his chest.

"You have a small heart, Christopher. I can feel the shape and size of hearts, and yours is small."

"Is that bad?"

"No." He put his stethoscope away. "From my observations, I'd say people with small hearts are the dreamers. Good people, and as healthy as anyone."

"Who else has one?"

After a pause, he said, "Your mother, maybe?"

Christopher laughed. "Do you have a small pump too?"

Dr. Royce smiled suddenly. "You might be right. Takes one to find one."

Later, lying nearly well in bed with his fever dreams still fresh in his mind he remembered that Dr. Royce had not said what kind of dreams were dreamed by people with his kind of heart. There was always the possibility of nightmares. Asleep, unconscious, you couldn't choose your dream. Awake there was a choice, perhaps only a daydream, nothing real, but a dream nevertheless.

Fielder wasn't a dreamer. He would laugh. Gabe would say, "Okay, right, look, if you're going to play that middle D in tune, you've got to open your throat muscles a little to lower the pitch, because no saxophone can be built to make true notes top to bottom, so you got to blow those true tones yourself." Emily would listen and wonder if she had a small heart too.

In the bathroom mirror, his hair was not as dark as his mother's, and his skin was not as white as his father's. In the winter he looked pale and a little shocked, skinny beneath his clothes, and he had no muscles that showed through. One ear was larger than the other: after much examination he'd found this to be true. One eye drooped a little, and he was sure it was lower in his face than the other. When he pretended to talk and smile and gesture with his hands all at the same time in front of the mirror, he thought the ear and the eye were not so noticeable. He didn't often have pimples. Neither did Emily. But he had freckles on his nose and a few on his cheeks. Emily had them sprinkled very finely only on her nose. He had big feet. The time in front of the family's three mirrors proved these things, and eventually magnified them—the bad and the good—so that he began to look at himself through slitted eyes and a wide focus. It was like glancing: nothing registered indelibly, neither the bad, which was painful, nor the good, which he'd been taught not to believe. Emily thought that way too. He'd said, "You're very pretty," and she'd said, "Am I? Patty always says I'm lumpy."

"What does your mother say?"

"That I'm beautiful, but she smiles when she says it."

"She loves you."

"People who have to love you always say you're beautiful."

There were things to walk softly around when he was with Emily. He sensed rather than took notice of them. Families were small countries, and they had laws of their own which their people obeyed as if they were in their blood. Emily was first a Gordon, as he was a Waterton. Emily was also the last Gordon. The final one. Dr. Gordon only had sisters. She was the end of the line. Another accident. Their small Gordon country was nearly finished.

He lay down on his bed with his feet together and his hands folded across his chest. "Bloody doom," Fielder had said. Doom, doom, doom. He remembered laughing hard, because doom didn't need to be faced right now. It was something that hung over you, like Hitler, and you tried to live as if it weren't there. He got up again. The Gordons didn't say, "You're the last of the family, and when you're gone—Doom." Are we just names? That's stupid.

Maybe what they said was, "Patty is bright and a doer, and we tell Emily she's beautiful because we think she is, and one of the things that makes her beautiful is that she's quiet and supports her sister." What was true in their family was that Emily loves and Patty does. It wasn't fair; but life, his mother had said, laughing, wasn't supposed to be. Families made people what they were. When he visited the Gordons, he didn't say anything about them being different from his own family. He lived with Emily's differences; she lived with his when they were together, and it felt as if they were making a small country of their own.

He picked up his alto out of its case and hung it from its strap around his neck. Even this early in the morning, he needed to honk on it. It cleared his head because it demanded its own kind of thinking. He wet a reed and put it on the mouthpiece. The noise he made when he blew into it, after five weeks of lessons from Gabe, was a good one. On Christmas day, he'd managed three notes. Now he had them all, from high F down thirty-one half-tones to low B-flat. He couldn't read music fast, but he could play ballads well. "Once in a While," "Marie," and on a good day "Shoeshine Boy." Gabe had him transpose pieces for the alto and copy them out to help him read better.

"Get as close to the music as you can," he'd said. "Hear the notes and feel them too, because when you get to improvising sometime, those tunes'll be what you start from. They'll help you choose the notes you're going to play."

Another time he'd said, "Funny thing about improvisation. It sounds as if it's free as a bird, but it's not. It's tight and logical, just like mathematics. What happens is, you know what you're doing, and know it and know it some more, and finally what you play can be as close to free as any ordinary human thing can get."

He blew some free notes. They sounded empty, a noise. Then he blew a tune he knew: "Sugar Blues." It made sense. And what he was doing did too. It was outside of himself and this room and this house. It was like being in a new place and seeing it all at once: not its total possibilities, but its *presence* in his mind as somewhere he wanted to learn to be. He tried to make his horn wail. It squealed. He took it out of his mouth and looked at it. Its satin-silver finish didn't glow. But it was a good horn. Gabe's first one had had most of its finish worn off and some of its keys he'd had to spring with rubber bands. He'd had to concentrate hard and play carefully to make any decent sound at all. "Make every note a good one," he'd said. "You do that and you'll be a horn player some day."

His mother called from Sarah's room: "Eight-thirty, time for school, Christopher."

He put the saxophone away and got his books from under the bed. He put on his coat and went outside. The snow was hard-packed and squealed under his boots. The cold was painful against his cheeks and forehead. Sarah caught up with him halfway down the block. Only her eyes showed above a scarf wrapped around her head and pinned at the back. His own clothes hardly kept him warm; the bones in his face ached, because there was a small wind coming steady up the hill toward them. At a quarter to nine, it was only just past dawn. The sun rimmed the horizon beyond the river. By the time school got out at 3:30 it would be riding the horizon again in the southwest.

"Did you look at the thermometer?"

"Mommy did," Sarah said. "It's twenty-two below. She said not to run or I'll freeze my lungs."

"Best not to do that."

"I'd die."

"Did she say that?"

"I just know."

"You're a real expert on dying."

"Miss Linkletter said freezing's the easiest way to die."

"What's she doing talking about dying?"

"Well, we all have to, don't we? She was talking about Eskimos. When their granddads get too old to hunt for food they leave them on the trail. She says it's a happy way to die."

"I'm glad I'm not in grade two."

"Why?"

"Because I don't want to sit around all day and talk about dying."

"I wish we did do that. It might be interesting. Two times five equals ten. Ugh. Miss Linkletter says if I draw pictures once more when I should be doing arithmetic she'll put me out in the hall." Sarah's voice began to go thin and high.

He put his arm across her shoulder. "Better do your times table then."

"If Mr. Littler sees you out in the hall he takes you to his office."

"I know."

"He straps you then."

"Not little girls."

"Cora Radford."

"Cora's not a little girl."

"She's in grade two."

"She's failed twice already."

"Miss Linkletter says she's a bad seed. Cora told her to go chew mice."

"Then what happened?"

"She got sent to the hall and Mr. Littler strapped her. Three on each hand. And her wrists were swollen. She couldn't hold her pencil all day. Paula Bukowski says she might get gan green and die."

"No she won't, and I still think Miss Linkletter talks too much."

"Mommy says she's very young, and she's lucky to have a job as a teacher. She comes from Vancouver where they don't have much winter. She doesn't like the cold here."

"Maybe she's afraid the Eskimos will get her and leave her on the trail."

"To die."

"What are you laughing at?"

"I think she's too skinny to be an Eskimo."

He could see Emily waiting on the Liverpool Street corner. Her blue ski pants and jacket made her look shorter than she was. He began to walk faster, and Sarah couldn't keep up. Emily didn't have a scarf across her face. She stood with her back to the small wind, her feet apart and her arms at her sides. She carried no books. He saw her hazel eyes watching him get closer. They were wide open. They didn't blink. Everything her body said about her was true. He felt in him a soft tension begin that made his breathing go shallow and his heart beat slow and strong.

He went very close to her, and she looked up into his face. Her nose was red. He bent and kissed its tip. It felt cold and crisp.

Sarah went by, head down, giggling, and when she couldn't any longer see them, he put his free arm around Emily. She put her arms around his waist. The first bell rang. They had to be in their classrooms in five minutes.

"I dreamed about you last night," he said. It wasn't quite a lie. He had been skiing and she—no, her eyes—had watched him.

"Did you?" She hardly ever said anything about him. Or them. She didn't have to.

He nodded. "It was good, but this is better." He kissed her lips, and she kissed him back. People were passing. He felt it didn't matter.

"We've got to go," she said.

"Can we skate after school?"

She shook her head. "Dentist." She shivered, and laughed. "My dad's big on checkups for his kids."

"I'll phone you."

She nodded, and he let her go.

2

Fielder said, "I was at the window, Waterton. You and Gordon are getting disgusting."

"Meretricious," Smith said. "Rancid, bloody near penultimate."

"Stop calling me names."

"The English language will always be preternatural to you," Smith said. He wiped at his nose with his wrist. "I saw you out the window too. Who do you think you are, necking at twenty below in full view of the whole school?"

"It's just show-off," Fielder said.

"Bull," Christopher said. "Who says you have to look?" It was only a show if they watched. When he stood close to Emily what happened was private.

"Bleeding arrogance."

"Smith," Christopher said, "you don't even know what arrogance means."

"Insolent, dear boy, and conceited." The English accent was an imitation of his father's.

From the doorway, Blenkin said, "If you'd read something besides the dictionary, Smith, you might have some chance of making grade ten."

"He doesn't read it," Fielder said. "He just looks at the words in large print at the top of the page."

"Preternatural?" Blenkin asked.

"Weird," Smith said. "Really weird."

"Look it up," Blenkin said, "and write out the full meaning twenty times."

Smith began to get out his dictionary.

"After school," Blenkin said, and sat at his desk. He opened the class register and picked up a pencil and cleared his throat as if he were about to call the roll, but he only glanced around the class. Alpert, Anderson, Beaumont, Bell, Callaghan, Cameron, Emily's sister, Pat Gordon. Forty names. Today Isonovich and Nelligan weren't there. May Kaplik had quit. So had Doucette, and no one asked if they were fifteen and should by law be in school.

Christopher glanced up and saw Blenkin looking at him. His eyes were blue chips: he swallowed and his adam's apple rose and fell the length of his neck. "I happened to see you, too, Waterton. The school has no jurisdiction outside its grounds. If it did you'd be in Mr. Grandison's office explaining yourself."

There was giggling laughter.

"Enough," Blenkin shouted. He rose red-faced from his chair. His back looked as if it were beginning to hump, and his wiry hair had waves in it as if it might have been marcelled. He looked down at the class and chewed his lip, a signal that there was more to come as soon as he regained control. But instead he walked to the windows and looked out toward the Liverpool Street corner. Then he turned and went back to his desk.

The bell rang for the start of classes. The door opened, and Mr. Grandison stood there waiting for Blenkin to leave. Grandison taught Math.

The door closed. Mr. Grandison said, "Good morning, class. Are you ready?" He stood on his toes and clasped his hands in front of him as if he might sing. His glass eye stared at Christopher, and then he turned his head away and began to dictate a problem to be solved. Every morning he began with a three-minute problem.

9:15. Christopher felt as if he'd been here all day. He looked across at Fielder; Math was the only subject he got more than fifty-five percent in. He had his head down and his hair fell across the side of his face. Smith had the answer already. Cameron was looking out the window. Christopher glanced out too: the sky was a heavy cold blue. At least a minute had gone by. He looked at the problem. Gabe said music was mathematical. This wasn't music.

"Who's got it?" Mr. Grandison asked. He was a monster in his office, but a pussycat in the classroom. He loved Math; it made him walk on tiptoe, smile, laugh, write huge letters and numbers on the board. "Come come now, surely you've got it. I went easy on you this morning."

Smith waited for someone to give the answer, and when no one did, he said, "Fifty-four minutes."

"Yes, right. Good." Mr. Grandison swung around to the board. "Step by step, now. You didn't just guess, did you?" He smiled over his shoulder. He hadn't stumped Smith all year.

They worked through the problem. The rest of the period was spent being amazed at the beauty and symmetry and efficiency of equations. It was from Mr. Grandison that Smith had first heard big words. The class was hard to get through. Everyone had to sit still, listen, work. When the bell rang, the class always looked around at each other as if they'd been on a dangerous mission together and had managed to arrive safely back at camp. There were ten minute recesses between each period and lunch was an hour-and-a-half so that almost everyone could go home to eat.

He didn't see Emily except to wave at when they were going home after twelve. She and Dody were a hundred yards away, headed in the opposite direction from the one he and Fielder took to get home. Cameron came halfway with them. It had warmed up a bit. Cameron said it could be zero. Fielder ran up on old Mrs. Selwin's front porch and looked at her thermometer. She came to the door and scolded him, and then she began to cry. "My sister's very ill in Edmonton. I thought you might be the telegraph boy."

"Nice going," Cameron said, when Fielder was with them again.

"How was I supposed to know?" He grinned and laughed.

"Disgusting," Christopher said, and he didn't see Fielder's foot trip him into the snowbank at the edge of the sidewalk.

"Kissy-face," Fielder said.

"You still onto that? What about you and Dody?"

"There's nothing about me and Dody."

Christopher got up and decided not to retaliate.

Cameron said, "What's the big deal? Waterton likes Gordon and who cares?"

"Why doesn't he pick on someone his own size?"

"Like who? Alpert? Or Monica Lewis, for God's sake? She's six feet tall."

"Lewis is the one Fielder really wants," Christopher said.

Fielder punched him on the shoulder. He laughed and backed up the street. At the corner of York, he broke away and ran toward home. When he looked over his shoulder, Fielder was still standing where he'd left him. Maybe there was nobody home at his place.

"You want to come for lunch?"

They walked up York. He wanted to tell Fielder about Emily. Get it finally straight. But it didn't feel like the right time.

"What's for lunch?" Fielder asked.

"Bean soup."

They went to the back door and broomed the snow off their boots. His mother knew why Fielder was here. "How nice to see you," she said, as if it had been weeks since they'd met.

The bean soup was so thick it was almost like porridge.

"Where's Dad?"

"He'll be here in a minute."

"Everyone else takes lunches to work," Fielder said.

"He likes to come home, even if it's only for half an hour."

"Does Dodd really let him?" Christopher asked.

"Mr. Dodd is a grump, but he knows your dad is a graduate engineer—" She smiled. "I guess he's the classiest general foreman anywhere." She laughed, embarrassed at saying it.

"My old man's probably gone to the Legion," Fielder said. "War pension cheque came today."

"What a terrible thing that was—shrapnel."

"Don't bother him none."

"I don't believe that, Donald. He's brave the way he handles his disability."

Fielder looked at her. Once, he'd said, "Your mother's too damned good to be true." He tipped his bowl so he could spoon up the last of the soup. "It's not much of a cheque, either. He says a man who's fought for his country deserves entertainment money."

His mother ignored Fielder's attempt at being adult.

Christopher watched Fielder's face watching his mother at the window. The expression was new to him. Fielder cared about his father. There'd never been any sign of it before.

"He's here," she said, and smoothed her hair with her hands and took off her apron. When Christopher's father opened the door, she went to him and gave him a kiss. He put his arms around her and kicked the door closed with his foot. He wore green workpants shoved into brown boots. Under his mackinaw jacket was an engineer's vest worn over a plaid shirt. His hair was thinning at the front.

She moved out of his arms and went to the stove to serve his soup. He sat at the table.

"What's new?" he asked Christopher.

"You know. School."

"You've been back three days. The thrill must be gone by now."

"Yeah, right," Fielder said.

"There's still things to be done," Christopher told him. "Is Mr. Brant going to finish, or did you run out of money?"

"Brant's contract is to do it over exactly as it was. The insurance was supposed to pay him."

"Is it going to?"

"Not quite."

"No panelling in the hall looks funny."

"Well, we'll see what can be done."

"Do you boys want cake or pie?" his mother asked. "And don't say both."

"Cake," Fielder said.

Christopher nodded his agreement. "I bet Mr. Courtney is mad," he said to his father.

"Christopher," his mother said, "can we leave this for another time?"

His father said, "Mr. Courtney thinks Sanderson Construction could've done the job for the money available."

"Is that true?" She served the cake and sat down at the table.

"Yes. Because Courtney would've sneaked him the extra cost out of the town's coffers." His voice was abrupt, annoyed.

"Is it going to be bad? Is he going to give you a bad time?"

His father shrugged. "I work for him." He finished his soup and cut himself a piece of pie.

"What about the other Board members?"

"They're on-side, Laura. When Courtney and Sanderson decided not to bid on the job because they thought they could get the contract out of the Board without it, the Board accepted Brant's tender. They weren't for once going to buy a pig in a poke. Brant's bid was normal practice. Courtney put himself in a position where even people who depend on him could vote against him."

"Just the same, you defied him."

"He can't do much about it. The School Board's not his baby."

"But will he give you money to finish the job?"

"Of course not. We'll pay for completion out of next year's budget."

His mother's smile was quick and relieved. "You're mighty snappy with the answers." She poured herself more tea. "I've got some news. Mr. Coppard at the library phoned. He's going to let me hang a show of my watercolours, and do a display case of some of my china too."

"To sell?"

"He says I can put prices on things if I want. But I think he feels that's a bit of a joke in Long River."

"By April, the mill might be running two shifts. Things are beginning to look up."

"Suddenly someone wants lumber?"

"Spruce for crating. The U.S. Department of Defense. That's what Dodd told me."

She drank from her teacup and put it down slowly into its saucer. "Is it going to be war, then, Peter?"

"God knows." He got up from the table and went to the door. "Not before dinner anyway. I'm going down to Creighton's mill. I don't think Dodd knows what they're doing with the logs they're trucking in.

What's going to happen when breakup comes? The river's full of debris as it is."

"Well, thanks for dropping by," she said.

"Not at all. My pleasure." He gave them all a half-salute and left.

No one spoke for a long moment. Fielder still had a mouthful of cake left on his plate. He ate it. "If there's a war—?" He looked up at Christopher's mother.

"You're both much too young," she said, quickly.

"I meant, maybe my old man could be an officer again."

"Please, Donald, let's not talk about war."

Fielder nodded, and then got out of his chair. "Thanks for lunch," he said, and put on his mackinaw.

Christopher put his on too. Outside, the wind blew snow off the roof and it fell like a curtain past the kitchen window. "Cold," Christopher said, involuntarily.

"Wrap up warm," his mother said.

They walked down York Street, and the first thing Fielder said was, "Your dad's a riot."

"Meaning?"

"He's so damned—I don't know—happy."

"Yeah, I guess. He's not always this cheerful."

"He's got a few things going for him now," Fielder said. "You guys are lucky."

"It doesn't feel that way."

"Who the hell else got a saxophone for Christmas?"

"I told you, everyone in the family sent money. My mother even wrote a couple in England and one in the States. My old man doesn't get big pay being foreman."

"Everyone knows he's an engineer," Fielder said. "That's how he got to be Board Chairman too." He laughed suddenly. "That must really frost Courtney." He put his arm around Christopher's shoulder. "Know what? If ever there was a war, everything'd be different. My old man says last time they emptied whole towns and marched off to England. I'd quit school and go in a goddamn minute."

"We're fourteen."

"I'm fifteen in April. I could lie. My uncle did."

"Yeah, I know," Christopher said. "And he was killed on the last day of the war. November 11, 1918. Went for a walk because it was over, and a German sniper got him."

"You tell it better'n my old man."

"You don't even think of stories like that. What'll we join up in? Not the army."

"They won't use gas on the navy."

"The air force isn't going to get gassed either."

"You have to have grade twelve for the air force."

"Three-and-a-half more years. We were born at the wrong time."

"The last war went four years."

"Maybe it won't start for a while," Christopher said, and broke away from Fielder's arm. Ahead of them the schoolyard was empty, except for a few people heading in to classes. He could see Emily and Pat. "I don't see Dody," he said.

Fielder looked where he was pointing and laughed. "Some bloody pilot you'd make. You'd have to have Gordon around to get your plane off the ground."

So, that meant they were going to join up in the air force.

He didn't touch Emily when they met on the sidewalk between the two schools. Fielder and Pat watched them, and Emily's smile was very big and knowing. It was obvious Pat had told her what had happened with Blenkin in the morning. She put her hand on his arm. "I'll phone you when I get home," she said, and left him. He walked with Pat and Fielder to the high school.

In Miss Lee's class, they were doing John Masefield. He didn't listen. It was a poem about dying. He tried to draw a picture of an airplane and, while he sketched, Emily was in his head wearing a pilot's uniform. The biplane he was trying to draw didn't look as if it would fly.

He glanced up. Miss Lee was sitting on her desk, one leg on the floor and the other dangling. Her lips were apart and her teeth showed through, making an odd smile. She was looking at him. "Christopher," (she never used last names as the other teachers did) "what is the meaning Masefield wants you to get out of the phrase 'crossing the bar'?"

"It's when you die, you cross the bar."

"Is that true?"

"Well, it's what he says dying's like."

"Like. Yes, and what are we talking about when we say 'like'?"

"I don't know."

"Come come. One thing is like another."

"A simile."

"Yes, and what if something *is* another thing. Death *is* crossing the bar?"

He was good at English, but he didn't want everyone to think he had all the answers. Smith could do it in Math, but that wasn't English. "I don't know," he said, fumbling. "A metaphor?"

She smiled at him. Her top lip folded back and showed her gums. "Yes, a metaphor. Thank you, Christopher. Now you can go back to your drawing."

He threw his pencil down and gave an exaggerated shrug. It didn't raise much of a laugh. Fielder applauded, but no one else did, because Miss Lee began to talk again.

Blenkin made it through Junior Business without yelling—he appeared quite calm, as if he weren't paying much attention while the class worked out a bookkeeping problem. He waited until the bell had stopped ringing, and then he asked Christopher to stay behind.

"What have I done now?" he said to Fielder.

"Maybe he wants to say he's sorry for this morning." Fielder headed for the door, a grin on his face.

Christopher picked up his books and went to the front of the room. He tried to look as if he were in a hurry, and hoped Blenkin would sense it and not keep him long.

Blenkin looked up at him and opened a folder. The saxophone picture was in it. "Is this yours?" Blenkin's voice rattled out of his mouth through tiny bubbles of spit.

Christopher tried to swallow fear. Why the question? "Yes."

"You're sure?" Blenkin stood up.

"Yes."

Blenkin's eyes were blanks. "Nobody helped you?"

"No. Why?"

"What's the best mark you've gotten this year?"

"Three-and-a-half."

Blenkin shoved the drawing at him. In his small precise hand he had printed at the bottom of the paper: 9/10.

"You're not helping yourself if you're lying."

"I knew it was better," Christopher said. It was hard to talk to Blenkin when he was standing, because he was a foot taller. He put the drawing back on Blenkin's desk.

"You got no help at all?"

"I practised. I've been drawing them—" He looked up into Blenkin's face. It was fleshy, even though the man was skinny. It made him look young, like Sarah when she was pouting. Except for the eyes it was always a mask just hanging there under that marcelled hair. This man was accusing him. He was saying that if his art was no good, he was no good, and if it was good he was cheating.

"Mr. Blenkin, look." He put his books down on the teacher's desk and picked out a scribbler. When he glanced up again Blenkin's face was still waiting, but now his hands were on his hips.

Christopher opened the scribbler's cover. The saxophone pictured there was an early attempt. The bell was awkwardly drawn, lopsided.

Blenkin grinned. "That looks more like you."

Christopher knew he was smiling back. He'd never talked to Blenkin alone before. The room behind him was empty, hollow. "It was when I first started drawing them." He flipped the pages. The small ones in the margins were no better. Then on the middle pages, where the staple held the scribbler together, there were two saxophones he'd drawn in October. They weren't perfect, but the keys were in the right places and the bells were the best part of the pictures. He liked them, and it occurred to him now that he wanted Blenkin to admire them too. Blenkin liked Fielder for the way he played basketball.

"I see," Blenkin said. He took the scribbler from him and looked at it through squinted eyes.

"I got one for Christmas."

Blenkin said nothing. He looked up from the saxophones and closed the scribbler. "Did you?" He picked up the drawing again. "How will you learn how to play it here in Long River?"

"Gabe Sommerville teaches me."

After a moment: "He married the Pritchard girl."

What Blenkin was saying was quite clear. It was nothing new; his mother had said it too.

"Are you headed in that same direction, Waterton?"

The question was unanswerable.

"From what I've seen, Sommerville is teaching you more than saxophone lessons."

"I'm sorry about this morning." Christopher heard himself say the words, and knew they were the confession Blenkin wanted. But there was going to be no forgiveness. He felt foolish. There was no reason to say he was sorry.

"You should be." Blenkin looked away from him and down at the drawing. "The others didn't practise for two months before they did their drawings." He picked up a pen and crossed out the 9 and wrote 5. Now he looked up once more. "That's all, Waterton."

Art was a subject. He needed the 9 to pass it. "I did the picture, why can't I have the mark?" He picked up his books.

"What difference does it make?" Blenkin asked. "I can't see you passing Art." He rubbed the end of his nose with the palm of his hand. "You can go now."

"It's not fair." He was surprised he'd said the words. There was lead at the bottom of his stomach.

"You're used to getting things given to you on a platter, Waterton."

The door opened and Miss Garrett stood there, her eyes blinking. They always blinked. They were big and brown and sat round on each side of a triangular nose that had a bump halfway down it. Her hair was mouse-coloured and done up in little sausage rolls that were coming loose. Strands of hair hung down the sides of her face. "Oh," she said, in her odd, strangled voice. "I came for my pen. Is that it?" She pointed to the one Blenkin had used to change his mark. She walked to the desk.

Blenkin handed it to her. "I said you could go, Waterton."

Outside in the hall, Fielder was waiting. "What was that all about?"

"Art. He thought I'd got somebody else to draw my saxophone."

"Who else has hardly even seen one?"

Anger was relief. He let it happen. "Some day—" He looked around. Blenkin and Garrett were at Blenkin's door. Christopher went down the stairs two at a time and out into the cold. "I'm going to kill him. He told me I'm not going to pass Art. The first goddamn mark he put on that drawing was 9, then he hauls me in there, accuses me of cheating and when I *prove* I did the drawing he gives me a 5. What did I do?"

"Emily Gordon," Fielder said. "He goes to church three times on Sunday and once on Wednesday."

"He likes you." Christopher could hear himself beginning to yell. "I play basketball too."

"Come come now, Waterton. I'd hardly call what you do out on the floor *basketball*."

That was true. He was supposed to laugh, but he couldn't. "Screw off, Fielder. I ski pretty good."

"He doesn't give a damn about skiing."

"He does, and I need Art to pass."

"No you don't. A sixty percent average will pass you."

"With him giving 5's for the best thing I do?"

Fielder shrugged. "Okay, so kill him. Burn his house down."

"If he had a house. Bloody cheap, boarding at the Carltons'." The anger was gone. There was only hurt left.

Fielder said, "I'm going down to Keefer Hall to practise. Coming?"

Christopher looked up into the sky. It was filling up with darkness. Too late to ski. In another couple of weeks, when the light lasted longer, he'd be able to go to the Castles after school. What he wanted to do was play his horn. "I've got a lesson with Gabe tomorrow."

They separated. Fielder headed downtown to Keefer where both the High School and Commercial League played basketball. It was always open—a court that took up the second floor of the building. The city owned it; and on the ground floor was the library.

Christopher looked back at the school. It didn't even have a library. Times were too tough. That was one of the reasons his father had run to be elected to the School Board. He wanted a proper library and had campaigned on that issue. The Elementary School had a few books on shelves in each room, but they were old and not much use. But that was where Mayor Courtney thought the books should be. "High School is mostly a frivolity," he'd said, when he'd spoken at the final election rally. "I know we'd all like to have our kids go there, but in these times we got to face reality. There's plenty of land needs opening up north. That's how us oldtimers got here. We were opening up the country, and I don't suppose most of us got past grade eight. I got out at grade four myself, and I haven't done bad at all. Of course, we got some educated people. Have to have them. Doctor Royce. Ernie Kroll over at the pharmacy, practical men. It's when you get a person having ambitions outside the job that feeds him that you get calls on the public purse for things like libraries in High Schools. There's books enough in the schools now, and if there aren't then we got a library downtown, and the Ladies' Institute and church groups make donations there. That's the way it should be. Them as wants gives, and then they get back what others gives. It's a law of life and business that it's a sin to spend everybody's money for the pleasure of a few. And that, sure as the Pits of Hell, goes for spending public money so a few can do something the rest of us don't give a tinker's damn about."

When his father got up, he didn't make a speech. "The Keefer Building," he said, "the bandstand in the middle of the city hall park, the ski jumps on Castle Hill, the skating rink, the sports grounds, the park by the river where some people swim in the summer. Do we all need city water? There are still plenty of wells and outhouses in town. The bridge across Long River. The old barge was good enough. Do we all burn our houses down? Why have a Fire Department? Are we all crooks—or just some of us—so why have the police?" He paused and gazed out over the audience as if he were trying to make up his mind to say something. Then he smiled and said, "The Mayor's car."

The near-silence was, in the end, not applause for the Mayor, but he took it that way. He got up, laughing. "I've seen a lot of performances in my time, but never one so calculated to bring doom down on the head of a man seeking public office. That car is not mine. It's the city's. Every citizen owns it. And, well, if they want to give it to somebody else that's what these civic elections are all about."

The applause was like the crack of a whip. Christopher's mother had said, "Oh, dear," and he remembered sitting beside her being embarrassed for his father.

On election night, Mayor Courtney was returned with a bigger majority than ever before, even bigger than his first in 1924 when Long River stopped being a village and became a town. Maybe he got all those votes because people didn't dare go against him, but after they'd done their duty they voted for Peter Waterton too. He topped the polls, and was made chairman. The school burned down. There was no money for a library. Courtney, in the end, had his way.

The lights were on in the school now. From here, up the hill toward York Street, he could see Blenkin at his desk. He picked up the remains of a broken hockey stick from the snowdrift by the sidewalk and sighted down it toward him.

Blenkin's head turned. He stood up. Christopher was for a moment certain he was seen. He dropped the broken hockey stick and stared down the slope into the grade nine room. Blenkin looked now as if he wanted something he couldn't have. He turned away, and went to the door. He paused there and then went again toward his desk.

Christopher backed up the sidewalk. At this distance, Blenkin was funny—a stickman jerking around as if there might be something inside of him he was fighting. But on the basketball court, or skiing or playing hockey he wasn't that way.

Smith came out of the south entrance and Christopher waited for him. He was taller than most of the grade nines and he looked athletic, but he played no games, except when he had to during Blenkin's P.E. periods: volleyball now, because it was winter. "I figure that when I was born I was given just so many heartbeats," he'd said, "and I don't want to use up mine any faster than I have to." He looked as healthy as anyone else. Christopher waited for him.

"What did Blenkin want after school?"

Christopher told him.

Smith laughed. "Why don't you get your old man to fire him?"

"You can't fire a teacher. Not any more."

"Well, I guess it's just tough-titty on you," Smith said. "Old slack-jaw had it in for you today." He laughed again. "Osculations with Emily Gordon. Naughty-naughty."

"Whatever the hell that means."

"Look it up."

"You look it up."

"I did," Smith said. "Kisses, dumbo." He turned to go up Bristol Street. "I'll say this for you, Waterton, you got guts. Very few brains but a lot of guts."

"What's the matter with a kiss, for God's sake?"

"You are the ultimately egregious innocent. Look that up."

"It's a cinch you didn't."

"Inn-o-cent," Smith said. "Lovely word. Means naive."

"How would you know?"

"Then tell me what it means, smart-ass."

"It means you're not guilty. You didn't do it."

"Then who did?" Smith began to walk away.

Christopher didn't try to stop him. "What're you going to do with all those words, professor?"

"Crossword puzzles. Big money in crossword puzzles," Smith said, and jogged away up the middle of the street.

3

He lay in bed with the pillow pulled down under the blankets so that he was completely covered. With the door closed into the kitchen, his bedroom took only a few minutes to cool off. By morning it was always cold; the whole house chilled to freezing. Then his father got up, shook the ashes out of the grates in the kitchen range and the furnace. Gradually the rebuilt fires warmed the house. He was too old now to take his clothes to the kitchen and dress in front of the stove. Morning was iced linoleum under his feet, and always his skin was tight and bunched against the bedroom's frigid air.

But now he liked his small warmth. Inside it, his body disappeared and his mind took over as if it were another self that in this safe place had its own life. He tried to make it think about the day: Blenkin; Garrett's useless science experiment; Miss Lee's metaphor (something is something else); Emily close to him on the sidewalk near the school, her face turned up to his and her eyes waiting for him to give her a kiss. He gave it to her and then thought of summer, drifted clear of winter: here in this warm darkness his mind produced a picture of a woman, maybe fifty years old, her hair knotted at the back of her head, her shoulders hunched and wearing a dress that stuck to her body because she was hot, sweating. In her hand was a thick rope and, at the end of the rope, a cow. May Kaplik's mother.

May had a bike. A secondhand boy's bicycle. One of her sisters had sent the money, and her mother had got it for her. It was a boy's bike but May rode it as if for her that wasn't as important as the fact that she owned it. She wore shorts, and she stood with one leg over the bar and the other propped her up. He always saw her that way. She had fair hair just short of her shoulders, a round face, a small neat mouth, a good strong nose and eyes that had no shyness in them at all.

She said, "I'm not going to *bite* you." Her voice had scorn and laughter in it.

Then, in the evenings, when the sun stayed up until after eight and its glow remained until eleven, they played games on the streets. Sometimes scrub softball, but more often run-sheep-run or kick-the-can. Kids fifteen years old sometimes played, and ones older than that sat on the steps of porches along the dusty street and cheered or booed and yelled as if they were a crowd at a hockey game.

One night he was It, and after a long hour he'd got everyone out. The game—without anyone saying so—was over. The air was still, and the small clouds at the horizon were the colour of freshly slaughtered chunks of moosemeat. May was there, with the Dobroski twins who had skirts on and wore silk stockings with runs in them that they rolled down onto elastic bands just above their knees; Fielder was away for the summer at his aunt's in Victoria, but Callaghan was there, and Doucette, Garner, and Lorne. Not a usual mix. The gang from the flats down by the river didn't often come this far uptown.

Nor did Elmo Kidner: Elmo the Kid. He had St. Vitus' Dance. And it really was a dance the way he walked—knees bent, arms working as if he were pulling himself along, and chin high and his head snapping from side to side as he moved forward down the sidewalk. Spastic. Elmo sold papers. He met the 2 A.M. and the 5 P.M. passenger trains. He sold papers when people were going to work in the morning and when the movie theatre closed at night. In the winter, what money he made from selling papers he lost trying to play Kelly Pool with the hustlers who hung out at the poolhall across from the railway station. Sometimes they made two or three dollars a day—enough to eat, buy beer and smokes, and rent a room at the Budapest Hotel next door.

"Hey, Elmo, where you going?" Callaghan shouted.

"None of your beeswax," Elmo said, flopping along. He had a cleft palate.

"Stick around. You can be It."

Elmo stopped, and then he charged, like a shambles made half human, toward the can in the middle of the road. Christopher was standing astride his bike by May Kaplik. "Oh, for God's sake," she said.

But Elmo kicked the can. It went high, almost straight up, and landed in front of Callaghan.

"Way to go, Elmo," Doucette said. "Want to play?"

"Can't," Elmo said. His head and arms were quiet for a moment, and then they began to flop around again. "Got to see a guy about a job." He said it deliberately. He wanted everyone to hear and understand.

"What you going to do, run a butterchurn?" Garner asked.

Doucette didn't laugh; he walked over to Elmo. "Hey, you didn't do it there for a little bit. Mus' feel good when you don't jump around, eh?" He moved closer and held onto Elmo's arm. "How d'you feel when it stops?"

Elmo pulled away. Doucette grabbed him again. "Hey, don't do that now. We're going to help you." He laughed: it was a new game. Lorne laughed too.

"I bet we can stop it for you," Doucette said to Elmo.

Christopher watched Lorne move in on Elmo. Callaghan moved too; so did Garner. He began to drop his bike, and then he looked at May. Her face was blank and dead. She was with Doucette. The Dobroski twins were grinning. He heard Elmo make a loud noise, like a horse bellowing. The sound scared him. Garner was forcing Elmo's head to be still; the others held his arms and legs; Elmo was lifted off the ground. The convulsions got stronger. Elmo's body heaved against what was restraining it. Doucette became angry. "Goddamn," he shouted. "Don't you know we're trying to help you?" He took one hand away from Elmo's shoulder and hit him a hammer blow on the forehead with his fist. Elmo was quiet for a moment, but then he yelled again. "Goddamn," Doucette shouted, "hold tighter."

No doors were opening. No one on the porch steps or the verandas along the street was moving to see what was happening in the middle of the road.

"Doucette," May shouted.

He turned and grinned at her.

"Leave him alone."

Elmo kicked and almost got his legs free. Doucette laughed and turned to hit him again. Christopher heard May's voice. "Come on," she said, and hauled her bike over the sidewalk and rode between two houses down the pathway that led to First Avenue. He followed, and he thought now, in bed in the middle of winter, that because it had been Doucette who'd wanted to stop Elmo's dance, it was all right: until then, he'd thought anything Doucette wanted to do was okay and, if it hadn't been for May, he might have helped try to stop Elmo's spastics. McDonald and Lamb and Muncie's gang buried people standing upright in the sand on the island in the middle of the river. They'd done it to Isonovich and had left him there. Callaghan and Smith found him hours later after supper. They'd buried him on the far side of the island. He was just a head above the jam-packed sand, and when they got him out he couldn't move his legs. Smith wanted to take him to Doctor Royce, but Isonovich was afraid of what McDonald's gang would do to him if they got into trouble. Besides, his family couldn't afford to pay for a doctor—which was one of the reasons his little sister had died the following winter.

After that had happened to Isonovich, he'd told his mother about how Purvis had helped him ashore when McDonald forced him to swim across the river from the island to the west bank. She had looked at him, fearful, and had hugged him. "The police," she'd said, and then her arms had gone limp, and she'd sat down at the kitchen table. "But they wouldn't do anything. They feel the same way about those awful jokes."

He'd wished he hadn't told her. She always had to try to find out reasons for things scary or rotten in the world. "These times have made people cruel." The times, these times: they were to blame for everything. But people helped each other out too. In the fall the men hunted and divided the meat among the really poor. At Christmas, there was always a party at school, where everybody brought clothes that didn't fit anymore, and there were food hampers. Isonovich's father, who'd been an educated civil servant in Russia, couldn't stand the charity. He took the turkey and sold it for a bottle of rye. He passed out in the middle of the street, and Mr. English took another turkey to the family. Billy MacLean put Mr. Isonovich in jail overnight to sober up.

He rode with May down First Avenue toward the river. The light was still strong. She pedalled along beside him, not saying anything, and he was silent too. It was awkward. He didn't want to talk about Elmo, and he couldn't think of anything else, except what would happen if Doucette caught up with them, but she kept looking at him as if he should say something. There was amusement in her eyes. What was happening might be funny—or worse, this might be the beginning of a joke she was playing on him. Her sisters were whores. Alice and Annie. They had been pretty at school. When he was in grade five with May, they had quit grade nine. Men went to the Kaplik house on the edge of the cranberry swamp; there was a barn and a shed and an acre or two of damp pasture, where Mrs. Kaplik kept her cow.

There was no Mr. Kaplik, and there hadn't been since May was a baby. Everyone knew then what was happening. No one talked about it. Alice and Annie had been fifteen and sixteen. Just once he'd heard his mother ask his father about it, and he'd shrugged. There was nothing anyone could do, not with Courtney condoning it, and he'd said, "Do you know what the mayor told Sparks and Kroll and Paulson at the hotel? That charity was getting to be the biggest item in the city budget, and if holding parties for the men from the mill kept the Kapliks off the dole, then that was all right with him."

One day in class, May had gestured to him, asking for a pencil sharpener. She made a circle with her thumb and forefinger and shoved her other forefinger into it. He understood what she wanted. It was a usual gesture, but before he could hand his little sharpener to her, Miss Curry was there between them, her rouged face more livid than ever, her lips thin and her eyes outraged. She grabbed May's hair and pulled her out of her seat. "You filthy little creature, how dare you, how *dare* you in my classroom?" She dragged May down the aisle and out the door. The shock of it made the class absolutely silent. Mr. Littler strapped May. She came back to her seat, and her hands were fists. She had not cried. Christopher stared at her. She looked as if she were holding her breath in and might not let it out again. All through the rest of the afternoon, he'd watched her when he could. Gradually, muscle by muscle, the stiffness went out of her, until she'd sat as if she'd made up her mind to be a different person. She did no more school work. Her geography book was open. She watched out the window. Miss Curry said nothing to her, but she moved awkward around the room as if her knees had become locked. The next day, May was transferred to Mr. Bond's class, which was a mixture of slow grade fives and fast grade fours. Alice and Annie left town in the spring. Everybody knew that in summer they worked the cruise ships to Alaska. They bought tickets, got cabins and entertained in them the old Americans and Englishmen who had money enough to travel. That was the first time he'd understood that there actually were people in the world who weren't in the movies but were well-off anyway, even rich. It allowed him to dream about sometime having money. Alice and Annie had done that much for him. It was resented by people in Long River that they weren't down Hogan's Alley in Vancouver, getting beaten up by drunks. In the winter, Purvis told him, they worked in a steam bath. "Life's pretty good to girls," he'd said. "They got a choice."

Where First Avenue crossed River Road, May stopped. He rode around in a half-circle and came to rest facing her. Over her shoulder he could see up the long empty avenue. If Doucette appeared on the horizon, he could head on out fast.

Then he had to look at May. What she was doing now was watching him, waiting. He was supposed to know what was happening, but the question couldn't be asked: what do you want? His mind refused to think, or even offer up any images. He knew he was staring. His throat-muscles convulsed and made a clicking sound as if he were afraid.

She grinned faintly. "I'm not going to *bite* you," she said.

He shook his head. "I know." Doucette wasn't coming. "We could go to the island."

She swung her leg over the seat of her bike and stood beside it. "What for?"

"We could swim."

She wheeled her bike slowly around so that it was headed away from the river. "Bare ass," she said.

Now that he knew they weren't going to the island, he could say, "It'd have to be, I guess."

She didn't say anything.

"I don't go much," he told her.

"Neither do I. McDonald only lets certain people on."

"If they go bare ass," he said, and laughed. She didn't. Her eyes had no expression in them. She looked younger than he'd ever seen her. It made him feel safe. "I like you. If Doucette heard that he'd kill me." He laughed again.

"Doucette," she said. "He just wants to be another McDonald."

He watched her look away and, relieved, he thought, Doucette, it has to be Doucette for you. That's the way it is.

Out of the trail in the bush fifty yards up River Road, there appeared a woman leading a cow on a rope.

"Go away," May said.

He didn't move. Mrs. Kaplik was almost a stranger to him, because she seldom went up town. He watched her come toward them.

"Go on," May said, between her teeth.

Now, in bed in the cold dark, he understood why she wanted him to go—not to get rid of him, but to have him be somebody from York Street her mother didn't know anything about at all. Doucette had gone too far. Elmo hadn't been a game for her and, when she'd said she didn't go to the island much, that was something she'd wanted right then to be the truth. Maybe it was. Except that she lived with her mother and was sister to Alice and Annie.

He didn't like himself for not doing what May had wanted, but what she wanted and what was possible were two different things. He didn't come from the flats, and anyway, Doucette would make sure they couldn't become friends. May's mother had come toward him like the last line of a joke. He couldn't leave. She looked comically friendly. Her eyes were small but they were bright. She stopped near them on the road and looked down at herself.

"I'm a big mess, eh?" She laughed. "This cow she got out. I got to chase her in the bush."

May didn't say anything.

"What else? She's in heat and I got to take her to have a party with Jake's bull."

"Now?" May's voice had a quarrel in it.

"Why not now? It ain't going to stay home when it wants the bull. Who's this?" Mrs. Kaplik pointed at him.

"Nobody," May said.

"He don't look like nobody."

"Well, he is."

"Okay, I'm going to Jake's. You go home." She fished a key out of her pocket and gave it to May. "Those guys'll break the cupboards and drink all my whiskey."

He saw then that she had been drinking too. She wasn't angry at the cow for running away, and taking it to Jake's bull was necessary, so why not do it now?

"I don't want to go home," May said.

"Go." Mrs. Kaplik waved her hand. The decision was final.

"I don't want to be alone with—"

"Hush yourself up, Marie's there."

"Why didn't you give her the key?"

"Marie drink my whiskey faster than anyone." She moved off, her voice a slur that drifted back to them. "Go. I said go on. I mean it."

Christopher watched her head unsteadily down the road. Jake Shipley's place was less than a mile below the bridge, a high, dry fifty acres where he had a dairy.

He looked back at May. She was putting the key into the pocket of her shorts. He thought of one of the drunks at her house picking her up and carrying her someplace upstairs. Without thinking, he asked, "Do you want me to come with you?" If he'd been a foot taller and ten years older, the offer to protect her might have been real.

May looked at him. *She* was ten years older. "Jesus," she said, and began to climb onto her bike, "why don't you just go home?"

He didn't move. Couldn't.

"Scram, or I'll tell Doucette on you." Her smile was a knife that cut the stomach out of him. She didn't look back. He watched her pedal her out-sized bicycle along the road and past the trail where her mother had appeared.

He stood up and pumped hard toward town. What did she do there? What did she have to do? The questions were much bigger than the acts he imagined. Were those things normal at her house, as filling the coal scuttle and helping with the dishes were at home? She opened a cupboard, and whiskey was there. Behind her in the room were the men. How many? And, of course, there was Marie. Did she take the men upstairs one by one? Were there old men there who wanted Mrs. Kaplik to take them upstairs? Or was Mrs. Kaplik's just a place to hold a party and they gave her money for whiskey, which would mean she was only a bootlegger. May was free to run with Doucette. That summer she was not as old as Alice had been when she'd left. And Alice and Annie were both big women, like their mother. May was small. By the time he'd arrived home, the rescue fantasies had begun. May never spoke to him again during the holidays. At school in the fall, she began to wear makeup, high heels and stockings. Blenkin made her go and wash her face. He'd never been against lipstick before. He threw chalk at her when she didn't pay attention. One day, in early November, she somehow caught a piece as it was winged toward her, and then she got up and walked the length of the room to Blenkin's desk. She dropped the chalk on his blotter. His face went red with anger, his eyes blinked and he chewed at his lip. She was trembling. For a moment neither of them moved, then she turned and walked stiff and weeping out of the room. She never came back. Nobody else in the room moved or made a sound. Christopher knew that she was alone. Doucette was gone trapping. Lorne and Garner came to school only two or three times a week. Mrs. Kaplik didn't protest. May went to work at Ch'en's Cafe as a waitress.

At the dinner table one night, he asked why nothing had been done about May. "I don't think she's old enough to quit school."

His father had almost smiled. "Some people grow up quicker than others."

His mother's face had gone rigid. "Well, she's certainly no better than she should be. A girl like that at school can be a disruptive influence."

They went on eating through an unusual silence, and later, while he was doing his homework in his room, he heard his mother's voice insisting, arguing, and once it became loud enough for him to hear. "Peter, this is serious, and it's not my business, it's yours."

He waited, finished with Math and Social Studies, and knowing the discussion had been about him. When his father came into the room, he pretended that he was reading for English. Christopher had seen him angry, but never before nervous.

"You have anything to do with May Kaplik?" he asked, finally.

"No, she's not at school any more."

"You know what I mean."

Christopher stared at his father: he looked desperate. "I don't know what you're saying, Dad."

His father stood up and began again. "Your mother thinks I should give you the facts of life." His voice was hollow, and there was a kind of ferocity in it he hadn't heard before. He wanted to stand up too, but he felt attacked. "I know what you're talking about," he said, and heard his voice come out high. "In Science class Miss Garrett—"

"You talk about girls, you and Fielder."

"I suppose so."

"You've talked about May Kaplik, her mother, her sisters."

"Yes."

"Well, you don't fool with women like that."

"I liked May. Blenkin did—"

"Blenkin did exactly the right thing. Girls like that are diseased. You go with them." He stopped. His eyes bulged. "You'll get a dose of the clap. You understand?" His voice was nearly a shout.

Christopher felt himself nodding his head. This wasn't his father talking; it wasn't anyone he'd heard from before.

"You save yourself till you're an adult and married to a decent girl. Till you're married, you see." His voice was more familiar now. "Nice girls get pregnant. No one wants to have to get married. Do you play with yourself?"

"No." He could only lie. His father was looking ferocious again.

"Good. Well, good." He moved toward the door. "It's not good for you, not good at all." He smiled eagerly. "Didn't mean to interrupt your studies. Mother insisted."

"That's okay." He thought he should say something more. "Thanks, Dad."

"You're welcome, Chris."

He remembered watching his father leave the room and seeing his mother waiting outside the door. "Oh, Peter," she said, and her face was wide open and anxious, as it often was. "Do you think—?"

"Hush," he said, and closed the door.

May had clap. Not all by herself. Someone gave it to her. How did his father know? Or was it something he only said to make a point? So the truth was allowed to be stretched or the rules bent if they had to be. When Tim Barber had gone home one noon in July, 1936, and had found Ray West in bed with his wife, he'd killed both of them. He was let off by the jury, the Crown didn't appeal, and his mother had said, "It may not seem quite right, but decent people have to fight back. Laws must be allowed to be for us too."

So, if he or Fielder or Smith quit school the law would be enforced. Doucette and May could quit and nothing was done.

"One of the reasons—my God, maybe the only reason—Long River is a tolerable place to live is that here we have a little control over our lives," his father had said, and he had laughed. "Tim Barber is a good person. Who's to say any one of us might not have done the same thing?"

Elmo's arm had been broken when the gang had tried to stop his St. Vitus' dance, and it had been Doucette who'd quit school and had gone trapping. May belonged to a rotten life. Not decent. Her mother wasn't decent either, but nothing was done about her. Nobody said she ran a whorehouse and nobody said she didn't.

"Helps keep the loggers off the street," Purvis had said.

"Is it the same about the mayor?"

"What about him?"

"My dad says he's a crook. Why don't they close him down?"

"Nobody said he was running a whorehouse, either," Purvis said, "but he's like Mrs. Kaplik, if you think about it. I mean, he helps keep things running smooth. He's good at that, and people think the money he makes doesn't hurt anybody, and it helps a lot of his friends."

He had his head above the covers now, and sleep was muddling the images in his head. In the clear cold distance, he heard a train whistle. It was miles away, going somewhere else. He thought of war with Germany. Men on a train going somewhere foreign that was green, but its ground was splashed with blood. And he was flying over fields where he could see smoke from guns. May was there. She had no clothes on, but her back was to him; she watched out a window and wouldn't turn around. He wanted to see what the front of her looked like. Then he was flying the aircraft again, and it began to dive toward the smoking guns on the ground. He pulled hard on the joystick. It wouldn't move. The plane flew faster and the ground came closer. He was very frightened. May turned her face toward him and said, grinning through rotted teeth, "Well, what are you going to do?" There was nothing he could do. The plane began to crash and his fear wakened him. He lay trying to understand that the dark around him belonged to his room. His room. He rolled over and held the pillow, and forced himself to think of Emily. The dream broke up, began to dissolve, but away in the distance there was still May standing in sunlight with her leg over the bar of her bike.

CHAPTER THREE

1

THEY CLIMBED THE CENTRAL CASTLE HILL, THE ONE WITH THE trestle on top of it. Emily carried one of his skis balanced on her shoulder like a piece of timber while he carried the other. They were each two metres long and had three grooves cut into their skiing surfaces so that when he landed after a jump the grooves helped hold him steady. It was early in the day. The hill was smooth and white, not a mark on it.

He had wakened at first light and had known immediately that it had snowed during the night. Still sleepy and without inhibitions, he had phoned Emily. It had felt right to do that, and it had been. They'd both talked softly, afraid to wake the others who were sleeping in on a Saturday morning. Because it had snowed, the temperature was above zero; by the time he'd left his place the thermometer had read fifteen above. They'd gone together to the bottom of the hill, had left her skis and poles standing in the snow, and now they were climbing the switchback trail through the tall spruce at the edge of the ski-run toward the Boys' Jump halfway to the top.

He broke trail and shook the loaded branches overhead so that the snow wouldn't drop on Emily. He turned often to watch her struggle up toward him. Her cheeks were full of colour, and her eyes looked up at him seriously from beneath her toque. The new snow had blunted the sharpness in the air, and the smell of spruce was like a message from spring two months away. The hill was so steep they could almost lean on it. He lay back in the snow with his feet against a tree and waited for her.

He took the ski she carried and held both of them from sliding away down through the bush and across the hundreds of yards of flat ground at the bottom of the hill.

She put her feet against his tree and lay beside him, breathing hard. She laughed her quiet laugh. "I've never been up this trail before. I've only watched them jumping from the bottom."

"Skiing's stupid," he said. "A big climb and then it's all over in half a minute."

"But you like it."

He nodded and laughed at her. "You're a wonder," he said. "Anybody else would've asked why I do it if I think it's stupid."

"Don't you like it?"

"Sure. I just don't know why it has to be stupid."

"In Switzerland I think you get towed up."

"Not if you're a jumper, I bet."

"My dad takes us out to Kinney's Meadow. You could come with us."

"Sure, after Sports' Day is over."

"You'll win the Junior Jumping."

"Come second, if I'm lucky."

"Maybe you'll beat Lester."

"I haven't ever beat Sonny yet." He rolled away from her and stood in the foot of new snow on the switchback trail. She got up too, and he needed suddenly to touch her. The skis got in the way when they hugged, and their noses were wet when they kissed. He thought that soon he wanted to feel her close to him in some place where they didn't have to be bundled up in jackets and heavy pants, boots, mitts, scarves, and toques. He knew he was grinning.

"What's funny?" She looked worried.

"I've hardly seen you with your jacket off."

"There's Pat's party tonight."

She often laughed, but she never made jokes like everybody else did. There was just one Emily. The same all the time. He loved the steady thing she was. He'd never liked parties, but because of her he was looking forward to this one.

They moved on, and finally the trail broke out onto the edge of the steep run. He left her ninety feet below the jump where he would land, and took his skis with him to the take-off above the jump.

This was nearly two-thirds of the way to the top, where the trestle stood, and from here he could look out over the town. The river came in from the west and curved south a mile east of the Castle Hills and beyond the flats where the big railway bridge spanned a quarter mile of water. The river was not frozen solid. Its ice was churned up on both sides of a ribbon of open water that flowed green through what looked from here to be a white wasteland. Below and straight ahead were all the stores, the theater, the ballroom where Gabe played, Keefer Hall, and the three hotels with their restaurants and beer parlours attached. People walked black against the new snow. The few cars and trucks he could see on the streets looked half-size.

He bent down and snapped his feet into the skis' harness. When he stood up again, Emily waved. He raised his mittened hand to her and turned the tips of his skis toward the jump below. The foot of snow would slow him down, but the mark he made when he landed would be indelible. He wanted Emily to see how good he was. He slid his skis back and forth at the top of the run. They were waxed with paraffin. Blenkin had different waxes for different weathers that he ordered from Vancouver, but candle wax worked as well as anything else in dry cold snow.

He moved forward and waited until his muscles relaxed. Then he started down the run. Anticipation and speed built; he loved it. Locked into what had to happen now, he felt freed to go hard at it. He crouched, arms extended in front of him, head up and his eyes trying to gauge the exact moment when the tips of his skis would meet the edge of the jump. He brought his arms back and smoothly leaped forward over the slant of his skis. He knew he'd started the leap too soon and that he might not make ninety feet. Below him, he could see Emily looking up as if she were seeing something absolutely new. His arms milled slowly at his sides. He felt the back ends of his skis touch down, and then the full length of them hit the slope of the hill. His feet were together, the right one back of the left. His arms balanced him while the slant of the hill took over. This was the second thrill—the rush of wind on his face and against his body, trying to force him to lose control and fall. Then, all at once, there was the sudden flat at the bottom of the hill. His knees gave. They pumped like shock absorbers and he didn't fall. He stood straight and turned early in the new snow so that a great sheet of it rose up, and then a cloud billowed above and around him. He came to a stop facing Emily. She was there against the run's white perpendicular surface. She waved again, and he knew he felt as good as he ever had. Emily was shouting words down toward him, but he couldn't make sense of them.

He waved at her and turned to see a tall figure poling himself toward the base of the hill. It was Clarence Blenkin, and there was no way to avoid him.

Christopher looked up and saw Emily moving down the edge of the run. She was sliding and tumbling through the deep snow. He could hear her laughter from where he stood. Blenkin stopped when he saw her. She came to rest a yard away from him. Christopher, without his poles, ran on his skis toward them. With Emily there, he suddenly didn't mind that Blenkin had arrived.

"You know Emily Gordon, Mr. Blenkin?"

"Of course." Blenkin's smile was brief. "I thought you were Lester." He bent and loosened his harnesses. "That was a good jump you made."

The words were unexpected, like a punch in the chest. Christopher laughed.

"I've never been that close to anyone jumping before," Emily said. "I don't know how you keep standing up."

"Practice," Blenkin said. He kicked off his skis and planted his poles in the snow not far from his and Emily's. "Are you going up again?"

Christopher took off his skis and put them over his shoulder. They walked in silence up the steep switchbacks. He put his free hand behind him, and Emily held onto it. He did it as much for himself as for her. At the top, Blenkin, fifty feet ahead, turned, and Christopher saw him watching, not him but Emily. He wore his blue ski pants tucked into grey socks that had red tops. His ski boots were black and their laces white. His jacket was red, and he wore earmuffs over a rolled-up toque. But his face still just hung there, as it did in class. Christopher couldn't tell what he was thinking. Emily let go and leaned against the lip of the jump.

"Go on," Blenkin said, as if he were coming out of deep thought, "give it another try."

"I think I began my jump too soon last time."

Blenkin nodded. "You've got to use the run for all it's worth. The leap is just an extension of it."

He was being friendly. "The edge of the jump is hard to judge," Christopher told him. He found himself watching Blenkin's face for a sign of real acceptance.

When he had his skis on again and was ready to jump, his muscles wouldn't relax. His body felt as if it had separated into its parts and they were held together by lengths of string. Emily was standing with Blenkin at the point where he'd touched down before. He thought they were smiling at one another. When he was very young his mother had brought him into the living room, where she and her friends were having afternoon tea. "He knows the difference between two, too, and to," she said, laughing, delighted. He had known. She'd taught him. But suddenly he was afraid it might all be a joke on him in front of these ladies, and he couldn't remember what it was she wanted him to say. He felt as if there was an echo of that moment now in his head. He wondered if he could ski at all, if Blenkin would laugh. It was difficult to concentrate.

Blenkin looked up at him and signalled. Christopher obeyed. He leaned forward and let his weight start him down the run.

He did what he'd done during the first jump: crouched, extended his hands forward, watched the tips of his skis, and this time he leapt too hard and felt off balance in the air, awkward, one ski-tip higher than the other, his arms stiff as if he were trying to balance himself stationary in the air instead of trying to fly. Emily's face below him was like Dody's watching Fielder sink a basket. He landed a ski-length short of his first jump, and there was no style in his run down the hill. When he'd stopped and could look back, Blenkin was nearly at the jump, and Emily was watching him pick up his skis to begin his climb to the trestle at the top of the main hill.

Christopher planted his skis in the snow and moved to where Blenkin might land. Emily came with him, and they stood staring up into the grey sky against which Blenkin was a remote thin, half-red figure that signalled and then tipped forward. On the trestle's long steep slope he moved in silence and disappeared down into the bottom of the trestle's curve and then appeared again at the edge of the jump. His leap was smooth, the tips of his skis rose up, his body lay along them and he floated down through the void made by the almost vertical slant of the hill. It was then that they heard him. He grunted. The sound became a low howl, as if a pressure were being relieved. The back ends of his skis touched down two hundred feet below the trestle. One arm was up over his head, the other swung low; he was off balance as he hit the hill's new unmarked snow. His knees bent, he crouched and his body leaned first to his right and then to his left. His speed increased, he hit the base of the hill, and the force of coming out of his dive down the slope shoved further at his balance. He fell with such suddenness that Christopher heard himself shout with surprise. Emily said, "Oh, no," and then anxiously: "Will he be hurt?" Already the snow was settling around Blenkin. His skis were off and coasting on before him, but he rose up onto his feet and his momentum made him run. He tried to keep from falling again. He tottered, skidded, a marionette. Emily laughed. He fell once more and finally stood and walked through the snow toward his skis.

Christopher looked again at Emily. "Are you going to ask me to do that now?"

"Would you ever want to?"

"Sometime," he said, and wished he hadn't brought the subject up.

"Mr. Blenkin's pretty good. That was a big jump."

"He's been skiing a long time."

"When you're as old as he is," she said, and held his arm, "you"ll be able to do it backwards."

Lester had dared him. They had climbed to the bottom of the trestle. The slope was simply a cut the final fifty feet and it was hard to get up it. Then, at the top, he'd looked down over the town. In the summer this height didn't bother him, but in the winter the blank whiteness of the landscape made everything look far away and, just glancing down the length of the hill, he'd known he wasn't going to be able to ski it. He felt sick and dizzy.

There was a landing halfway up the trestle for people who couldn't handle it from the top. They climbed the narrow stairs. Sonny Lester was two inches taller, fifteen pounds heavier, and a grade ahead of him in school. "You done this before, Lester?"

"Every day." He began putting on his skis.

Christopher watched him. Maybe this was a game of bluff. In a minute, when they got to the place where you either went or you didn't, it would be over. "Every day. Yeah, I bet. How come I've never seen you?"

Lester said nothing more. He was at the edge of the platform. Then he was gone down half the trestle and off the end of the jump, with the hill falling away below him. He hadn't leapt, just stood on his skis and let whatever speed he'd built up carry him through maybe a hundred foot jump. Christopher saw him land and watched him crouch. The problem was to get it straight in your head that it was possible to stand up at that speed. Lester managed it until he hit the flat at the bottom, and then his balance folded. His arms flailed and he went over on his side. His skis came off, and he skidded on his hip and shoulder for fifty feet before he stopped, jumped up, and Christopher heard his whooping laughter drift up to him. Lester waved his arms, gestured for him to jump. A dozen people on the hill and down on the flat near Lester paused, looked up. He could feel their waiting. The wind in the trestle's timbers moaned. If he made it, he'd be a hero. He shuffled forward, refused to think or feel, pushed off, and started down the run to the edge of the jump. His breath caught deep in his lungs. His knees buckled before he'd gone twenty feet, and he slid sideways down the run. He dug his hands and knees into the snow. At the lip of the jump he was going slow enough so that when he went over the edge it was like falling out of a tree. He twisted around, landed sitting down on his skis: he was a toboggan. The ride was rough down over the part of the hill never touched by jumpers. He tried to stand and head toward the bush; suddenly the direction was right, but there was no balance to go with it. The tree he hit was a spruce three feet thick, and when he came to consciousness again, he heard voices in the distance, but there was no one near him. He lay still until he knew that only his head was hurting. His skis were on his feet. He looked for another way down, one that would let him go to the bottom without meeting anyone.

Emily stayed for his next jump, and then slid down the hill again so that she was at the bottom by the time he'd turned and skied back to where their poles were planted in the snow. Blenkin had retrieved his skis and was standing with her. Lester was coming across the flat toward them.

"A foot of new snow is hard to ski on this hill," Blenkin was saying to Emily.

"I'm sorry you had to fall."

He grinned. It was what he did instead of smile, because no matter what you said to him, the remark that came back was pointed. "That's practice too." He plucked his poles out of the snow and leaned on them. "You're late," he said to Lester.

Sonny apologized and took off his skis. "Teaching her how to jump, Waterton?" He was looking at Emily.

Christopher watched her stare back at him, and saw him look away. Blenkin hoisted his skis onto his shoulder. "Come on," he said to Lester, and headed for the trail. Lester followed.

Christopher waited, feeling out of it, unchosen and embarrassed to be ignored in front of Emily.

"You too, Waterton, if you want."

He stood, still rigid, not wanting to be an afterthought.

Emily said, "I'll practise some turns on the main hill."

Without her here, Blenkin might not have offered, and it felt strange that it was Emily who was releasing him to go with them. She was like Fielder; she knew who she was, and he thought that was what made people around her act—what?—human, more human than was the style in Long River. He bent down and took off his skis so he could climb the hill.

From the top of the jump he watched Lester leap as if all of his muscles were pistons. There was an awkwardness in him until he was in the air, and then he was a bird. Blenkin stood watching him too, and when Sonny was safe down the hill, he signalled to Christopher.

This time he made a careful jump, trying to keep his skis and body exact, because style rather than distance was what practice was all about. When he got to the top again, Blenkin had already talked to Lester and was watching him prepare to jump.

"How did I do?" Christopher asked, but having to say the words made them come out awkward.

Blenkin glanced at him and then looked back at Sonny. "I think you're jumping off one leg."

It hardly made sense; he wondered if Blenkin were trying to make a joke.

Blenkin looked at Lester and gestured up toward the main trestle. Lester laughed and shook his head, but followed Blenkin across the main hill to the trail to the top.

Christopher looked down to where Emily was doing gentle turns. She skied much better than she said she did. He thought he probably talked better than he skied. Blenkin and Lester were opposite him on the far side of the main hill now. He could meet them at the top. If he made the jump this year, both Lester and Blenkin would have to ease up on him. If he stood up all the way down . . . . He felt fear just thinking about it, the kind of fear that occupied all of his mind so that when he realized what he was doing again, he found himself climbing the harder alternate route toward the trestle.

There was a committment to being with them that he couldn't try to understand: thinking about it would turn him back, and going down again would be a defeat that they would watch.

At the top, he waited for them. They were faces below him that stared up. Condensed breath steamed out of their mouths.

Lester said, "Going to fall off it again, Waterton?" He laughed, and glanced at Blenkin.

"Shove it, Sonny."

Blenkin said, "All right, that's enough. Do you think you're ready, Waterton?"

"Yes." He turned and walked to the stairs up to the lower take-off ramp. Blenkin went up first. Then Lester, not grinning now; he was not so sure of himself that he didn't feel the competition—for what?—who would be Blenkin's top pupil? Maybe. Sonny could make the jump. He'd done it. He'd want to stay being the best.

Lester put his skis on first. Blenkin stood beside him and pointed down the hill. "Just letting yourself go is awkward," he said. "Do all the things you'd do to make a real jump, and you'll find that what you've learned on the Boys' Jump will help you here."

Lester shuffled his skis.

"Good luck," Christopher told him. He meant it. He wanted Lester to make it easily.

Lester stared back at him, half a grin on his face, but he didn't say anything. He took hold of the railing and pulled himself forward until there was no turning back. At the edge of the jump, he made a slow leap—just enough to bring his ski-tips up and push his body forward. His arms became wings.

Blenkin chewed his lip, and as Lester landed 125 feet down the hill, he grunted and let out his breath. "Easy," he shouted. "Relax into it." But Lester couldn't hear. He was managing too many forces at once.

Christopher watched him struggle with his skis. They drifted apart; his knees bent too far; his arms stood rigid as poles straight out from his shoulders, and gradually his body was pushed back by the wind he was making, until he sat in the snow and a great roostertail trailed behind him. Then, near the bottom, he rolled, his skis rose up into the air like parts of a wreck, and Lester disappeared into a cloud of new snow near the bottom of the hill. Then he became visible again and got slowly to his feet.

"Good try," Blenkin shouted. "Good try, Lester." He waved his arms above his head, and Sonny waved back.

Blenkin turned. "Think you want to go? You don't have to, you know." His voice was kinder than Christopher remembered having heard it.

He bent and snapped his harness shut around the heel of his boot. When he stood up and looked down over the lip of the jump, Emily was on one side of the main hill and Lester was on the other. He felt as if he might be keeping them waiting.

"Do the same off the jump as Lester," Blenkin said. "Keep your balance in the air. You'll be going only thirty or forty feet farther than you're used to."

"It's the hill," Christopher said.

"I know. It's not kindly."

Christopher stood with one hand on the railing, and waved at Emily with the other. She waved back, and now he had to go. The challenge to Lester had been made; Blenkin was paying attention, watching, and Emily was saying yes.

He pulled himself over the edge and saw the tips of his skis fall forward down the slope of the ramp. He crouched, tried to put his arms straight out in front of him, but there was no real strength in them. The jump ahead was wide. Its lip was a horizon. He came to it, stood, and leaned into a void. The tips of his skis came up and he saw between them, far down and a long way away, the town and, beyond that, the river. He drifted through the cold air. It felt good, as if he knew how to fly and was doing it well. Then he remembered to look down for the hill. It was there, a rush of snow coming up to meet him. The backs of his skis touched, and he slapped down on the steep slant that dropped toward Emily. He crouched again and held his balance carefully in the curve of his body. It occurred to him that he was not falling. He was close to the run, so close that he could hear the hiss and clatter of his skis through the dry snow. He held his boots close together all the way down, and then at the bottom they were forced apart by the sudden impact of straightening out on flat ground. There was no easy balance now. His arms windmilled, one ski and then the other came up, but slowly he lost speed and got them together in the snow. He turned, slid to a stop. Emily was poling toward him, shouting, laughing. He began to skate toward her on his skis. Lester wasn't where he'd been standing. Already he was climbing back to the trestle, and he felt for a moment awkward about having made the jump. For all of the time he'd been jumping it had been expected that he'd be second to Lester.

Emily was laughing hard through deep breaths; her scarf was dangling to the tops of her skis. She held out her hands, ski poles attached, and they began to hug, but above them there was a sudden rush, and they looked up to see Blenkin in the air, perfect this time all the way down.

Christopher waited. Blenkin made a wide turn through the snow and glided back toward him and Emily. He nodded, his face hung serious beneath his toque and muffs, and his eyes watched them as if they were against a rule.

"That your first time?"

"I fell on the trestle last year." Christopher stood close to Emily.

"No problem this year," Emily said.

Blenkin grinned at her. "I'm not sure whether beginner's luck is a help or a hindrance." He looked at Christopher. "Want to go again?"

The shock of success was beginning to make him tremble. He glanced at Emily.

"I'm getting cold," she said.

"Best to consolidate your gain," Blenkin said.

"Not today, I guess." Christopher knew his laugh was awkward.

Blenkin left them then and shouted for Lester to wait for him. There were two others at the top of the Boy's Jump now, and soon there would be more people on the hills.

"That was gorgeous, Christopher," Emily said.

He looked at her standing square on her skis in front of him, and he wished he could have watched himself jump as she had. Now he couldn't remember thinking or feeling anything very strongly about the jump while he was doing it, and he had no sense that he could rely on the experience to help him do it again.

"I've got fifteen cents," he said. "We can have a hot chocolate and share a doughnut at Ch'en's."

She nodded, and on the way there she said, "We're going to be together nearly all day, right to midnight."

Side by side in a booth at Ch'en's, he sat with his hands around the cup of hot chocolate May Kaplik had brought him. Now he began to feel that he'd really done it—gone from the Men's Jump and run the hill right to the bottom without falling.

"February 20th," she said.

He knew what she was thinking and laughed. "A great moment in history." Her eyes laughed with him over the rim of her cup.

At the counter, people they knew were watching them, and they were smiling.

"You'll beat him on Winter Sports' Day," Emily said.

"Who?"

"Lester."

"I was thinking about Blenkin."

"What about him?"

"Lester fell and he shouted Good."

"You surprised him." She grinned. "Dumbfounded him."

He laughed again. It occurred to him: he could say anything to Emily that he needed to, anytime, anywhere.

"Am I funny?" she asked.

"No." He wanted to say he loved her. "You're the best thing that's happened to me." She reached over and touched his hand with the tips of her fingers. May brought a yellow bill with 15 written on it. He smiled at her. She watched him a moment and then glanced at Emily.

"You two are cute," she said, and turned away to serve people in the next booth.

"What—?" Emily didn't finish her question. Maybe it wasn't really important. He couldn't think of anything to say. Instead he shrugged, and then he reached for their jackets.

2

His mother served homemade soup: scotch broth. There were also canned salmon sandwiches and a white cake with chocolate icing. Sarah hunched over her food; her eyes shifted from one face to another unable, Christopher thought, to understand why everyone was treating Emily's being here as *normal*, or were trying to.

His father had been working in the basement with his hand tools making the frame of a chair for the living room. Soon it would be finished, and he would upholster it. Smiling at Emily, his father said, "All you really need is a good knife and a saw and the flat of your hand."

Emily stopped eating. He had her attention, and they smiled at each other.

"You make shapes with the saw, decorate with the knife, and the oil from the palm of your hand is the best finish there is."

"But you've got more tools than that," Emily said.

"Mr. Waterton knows how to exaggerate," Christopher's mother said.

"To make a point." He got out his jackknife. "My father gave me this when I was twelve. I've had it for twenty-five years."

"Which makes you thirty-seven," Emily said, and her face went red.

He laughed. "If I wasn't exaggerating."

"Peter, don't tease, it's only Emily's first visit."

They liked her. He had thought they wouldn't, but it was a surprise to see how formal his mother was being and how eager his father was to entertain.

They had skied past the school and had fooled around there, had skied down Carney's Hill a few times, and when they were hungry he had brought her home. His family knew about her, his phone calls, Sarah's teasing. His mother had said almost from the beginning that she knew Pat but not Emily. The hint was that she wanted to meet her. He had expected they would make sandwiches for themselves, but his mother had said she'd get lunch for them all, and he and Emily had sat in the living room, awkward until it was ready. He'd played her Bunny Berrigan's "I Can't Get Started." Mr. English had given him the record for ten cents because it looked as if no one would ever buy music like that. People wanted Wayne King waltzes or Wilf Carter singing cowboy songs. The trumpet rendition and then Berrigan's odd nasal vocal had brought his father up from the basement. His favourite song was, "I Want the Waiter with the Water for My Daughter." His other favourite was "One Meatball." The man in the restaurant who got only one meatball in the middle of a white plate appealed to him. When he was working on a project in the basement he sang his own words to both songs and sometimes mixed them mindlessly together. When his father came into the room, Christopher had stood stiff in front of the fireplace. The scene in his bedroom last summer about May Kaplik got in the way of him saying, "You know Emily Gordon, Dad." He'd rehearsed the words when he'd heard his father's footsteps, but he didn't get them said.

"Can a fellow make a living singing like that?" his father had asked.

"It's a good voice for bluesy songs," he'd said.

"It's a torch song. I know one of those when I hear it. I've listened to Helen Morgan on the radio." He'd been talking to Emily, in the same way he was talking to her now at the table. It embarrassed Christopher, but Emily was smiling and looking as if she liked what was going on.

"You have to be nearly thirty-seven to have a fourteen-year-old son," she said, impudent.

"Bless you for a mathematician," he said, and suddenly reached across the table and mussed up Emily's curls with his hand.

Sarah hunched lower over her plate, and his mother said, "More cake, Emily?"

Emily shook her head. "Thank you. It's good, but I'm full." Under the table, she took his hand and squeezed it. He wanted only to end the meal, and the visit.

"Emily's coming to Gabe's for my lesson," he said, getting up. "It's pretty near time."

"Thank you," Emily said again, and got up too.

"Oh, you're very welcome," his mother said, and both she and Emily touched their hair with their hands. "Do come again."

"I will," Emily said, and smiled across at his father. "Was I right? You are thirty-seven."

"Yes," his father said. "It's all downhill from here."

"Is that so?"

"Three score and ten, that's what they give us."

"Is everything arithmetic with you?" Emily asked, teasing back.

"Come to think of it, yes." He got up from the table, and Christopher felt they could go.

"Come on," he said, "I'll show you my horn."

"You can leave the door open if you want," his mother said. "The noise won't bother us."

Emily was disturbing them both. His horn, his first bike at nine, cubs when he was eight, his first skis when he was five had all originated with them. They'd been in control. Only school, and now Emily, had happened to him alone, and of those two things, Emily was the more serious. He was going free of them in this new way, and there could be no objection to it, because it was a natural event. Puppy love, he'd heard his mother call it, and his father had grunted from behind *Popular*

Mechanics. But their messages to him about it could only come in a roundabout way: You can leave the door open if you want.

It made him want to laugh; he felt for the second time that day as if he were flying. The trestle was behind him and he was in the air. He was choosing a dream, even if, he thought, as he got the saxophone out of its case, everything else in his life belonged to his mother and father. The sudden difference now was that he noticed it. Ever since he could remember they'd just been there, but in the world where he really lived, people his own age had always been more important than the grownups. Emily was not something new; she was a result of that part of life that was his own. He glanced at her. She was looking down at the opened case and was reaching to touch the silver bell of the horn. He wanted to reach and touch her. She'd come naturally into his life. It felt good to think that, and he wanted what was happening between them to go on as it was for a long time. She was just exactly as much a woman as he was a man.

He turned to see his mother standing at his door. Her black hair was trying to stay in its coil on top of her head, but it was loose, and it gave her, along with the worry in her eyes, the look of someone not quite in focus, like her people sometimes were in some of her charcoal sketches. Her uncertainty made him feel more than her equal, and so he grinned at her. "Don't worry, Mom, the saxophone's on the bed, we're not."

He might, from the look on her face, have hit her. She stood with one hand at the side of her face. Emily turned to see her and looked uncertain, as if she might be put-upon by this stranger.

"You're so young," his mother said, after a moment. "Must you—?"

"What?" he asked, wanting her to say what she must. It couldn't hurt them. He put his arm around Emily's waist.

"Be in such a hurry?" And she laughed then, the kind of laugh that was half embarrassment and half distress at not being able to say exactly what she wanted.

Christopher was afraid that if he didn't do something to reassure her, she might, because she wasn't in control, become angry. He shut the saxophone case and stooped to latch it and pick it up. The room was the problem. She was as upset about this bedroom as his father had been about May Kaplik. "Time to go," he said. "Gabe'll be waiting."

"I'm sorry," his mother told them. Her eyes were more certain. "You must think we don't trust you. I wonder if you understand? It's not that." She put her hands out and touched them. "It's just that—" and she laughed again— "we *have* to."

"I know," Emily said.

He heard himself say, "Mom," high-pitched, as if he were Henry Aldrich on the radio. They were suddenly a crowd at the door, and he wondered if she could keep herself from talking.

"Mother don't," he said.

"You're good kids." She nodded, agreeing with herself, and stood aside.

In the kitchen, they got on their boots and coats. His father came through on his way to the basement. "You drop in any time you want," he said to Emily.

"Yes, I will," she told him. Her smile was genuine.

"Then I haven't ruined it," his mother said.

His father looked at her.

Christopher picked up his horn and went to the door. The whole scene felt unreal. He wanted to ask her if she was worried or not, was she happy for him, or was everything just a mess of feelings she unloaded every time something new happened to her?

The phone rang.

"Don't go," she said. "It's probably for you." She answered it. "Donald," she said, with the happy surprise he always heard in her voice when she answered the phone. "Yes, he and Emily were just going out the door."

Christopher went to her and took the phone. Fielder said, "What's this about Gordon?"

"Nothing. We had lunch here."

"I thought maybe you'd moved her in."

"Sure, Fielder."

"So what's up?"

"We've been skiing. I made it off the trestle."

"I'd need witnesses to believe that."

"Blenkin and Lester were there. Lester fell."

"And you didn't. Look, get rid of Gordon. You're going to see her tonight. There's hockey on at the slough."

"Can't. I'm going to a lesson with Gabe."

"Busy-busy. Okay, see you."

"I'll come by tonight."

"Why?"

"You're going to the party, aren't you?"

"Maybe. Probably not."

"Come on, Fielder, you were invited. You have to."

"Since when?"

"Since Pat gave you the invitation at school. What's the matter?"

And then he knew: clothes, or maybe shoes. "I'll phone you at supper-time, okay?"

There was silence, and then Fielder said, "Girls, parties, music lessons—pretty soon you'll have to squat to pee."

There was nothing he could say to that. Fielder wanted him to play hockey. "I'll give you a call later," he said. "No, wait. Come on over for supper and we can go to the party after." He waited, knowing Fielder liked to be away from home as often as possible. He glanced at his mother and she nodded. Emily smiled at him. Fielder said, "What's your old lady cooking for tonight?"

"Skunk cabbage."

"That'll be for you. Tell her steak and onions for me."

"It'll be beans for all of us. This is Saturday."

"I forgot."

"See you at six." He hung up and felt as if he'd been having a private fight in front of an audience.

"You went off the trestle?" his father said. "That's an important event."

"It just happened," Christopher said.

"Mr. Blenkin and Sonny Lester were going." Emily said. "He went with them. I knew he was going to do it too."

"I wish I'd known," his mother said.

"Only so you could try to stop me."

"Ole Sanderson landed on his face. He's still in hospital," she said.

"Ole was drunk," his father told her.

"Why didn't they stop him from jumping then?"

"Nobody stops Ole from doing anything when he's drunk."

"We've got to go," Christopher told them.

"I'd like to see you make that jump." His father's voice sounded different than he'd heard it: as if he might be a fan and not his father.

"If I ever do it again. It was scary. Blenkin said it was beginner's luck."

"It wasn't," his father said. "You've been jumping almost since we moved here."

"Utter madness," his mother said.

"Gotta go." He opened the door. The cold rushed in, Emily went quickly past him out onto the back steps, and together they shouted goodbye as he slammed the door. He held the saxophone case in his right hand and put his other arm around Emily. She grinned up at him as they walked east on Manchester toward Gabe's house.

"That was nice," she said.

He nodded, thinking she was being polite. It was a day full of firsts. "Except for my mother." He didn't want to think about the scene in the bedroom again.

"She's—I like her."

"My friends always do."

Emily laughed. "You think they shouldn't?"

"Sometimes she's embarrassing."

There were frozen horse buns on the road from the milk wagon and garbage cart horses. She kicked one. "Mine is too. They're supposed to be." She giggled, and he stopped their walking and turned to hug and kiss her. A car went slowly by and honked. It was MacKenzie, the projectionist at the Regent theatre, and his new wife. They waved and looked delighted to have caught them.

"I think people like us," Emily said.

He didn't care if they did or not. "I guess they do."

"Us," she said, and kissed him again.

He tried to imitate his mother. "You're so young."

Emily looked sad. "I hate that."

"Must you—be in such a hurry?"

"Stop it, Chris."

"Why?"

"Oh, you know."

"Okay. Think about not laughing when you hear me play for Gabe."

"Will he mind me being there?"

"Better not."

"I could go to Gran's and wait."

He took her hand and ran, pulling her behind him down the block until they were at Gabe's gate. He wanted to play for her, and when they were inside, he got his horn out quickly to warm it near the stove. Gabe looked amused and almost immediately took him down into the tiny basement room where he practised. He didn't invite Emily to follow.

"She can listen from up there," he said. "Irene'll like the company." Gabe picked up his horn from its stand and put a reed in his mouth. He stared at Christopher. "You got a lot of—I don't know what?—today. You're intense."

"What do you mean?"

"I mean you go at things strong."

"I want to learn the horn."

"And every other damned thing." He took the reed out and put it onto his mouthpiece. "I'm like that, too, kid, you know?" He tightened the ligature.

"Sure," Christopher said. "I know." But he didn't.

"It's how I got where I am today." Gabe's brows rose up above his grey eyes and he laughed. "A husband and father stuck in this craphole. What I'm saying is, that's a nice girl you got up there, and so is Irene, but you keep your pecker in your pants. You want to be somebody, you keep yourself free." He blew a couple of notes somewhere near the middle of his horn. Then he smiled. "Just a little advice from an old vet, eh?"

Christopher put his reed on and blew a note. It sounded good in his ears, and it made him not want to talk now. The next note he played led him into "Sunday." "Sunday used to be my fun day, now it's my blue Monday." Gabe stopped him.

"Okay," he said. "Let's hear the E scale, top to bottom, four sharps."

He played it and missed the first D-sharp on the way down.

"It just feels like too many sharps," Gabe said. "But you look at any piece of music and you'll find changes in it that use chords from a lot of different keys." He blew into his horn again. This time he made a tune. "These Foolish Things." "Listen," he said. "I'll play it in C—no sharps or flats." He played four bars of the melody, and then he did it again, improvising. "C," he said, "then A-minor seventh—D-minor seventh —G-seventh—back to C again. Now listen to the bridge. You begin with an E-minor chord, and then go to a B-seventh. That's five sharps." He blew the tune and named the chords. "A, three sharps; D, two sharps; G; G-diminished; G-seventh, and all of it is in a piece that says it's in the key of C. Play a dozen numbers at a dance and you've used chords and scales from everywhere, so don't think of keys as being hard or easy. We use them all equally. That's why when we know them, we run them through every day until we think E, and our fingers just naturally play all four sharps. Now, let's hear it again."

It wasn't a scale anymore, it was music, and he tried to play it as if it was.

"That's right," Gabe said. "Make every note a good one. Now, play it as a minor scale. E-minor."

He played it: E, F-sharp, G, A, B, C, D.

"How many sharps?"

"One."

"What key is it related to, then?"

"G, because it's got one sharp."

"You're going to be all right, kid. You learn fast."

"I want to." He felt as if the trestle were behind him and he was in the air again. With Gabe, there was no extra struggle to be acceptable. What Gabe liked was music, he knew music, and every day he learned a little more about it for himself. It was good to be taught by him.

Gabe picked a piece of manuscript paper off a pile on the shelf near him. "I tried to copy this off a Jimmy Lunceford record. You play the melody, and I'll do the second tenor part."

He beat out the time with his foot and they played the riff together. They only went two bars before Christopher screwed up. They tried it again. Four bars. Then the complete riff. Then a repeat. Then the bridge, and finally the eight bars of the riff again. Gabe wanted him to be free to make mistakes. They worked it through half a dozen times. Then Gabe grabbed some more manuscript paper and a pencil. He sketched in four bars of notes that made a rhythm when Christopher played them.

"Play them behind me after the first time around. I'll do a chorus over them."

They went through it, and Christopher played the rhythmic phrases for Gabe to ad lib against. It was like being in a band. Gabe came out of it laughing. "Kid, you're doing good. You'll make a fine lead alto player some day." He picked up the music, put it back on the shelf and looked at his watch. "We didn't even get to the exercises." He put his horn down. "Okay. The B-scale for next time. Five sharps. You got that Lunceford riff in your head. Play it during the week and we'll do it from memory." He stood up.

Christopher got out his money and paid for the lesson. "Thanks," he said. He wanted to say more. "I like being pushed. I want to work hard."

"Can't go any faster than you are. It's your speed, not mine."

"I never learned anything so fast."

"You wanted to." Gabe patted him on the back and herded him toward the stairs.

"I want to do tunes, Gabe."

"We'll do tunes. We did one today."

"I mean like 'Sunday' and 'These Foolish Things.' "

"I'll write some out for us."

"By next time?"

"Quit nagging, kid." They were climbing the stairs. "Jesus, you must be busier than a cut cat. Horn, school, Emily."

"I made the trestle today."

"Break your damned neck."

"Not if I don't go again."

Gabe laughed. "I know what you mean."

Emily and Irene were in the kitchen. While he was putting his horn away he could hear them talking. He glanced in at Irene. She was pretty in a sad sort of way. She had the kind of face that made you want to ask her if she needed help. Gabe had asked, three years ago, when she was seventeen. Emily wasn't that kind. She got up from the table and came toward him. He wondered if Irene had stopped talking long enough for Emily to have heard them playing. He looked at her and saw that she knew the question he was going to ask.

She answered it: "I think you should be in Gabe's band."

"Well, give him a week or two," Gabe said.

"It sounded good," she said.

"Just one piece," Christopher told her. He got her jacket from the chesterfield and helped her on with it. He knew Gabe was watching. He didn't care. Everything was good—as if he were giving orders to the world and the world was obeying all of them.

Irene stood close to her husband as they said goodbye, and after a moment Gabe put his arm around her. Their child came out of the kitchen and stood looking at Emily with its thumb in its mouth. It needed its nose blown. The three of them together looked distant, years away.

He turned with Emily and walked up Manchester Street. When he put his arm around her, he knew it was a different gesture than Gabe's with Irene.

"Is that what you want to do?" Emily asked.

"I want to play good jazz." Then, after a moment, he said, "I want to know how to do it." Just wanting was easy. It was a dream. But wanting to know how, and working at it, was what Gabe had done for him. "Gabe's great," he said.

"Irene's a nice person, too," Emily said.

He waited.

"They don't have much, but she has plans for their place. She says the extra five dollars Gabe makes every week playing in his band is a real help. He gets seventy-five at the store because he does the deliveries too. She says there are people with four kids who have to try to get along on that."

She sounded serious. He liked listening to her talk this way. Her voice was low, not a baby soprano like Dody's. Again he wanted to tell her he loved her. But instead he kissed the side of her face, and she glanced around at him.

"What a good day this has been," she said.

It was not her voice at all. Her mother's maybe, or old Mrs. McLeod's. It made him laugh, and he wished he hadn't. She looked at him again, a little uncertain. "It's been as good as it could get," he said.

Then she stood still in the middle of the road, and he thought she was going to kiss him, but she didn't. She said, "I like your name: Christopher."

She was like this often. He didn't know what she would say at times when things between them got a little awkward. He said, "And I like your name, Emily."

"It's my other grandmother's, my dad's mother's." She took his hand and began to run. "I'm going to catch it from Pat when I get home. The deal is we get to clean the whole house if we want a party."

At his place, he took his horn in and put it away while Emily got her skis on. They poled their way down York Street and south to the edge of town where her house stood sheltered in its grove of tall spruce and hemlock. Each time they came back here they stood close together under the tree where he'd first touched her cheek and had tried to push her curls back under her toque. He had a sense that this was where what was going on between them had begun to happen. Not at the fire, or at the rink, but here. He tried to laugh at how they did this every time, but it had become a natural thing to do. He leaned against her and felt her mouth as something warm surrounded by the cold that pressed in on them now that the sun was set.

Pat came out onto the back porch to shake her mop. "Jesus, Waterton, break it up, why don't ya? Maybe we'll have a party tonight."

Mrs. Gordon appeared behind her with her coat on. "Must you swear, Pat?" She was slim. Her elder daughter would look like her in another half dozen years. She was tall, but still her fur coat came almost to her ankles—a relic from when times were better, she'd said. It was beautiful—the coat—and probably she was too, but her slimness and her height and the sharpness of her profile made him think of something far away. She had a strong laugh, and her eyes were bright and creased from smiling. She was up, like Pat; and Doctor Gordon was down. Emily had both of them in her. "Come along, Emily," she said. "This is your party too." She stopped by their tree. "Pat says you're bringing your dance records with you tonight," she said to Christopher.

"Yes," he said.

"It's why he's being invited," Pat said, and slammed the door.

"You better go in, miss," Emily's mother said, seriously, and moved away from them to the street.

"Where're you going?" Emily asked.

"I'm meeting your father at the Lesters' for a cocktail. We'll be back after you've finished in the house." She walked off down the street in her coat and high-heeled overshoes.

"Cocktails," he said. He only meant that the word sounded peculiar if you thought about it. His mother and father didn't drink, unless they had company, and then they only sipped one to be polite. He pictured Fielder's dad at the Legion. Boilermakers, Fielder said. Rye and beer.

"I know," Emily said. "It's funny." She began to walk toward the steps up to the back porch. "They talk about what kind they drank when they went on a ship from New York to London and then down by train to Rome." She stood on the bottom step and was his height, but she didn't kiss him.

"When was that?" It was just a question to keep her from going in.

"1923."

"Long time ago." He put his arms around her and kissed her.

Emily giggled and made him stop. "Mother got squiffed at New Year's and she wouldn't stop talking until she told us the whole story. What they did every day. It was like she was reciting from a diary. She even began to cry, and Daddy tried to stop her from telling it, but she got mad and said it was her honeymoon and her best memory. So we listened. They were supposed to go out, but they didn't. She just talked and drank Brandy Alexanders until we knew everything they did in New York and London and Rome. She made it sound like ancient history, and Daddy kept saying, it'll happen again."

"Maybe it will," Christopher said.

She shook her head. "Not like that. It couldn't."

"Why?"

"I just know. That's all gone. It's what my mother was talking about. Sixteen years, she kept saying. You want to know how long forever is—well, it's sixteen years."

"We can go to Rome if we want."

"How?"

"There are people who get rich."

Emily laughed suddenly. "I bet you will." She kissed him and began to go in.

"I'm sorry you had a sad New Year's."

"Did I say that?"

"I thought so."

"It was the best time I ever had with my parents."

"You said she cried."

"It was the most wonderful story I ever heard."

"Tell it to me."

Emily waved her hand as if she were an actress making a dramatic exit. "It's not my story to tell. Mustn't tell other people's stories."

"You'll have a story to tell someday," he said, and it was the right thing to say. She didn't make her exit. She came back down the stairs and kissed him. They walked to the gate together.

3

Fielder came out from the bedroom wearing a pair of Christopher's pants. "They look good on you," his mother said, and laughed. Her laugh was often a way of trying to control what was happening, an unspoken order not to be serious. But Fielder stopped in the middle of the kitchen and looked down at himself.

"Nobody'll know," Christopher heard himself say.

"Know what?"

Now it really was awkward. "They look like they're yours."

"Well, I'm wearing them."

"Sure, okay, let's go." The argument to get him to go to the party had been about his patched pants. It had taken a long time to get him to change, and now if they didn't hurry they were going to be late.

His mother went into the breakfast nook. "Hang on a minute," she said, and then came back into the kitchen with two wrapped boxes. "Brownies, and some cookies," she said. "Always take your hostess a little gift." Her voice was instructional.

Christopher took the box he thought was cookies so Fielder could have the brownies to give to Pat. It would embarrass him more.

Fielder weighed the brownies in his hand. "I'd rather give her a paper airplane."

"She's a good girl, Donald, and she's gone to a lot of trouble to give this party. Try to make her feel special."

"You're a nice lady, Mrs. Waterton," Fielder said, trying to imitate Edward G. Robinson. "You're a real class act, but let me tell you something—that Gordon broad ain't even worth a paper airplane."

Her face went pink for a moment, and then she laughed. Fielder grinned back at her. She said, "Women aren't broads, Donald."

"Some of them are." He spoke to her as if he were an adult and they were equals.

She ignored him, and said to Christopher, "Have you got the records Pat asked you to take?"

He went into the living room for them. It was a big awkward package, and when they were walking down the hill toward Emily's, he gave the cookies to Fielder so he could carry the discs in two hands.

They went to the kitchen door, and Pat answered it. She was wearing a red dress that might once have been her mother's. She looked glad to see them, and when she opened up the boxes she said, "Good, we need these. Monica's brought a bloody great angel food cake."

There was noise coming from the living room. The music on the gramophone couldn't overcome Dorrie and Maxine Dobroski telling a story together. The twins always wound up shouting and laughing at the same time.

"Where do you want these?" Christopher asked. He held out the records.

"Music," Pat said. "I hope we can dance to it, Waterton. Here, I'll take them. You can put your coats in there on the bed." She walked away into the living room.

On the kitchen table there was a large mixing bowl full of punch. Fielder leaned over it and sniffed. "Gordon's trying to be *veddy sna-ha*, but it's only a bunch of stuff out of cans." From his mackinaw pocket he got out a mickey bottle of rye. "Stole it." He grinned. "The old man'll wonder when it was he drank it." He took the top off and began to pour the liquor into the punch.

Christopher grabbed his wrist. "What're you trying to do?"

"Make a party out of this funeral."

"You don't even know who's here."

"Gordon, Lewis, Dobroski, Alpert. If Blenkin came he could call the roll."

He let go of Fielder's wrist and watched the rest of the rye gurgle into the punch. Thirteen ounces among about fifteen people wasn't going to make anyone drunk. Fielder screwed the top back on the bottle and put it back in his pocket. He looked as if he'd taken charge. There was a spoon by the bowl. He stirred the punch and sipped it. "Better," he said, and headed for the bedroom to get rid of his coat.

Emily came from the living room and put her arms around his shoulders. He kissed her, and then made her stand back so he could look at how she was dressed. She wore a blue pleated skirt and a white blouse, silk stockings and shoes with heels that made her a couple of inches taller. "Pretty," he said, and she laughed and blushed. The Emily who wore boots and ski pants, and thick jacket and toque, and who was only hands and face and brown-gold curly hair every day in the week was now changed for Saturday night into a woman. Always before she had stood square with her feet apart like an athlete, and now she was standing prim with her shoes pressed together and her arms stiff by her sides.

"Do you think so?" she asked.

Pretty was such a small part of what she was that he laughed now and went to her. She raised her face, the question still in it. "Am I?"

"Yes," he said. "The prettiest."

She smiled. "This is the first time we've been dressed up together."

"You were worried?"

She nodded. "Mother wouldn't let me wear a dress. I had to fight not to wear knee socks. I'm thirteen."

He took off his mackinaw to show her his green pants and white shirt. "I don't even own a sports jacket."

"I was afraid you did, and I'd look like a little girl beside you."

"Well, you don't." When he kissed her again he tasted the pale lipstick she was wearing. He didn't say anything about it, because that might be something she was doing for the first time, too. "Where's your Mum and Dad?" he asked, still holding her and wondering if he should.

"Gone to the movie."

"That's brave of them."

"That was an argument too. Pat said if she couldn't be trusted she'd cancel the party."

"Sounds like her."

"I wouldn't've minded them being around. We've sat up for some of their parties." She took his hand and led him into the bedroom. "You and Fielder were the last to come."

He put his mackinaw on the bed. "This is your room, isn't it?"

She nodded.

"Mine's the one off the kitchen, too." He looked around. The dressing table had a mirror and ruffles. There were dolls sitting on top of upended blue-painted orange crates that held her books. There was a rag rug beside her bed. Three teddy bears sat on her bureau. "Sarah has my teddy bears," he said. He'd never admitted he had teddy bears to anyone before.

"Pat would never've given me hers."

He felt comfortable here. Nothing was unexpected. He turned and held her again. She had on a perfume that wasn't too sweet, but he wished it was just her he was smelling. He liked the taste of her lipstick. "How come we've always known how to kiss?" he asked her.

"Didn't you teach me? I thought you knew all about it before me." She pressed her mouth against his once more.

"Do you remember the first time?" he asked.

"Christmas day at the slough."

"It was so good I thought I was going to burst."

"Sometimes things just work out right," she said, "and it's a big surprise, because they usually don't." She laughed, a little embarrassed at this being a truth for her.

"Don't they ever?"

"Not the things you have to wish for for a long time. By the time they happen they're all different. I wanted to be with you, but it didn't seem at first like it was going to be anything but, you know, seeing each other at the rink and kidding around. Then Christmas came." She paused. "We've been different. Pat says so. She says, Who the hell do you think you are, Carole Lombard and Clark Gable?"

"Yeah, and then we'd be rich."

"I've thought about it."

"What?"

"The thing that's happened."

For a moment he was afraid. "What's Pat saying? It's too grown up? Is that what you think?"

She shook her head. "No."

"Anyway, it was fast."

"Everybody says growing up is something you do a little at a time. That's not true."

"We weren't and then, blam, we were," he said.

"You can't have an *us* a little at a time."

He thought she was going to say something else, but she looked toward the door and took his hand again. "I don't care if we go out there or not," he told her, but he let himself be led into the living room.

There was no rug on the floor, and the furniture was pushed up against the walls. It was a big room. Pat had opened up his records, and the music on the gramophone was "Johnson Rag." The Dobroski twins were jitterbugging. They were small, skinny, wild like barn kittens. They were from the flats, but they mixed in anywhere. Pat was being class president and was shouting over the music, "Okay, that's how to do it. Come on, let's go. This party's to get you guys to learn how to dance." She grabbed Johnny Bell's hand and dragged him out onto the floor. He pulled her in, pushed her out, twirled her, and tried to swing her past him, but he tripped and landed on the chesterfield against the wall, an act that was supposed to be funny but didn't get a laugh.

The Dobroskis quit dancing. One of them grabbed Pat, and the other hauled Bell off the chesterfield. "Okay," Dorrie shouted, "take it easy." She began half-time. Bell didn't trip. He began to smile.

"You've been to the Royal," Emily said. "Can you jitterbug?"

He shook his head. "I listen to Gabe."

"I can dance a little."

He looked at the others: Smith, Callaghan, Cameron, Fielder, Isonovich all standing as if they were at attention, not looking at Dody Wentworth, Jenny Alpert, Monica Lewis, or Marie Anders.

"Girl's choice," Pat yelled, and left Maxine Dobroski for Fielder.

Pat knew what she was doing. Fielder had to be on the floor first. If he did it, everyone else would.

Jenny chose Smith. They moved like puppets and both of them looked anxious, not just Jenny who looked that way all the time. Maxine chose Cameron, Dorrie went over to Callaghan, Marie Anders grabbed Bell, and Monica in her new electric blue dress and flat black slippers smiled at Isonovich and held out her hand. He was taller than she was, even with his boots off. He'd been to a few Russian weddings, and jitterbugging was a cousin of what went on there along about the third day. Monica bounced with him. She did everything eagerly, as if each new thing might be the answer to what her parents had made of her. She twirled. He held her fingers high above her head and looked like a ruined aristocrat with vague memories of St. Petersburg.

"Oh my God but you're beautiful," Pat told them, and Smith shouted like a Cossack dancer. Then Pat saw Dody Wentworth standing alone. She dragged Fielder to her. "Here, I've got to organize in the kitchen." Christopher watched Fielder look surprised first at Pat and then at Dody. She was dressed in a skirt and sweater, socks and loafers. She looked older than she did in school clothes, but she was still a tomboy. They stood looking at each other; she began to laugh and went close to him. "I can do it, watch." And she could. Fielder put out his foot to trip her as she went around him. She jumped over it and caught his hand. No one knew whether it was going to be a dance or a fight.

"I'm not sure I want to watch," Christopher said, and Emily laughed. He took her hand and went to where Pat had left the records. When the music stopped he put on Muggsy Spanier's "Who's Sorry Now," and said to Emily, "Okay, show me." For the length of a chorus, he tried to follow what she was doing, and then he held her still in the middle of the room. "Do you know how to just dance?"

She nodded and put her hand on his shoulder. His feet tripped over hers. "It's too fast," she said.

"Then do it slow."

She took him through the archway out onto the glassed-in porch. It was cooler here, but not cold. The music was bouncy, Dixieland. He felt stupid not being able to jitterbug. He put his arms around her and stood still, kissing her. In a moment she began to move her feet.

"Dance," she said.

"I'd rather kiss you."

"I want us to."

"Why?"

"I watch you jump off the trestle and listen to you play your horn. We can dance together." She sounded a little as if she might be saying something that would make him angry.

"We skate together, walk, talk." He knew he was only defending those other things he had to do alone.

The music ended again, and they could see Pat bringing in the punch bowl. Emily left him and went to the kitchen to bring out the tray of glasses. Fielder had abandoned Dody already. "Maybe a couple of slugs of that will relax things," he said.

"Pat invited Dody for you."

"You're the only one's got a girl, Waterton. The rest of us are here for the exercise."

"Pat holds a good party."

"She's a class act."

Emily came back with two glasses of punch. Fielder reached and took one of them from her. "It's for Christopher," she said.

"What is he, a cripple?"

She said nothing. It was better than answering. Christopher laughed at him. He took Emily's glass from her and handed it to him. "Here, have another, Fielder, you look real thirsty."

Fielder gave it back to Emily. "God, but you're a boor, Waterton."

"I took lessons from you."

Dody came out onto the porch and stood by Emily. She looked at Fielder. There was no snowbank for Fielder to push her into. "Don't follow me around, kid," he said, Edward G. Robinson again.

"You really are being horrible," Emily said.

Fielder's eyes went serious, the way they did on a basketball floor. "I thought this was a party, ma'am," he said to Dody. "May I kiss your hand?" He took it and pressed it to his lips.

Dody squeaked and jerked her hand away. "You bit me." She hit him.

Emily laughed. "She brought you a little punch, Fielder. Does that make you a cripple?"

Fielder did a made-up laugh and backed away. "Smart cookie you got there, Waterton."

Christopher left Emily and Dody and followed him to the punch bowl. Fielder grinned at him while he poured two glasses, and as they drank, he said, "You got a match?"

Christopher shook his head.

"Maybe in the kitchen." He went there and came back with a couple in his hand. "Lewis," he said. "Her and Isonovich are sickening."

Christopher glanced. They were sitting on chairs at the end of the table where the punch bowl was. The table had a cloth on it that hung down almost to the floor.

"Do you have to, Fielder?"

"I'd do both of them, but Isonovich isn't wearing shoes." He ducked down under the tablecloth.

Christopher looked around. No one had noticed. There was a slow tune on the gramophone. "Stardust." Callaghan was really concentrating on Dorrie. They were standing in the middle of the room, hardly moving. She was standing on her tiptoes, her head a profile against his chest and her dress higher than her rolled stockings. Callaghan's eyes were closed. Bell was with Jenny Alpert now, and he was still awkward; he moved around the floor like a stick-man, and pumped his arm up and down in time with the music.

Isonovich was turned toward Monica. At school they were seated apart and probably hadn't spoken to each other seriously before. Isonovich's hands were talking faster than he was. They were long narrow hands with tapered fingers. Blenkin liked his drawings of flowers and pussywillows. Monica's eyes were wide open: the class clown, and the goody-goody. It was pretty sickening, but they weren't making the party a stupid time for two other people. Christopher tried to imagine being stuck with her. He stood near Isonovich and saw Fielder's hands under her chair working the match between the upper and the sole of her right shoe. Kelly had given Purvis a hotfoot at the rink when Purvis was asleep. Everyone had laughed except Purvis, who had to be pried off Kelly by Howard Streeter because he was choking Kelly so hard he wasn't breathing any more. But this wasn't the rink. It was a party.

Emily came and stood beside him again. "What's going on? Where's

Fielder?" she asked, as if maybe she knew.

He pointed. "Under there giving Lewis a hotfoot."

Emily knelt, reached, took the matches from Monica's shoe, and Monica didn't notice. Fielder rose up at the other side of the table. His face was full of amazement.

"What's with you, Waterton?"

"It was me," Emily said. She held up the matches. "You could've set the house on fire."

"What?" Isonovich said.

Monica glanced where he was looking and saw Emily. She smiled.

"Fielder was giving you a hotfoot."

Isonovich stood up, unsure. He played basketball with Fielder—not well, but his height made him valuable as a substitute guard. Bell laughed. Smith came over with Pat. Monica finally understood what had happened and turned toward Fielder. "When are you going to grow up, Donald?" Her voice didn't want to be prim but it didn't know any other tone. Fielder reached out to a lamp near him and took the shade off it. He put it on his head and shuffled out from behind the table.

"Like this?" he asked her.

"That's pretty adult," Smith said. "My old man does it."

Fielder took the shade off and put it on Monica. "Looks like the one you wear to church."

Monica didn't move; she only kept staring straight ahead, until Pat took it off her head. She turned to Fielder. They were equals facing each other. "Come on, Fielder, ease up, eh?" She kept looking at him.

Fielder didn't stare back. He laughed, and picked up a glass from the table and tossed it at Christopher. It was sudden and demanding. Christopher caught it and tossed it back. "Not me, stupid," Fielder said. He threw it at Smith, who knew what to do. Fielder kept throwing them. When there were six in the air being tossed in every direction, he left the table and went over to the silent gramophone and stood looking down at the pile of records. Pat began shouting and her hands signalled panic. She caught a glass from Bell and put it back on the table. The game then was to throw them at her. One smashed against the wall. Fielder turned and watched her and Monica pick up the pieces. When it was over he said, "No couth, no couth at all." And Pat said, "For God's sake, let's dance. Put on some music, Fielder."

Christopher went over to him and began selecting a record. "What was that all about?"

"Put some life into the party."

"I don't think so." He put on Tommy Dorsey's theme song and said to Fielder, "That was scary."

"It was supposed to be." He smiled, his eyes calm. "Why'd you tell Emily?"

"Because she asked."

"Great friend you are."

"It wasn't such a good joke."

"Yes it was."

"Okay, it was."

"You embarrassed me."

"Not much."

"Enough."

"This is a party, Fielder."

"Sure, sure."

"If you don't like it, why don't you go?"

"Maybe I will."

"I shouldn't've got you to come."

"You didn't," Fielder said. "I made up my own mind."

"What was our argument about then?"

Fielder turned away. "Why is everybody so serious? A little joke on Lewis. She isn't even human."

"Isonovich thinks so." They were dancing again.

"Coming?" Fielder asked.

"Where?"

"We could play some pool. I haven't beaten you since the last time."

"If you go that'll mean both Pat and Dody won't have anyone to dance with."

"You don't want to come?"

"No."

"Then you leave me no choice," he said, stiffly.

Christopher didn't say anything. They'd quarrelled often in the six years they'd been friends.

"No choice but to stay." Almost everything he did was sudden. He put his arm over Christopher's shoulder. "I think I'll give Monica a thrill. Isonovich looks tired."

"Sure, why not? Be friendly."

"No, that's not a good idea either."

"Relax. Dance with Dody."

"Okay. I will."

He watched Fielder cross the room and put his hand out to Dody. She looked suspicious and didn't move toward him.

Emily came to him again. "He's a nut," she said.

Christopher laughed. "You're talking about my best friend."

"He's always so rough."

"Not really." He looked again. Fielder was leading Dody, actually dancing. She was smiling and looking up into his face. His movements were careful. They didn't look like Fielder and Dody at all.

When the music ended, Emily said, "Let me choose one." She picked up a record from the pile that belonged to her mother and put it on the turntable. It was a waltz, very sweet. The saxophone that played the melody was high and clear, like a violin.

"What is it?" he asked

She joined the melody, singing the words: "My Buddy, your Buddy misses you."

They began to dance. "Wayne King," he said.

She nodded, and pressed in very close. He moved, learning to let his feet go with the music. Then he forgot them. They danced. The simple rhythm under the long line of the melody eased them closer together. His face was in her hair. He'd not felt her like this. The blouse and skirt were like nothing between them. Her body moved against him. He could feel the small softness of her breasts, and her thighs were firm against his.

He wanted to say, I love you. It was the truth. He said the words in his head, and it was as if someone else had said them. He watched himself dance with Emily. Christopher and Emily dancing, kissing while they moved to the music of the Waltz King. "Say the words," he said.

"The words?"

"To the song."

She waited for the chorus to begin again, and spoke the words in his ear. "Nights are long since you went away. I dream about you all through the day. My Buddy, my Buddy, your Buddy misses you. . . . "

"I like the way we dance to it," he said, "but the words aren't for us. I'm not going away." He hugged her and they twirled without tripping over each other's feet. "And neither are you."

"No," she said, and broke away suddenly. She picked the arm off the record and put it back at the beginning. Smith, at the other end of the room, turned off the lights. There was a glow from the kitchen where Pat was laying out the food. Everybody was dancing as if this were the Royal Ballroom. Over the heads of the other dancers, Christopher could see Pat look up and then leave her work. She stood by the doorway and watched. It was Fielder who gathered her in to be part of the movements he and Dody were making. They were a revolving triangle, their arms not quite around each other. Fielder was behaving himself.

"Why didn't Pat invite someone for herself?"
Emily shrugged. "Maybe she did."
"Who?"
"I don't know. Anybody but you." Then she grinned. "But I might've wrecked it for her."
"How?"
"I invited Dody."
"You're a brat kid sister."
"Yah."
He saw Smith and Jenny again. Callaghan and Maxine. Cameron and Dorrie. Isonovich and Lewis. Bell and Marie. None of them could handle Pat. But Fielder could. They'd be wild together, both of them trying to run things. "It's her party. She wanted us all to learn how to dance."
"Sure," Emily said. "There's going to be another party sometime for the rest of the class. She takes being president seriously."
"It's lonely at the top," he said, but Emily didn't laugh.
"She's really pretty. I don't know why she has to be like she is."
"She's got Fielder to herself. Dody just went to the kitchen."
"Dody's scared," Emily said.
"Of Fielder?"
"Wouldn't you be?"
"I'm not a girl."
"Now she knows he's crazy."
"Not true. He always knows exactly what he's doing."
She didn't answer, but moved in close again and leaned her head against his shoulder. He looked at the others dancing. They're over there, he thought, and Emily and Christopher are over here. Exclusive. Callaghan looked unconscious; Maxine rode on his shoved-out hips. Jenny was trying to stay a little way away from Smith. He was smiling with his eyes closed and she was looking anxious for both of them.
"What's the word, Smith?" he said to him through Emily's hair.
"Propinquity," Smith said, without opening his eyes.
"That's not a word," Jenny said.
He opened his eyes. "Yes it is. It means closeness."
"Get me some punch," she said.
"The lights are out," Emily told her. "You're supposed to dance."
"Out of the mouth of a babe." Smith danced Jenny away toward the punch bowl.
Still separate from the others, they kept on dancing until the music stopped. Emily opened her eyes. Her closeness was a drug; he felt the

excitement of it, but there was a lethargy behind it too. He steered her out onto the porch, and when the music began again, it was Benny Goodman's "Gone with the Wind." In the other room, Maxine and Dorrie were at the center. They were like knives cutting through the rhythm of the piece. Callaghan and Cameron were looser, able to go with them. Maybe Fielder's punch was working.

"You don't like it that fast, do you?" Emily asked.

"Sometimes. Not tonight." He tried to think what else to tell her. "Right now I feel like I'm floating."

"I know. I do too."

He didn't want to go back into the living room, especially not to dance. He wanted more than that now, but in this room there were only chairs, straight-backed and uncomfortable. "What's this room used for?" he asked, looking around it.

"It's my dad's place really." She went over to the corner to where there was something white hanging like a canvas without a picture on it. "His hammock," she said, and unhooked one end of it from the wall. "Every night before dinner he has a nap."

"He must've been in the navy in the war."

She nodded. "He lied about his age." She walked across the angle of the porch and hooked the hammock to the wall.

Christopher sat in it and swung it back and forth. Emily stood beside him. "How'd your people get to come to Long River?"

"I guess they believed what people said about it booming and becoming a big place. It was supposed to."

"After London and Rome, this is pretty small potatoes."

"That was just their honeymoon. They were going to get settled and make some money and then they were going to travel every year."

"And you would've gone with them."

"Yes."

"My dad was going to build bridges in China or maybe Africa. It seems like not very much ever works out."

"It's like punishment for something we didn't do," she said, and he thought maybe those were her mother's words. He reached out and took her hand and pulled her down to sit beside him. He pushed with his foot and the hammock swung up into the corner and then out toward the middle of the porch. Through the windows he could see the curve of the moon's first quarter shining through high thin cloud above the Castle Hills, and he said some words that he remembered from his mother: "New moon, new beginnings."

Emily kissed him. He wanted to lie down in the hammock with her.

He watched her eyes watch him. They were waiting, and he could feel his heart begin to pump hard enough for them both to hear it. He couldn't ask. It would mean he didn't know how far it was she wanted them to go. There hadn't been any signals before, because none were needed. Since they'd met, they'd stood close and kissed in the cold outside, and he'd kept those feelings alive until he was alone. He knew she did too. When he lay in bed, what he'd felt came back strongest, and maybe that had been strongest for her then, too. But a limit had been reached; he couldn't feel any more than he did now, and his emotions had become tensions that were stringing him out, making a taut silence in him that he couldn't break because what he wanted might not be what she could agree to.

"Christopher," she said. "what's wrong?"

He shook his head, and pulled her down along the length of the hammock. She moved with him, lifted her legs as he did, and the hammock sides rose up and held them together. He twisted until they were face-to-face, the whole length of their bodies tight against one another. His arms were around her and there was a fierceness in him now that he hadn't felt before. Her mouth was hard on his; then it gradually opened and her lips and tongue were soft. In the dim light he saw only the outline of her face, and he listened to her breathing. It shuddered, and in a moment he knew that she was crying. Salt from her tears was in his mouth. He stopped their kiss. "Is it okay?"

She whispered Yes, and lay hard against him.

"I didn't know this would make you cry," he said.

"I don't know what else to do."

He lay gentle with her now, the tension in him gone, and felt, not as if he were in love, but as if he were safe, more comfortable than he'd ever been. The canvas held the whole length of his body with hers. Their breathing matched. He moved his lips close to her ear. "Some people say it's puppy love."

"No, I don't think so." She snuffled, and then the air in her lungs pushed out a soft quiet laugh. She was shy, too, talking about what it was that was happening to them.

He kissed her nose, and then drew back to see it in the dim light that came from the living room. It was what he'd looked at when they'd first touched and he hadn't been able quite to meet her steady hazel eyes. It didn't have a describable shape, but it was there, present in the middle of what until now was all he had been able to see of her—a halo of hair shoved out beyond her toque, nearly straight eyebrows, eyes that said she was gentle, interested, a mouth that was—what?—alive. It smiled, it went slack when she was surprised and straight when she was determined. A chin which, like her forehead, had strength.

He pulled his arm and hand away from hugging her and touched her cheek. This was the miracle: that he could touch her.

Beyond the door of the porch, Cameron and Dorrie, Maxine and Callaghan, Bell and Marie were dancing so they could be close. Jenny was afraid to touch Smith. Isonovich with Monica was a happy kind of comedy. He wondered who Fielder was dancing with, or if he was dancing at all. He might have taken off from the party, gone with Dody, or not. The hotfoot, the lampshade, the thrown glasses had not put him in charge. This party was a different place for him, and those things that worked at school or at the poolhall or at basketball practice made no sense. The picture of him dancing with both Dody and Pat was the right one. It was the only time tonight he'd seen Fielder neither wild nor careful.

He took his hand away from Emily's cheek and slid his fingers up into her hair. It had no gold in it in this light.

Its curls were loose. She never fussed with it the way Marie or Jenny or Monica did. Like everything else about her, it just was. "Who cuts your hair?" he asked.

"Mother. She always has."

"It's so natural."

"Is it?"

"Yes. You are too."

"I don't know what I am."

"You just are. I don't think you have to care."

"Do you?"

"What?"

"Care what you are?"

"All the time."

She pushed away from him, curious. "When? I've never seen you."

"I just do. When you're not around."

"You mean like planning to be a musician?"

"Yes." He felt awkward, and wanted to turn around what they were saying so that the talk was about her again.

"Planning's not the same as worrying about what you are," she said.

"Maybe planning's getting away from what you are," he told her, and that flash of insight was cold lightning in his stomach.

"You don't have to do that." She kissed him.

He lay still. He was in her arms now; she'd moved so that she held him against her. He returned her kiss. Then, completely open, he said,

"If I got to be a musician, you could be a mother, have kids."

She didn't answer for a while, but he knew it wasn't because he'd said the wrong thing. Gradually, he thought, we're melting together. He could feel her ribs, the bones of her hips. She held him quietly. He closed his eyes.

Then she asked, "What would we name them?"

She was saying yes. He didn't want anymore to be close: he wanted to be inside of her. He took a deep breath and let it out slowly. "If we had kids? I don't know. Would they be girls or boys?"

"If you have a boy and then a girl, that's called a millionaire's family."

"Who told you?"

"Daddy."

"Then that's what to have."

She didn't say anything. He closed his eyes and drifted, stayed relaxed against her, and in his head there appeared a room like this one. It had the kind of comforts that were here. He drifted farther, not away from Emily, but closer to where their baby was feeding at Emily's breast, as he'd seen Sarah feed at his mother's. It was soft and white. He moved against it, as if he were the child. He wanted to take the rest of Emily's clothes off and see what she looked like. It was odd that he didn't know, but somehow he didn't. He set their baby aside and began to undress its mother, his wife.

Emily said something too softly to hear. He held her skirt in his hands, but it was still in the way of his seeing. It billowed around her legs and hips.

"Christopher," Emily said, into his dream. "My Mum and Dad are coming. Get up."

He woke, already moving, rolled hard against the side of the hammock and held her hands so she could pull herself up and out. They stood together, rumpled, in the middle of the room. Her pleated skirt was folded up at the side so that the top of her stocking was exposed. He reached down and straightened it around her knees. It was hard to think, to move against the sleep that was still in him. He looked at Emily and saw her steady eyes watching him. She held out her arms. "Dance with me," she said.

The music was a bouncy version of Eddie Cantor's "Making Whoopee," a record from her mother's collection. They moved half-time to it toward the windows, and when he turned around so that he faced the door, Mrs. Gordon was standing there, tall in her fur coat and high heels. She wore her hair short, and it made her look elegant. When he thought about living in the city, he pictured the women there looking like her.

Pat came and stood beside her mother. She saw the hammock, and stared with wide eyes at him. He stopped dancing. Emily turned around.

"Having a good time, darling?" Mrs. Gordon asked. There was no edge to her voice.

Emily leaned against him and nodded.

Her mother shook her head. "You two—" She stopped. "I suppose you know you're famous? You've got people talking."

"People are drips," Pat said.

Still Emily didn't say anything.

"Paula Thompson said she'd lock Edna up—"

"Mother," Emily said, loud and firm. "I'm not Edna Thompson."

"Do you think I'm too old to remember?" Her laugh was unsuccessful. "This kind of thing—"

"It's my business," Emily said, her voice still firm, but she went to her mother and kissed her cheek. "It's a good party. Thanks for letting us have it."

"Us," Pat said. "You haven't lifted a hand."

"Yes I have. I brought the glasses out for the punch."

"Which reeks of rye," their mother said. "Who spiked it?"

"Fielder," Pat said. "It was only a mickey and I gave him what-for."

"How'd you know it was him?" Christopher asked.

"It had to be either him or you, Waterton, and I figured you were too lovesick."

Fielder came and stood beside Pat. He liked being caught. It was part of the fun. Mrs. Gordon stopped looking at Christopher and said to Fielder, "You two are scourges, I hear."

"Not him," Fielder said. "Waterton's a spoilsport."

She looked at Christopher again. "I don't suppose Fielder tried to stop you from putting up the hammock?"

"We were talking about Daddy being in the navy," Emily said. "I put it up."

Mrs. Gordon's eyes blinked, and blinked again. Then she said, "You'd better put it back before your father sees it."

Emily took it down from its hook on the windowed wall and folded it back against itself. "Where is he?" she asked. "I want to dance with him."

"Thanks," Christopher said, "you really know how to hurt a guy."

"He taught us," Emily said.

He tried to think of dancing with his mother. The idea embarrassed him. But Emily wanted to get away from her mother and she went quickly, almost breaking into a run, toward her father, who was talking to Isonovich and Monica at the far end of the room. The music now was a latin version of "The Isle of Capri." She took his arm and said something to Isonovich, and her father looked down at her, smiled, and then they began to dance. This was a different Emily. She copied his older grace, which made her dance tall and straight and follow the rhythm of the music exactly. She looked serious, except when he swung her around, and then she smiled a smile that was a thrill on her face. Everyone in the room was watching, as if this were a lesson at school.

"Show me," Fielder said to Mrs. Gordon. He held out his arms as Emily had done to her father.

But Mrs. Gordon smiled at him coldly. "Don't think you can get away with spiking the punch that easily. I won't be diverted. I want you to get your coat and go home."

Fielder's head jerked as if he'd been hit, and his face went red. He dropped his arms.

"*Mother*," Pat said. "Nothing *happened*. Nobody's drunk."

"That's not the point. It was done." To Fielder, she said, "And don't think Emily won't be called to order about the hammock." Her voice was kindly, as if having passed sentence on him she could now let him know he wasn't the only one in trouble.

Christopher saw Fielder glance at him. His eyes were hard and demanding. Christopher stared back. Any other time he would go with Fielder. Now he couldn't.

Then Pat moved. She put her hand on Fielder's arm. "Come on," she said, her eyes watching her mother, "I'll help you find your coat."

Fielder said to Christopher, "Coming?"

He shook his head. "Emily," he said, and couldn't think what else to say.

Pat dragged Fielder away, and then changed her mind. In the middle of the floor she turned and made him dance with her. She moved in close and put her head against his. It was the right thing to do. When they wheeled around, Fielder was grinning.

Christopher watched Mrs. Gordon look at them. After a moment, she appeared suddenly to remember him. She turned and said an astounding thing: "Your father somehow became Chairman of the School Board."

And Christopher said too quick, "He was elected."

"Yes, I suppose," and she left him before he could ask her what she meant. But he knew, and it was hard to believe. It was stupid to think she might like him and his family because he loved Emily. That wasn't the way things worked.

Fielder and Pat glided off the floor as the music stopped. They went into Emily's room and came out again with Fielder struggling into his coat. Christopher watched for him to signal again, but Fielder went instead to where Emily and her father were standing. He held out his hand. Dr. Gordon looked surprised and laughed, saying, no doubt, that the party wasn't his. He shook Fielder's hand and gestured to his daughters. Pat grinned hugely. Fielder saw Mrs. Gordon coming back from having hung her coat up in the hallway, and he left, waving at everyone. Pat followed him through to the kitchen.

Christopher stood in the archway that led from the porch to the living room. The party was over. No one was at the gramophone selecting new music. The dancers, all of them, and Pat and Emily and their parents were simply standing there in the room. What had been a little crowd was now seventeen separate people, and the time was awkward: Fielder had been sent away and Pat had tried to make it look as if he'd chosen to go. But he hadn't. Everyone knew it, and there was something heavy bearing down on them, the same kind of trapped silent moment that happened in a classroom when someone was punished in front of everybody.

Christopher went toward Emily. She saw him and broke away from her parents. There was in her again the firmness she'd showed her mother on the porch. It was as if what she was doing was a signal that if Fielder's spiked punch had been handled without fuss, the hammock incident wasn't going to be dealt with so simply. Her father watched her with his eyebrows raised and a sudden fixed smile on his face.

Christopher halted in the middle of the room. No one except Emily was moving, but too much was happening, and he could feel himself choking on the need to escape. He could see Mrs. Gordon staring at him; Emily was too, but he didn't know why, because the silence in the room wouldn't let her speak. She took his arm. "Let's put some music on," she said, and turned him toward the gramophone.

"A waltz," her mother said.

"The home waltz?" Maxine Dobroski asked.

"Oh, I think so," Mrs. Gordon said, brightly.

He put his head close to Emily's while they searched, and she whispered, "Please, Christopher, you look awful. It's going to be all right." She picked up "My Buddy" and put it on.

They danced. In the new bright light everyone moved gracefully to the easy beat. Doctor and Mrs. Gordon revolved slowly in the middle of the room. It was their music, too. They smiled at each other and danced close.

"Maybe I should tell your mother nothing happened."

Emily shook her head.

"What about you?"

"Nothing. I'll get a talking-to."

"Your mother's really mad."

"Not really."

"What is she then?"

"Disappointed."

"That's worse."

"Maybe. I don't think so."

He swung around so he could watch the others dancing. Callaghan came by. "We're going to Ch'en's," he said.

"We've got to clean up here," Emily told him.

"Come on down after."

"Maybe," Emily said. And when they were alone again, she said, "Go with them if you want. I think you should."

"I'll stay and clean up."

She shook her head. "It's our party."

"It's been a good one."

She laughed, maybe to get rid of tension. Then she looked serious. "It's the best time we've had together."

The music was ending. He held her close and stood with her waiting for the final chord.

"Hey," Maxine shouted. "It's been great." She dragged Callaghan to Pat and gave her a hug.

It was a party again. The end of one, and it was easy to go, to break out into the moonlight and watch the Dobroskis jitterbug in the snow while Smith and Bell hummed a loud and fast "Johnson Rag" through their noses: they were trumpets, and when Maxine and Dorrie fell down, they marched over them and out of the gate to the street. Monica had phoned her parents. Her father came in his car, and Isonovich opened its door for her. She got in and he closed it, a ceremony that made her the old Monica again. She smiled as if she knew, raised her hand uncertainly, Isonovich bowed, and then, when the car was gone, he ran slipping and sliding after the others.

Emily had her heavy coat on, the one she said she wore to church. They stood hidden against their tree and he kissed her. In the middle of

it she suddenly began to laugh. "We're famous. People talk about us."
"Why?" He really wanted to know.
"Maybe they're jealous."
He hugged her. "They should be."
Mrs. Gordon opened the door and called Emily's name.
"That's her right-now voice," Emily said. She kissed his lips and left him.
"Call me in the morning," he said after her, and when she slammed the door, he walked down the street away from the Gordon house. It felt as if something had changed. He could still sense the stiff canvas of the hammock at his back, and Emily pressed against him so that the air they breathed belonged to them both and his warmth was hers. Her body hadn't stopped where his started, and when he'd drifted into sleep he'd dreamed what he wanted now: to see her.
First, she had been Pat's younger sister, and there had been distances between them they'd bridged. One day, under the tree, he'd reached out and touched her. At Christmas they'd kissed, and in a while people noticed them always together. The town was gossiping, and Paula Thompson had spoken to Mrs. Gordon. She wanted to stop them, maybe because it made her daughter somehow unsafe. Emily's mother might want to stop it too, because of the hammock and the rye in the punch. But none of those things were the change, and they might not have anything to do with it. What he felt was a shift in himself. Something had turned over, or maybe it had risen up so that now he had to look around it to see what was happening to him and Emily.
He didn't want to think about it any more and, if he went home to bed, he would. The rest of the party was at Wei Ch'en's by now. He began to go there—but in his head and gut he believed he should have stayed at the Gordons' to clean up. He wanted to make it easier on Emily. He imagined how her whole family might now be talking to her all at once about the hammock. If he were there, they might have to be polite, and he'd have time to show the Gordons that he loved Emily, and they'd surely understand what that meant. No harm would ever come to her.
It was late. The Saturday dance at the Royal must stop at the top of the clock, when Sunday began. He could walk in past the ticket-taker without paying. He was on London Street now, a block away from the ballroom, and when the door opened to let someone in or out, he could hear Marty Franklin's trumpet for a couple of bars. The tempo was up. Gabe always did this on Saturdays—played faster and faster tunes until finally they might do "Cherokee," and then off the end of that, break

into a very slow version of "Home Sweet Home."

He reached the big double doors and opened the right hand one. The tune was "The Sheik of Araby." Good solid stompin' music, Gabe called it. The clock on the wall was nearing midnight. He walked the length of the hall, dodging dancers who were moving fast and swinging hard. Gabe was a magician making these four hundred dancers do crazy things. Now he closed his eyes; Marty Franklin blew the spit from his trumpet and joined Gabe at the mike. They played the first half of the out-chorus soft and fast and easy, and then the last eight bars loud. No arranged ending, just a final note cut short by a rim-shot from Buster Brady's drum. The applause from the dancers was as much for themselves as it was for the band.

Gabe and Marty sat down, tired. At the Royal, the music was continuous from nine to midnight on Saturday nights. On other nights when there were dances, the band took a break at eleven and another at one o'clock before playing on until 2:30 or 3:00 in the morning. They both rubbed their hands across their lips and reached down beside their chairs for a Coke bottle. Gabe didn't spike his with rye. Marty did. There were nights every now and then when Gabe finished the dance by himself, while Marty lay passed out behind the stand. But never on a Saturday night. The time went fast; people paid a quarter each to get in, and they didn't want to miss a minute of dancing time.

Gabe saw him and smiled. "Hi," he said. "Listen, we're going out on "Twelfth Street Rag."

"That ought to do it to them," Christopher said. He sat up on the stand and watched.

"Let's see how fast we can go." Gabe began to count. One two, one two, and suddenly there was the traditional march introduction at double-time—240 on the metronome. It was a simple six-note rag. He tried to move his fingers on an imaginary saxophone, but he couldn't make them go fast enough. And this was the easy part. The hard thing was to do choruses at this tempo. They gave it to Jim Collins at the piano, and then Marty did five choruses as if he were in the Schickelfritz band or playing with Spike Jones. The dancers loved it: they duckwalked, marched, ran, jumped, did the turkey-trot. It was what happened at five to twelve every Saturday night, no matter what fast number Gabe played—and now he kept it going until it felt as if the floor would collapse, or the people explode because their heartbeats had caught up to the tempo of the music. Everything in the hall was synchronized. The music couldn't just stop. This time, Gabe and Marty signalled the end a long way in advance, and when they stopped repeating the tune, there was a contrived eight bars that finished with Gabe playing his bottom note, Marty three octaves above him and the piano and drums raving in between. It was wild. There were hollers, shouts, whistles, and then gradual quiet.

Christopher leaned as near as he could to Gabe. "Do 'My Buddy' for the home waltz."

Gabe looked at him. "Where you been?" He grinned.

"Party."

"With Emily?"

"Sure. Are you having coffee after?"

"Going home. Kid's got the croup."

Christopher walked down the length of the hall while the band played "Home Sweet Home." All the couples were reunited now, after having danced with as many other people as they could. It was a way to touch that everybody approved of. He stopped by the door, thinking about dancing with Emily, and he could still feel her moving against him.

"Your mouth's open. Watch out or your brains'll leak out," Purvis said. He was leaning against the wall near the exit.

"I was thinking."

"About guess what."

"I learned how to dance at a party tonight."

"Where?" Purvis always wanted details.

"Gordons'."

"That's getting serious, you and Emily."

"Going for coffee now?"

"Maybe later," Purvis said.

"You got a date?"

"What if I said yes."

"I'd believe you."

Purvis reached over and gave him a ritual punch on the shoulder. "Never believe a word I say, kid."

Christopher pushed open the door and went outside so he wouldn't have to stand at attention for "God Save the King." Gabe always insisted on playing the whole thing. It made everyone very solemn. Purvis came outside and turned uptown without saying goodbye. Christopher watched him go. He didn't wear a hat until it was thirty below. His hair was long enough to cover the tops of his ears, but that was all. He said that if you were going to live in this climate you should be able to do it as much as possible on your own terms. He thought the same about his family. They were another kind of climate he tried not to let bother him. Christopher went down London Street to Wei Ch'en's.

The party was in the back room, where Ch'en had nailed rough knotty boards to the walls and had called it the Pine Room. The tables were family-size, or they could be pushed together for meetings. The jukebox was turned up loud, and out front all the booths were filled. Mostly they wanted Coke to splash rye into from the bottles they'd brought in paper bags. He went on through to the Pine Room door. There was no one there for him to dance with. Callaghan shouted for him to come on in, but he didn't want to sit by himself and watch. Others had joined them. Callaghan's older sister was with Pete McIntyre. He felt out of it, and turned away to go home.

The kitchen doors swung open and May Kaplik came out with two Westerns and fries on her arm. "You still here?" he asked her. She nodded and said, "Split shift."

He stood by an empty stool at the counter and watched her serve Alex Fraser and Donna Franklin, Marty's sister. He knew everyone here. May walked back behind the bar and poured four coffees. She put them on the counter in front of him. "There you are, Waterton. My feet are tired. Give those to Alex."

"He wants four?"

"No. You can have one of the others if you want."

When he came back from Alex and Donna's booth, May was sitting on a stool at the counter as if she were a customer. She was lighting a cigarette.

He sat beside her and it made him feel as if he now belonged somewhere. He wasn't a Gordon guest, or someone who wanted to be a musician, or the odd member of a party in the Pine Room. Just Christopher having a coffee with May. "Split shift makes for a long day," he said.

"You want the job, you do what you have to."

He sipped his coffee. "Why did you want the job?"

She looked at him, and he saw that she'd gained weight. Her cheeks were rounder and her eyes appeared to him almond-shaped. Even with her fair hair, she might pass for half Oriental. "Guess," she said.

"You didn't have to quit school."

"Yes, I did."

He drank another mouthful of coffee. "You want to save money and get out of here."

"You're bright, Waterton."

"You could get money from your sisters."

"I want my own. And I got to get it soon."

"Why?"

"Because Ch'en put his hand on my ass yesterday is why."

He glanced at Ch'en ringing up money on the cash register. He was a a small man, round, but not fat. Younger than most of the Chinese in town. He imagined May punching him. She was as tough as Purvis. He smiled at her. "What did you do?"

"The thing you do if you want the job is nothing."

"I guess the other thing is that you're illegal."

She smiled at him and nodded. "You know a lot for a mere kid," she said.

"That much."

"I'm supposed to be sixteen. That's what I told Ch'en so he'd hire me."

"I meant illegal for putting his hand on you."

May blew smoke across her coffee and then sipped it. "They don't give a crap about that." She pulled on her cigarette again. "If you're big enough, you're old enough. And they want it, so they think you want it."

"Who? Ch'en?"

"Sure, and lots more." She stubbed out her cigarette and got up. When she was on the other side of the counter from him, she said, "I close this place down at two every night I work. Billy MacLean saw me going home one time and stopped me—"

"*MacLean?*"

"Don't get excited. He didn't touch me. He only asked me if I was a working girl now, and he meant working the street. Jesus, it was twenty below and me in my coat and uniform and him in his fur hat and cop get-up are the only two people awake in the world. I said, no I wasn't a working girl. He said, I don't like working girls, and I said, that's nice, why don't you close down my mother. I'm damned if I know why I said that, but I really hate going home now."

"You could have a place of your own."

"Not if I want to save any money. You know what Billy said? That's your mother you're talking about. You give her respect, young lady. Where'd you be without her?"

Ch'en came past her from the cash register. "Number two booth need you."

"Have a heart, Ch'en, I'm on my break."

Ch'en smiled. "Come see me after. I give you pay." His voice was serene, and he went to serve the people in booth number two.

May shrugged. "Maybe he's going to get me."

"No, he's not," and he was embarrassed by his emotion.

"My mother wants me out," she said, and stood away from the counter looking at him as if he must understand what she was saying. Christopher nodded as if he did. "He's got a place upstairs where he does Indian girls. What the hell, he needs loving too. Mary John—you know her?" He nodded again. "That papoose on her back could be his for all I know." She grinned coldly. "Maybe I'm going to be his first blonde white girl."

"Because you don't have anywhere else to stay? Are you going to—?" He watched her face. It had gone blank again.

"I don't know what's going to happen." Her voice was as expressionless as her face. Then she smiled and leaned on the counter. "I started something when I quit school, eh?"

This was the first time he'd been able to stare back into her eyes. Their wary trust made him feel May was a friend. "You didn't get to say who your mother was," he said.

"I never got to choose anything."

"Yes you did."

"Like what?"

He reached and held her arm. He knew it was a wrong thing to do, but he didn't take his hand away. "I don't know. What about deciding to talk to me just now?"

"Big time." She grinned again. "I felt like talking." She took her arm away. "You want to touch too?"

He felt bold. "That's not your ass."

She looked faintly surprised. "You weren't standing behind me." She glanced away at the people in the booths and then looked at him again. "It's easy to talk to you. You don't count for anything."

"I like you—"

"Go home, Waterton."

Behind her at the coffee urn, Ch'en said, "Your break over now."

Christopher got up and felt in his pocket for a nickel to pay for the coffee. May shook her head. It was a small thing, a one cent profit she was taking from Ch'en, but he saw it was important to her. He said good night and went outside into the cold again. When he looked back through the cafe window he could see May at the booth near the door. She was clearing dishes away. How she moved didn't give him any messages about how she felt. She was just bending over working at what she had to.

CHAPTER FOUR

1

THE HORN WAS SOUNDING GOOD. GABE HAD WRITTEN OUT THE circle of dominant seventh chords for him, and now he could play them through slowly from memory. The scale of B, with its five sharps, was a pretty one. For the first time he was beginning to hear that there really was a difference in the texture of sound between the sharp and the flat keys. He blew softly into his horn. It made a low sound, a note that needed another to—what?—maybe begin a story. He began to tell one. It was his own. Up three notes, back down again. They made a lonely tune. What they were saying was physical too. Lonely physical. Like when he hugged Emily, and he couldn't get close enough. Ever. The story his notes were telling was about Not Ever.

Higher up the scale the tune wanted another set of three notes. They made the feeling stronger: split off: Emily was not able to be with him in the old way. Her parents had said No. "Think about it, Emily. Ask Christopher to think about it too, if he can. Have lots of friends. One friend is unhealthy." Mrs. Gordon was a wrong note. He played it. And then from down the hall Sarah in bed called for silence.

He stopped blowing so his mother wouldn't shout at him, but the tune remained in his head while he put the horn away and stored it on the shelf in the closet.

His skis needed waxing—anything to keep from doing Miss Garrett's homework. This was the time he was usually on the phone to Emily. But now it wasn't allowed. He called, or she did, and they talked. Or sometimes they didn't say much, just sat and listened to each other breathe for maybe a minute. It was as close as kissing. Closer, because there wasn't a hug or a kiss to measure their nearness. What he felt for her was a pressure in his chest. It was a pleasure he thought Emily felt as well. It was why he could be silent on the phone, because she had it, he had it, they had it together. The pleasure made them want to be close, but—and this was crazy—they had to be separate people so each could have the feeling. It was why never being close enough was a good thing.

He passed by the phone on his way to the basement and couldn't help but stare at it.

"You look so forlorn," his mother said. Her finger marked where she was on the page in front of her, and she smiled up at him from her chair. "You see Emily after school, don't you?"

He nodded. Right now it was none of her business. She always knew too much about him. They were alike. They got angry at the same things and had the same sense of humour. When they needed to, they could talk seriously and become friends again, even if days had passed when they were only mother and son.

"You must have patience," she said.

"Why?"

"Because then it will be easier for you to wait for things to return to normal."

"I don't think they will."

"A new normal, then."

They hadn't talked about what had happened at the party—the hammock. Maybe she knew from Mrs. Gordon. Or maybe she didn't want to know exactly what was wrong and only understood that something had happened. Now, she said, "I like Emily. She's wonderfully mature, but I guess if I had her for a daughter at this time in her life I'd worry about her too."

"That's all mothers ever do."

"Pat's been an easy child for the Gordons to bring up. Bright, outgoing, successful. Emily—I don't know. I think there's a part of her that says I'm different, and I may not be exactly what you want me to be."

"She knows who she is," he said. "So does Pat."

"I wonder." She smiled a little sadly.

"Why?"

"Do you think Pat might be trying a little too hard?"

"I don't know what you're talking about."

"My, but you're touchy."

"The Gordons aren't your business."

She sat for a moment, still looking up at him. He thought she was waiting for him to stop fighting her and listen. He turned away, but her voice stopped him from moving out of the room.

"What happened at the party, Chris?"

He didn't answer.

"Did you misbehave, or is it that things have changed between you and Emily?"

"Both," he said. The relief he felt in admitting it caught at the back of his throat.

"Do you want to tell me?"

"No."

"Was it a bad thing?" She was standing up now.

"No." He wasn't afraid, not of the hammock, but of tears.

"Then Emily's punishment won't last long."

"I guess not."

"And in the meantime you see her. You went skating today."

"I went skating and she went skating. We didn't go together."

His mother sighed. "It's all so childish, isn't it?"

He turned and looked at her, surprised. The expression on her face said: Did I say that? I'm glad.

"What do you mean?" He wanted to keep her talking.

"I mean, you two can handle this—" She stopped; her hand gestured for him to fill in the blank.

He left the blank empty. "You think so?" He couldn't think what she wanted to hear from him.

"You're both responsible people. You have your saxophone and skiing. Emily has healthy interests too."

"Healthy?" Mrs. Gordon's word.

His mother blushed and put her hand on his arm. "You know what I mean, Christopher. Think about how your father and I—"

He put his hand up to stop her. "Hold it."

She laughed suddenly, not at him, but at herself. "I know what you're going to say. It's not the same with your father and me, moldy old figs that we are." She gave him a hug. "I wish you weren't so bright. It'd make it a lot easier to be your mother."

He didn't hug her back. "I got to wax my skis."

"Yes, please," she said, mock serious. "Go down there and disturb your father."

"I'll send him up."

"No, just an interruption will do."

He watched her disappear through the door into the bathroom, and then he went back out into the kitchen and down the stairs to the basement.

It was a half basement. The living room and master bedroom had only a crawl space under them. There was a bin that held three tons of coal, and there were six cords of stove-length birch piled under the stairs, floor-to-ceiling, in the space beyond the coal bin. The furnace gave off some heat, but his father kept the basement warm with a fire in a small camp stove near his workbench. In the space beyond the furnace was the laundry—a wringer washer new in 1926, and near it, two galvanized tubs on low benches for rinsing clothes. His skis were in the corner beyond the washer, but he didn't go to them, because no matter how often he came down the stairs, this small bright workshop halted him as if it were something alive that had to be given special attention.

He watched his father fit a pretty piece of knot-free fir onto the lathe on the far side of the big workbench. On the near side was a drill press, and at the other end was a jigsaw. His father had built them from scrap. Only the chucks on the drill press and the lathe and the blade on the jigsaw were store-bought. Even the lathe's chisels were made out of the tempered steel of discarded planer blades he'd found at the mill. The frame of the jigsaw had once been part of a Model T Ford that had been nearly buried in junk at the town dumping grounds. The drill press slid up and down on a piece of scrapped driveshaft he'd got from the foreman at the railway's roundhouse. Now, he was building a table that would hold a circular saw. The shop would be complete then. It would have to be. With his workbench against the north wall, the basement was full. As it was, there was hardly room to stand.

"He *will* have a life that's good," his mother had said. "And he'll have all those things in it he wants and knows are possible to build because he sees them in department store catalogues." She had gestured around the living room as she had spoken in a voice that was always astounded when she talked about him. In the room were chairs he'd made, stuffed, sewed, and covered himself. The dining room suite was mahogany—a table, six chairs, and a highboy. The lamps were turned on the lathe. "He's a Waterton," she'd said, and had shaken her head, perhaps in despair. "There have been generations of them here in this country. They have never been rich, but they have always had all the land could offer. And now, you see, he's built us the trappings of a life in these terrible times out of what he found in it. Your father's a quite wonderful man."

She had sat then in one of his chairs and had reached out a hand to Christopher. He'd not taken it. She often spoke like this, as if she needed to keep saying who his father was. There was, he felt, without forming the word in his mind, a fear in her. Maybe one day her husband would go downstairs and disappear.

"Be like him, Christopher, but not *just* like him. He has a fault, you know. He hunkers down. Inside this house. Inside himself. What he does is a language. It says, Watch out, it's tough out there, you have to be brave to survive." She had shaken her head again. "He doesn't mean brave. He means perfect. It takes up nearly all of his time." She blushed. "I keep forgetting you're just a child."

"Talk to him," he said, and watched her be surprised.

"Oh, I do. And he listens. But he believes you should have to be able to do everything for yourself inside your own world. You don't, you know." She laughed, embarrassed still to be saying these things. "It's okay to ask for help. He hardly ever does that. And mostly he only knows how to do the kind of giving that's really payment."

"For what?"

"Providence's good will? Or mine and yours and Sarah's and the people he works with?"

"Maybe you're wrong about him."

She hadn't replied. She always stopped short of the end of things she started. *Be like him, but not just like him.* What did that mean, really? Another time, she'd said, "Life's not black and white, it's what's grey in the middle."

Now his father straightened up and looked across the bench at him. "You're moping, son. Cheer up, what's the matter?"

"Nothing."

"No homework?"

"I have to wax my skis."

"For Saturday. Can we come and watch?"

"Do you want to?"

"Of course."

"I do better if no one's watching."

"There'll be a crowd, and we'll be in it."

"Yeah, I guess." He laid his skis across one of the laundry tubs. His father turned on the motor and began turning the wood into a round table leg. He liked to take the corners off things. Smooth them out whether they needed it or not.

Christopher ran his hand down one of the skis. Blenkin had probably already given Lester some of the new special wax from Vancouver. More speed, more distance, and he wouldn't have to jump so hard and could get better marks for style.

He kept an ordinary white candle on the shelf where the soap flakes and bluing were kept. This was the second one he'd used this season. He dripped the wax on and got the flat iron from the top of the camp stove. The wax melted against the brown paper and ran perfectly smooth across the surface of the wood. He used the edge of the iron to melt the wax into the ski's grooves. The wax and the heated paper gave off a smell unlike any other he'd known. He thought now, after nearly nine years of doing this chore, that this hot wax paper scent was what the colour brown smelled like.

He put the iron back on the stove and lit the candle again. What he was doing was a ritual that relaxed him. He straightened up and watched his father fit the next table leg into the lathe.

"It's young Lester again, I suppose? This is the last year you'll have to jump against him."

"He's better than me by ten feet. I'll be second again."

"If you don't fall."

Christopher glanced up. "Gee, thanks."

"I meant that only as a third possibility. A fourth might be that Harrison beats you both."

"Robby Harrison's in grade eight."

"He'll be real competition for you next year."

"If he gets to be Blenkin's pet."

"What does that mean?"

"He really coaches Lester and nobody else."

"I guess it's hard not to give extra time to the one who's best."

"How's someone else going to get good?"

"Keep going, Chris. Keep getting better. He'll notice you."

"I think he's nuts." The candle had dripped a pool of wax at the end of the ski. He blew the flame out, and saw his father standing by his lathe looking at him.

"I don't think you should talk like that." The voice was strong but not harsh. "He's your teacher."

"Can't he be wrong?"

"Is he? How would you know? Maybe he wants you to work harder so he can see what kind of a man you are."

Christopher put the candle on the shelf and wished that he could go upstairs. It wouldn't do any good to tell tales on Blenkin: maybe if Fielder—or Emily—were here he could make a kind of joke out of it so that his father would put on his company manners and laugh.

"Blenkin said someone else did my picture of a saxophone for me."

His father grinned at him. "Then it must've been a really good one."

"Yes." The grin hurt. "He gave it a 9."

"He did? You said he thought you didn't draw it."

Christopher went again to the stove for the iron. His mind produced a picture of himself kissing Emily and Blenkin seeing them from the school window.

"Blenkin got mad at me. That's when he said I didn't do the drawing, and when I proved I did, he moved it down to a 5 anyway."

His father was silent for a moment, then he said, "What do you think he was trying to teach you, Chris?"

"What is he? God?"

His father didn't answer.

"Nothing. I don't know what he wanted."

"Think a minute."

"I've thought about it a lot. Either it was a 9 or it wasn't."

"That may be true, but you have to look beyond that. What reason did he give for making it a 5?"

"He said I'd practised all year drawing saxophones and everybody else just did the assignment."

"Your marks in Art have never been good," his father said, and he turned back to the lathe. "A 9 would give you an average that doesn't reflect your real talent."

"I drew the saxophone myself. It was my picture."

"It was the one picture you could draw that might get you a 9."

"I told him I got a sax for Christmas and he said everything's handed to me on a platter."

"I'm sure he didn't say that."

"Okay, maybe not on a platter, but he said I was privileged. He doesn't like me."

"Neither of those statements is true."

"You should be there. He picks on me because I'm your kid. Why'd you run for School Board anyway?"

His father cut the hum of the motor and put his chisel down. "Christopher, I think Mr. Blenkin was being fair and was trying to teach you something. You have to believe that."

"Why?"

"Because he's one of the people we've hired to look after our children's education. Sometimes he teaches you out of a book, and sometimes he does it in ways that will prepare you for what it's like out in the real world. While you're in school, he's in charge. It's like having a job. He's your boss."

"He's a boss, so he's right."

"When you're out of school you'll have one—if you're lucky enough to get work at all."

"He'll be right all the time?"

"Someone has to say how things are going to be."

"Like Mayor Courtney?"

"That's a different matter."

"Why? He doesn't like you. You're not supposed to be Chairman of the School Board. He's your boss in that job. He thinks you're just one of his slaves. How do you feel about that?"

"You're upset, aren't you?"

"Yes."

"You're getting pushy, but, all right, I'll tell you. I feel objective about it."

"What does that mean?"

"He's got some power, I've got some. I don't take his attitude personally. We'll each use what we have, and I think the result will be a compromise."

"But he doesn't *like* you being elected. Hardly anybody does. At Emily's party, her mother said to me, 'Your father somehow became Chairman of the School Board,' like it was a stupid accident."

His father smiled. "I have to think that's her problem."

"It's no fun being your kid." He heard his voice come out harsh, and suddenly he saw he had to laugh to keep the shock on his father's face from turning to anger.

"You're hard to talk to sometimes, Christopher. I try to answer your questions."

"Yes." The word came out automatic. He put the iron on the brown paper again. It had gone nearly cold. "I know you do."

"And I know I'm right about Mr. Blenkin."

"I don't think so." He had to laugh for fear he'd gone too far again, but his father's face didn't change expression. Christopher took the iron to the stove. What was happening between them had to stop. "Mom wanted me to send you up," he said.

"What did she want?"

"Nothing, I guess. Maybe she just wants to see you."

It was the right thing to say. His father's smile was one of relief; he nodded his head and turned the motor back on. The wood spun in front of him, and he picked up his chisel again. "I'll just finish this."

Christopher watched. The chisel's blade bit into the wood, chips flew up and the square piece of wood became round and smooth and moulded. "Let me," he said, after a moment. He took the offered chisel and placed it on the bar in front of the spinning wood. Gradually he eased it forward until shavings began to peel off. He moved the chisel to the right and watched the wood take on a new shape.

"That's it," his father said. "Good."

He moved the chisel farther right. The pattern continued, but he wanted to dig the blade in hard to see what would happen. He held it steady and then skewed the chisel so that one corner of its square end became a point, and he pushed it into the wood. The groove grew wider and deeper as he shoved harder.

"Why are you doing that?" His father said, and touched his hand to take the chisel back.

"It's dull just making it round and smooth."

"The job is to make it round."

"Now it's got my mark on it." Christopher watched his father's face. It looked surprised and then disappointed.

"You'll never make a woodworker with that attitude. I can't have one leg with a groove in it."

"I could."

"Go do your ironing." His father glanced at him. "You wouldn't put another groove in your skis."

He mimicked his father's voice. "That's a different matter."

"Now you are being insolent."

"No."

"Then what *are* you being?"

He went to the stove. "Nothing. I'm sorry." He picked up the iron again. "I do have a special way of waxing my skis."

"I'm glad you see my point."

Everything felt rigid. He wanted to go upstairs again and play his horn, let things inside of him go loose, but Sarah was sleeping. The iron melted the wax blob at the end of the ski, and he watched it drip down onto the floor next to the washing machine.

If you deliberately walk outside at forty below you'll get cold. It was the same as deliberately talking about Blenkin or Courtney. The man at the lathe was only going to say—every time—that all you have to do is understand and then everything will be all right. His father could understand Blenkin all he wanted. He wasn't in his class. He stopped ironing. "What about Harrison Dodd," he said, loud enough to be heard above the noise of the lathe. "You get mad at him. The logs at the mill. Is he right about them just because he's your boss?"

"That's a political decision," his father said, not looking up from his work.

"What does that mean?"

"It means that the town needs Creighton's mill open and he's being allowed to get away with it down there—"

"So he can make more money."

"Council says profits will go into new machinery for the mill."

"What're you going to do about it?" He put his skis back against the wall. "Nothing?"

"I'm going to talk to Creighton. I already have. This time I'm going to take a plan to him I think might save him money and cut the risk he's running of losing his logs and maybe damaging the bridge."

Upstairs the phone began to ring. A long and a short. Their ring. His mind stopped arguing with his father and began to wait to see if the call was for him. Emily. Fielder. Phone calls for his mother came mostly during the day. It could be for his father. Emily couldn't call him anyway because she was forbidden to. He heard his mother answer and then say in her delighted voice, "Why, Emily, how nice," and he began to run up the stairs, not just to talk to Emily but to keep his mother from asking prying questions—When are you coming to lunch again? Will you be at the ski meet on Saturday? And Emily's answers would tell her what she wanted to know.

"Here he is," she said, as he rounded the corner into the nook and reached for the phone. "I wish he'd run so fast when I call him." She laughed and handed him the phone.

He held it against his chest and stared at his mother until she went back into the living room. The radio was on, and he saw her begin to knit and listen to it. He said into the phone, "Can you call me now? Are they letting you?"

"No. They're out. Pat's having a bath."

"Would she tell?"

"If she got mad at me some time."

"Maybe I hate her."

After a pause, she said, "What's wrong?"

"Do I sound as if something's wrong?'

"Yes. Like you're mad."

"I've been waxing my skis."

"In the basement?"

"Yeah, my dad was there. I screwed up some woodwork he was doing."

"I thought you were waxing your skis."

"I was, but I took over the lathe for a minute and put a groove in his table leg that wasn't supposed to be there. On purpose." He felt better now that he'd said it.

"Did he get mad at you?"

"He doesn't get mad. He just talks." He laughed. "And talks and talks and talks some more."

"Adults always talk." There was a shrug in her voice. "I like him."

"You don't have to listen to him tell you everything's okay if you just think right about it."

"Does he know?"

"About us? What to think? Sure."

"Tell me."

"It's too boring. When can you see me again?"

"Tomorrow, before school."

"Not that. You know what I mean. God, even my mother knows we went skating today. The whole town probably knows."

"Mom and Dad know too," Emily said.

"Then let's go back to what we were doing."

"I only meant they know it's a small town, and so we see each other."

He thought about that, and then he told her, "We didn't use to. Before the fire I hardly remember you."

"I know. I was in grade eight." And now her voice had a smile in it.

"Beneath contempt." He laughed. "I don't think of you as being in grade eight now."

"Neither do I."

"You're a lot older than Dody."

"Dody? She's never going to grow up."

"If she goes to a couple more of Pat's parties she will."

She didn't answer that. "Just a minute." She put the phone down, and when she came back: "I thought I heard a car in the driveway."

"Pat's still in the bath?"

"Yes." Then: "Fielder was here."

"*Fielder*? When?"

"Tonight, before supper."

"Why?"

"Pat has him writing sports for the paper."

"What paper?"

"The one you're going to write the record column for."

"Since when?"

"She talked Miss Lee into letting grade nine have a couple of pages in *The Booster.* She went to Keefer after school and talked to him. He walked her home. Neat, eh?"

"What's she up to?"

"With Fielder? I don't know. Maybe nothing. She's trying to laugh it off. He was the one who walked *her* home. Can you imagine Pat asking him to do it?"

"Those two? I don't believe it."

"Why not? You saw Isonovich and Monica at the party."

"Yeah, but Lewis doesn't even look at him at school. He might as well be dead as far as she's concerned."

"Why? He was really nice to her."

"Try thinking what Mrs. Lewis would say—'My dear, he's poor. And foreign.'" He couldn't quite do a Welsh accent.

"I like him."

"Isonovich? You like everybody."

"Not true."

"Name one you don't."

She didn't answer him. After a moment she said, "How come Callaghan and Cameron can go with the Dobroskis now? They're poor too."

"So are the Camerons. . . ." He was still thinking about Pat and Fielder. "I barely believe about your sister and Fielder, though. What do you think?"

"About them going together? Pat's never been interested in boys, for one thing. And another is, Fielder put rye in the punch."

"Did your mother ask him to leave?"

"After a while, he just went."

He laughed. "Fielder and Pat. What're they like together?"

"Christopher?"

"What?"

"It's none of our business."

"He's my best friend." He waited, but she didn't go on about it. "Okay, don't tell me."

"I wish you were here." Her voice was suddenly very young.

"I'll try to come over if you want. Will your folks be gone long?"

"I think so. I don't know."

"What about Pat?"

"I told you."

"If she wants Fielder, she's not going to tell on you. He's in trouble as much as I am."

"It's not trouble. My mother just wants me to be older before I have a boyfriend."

"Do you want to wait?"

"No." She was silent a moment. "Christopher?"

"Yes."

"Please come if you can."

The soft fist that always landed in his gut when she wanted him close hit him again. It was hard to breathe. "Okay."

"You'll see the car in the garage if they're here. Hurry."

He put the receiver on its hook and stood up. In the living room his mother was still knitting, and on the radio there was an organ playing long howling chords—incidental music for a murder mystery. "I want to try my skis," he said, and went back down the stairs, before she could reply. His father was holding the table leg and smoothing it with the palm of his hand. Only with wood was he absolutely gentle. He would make it perfect, fit it exactly and then glue it, nail it and put screws in it so that it could never come apart. If anyone else did it that way it would be funny, but when his father did it, no one questioned that it was the right thing to do.

The surfaces of his skis were dry and smooth. In the cold outside the wax would go hard and tough and slide through the snow, hardly making a whisper. His father's powers of concentration were enormous. He hadn't noticed that anyone had come down the stairs, and he wouldn't hear anyone go back up. In the middle of his forehead, between his eyes, there was a deep wrinkle. His mother said it was the backside of her husband's Third Eye, which was always turned inward. Christopher liked that Third Eye always looking the other way. It saved being asked questions.

He took the skis upstairs and put them out on the porch. It was snowing and the temperature was well above zero. He would need only his jacket, earmuffs, mitts, and a scarf.

The phone rang again. He closed the door and went to answer it.

"They're here," Emily said. "I'm glad I got you."

"That's okay. I wouldn't've minded trying my skis out anyway."

"Are you nervous, Christopher?"

"About Saturday? Maybe."

"I would be."

He heard Emily's back door open. He laughed. "Aren't you nervous about your parents coming in and finding you on the phone to me?"

"No. I'm going to tell them."

"What?"

"That I called you, and I see you three times a day too. I'm telling them now. They're listening."

He could see her standing with the phone in her hand, square on her feet and a little hunched forward. He knew the look on her face too. Calm—except for her eyes.

"Be careful," he said. His voice surprised him. It had fear in it, not just for her, but for himself.

"It'll be a week on Saturday. I think that's enough time in prison."

"I love you," he said. He heard her suck in her breath, as if the words were a weapon. He couldn't think how badly he'd said them. "I love you," he said again. This time it felt as if he were giving her protection. It was hard for him to breathe too, and in the silence between them, he knew Emily was crying. The power of the words scared him. The things they meant, and the way the words changed suddenly what he and Emily had been were crowded against the working centre of his mind. "Emily," he said. He wanted her to understand that the words had special meaning, but the voice that answered him was Mrs. Gordon's.

"What did you say to Emily, Christopher?"

"I said for her to be careful."

"Is that all? Why is she crying?"

"I don't know." His throat muscles choked shut over his lying.

There was a pause; then Mrs. Gordon said, "Is your mother there?"

He looked around. She was still in her chair in the living room. He turned again to face the breakfast nook's tiled blue wall. "No, ma'am."

"Where is she? I'd like to speak with her."

"She's in bed."

"At this hour?"

"She said she had a headache."

"Oh, Christopher—" His mother's voice was near and pained. She took the phone from him. "Is it Mrs. Gordon?"

He nodded. Words in his head clogged. "It's nobody's business," he said, too loud.

"Don't be rude." She put the receiver to her ear. Mrs. Gordon was already talking. After a moment, his mother said, "I cried too, the first time a boy ever said I love you." She was telling Mrs. Gordon what he'd said to Emily. And now she laughed her laugh that was supposed to apologize for having been too blunt.

"Of course I'm concerned."

"Approve? Well, I approve of Emily. I know that. And of Christopher too."

"Be sensible—?" Her voice was quizzical. Before she became angry it often sounded that way. He wanted to take the phone from her.

"Don't you wonder at times what sensible is, Mrs. Gordon? If you dam a thing up then you risk a flood, don't you? If you let it go naturally, it will just run off."

"Small damage is repairable," she said.

"I've had to think about that. It's a shock, isn't it, the way they suddenly grow up?" She laughed another apology, but her face was serious.

"Christopher's a good boy. Emily's. . . ."

"Of course I understand. But they mostly run in gangs, don't they? I'm not aware of what happened at the party, but there were a dozen others." She listened, and swung around to stare at him over the top of the phone. He turned away from her eyes and went into the living room. There was music on the radio, a band he didn't know. He cut the volume.

"I suppose others might also have swung in the hammock?"

"Well, I'm sure she doesn't fib. Pat's a fine girl, too."

"No, not at all. Christopher talked to me about it. He said you wanted Emily to think about whether more friends—"

"Well, were you really giving her a choice of answers? Or Christopher, for that matter?"

"Mother, please don't. You'll ruin everything." He started toward her, but she waved him away. Her face had no colour in it and she was being very calm. He didn't know which was worse—to have her on his side or against him. "Let me handle it," he said to her. "Let Emily handle her mother." He said it loud enough for Mrs. Gordon to hear it too.

"Well, if we ask the children to think, perhaps we should also—"

"No, I don't believe it's easier bringing up a son. Mrs. Gordon, think about me phoning you and asking you to tell your daughter to leave my son alone because she might trap him with her pretty ways and maybe give him a hurt to live with for a long time."

"Of course, exactly. The only joy Long River holds for me is the freedom it gives my children to grow up in a whole little world full of people from the worst to the best. Taking them out of school is no answer. Peter didn't take his children out of school and teach them himself. He ran for School Board." She was through. He watched the muscles in her shoulders relax and her head tilt back as if she were working a stiffness out of her neck. She said into the phone, "It's the best kind of thing we can do."

"Of course you must do what you think best, and I know you will."

"Certainly. Well, I'll let you go now."

"No, I wasn't in bed. Christopher was afraid of what I might say. But we needed to talk."

"Thank you. Goodbye."

He sat down and waited for her to begin to ask questions, but she went instead into the kitchen, and he heard her run the water and fill a glass. When she came back into the living room, she sat in her chair and picked up her knitting. He watched her hands. They struggled with the needles and the wool for a moment, and then she put them down carefully in her lap.

"She wanted me to yell." Her eyes were wide, as if there weren't enough light in the room. "And oh how I wanted to."

"What did she say?"

She kept looking at him. "Does a soft answer really turn away wrath, Christopher? Or does it just refuse the other person's anger and leave it there for another time?"

"I don't know. What did she say? Will Emily ever be able to see me again?"

"It's a very small town."

"I meant see me, visit, be friends."

"You told her you loved her, Christopher—"

He yelled at her, "It's none of your business," and started out of the room.

"You're fourteen," she said. "Can't you listen to your own mother? I do understand." She was beside him now, and he had to let her finish. "You do love Emily."

He turned again toward her.

"The look on your face," she said.

He saw her reach out to hold him. He thought he wanted that now. How did his face look? The answer might tell him something about what he was feeling that he couldn't understand. But he didn't hug her. He held himself a little away from her and felt the outlines of her body as if they were distant. Her face was there, but he didn't let himself see it.

"There must've been a time—" Her voice quit.

"What?" He pulled out of her embrace.

"When things were different. Much more brutish, I suppose. You'd've brought Emily home, and I'd've taught her about having babies while you and your father went to the fields or the forest, or to war. We would all have been dressed in homespun and wouldn't've been at all attractive. Just convenient, and together we might've survived until *your* children were fourteen."

She was making him angry. "I don't know what you're talking about."

"It's not possible now," she said, ignoring him. "Emily's there and you're here. We have laws against children working and marrying. It's called civilization. It is civil, very civil."

"I don't want Emily here."

"I do." Her eyes were wide open again. But then she laughed her apology. "You think I'm—"

"Nuts," he said, not able to stay angry at her, but wanting to.

"Yes."

"How did I look?"

"What?"

"Tell me. You watched."

Her eyes blinked, and he could see her searching for a word. "Noble," she said.

He couldn't find anything to say, and if he left her it would be in the middle of something.

"Don't be surprised. You are, you know, noble—and I wonder if now isn't the only time in your life you can be that—naturally." She put her hand on his arm. "It's embarrassing, isn't it?"

"You are," he said, and thought that she didn't have anything to say to him, not really.

"You asked what you looked like."

"Noble," he said.

"Not noble all the time. You lied to Mrs. Gordon."

"Yes, but I still say it's nobody's business."

"I wish that were true." She went back to her chair and picked up her knitting. "It's very awkward to be called to the phone like that."

"It was because Emily was crying."

"Maybe," she said.

"She wouldn't've cried if things were back to normal."

"Go study," she said, "or go to bed. I think I hear your father packing it in down there."

"You're not going to tell him, are you?"

"Yes."

"Why? Does everybody have to know?"

"He does."

The basement door opened. He glanced once more at his mother. She was putting her knitting away and smiling a welcome. He stood in the hallway and listened.

"It's going to snow all night," his father said.

"Is it?"

"Two or three feet by morning."

"That's good. You'll be able to call extra crews to dig us out."

"There'll be a lineup for work."

"Everybody wants work."

"That's the word: everybody. Even Elmo Kidner keeps coming around, always telling me he can shovel as good as anyone."

"Maybe he can."

"Oh, he'll work, all right. Kill himself showing how good he is."

"Not many of us do that."

"We all should," he said. "It's just that most of us don't shake like a bowlful of jelly."

"You're so graphic, Peter."

He risked a glance past the doorjamb at them. She had her arms around his neck and his father was looking down at her. She had often said things about his father that hardly made sense. "I think he believes the Depression is his fault, and that means he's not good enough to be thoroughly happy and give like happy people do, Christopher." And that had been another time she'd been embarrassed at her frankness. Maybe she'd been exaggerating again; he was just a father, that's all, not much different from Dr. Gordon, or even Fielder's old man. They all believed you had to work hard and do what you're told.

He went into his room and lay on his bed. Sarah cried out in her sleep, and his mother went to her door and looked in. He could hear her pause there, and then close the door again. He tried to imagine Mrs. Gordon doing that. He supposed she had. There were baby pictures of Emily on her bedroom wall—fat, happy, her curls made perfect by someone who liked to look after them. And tonight she'd taken the phone from Emily when she'd seen her crying. He'd not thought of her as a mother who'd say, Call your son off. The lady with a drink in her hand, her dresses like they were out of magazines and her hair just so, wasn't the same one who'd talked to his mother.

One thing. One little thing had caused all this. A hammock. Hanging there on the wall of the glassed-in porch at Emily's house. If Dr. Gordon hadn't brought it home from the war, if he didn't still like to nap in it after work, if it hadn't been something to unfold and make into a private place, if they hadn't come home just then—but it didn't matter that it was the hammock they'd been found in. It might have been another place. Emily's bedroom. Hammocks are supposed to be only for swinging on to the slow rhythm of music coming from the living room. *Nights are long since you went away*. They were.

He pulled the pillow out from under his head and held it in his arms across his chest. The sound in his head of Emily crying made the muscles in his stomach bunch and force air up into his throat. He rolled onto his side and drew his knees up so that he was wrapped around the pillow. He didn't want her to cry. Why have tears if you're loved? She hadn't cried for happiness. It was because he'd told her he loved her when they weren't supposed to see each other, and he said it on the phone when it was easy to say. He lay suddenly straightened out, and his body and voice both said No into the small hollow darkness that was his room.

"But I mean it," he said, and then he got up and went out through the kitchen to the nook. His parents were in their room getting ready to go to bed. He asked the operator for the Gordons' number and refused to think of the consequences.

Pat answered.

He said, "Pat, can you get Emily to come to the phone?"

"No. God but you're a dumbhead, Waterton." Her voice was low and tense.

"I want to talk to her."

"You can't."

"She was crying."

"Guess why?"

"Do you know?"

"Yes."

"Emily told you?"

"She's not mad at you. Did you think she was?"

"I should've been there—"

"With Mom and Dad coming in the door?"

"Is she okay?"

"Yes. Look, right now, they're in her room talking. You're big time, Waterton, the whole family's upset."

"It isn't just me."

"Right. She's as crazy as you are."

"Why's it crazy?" He hadn't meant to ask, and he didn't want any more of her fast jabs. "What about you and Fielder. How crazy can you get?" She didn't answer. He sat down at the nook table. "Pat?"

"What?"

"Skip it," he said, to make her curious.

"No, tell me. What?"

"Can you go with her to the ski meet on Saturday?"

"I suppose."

"I'll bring Fielder."

"You don't have to."

"I want her to be there."

"She'll go. They don't hate you, Waterton," she said, abrupt as ever.

"Why should they?"

"It's just that you guys are so *serious*. Can't you just—I don't know—just do it like everybody else does?"

"How's that?"

"Normal."

"Like you and Fielder."

"Yeah, right. There'd be no problem then." She laughed at him. "I'm hanging up, Waterton. You bore me."

He let her go and went back to his room. He imagined Emily talking to her parents. She was leaning back on the pillow saying, "You're ruining everything." And maybe Dr. Gordon was saying, "Let's think about this and talk about it in the morning." Fathers said things like that. And they were right. In the morning things always looked different.

The scene might not be true, but it was the only hope he had. They couldn't just say no to Emily. And to him. He got undressed and went to bed. His mother came down the hall to his room. Her fingers tapped on the door.

"Christopher, are you asleep?"

He didn't answer. There was a part of him that was dizzy with exhaustion. He made himself think of his lesson with Gabe, but his mind fell away into a dream about Emily. They were living in Gabe's house. Their bed was in the living room. People going by in the street could see them. So could Gabe and Irene. He got up and took Emily's hand, and they went from room to room. They all had windows. Sometimes the walls were gone. He got angry and shouted at the watching people.

The shout wakened him, and he was afraid his mother might have heard, but she didn't come to the door. In a few moments he slept again.

2

He had to break trail for Sarah in the morning because there was three feet of new snow. The Long River valley was a trap for it and this kind of fall happened three or four times a winter. When the season was over, the instruments in Harrison Dodd's back yard that recorded the weather might have measured fourteen or fifteen feet of snow. The lowest temperature for the winter might be sixty-five below, and the high could be forty or forty-five above when the Chinook wind blew in at the end of every January from over the mountains and as far away as Hawaii. The melt then saved the town from being buried deeper than its ploughs and trucks could handle. But this snow was extra. It was

March 9th, and it was very late in the winter to be dumped on again. His father was up and gone by 6:30, and now he and Sarah stood in the silence the snow made all over town. It was as if the place were deserted, except for smoke that rose up straight from chimneys. There were no corners, no angles anywhere. The houses looked like sentimental illustrations on Christmas cards, the evergreens were unreal white constructions too, and the snow, thick on the hillsides across the river, had changed those slopes so that they looked flat and bland in the dull grey light of the morning. There was no sun. The clouds were still dark and heavy.

Sarah moved very slowly. Even with the snow tramped down beneath her feet she walked in a trench deeper than her beltline. He shuffled along in front of her, making the trail as wide as he could, not because he was being a good big brother, but because he didn't want to listen to her complain. She'd cried about having to go to school. "I'm too little," she'd said. "I'll be lost."

"Poor darling," his mother had said, when Sarah was in the bathroom. "She's somehow known since the moment she was born what a nasty place the world is. None of the good things in it catch her attention at all. Just get her to school without teasing her. I wouldn't send her if I didn't have to paint."

"You got enough stuff," he told her.

"Don't sound like your father. I want new things for the show."

"It's only the library."

"Now you *are* being nasty."

"I mean it doesn't hardly have any room to put up pictures."

"Room enough, and they're not pictures, they're paintings."

"What can you do in three days?"

"It's four days." She had turned away, and he knew he'd gone too far.

"Hey, I'm sorry."

"Yes, you should be."

She'd gone upstairs, and Sarah had refused to leave until she'd followed her mother for a kiss and a hug. Already the day didn't feel as if it were going to be a good one. There was Sarah, the snow, his mother, and there was also what had happened last night.

As they got closer to the schoolgrounds, the going got easier. Hundreds of kids from the two schools had broken trails that made geometric patterns across the playing fields and down the sidewalks. It was too cold for snowballs, but there was fighting anyway. Faces were washed, snow was pushed down necks.

Sarah took his hand. "Don't leave me," she said. Her eyes were black holes in a pale face. Physical injury was more than hurt to her. It was insult, further proof that she'd been orphaned in a good place and sent here to suffer. He took her to the door of the school.

"Oh, Christopher, do I have to?" she said, and sounded exactly like her mother.

"You could leave and walk home alone."

She looked at him with scorn edged with pity for someone so stupid. "Mother told you not to tease."

She'd heard her mother say that from halfway across the house and with the bathroom door closed. He stared back at her and couldn't help laughing. "Sarah, who the hell are you?"

"A little girl," she said, precisely. "And don't swear at me."

"Oh, I'm so very sorry."

She went through the door and down the short flight of stairs to the basement to wait for the time when all of the classes would line up and march to their rooms. She hated school. He could see it in the sudden hunch of her shoulders and in the way she ducked her head and walked carefully as if the stairs were thin ice. Two girls came up the stairs bullying a third. Sarah flattened herself against the bannister until they had gone by. He watched her eyes watch the girls who were tormentors. It occurred to him that she was trying to understand, because if she could do that there might be a way to keep it from happening to her. He hardly ever sympathized with her, but seeing her now being horrified at something she must see every day, he wanted to go to her—and what? Tell her she was safe? She wasn't.

He turned away, and looked for Emily along the Liverpool Street sidewalk. She wasn't there. He leaned against a telephone pole and waited, but she didn't come. The first bell rang at the High School, and he had to run to make roll call on time. In the steamy room that smelled of wet wool, he sat down at his desk and looked over at Pat, but she didn't turn her head. He sent a note, and it came back with Pat's big scrawl on it. "Get lost, Waterton. Let her handle it." Blenkin had to call his name twice to get his attention. Emily was at home—*handling it*. The stupidity of her parents occupied his whole mind. If he could go to them and sit at their kitchen table—just be folks—he could talk to them and make them stop being afraid.

He looked around, and saw that he was standing in the aisle beside his desk. His body had begun to go to Emily on orders that had come from some automatic part of his brain. He stood uncertain and confused, but the idea of going to be with her felt right.

"Is something wrong, Waterton?" Blenkin asked.

"Just being his own goofball self," Fielder's voice said, loud enough for the class to hear. There was laughter, and suddenly everyone's attention was on him.

Christopher saw Fielder's eyes spark with the kind of jokiness that had always run back and forth between them. He sat down.

"No, no," Blenkin said, "stand up."

He stood again.

"What's going on with you?"

"Nothing."

"You're somewhere else this morning. Maybe it's a place you'd like to share with us?"

He could think of nothing to say that would stop what was happening. "No, sir."

"Fielder says you're a goofball."

"A lovesick goofball," Fielder said.

Fielder was saving him from Blenkin. "Look who's talking: tell us who you walked home from basketball yesterday." He glanced at Pat, and knew immediately he shouldn't have said it. Fielder said nothing. He looked stunned.

"All right," Blenkin said, his voice suddenly sounding bored. "Sit down, Waterton, and try not to walk in your sleep again."

The joke was unexpected. Blenkin never joked. The class was delighted. It laughed, and Blenkin's face relaxed as he rose up from his desk to greet Mr. Grandison, who was ready at the door, math book held to his chest like a hymnal. In fact, he looked as if he were about to sing. But instead he went to the board and wrote his teaser for the day. This time Monica solved it before Smith did. Mr. Grandison was gratified. He escorted her to the blackboard as if he were an old but elegant Fred Astaire. Monica blushed and wrote small delicate symbols and numbers that explained how she'd got the right answer. Isonovich applauded, but nobody joined in, and Mr. Grandison gave him his evil eye, while Monica returned, pinker still, to her seat.

The period was long. He thought about how he could explain that it was necessary to make a phone call because it was an emergency. But Grandison would want to know what was wrong and, even if he could think up a good lie that would get him into the principal's office, Grandison would stand over him while he talked. There was the staff phone in Garrett's science lab, but the grade elevens and twelves would be in there all morning. He stopped doing the math exercises the class was assigned and wrote Emily a note. He began to write it just to make contact with her, but then suddenly he knew what he wanted to say.

Leave it. Don't try to handle it. Let them think we've broken up. Because that's what they want. Then we can meet again as if we've never met before, and this time we'll do it right. You can take me home.

The fantasy stopped there. The foolishness of it was like a hook in the mouth. A painful tug and then he was hauled by what was happening in a direction he didn't want to go. He felt as he had when he'd found himself out of his desk and on his way to see Emily.

The bell rang for the mid-morning recess. Not many people were going to go outside, even for some fresh air. It wasn't snowing hard, but flakes were drifting down and the pathways that had been made earlier were beginning to film over, like lace draped onto something wrinkled. He stood up and turned toward Fielder, but he was gone from his seat and was facing the back of the room with Smith and Callaghan and Cameron. Christopher went to join them, but Fielder didn't move to let him in. It felt queer. No one was talking.

Then Fielder said, "Who do you think you are?"

"I don't know—who?"

The circle opened up.

"You talk too much."

"Okay, Fielder, what's going on? What did I say?"

He knew, but he didn't feel like telling him he was sorry. He looked at the others. Smith shrugged. "I got to take a leak."

Fielder put his hand out and stopped him. "Just a minute. Goofball here needs some instruction in good manners."

"You were the one who said I was lovesick."

"You are."

"And you took Pat home last night."

Even Smith looked surprised.

"My business," Fielder said. He wasn't kidding. His lips were tight. "Gordon and I were discussing *The Booster.*"

"I never said you weren't."

"The *implications*," Smith said. "The implications are terrifying."

"You're right," Cameron said. He laughed.

"Downright libellous," Smith said.

Christopher didn't bother to reply. The incident was over, dissolved in Smith's stupidities. He looked around. Miss Lee was in the room now, speaking to Pat while she sorted English assignments at the desk. More talk about the student newspaper.

But Fielder said, "I think you should suffer for this, Waterton."

"Let's sit him on the fountain," Callaghan said.

The grin on Fielder's face was lopsided. There were holes beginning to rot into his upper teeth that his family couldn't afford to have fixed. "I think we're going to stop talking to you."

"Coventry," Smith said, delighted.

"What's that?" Cameron asked.

"The silent treatment. Like in England they say they're sending you to Coventry."

Fielder laughed, and the other three echoed him. "Nobody talks to you. How do you like that, Waterton?"

"What's this all about, Fielder?"

"I don't like having my private business blabbed out in public."

"What about mine?"

"We watched you neck with Gordon." Callaghan pointed out the window. "What's private about that?"

Fielder faced the class returning to their seats. "Don't talk to Waterton." His voice was dead but loud.

"Who wants to?" Bell asked.

"He who talks out of turn gets punished." Fielder was delighted too. "Nobody talks to Waterton from now on." He was almost shouting. It was an order.

"What a relief," Pat said. Her smile was wicked.

"What'd you do?" Jenny Alpert asked Christopher.

Fielder pulled her around to face him. "Nobody talks to Waterton."

"Why?" Jenny looked more anxious than usual.

"We don't talk to goofballs."

Christopher watched her glance at him and then look away toward others in the class. He saw them too. They were smiling, like a crowd does when its not sure whether what they're seeing is something deliberately done or an accident. His ability to feel was suspended, and he knew he also had a weak smile on his face, as if he hoped Coventry might be a joke.

The bell rang.

Miss Lee went to the door to close it. Smith came up behind her. "Where are you going?" she asked.

Smith looked demure. "I'm suddenly taken short," he said.

She stood aside. "You're a bore sometimes."

"Small bore," Fielder said, quietly, but Smith heard him and there were snickers from elsewhere.

Smith turned and backed out of the room. "Egregious," he said, and disappeared.

"He's quite right," Miss Lee said. She looked at Fielder. "Except egregious is an adjective and it might better be used with a noun. It means flagrant. Fool might fit, do you think, Donald? An egregious fool."

"Are you trying to teach me something, Miss Lee?"

"I think that's possible. You're very bright."

"Flattery will get you nowhere."

She ignored him, picked up a pile of assignments and walked down the aisle to hand them back. She had something to say to everyone. A word mostly. Good. That's an improvement. Spelling. Punctuation. She didn't say anything to Fielder.

"Hey," he said, "that's not fair. You say something to everybody else."

"You wouldn't want to hear it."

"Why?"

"Because it might be flattering."

"What is it?" Pat asked.

"Excellent. After Monica and Christopher, the best in the class."

Fielder doubled over laughing. "After those two. Some flattery."

Until that moment, Christopher had only been watching Fielder. Now he looked at him, stared back. Fielder's eyes held steady and then went cold.

"Look, what did I *do*, Fielder?" He heard himself speak high and too loud in the quiet classroom. It was a mistake. The whine in his voice made someone—he didn't see who—laugh. It was the kind of laugh that was a reaction to someone falling who everyone thinks deserves to. There was no other answer. It was as if everyone in the room *would not* hear. He glanced at Miss Lee. She knew what was going on. Her eyes met his and he thought they sympathized, but there was nothing for her to do. Fielder was in charge. It was necessary to be his friend again to stop what was happening.

He leaned over toward him. Miss Lee was moving up the aisle distributing papers, but she wasn't commenting anymore. "Come on," he said to Fielder, just for him to hear. "Why'd you want to do this?"

Fielder looked at him as if he'd never seen him before. Cameron's eyes had some expression in them: they smiled a little. Not much. Just enough to say that he liked what had happened to the joke. Callaghan's look was purposely blank—the stare of a person who was following orders. Smith shrugged, sighed, but didn't speak, and Christopher knew from the expression on his face that he wasn't going to. And if Smith followed Fielder, then everyone was going to.

He had to wait to find out. The world had turned over, but it might only be for a moment. By noon, by the end of Miss Lee's English lesson, it might right itself again.

Fielder hadn't been serious to begin with; goofball was only Fielder's new word. Last month it had been horse. That's real horse. Don't be a horse. Before that it had been original. Everything had been original, except something that was, in fact, original. Smith had his big words, but Fielder, always competing, made up meanings for his own. Smith said it was disestablishmentarianism of the worst kind.

"Just being his own goofball self." When Fielder had said it, it hadn't meant a thing. Blenkin knew that. The whole class did. "A lovesick goofball" was the stinger. He'd had to fight back then, the way anyone else would have. Even Isonovich. He turned and looked at him. Isonovich was staring at the ceiling and his lips were moving. Christopher could see the words form there: "I stood tiptoe on a little hill." Miss Lee liked John Keats. The poem wasn't part of the course, but she said it wasn't too hard for them to read and understand. Isonovich and some of the girls would take it seriously. And so would Fielder—so seriously that everyone would see the joke immediately, except Miss Lee and, when she did understand what he was doing, she would only look puzzled and a little embarrassed—for him—and become more enthusiastic than she usually was about Keats' writing.

He opened his scribbler and unfolded the mimeographed poem. His hands were shaking. He'd been looking at Fielder and the class as if he might see in them what was happening to him. Now his hands showed him. And so did his breathing. It was shallow and fast. He leaned forward over the poem. Its lines didn't mean anything, and he'd forgotten the words he'd memorized.

Miss Lee didn't ask him to recite. She passed him over, and he was grateful that it was her class he was in. She sat on Blenkin's desk, her stockings wrinkled and there was a pale pink spot on her white blouse that might've been ketchup, or maybe jam from breakfast. Their real work was *Julius Caesar*. She loved Shakespeare too. After the Keats poem, she went to the board and wrote Caesar, Antony, Brutus and underlined them. He tried to listen to her. It was important exam material, but there were emotions in him now that took up all the room there was in his mind. Sitting here in Miss Lee's class he was safe, but when the bell rang, he would have to put his books away, walk out of the room and face this crazy thing that was happening. One moment he was Christopher Waterton in a roomful of friends and, in the next, a joke—a stupid little one—had exploded, and he didn't know yet what it had destroyed. He felt tiny and foolish, as if what was going on was his fault. If he'd ignored being called a lovesick goofball, nothing would have happened. He looked across at Fielder. Maybe something would've started anyway. Ever since the party, things had been different. Emily. He'd hardly seen Fielder.

The bell rang. He sat still in his desk and waited. Fielder didn't avoid him. He walked past and out of the room with Smith. It was noon. It was a long way home for some people. In less than a minute he was alone. Even Miss Lee was gone. He got up from his desk. So far, he could think that everything was normal. The only difference was that he'd stayed behind. There'd been no test to see if Fielder's joke was still happening. He walked to the door, stupidly alone. He wanted to laugh, but he was afraid someone would hear him and think he was crazy. There were people from other grades still in the hallway. Mr. Grandison was there talking with Megan Stanley, the grade twelve class president. He thought about waiting around and speaking to him too. I've been sent to Coventry. If Smith knew what that meant, then Grandison would for sure. He heard in his head the principal say, Have you? I wonder why?

I don't know, sir.

You don't know?

No, sir.

Then you'd better find out and put it right. Isn't that the way to handle it?

At the bottom of the stairs he thought that Fielder would be waiting outside for him with a how-do-you-like-that grin on his face. Or with his fists up. He opened the door. Blenkin was there talking to Lester. He started to pass them, smiling in case they noticed him. When he saw they weren't going to, he said, "See you Saturday, Lester."

Lester looked for a moment surprised. "I don't know why you'd bother turning up."

"Because I'm going to beat you." He thought he should laugh to take the edge off the boast, but suddenly it wasn't something to laugh about.

"That's the spirit," Blenkin said. "Go down fighting."

He couldn't answer back. Blenkin wasn't Miss Lee.

It wasn't snowing, and the clouds were not so black as they'd been earlier. He followed a pathway around the school to Liverpool Street. Emily was waiting. He hadn't thought about her all morning, and that hurt. She held out her hand and he took it. She pulled him close, and he saw her eyes. They were softer than he'd ever seen them.

"What?" he asked, still inside his own head.

"I love you too," Emily said.

He'd forgotten. "Do you?"

"Oh, yes. Last night—"

He put his other hand on her lips, and the feel of them brought him out of his own head. "Last night was stupid."

"Was it?"

"I meant our mothers."

"Yes." She stood square in front of him, searching his face. "What is it, Chris? You look funny."

He couldn't tell her.

"Shouldn't I have said—?"

"Yes." He hugged her, not knowing what else to do, and wondered who was watching them.

Her lips were close to his ear. "I said I love you."

He smelled the pretty scent of the soap she used, and leaned against her and felt the muscles down his back relax. "That's beautiful," he told her, "so very beautiful."

"Walk me to my Granny McLeod's."

"I thought you'd stayed away. I didn't see you this morning."

"I was late."

"Why?" They began to walk.

"So was my dad." She looked up at him. "We all had an argument. Not Patty. She left early."

"You shouldn't make them mad."

"I didn't."

He walked with his arm around her, and tried to think of words to tell her what was happening to him. But when he thought of them, he couldn't say them. They weren't words out of a story. They said something real. About him. And they were connected to Bell saying, "Who wants to." Pat saying, "What a relief." Miss Lee watching it happen. And there were more connections out into the future. The whole town knowing. Emily having to be on his side because she'd said she loved him.

"I'm sorry I wasn't on time," she said. "I wanted to see you. A lot."

"It's okay." He held her tight against his side. She'd never apologized to him before. It felt suddenly as if their world were turning over too. He didn't want that. "Tell me what happened."

She laughed. "I'm going to lunch at Gran's, aren't I?"

"I sent a note to Pat in class. She said to back off."

"Did she? I'm not like Pat. She's a firecracker that goes off ten times a day, and she's so busy they don't know what she's doing. They're used to that, and they want me to be like her. I said I was who I was."

"What'd they say?"

"My dad said there wasn't all of me formed yet, and I should wait a while before I started growing up."

"Like Pat? What does he think she's doing being president of everything?"

"Playing. Getting ready to grow up."

It occurred to him what she was saying, and he laughed. "They want us just to play."

"Young Waterton's a nice boy, but he isn't the only friend you should have."

"It's not healthy," he said, and they stopped at her grandmother's walkway. She smiled up at him. "It doesn't feel unhealthy." She leaned against him with both arms around his waist.

"They know I said I loved you," he said.

"Yes."

"What about that?" He had to ask.

"My mother said you got carried away. Did you?"

The cold in his gut was real. "I shouldn't've said it on the phone. But you were upset. I wanted you to know."

"I knew. The words made me cry, and Mother grabbed the phone."

"And my mother told her I said them to you."

"She thinks your mother's a bit lax."

"No. She's only embarrassing."

After a moment, Emily said, "Come to lunch with me and Gran. I phoned and said I wanted to bring you."

"How'd you manage that?"

"Dad went to work, and Mother was in the shower."

"I'm expected home."

"You can phone too." She took his hand again and pulled him through the snow to the porch. "Gran doesn't know what's happened."

The door opened and Mrs. McLeod stood smiling at them. She wore a heavy knitted sweatercoat over a flowered housedress. Her white hair had a fingerwave in it and was cut short at the sides and shingled up the back. "Christopher," she said, "just what I need, a boy to do my walk." She had a face that was lit bright by clear blue eyes. She stood very straight, with her hands clasped in front of her as if they had a surprise between them. People said she was Scottish, but her voice didn't sound it.

"We can shovel it after lunch," Emily said.

"Sure. Easy." He felt part of something again, and now he knew he'd not wanted to go home. His mother would've pried Coventry out of him, and he thought that after lunch the silent treatment might be over. They took off their boots and jackets in the vestibule. There was a tall round stove in a corner of the neatly decorated living room. It was backed by metal to reflect the heat and to stop the walls from scorching. A coal scuttle stood beside it. "Will it be warm enough in here for you?" she asked. "You can stoke the fire if you want."

Emily's eyes said to do it. He lifted the lid and poured coal out of the scuttle into the fire. There was a sudden burst of black dust and flames. Emily put the lid back on for him and closed the draft with a stockinged foot. "The phone's over there by the window," she said.

He went to it and asked Central for his number, 100-L2, and listened for the double ring. His father answered. He thought for a brief moment that he should hang up and try again later. "Dad. Hi. Is Mother there?"

"Of course she is. Where are you?"

"You got the ploughs working, eh? Did you hire Elmo to shovel?"

His father's voice came back surprised. "What? How'd you know?"

"I heard you say last night."

Laughter: "I don't think Harrison Dodd liked it much."

"I think it's great."

"Why aren't you home for lunch?"

"I'm with a friend." He paused. "With Emily. We're having lunch at her grandmother's."

Silence. Then, "Mrs. McLeod? Did she invite you?"

"Yes."

"Are you two defying Dr. Gordon's orders?"

"No, this is okay."

"You sure?"

"Yes."

"All right. Don't eat her out of house and home."

"No. Thanks, Dad."

He hung up and turned to Emily. She held out her hand again and led him to the kitchen. The plaster walls were painted light blue, and the wood trim in the room was white. The table was laid with a white cloth and a set of luncheon dishes.

"It's a cute little house, isn't it?" Emily said. "Really just three rooms and a sort of attic."

"It's closed off now. I'd freeze if it wasn't. Good for nothing really." Mrs. McLeod brought a pot of soup to the table and went back to the counter for a plate of sandwiches. "This is my second winter here." She gazed at him and shook her head. "My, they are long, aren't they? And the snow, I don't know how I'll get out shopping." She sat down. "Help yourself."

The delicate confusion of ladling soup and choosing a sandwich made him tense. He watched himself do it, concentrating on each movement so that he wouldn't drop or spill. Emily grinned at him. This was a second home to her. He smiled back at her and looked around. He had only one home. Emily could escape from her parents and Pat. "You're lucky," he said to her.

She nodded. "I know."

They both glanced at Mrs. McLeod and saw that she was watching them, and smiling too. "So, you two are being lovebirds."

"Oh, Gran."

"That's good," she said, and sipped at her soup. "It's a better way than we had, I suppose. Tell me, Em, what is he, a winter or a summer boy?"

"Winter," Emily said. "He skis. He's a jumper."

"Off the trestle? Now that's a feat."

"Only once off the trestle," Christopher said.

"But you will again."

"Maybe."

"And you like that best—ski jumping?"

He nodded.

"Your grandfather was a winter boy too, Em. He could skate like the wind. Played hockey. Where we were in Saskatchewan, they made great hockey players. I think he could've been one of them. Had half his teeth knocked out by the time he was thirty."

"I'm not much on skates," Christopher said.

"We practically met on them," Emily said. "I finally learned how a little bit from him."

"It must be fun," Mrs. McLeod said, "to be a teenager. It's new isn't it? Teenager. My God, we didn't know one year from the next." She got up and went to the stove. "I don't suppose you drink coffee, Christopher?"

"Sometimes in the mornings. Not now, thank you."

"You seem a nice boy."

"Yes ma'am."

"I never," she paused, "held Robert in my arms until after we were married." She poured herself a cup of coffee.

"But you wanted to." He hardly knew he'd said it, and got up out of his chair and took his dishes to the sink.

"I suppose that's the difficult part."

"You've been talking to Mother," Emily said, sounding suddenly betrayed.

Mrs. McLeod stayed by the stove. Emily went to her. He watched them together. Emily was her girl; they were built alike, except Emily was going to have more shape.

"Will you talk to Mother, Gran?"

"You're not supposed to see Christopher?"

"Not like we used to, just in company, not alone."

"Your grandfather and I—" She stopped, and Christopher wondered if there were tears in her eyes. "Your mother phones every day."

"Thank you," Emily said. She gave her grandmother a hug. "We're going to do the walk now before we go."

"That will be nice," she said, and Christopher thought that she was still back there in her mind with Emily's grandfather.

The snow outside was powder and fresh. It took him only five minutes to shovel it off the walkway, and for Emily to sweep it clean behind him. They put the broom and the shovel back on the porch and turned to go, but the door opened and Mrs. McLeod said, "I've enjoyed having you. Come again."

Emily, surprised, said, "May we?"

She only nodded and closed the door.

They walked back toward the school. No one was watching. He kissed her lightly, and then she stood square in front of him. "We've got a new place," she said, her eyes bright.

"Will she let us go there any time we want?"

"Not all the time," she said, and then she grinned.

"Why are you looking like the cat with the cream?"

"Going there all the time would be nice."

He had to leave her then, and he began to go backward down the sidewalk away from her. She stood watching him, and he wanted to tell her he loved her. It would make up for having said it on the phone last night. The feeling was strong, stronger when he wasn't close to her; and then he tripped over his own feet and nearly fell. He saw her wave and turn away. Dody Wentworth was at the door of the school. She ran across the new-packed snow to her friend. She could be with girls like Dody—real nutheads—and not be one of them. It was a kind of miracle, as if he'd found someone adult who was his own age. Her mouth was still on his, a feeling that was alive, a special warmth that was an easy memory he knew now he had to give up. Behind him was the High School.

He went across the grounds, through the main entrance and up the stairs to the main hallway. Fielder was there. He looked bigger, not in size, but as if he had something going for him and it had puffed him up from inside. He was talking to Lamb, who was in grade twelve. Christopher hestitated at the top of the stairs. It was the wrong thing to do. It gave everyone a chance to look at him, and he became again unsure. He couldn't risk speaking. Alpert came toward him, heading for the girl's washroom. She, at least, was safe to talk to. He said Hi. She went by him as if he were invisible. Lamb grinned.

He crossed the hall, awkward, to the grade nine room. Not everyone was back from lunch, but those who were didn't speak. He stopped inside the door and then turned back into the hall. He felt trapped between the people in the room and Fielder's joke. It didn't feel like a joke anymore, and hope that it might be one died. Lamb, in his high strained voice that made everybody listen (he'd been hit in the throat by a baseball in grade eleven) made an announcement: "Waterton's been a bad boy. Nobody's talking to him."

Fielder's eyes looked at Christopher now. They were wide brown slate discs. Nothing in them. All this might still be a joke. Fielder's father had once come away early from the Legion Hall and had lain in the dark under the bed and had waited for his wife to come home from visiting. When she'd undressed and was getting into bed, he grabbed her ankle. She had screamed. Then, instead of fainting, as maybe he'd expected, she'd gone into convulsions. Fielder said his father told him later he'd been ready to catch her when she fainted, but the fit, and having to take her to the hospital had been a miscalculation. Dr. Royce had given her an injection and had kept her overnight.

There were grins on most people's faces, except for some of the older more serious ones who were already moving with their books toward their classrooms. He didn't want to be anywhere in the school. He turned and tried to look as if he had to go to the lab. He headed down the short passageway that ran past the staffroom and opened the door. He was inside the room before he saw Blenkin and Miss Garrett. She was sitting on the high lab table. How had she got there? Maybe Blenkin had lifted her. He was leaning against her, his head on her breast and she was running her hand over his hair and kissing his upturned face, his forehead and his closed eyes. Blenkin looked as if what she was doing was hurting. Her sausage curls were loose, and he saw her mouth working as if it were some strange instrument made to pick things up off a smooth surface. Her eyes were closed. Blenkin was groaning softly and his body was stiff. He looked as if he were trying to burrow into her.

Then Miss Garrett opened her eyes. Blenkin's burrowing didn't immediately stop.

"Oh," she said, and that was all.

His rush to get beyond the lab door had propelled him well into the room. He stepped back. Blenkin's eyes opened and he turned his head. They both looked at him, and his first thought was to tell them it was okay. It was funny, they were funny, but it was all right. Blenkin and Garrett. My God, yes. Neither of them spoke. It occurred to him that they weren't looking at him now: they were *watching* him. And they weren't moving. Blenkin's head was still touching her chin. His right hand was holding onto her bunched sweater just below her armpit. Christopher backed away another step and looked to see if anyone else was at the door. Then he left without even glancing at them again. His mind said, Christ, that's the only thing they can be fired for, as if he was concerned for their welfare.

He went quickly down the passage and into the central hallway again. Fielder was still there, but not with Lamb anymore. The bell rang. He twitched, and then turned toward the stairs, and knew that Fielder was watching him leave. It wasn't what he wanted. Leaving would worry Blenkin and Garrett, but he couldn't face either them or the classroom. Once he was out the door, he ran across the schoolgrounds and then around the corner so that he was hidden from view by the Crossan's two-storey house.

3

He'd never played hookey before. He'd been late in grade school because he and Fielder had played too long on the way back from lunch. Miss Druik had demanded a note, and his mother had written one that had said: "Christopher was late because he dawdled. (Mrs.) Laura Waterton." Miss Druik had taken the note to Mr. Littler, who had phoned his mother. He had never known what was said, but the next day Mr. Littler had hauled him out of the line of grade fours marching to their room and had said—the gold in his teeth decorating his anger—"I want you to know, young man, that no matter how much support your parents give to your insolent slackness, I will not tolerate it. If you are late again, a note from your mother will not be asked for, nor will one excuse you. You will be severely punished." Miss Druik had made him write fifty times on the board: I will never be late again.

Blenkin would mark him absent. A note would be required to excuse him. He could think of nothing he could say to either his mother or his father. What Fielder was doing could neither be admitted nor explained. It was something nearly everyone in the school suddenly wanted to happen, and those who didn't want it, didn't dare go against Fielder and Lamb. He couldn't fight it.

He knew where he was going to hide out. There were shortcuts he would normally take, but the snow was too deep in the trails and across vacant lots. The streets and the sidewalks downtown were ploughed and the piles of snow beside them were six feet high. He walked between them and the houses along upper London Street, expecting someone to stop him and ask why he wasn't in school. At every corner he thought he might see his father supervising snow removal. But there were few people out walking, and no one he had to speak to.

He opened the door to the rink and went past Howard Streeter's office into the men's dressing room. The Rats were sitting around on the benches; they looked tired, and no one said anything to him. At the far end of the room, in the shadow there, he heard Purvis' cough. He went past the others, stepped over Riley's outstretched feet, and sat down on the bench. It felt good to sit beside Purvis. Safe. Or maybe it was that Purvis was an outlaw, and he had joined him.

"Playing a little hookey?"

"Yeah."

"You should've done it earlier. We needed help here."

"Lots of snow."

"I'm bloody beat. Three feet of it's no joke." He coughed again, hard.

Purvis always had a cold. "You should watch that."

"What?"

"Stay home and get better."

"I don't go there much."

"Howard still let you sleep here?"

"I keep the fire stoked." He reached into his pocket and took out a cellophane package. "Seen these? Greek."

Christopher looked at them. There were six. "You get a lot on approval."

"It's the only way I'll ever see most of them."

"They don't care when you send them back all the time?"

"The company says you can. There's no rule you got to buy them."

"But you do." One of the stamps had a map of Greece on it.

"One, maybe."

"Your collection's twice as big as mine."

"But it doesn't have much point," Purvis said.

"What?"

"You're supposed to collect a certain kind—everything from Queen Victoria's reign, that sort of thing."

"Why don't you?"

"I just like to see what something looks like that comes from a faraway place. Now, you take Greece. I'd never even hear of it unless they had a war or something. After I got these stamps, Miss Tanner at the library helped me find some stuff on it. Do you know it's got about twenty islands where a man could dive for sponges?" He coughed and laughed. "It's warm there."

Christopher looked again at the map. There were tiny shapes scattered south and east of the main part of the country. The writing on the stamp used a different alphabet. "What about the language. They don't even use the same letters we do."

"Nick Kolas learned English when he came here. A man could learn Greek there, I guess."

"I never knew sponges came from the sea."

"They're alive. The water's not deep right around the islands and you dive down and find them among the rocks." Purvis reached over and picked the stamp out of Christopher's hand. "I'd like to go," he said. "Get to the coast. Maybe ride down in Bailey's truck, and then find a boat going there."

Howard came out of the office. "The snow's quit. Sweep it," he said. "I'll make a little ice before we open again."

The Rats got up off their benches and went outside. Purvis got up too and said, "Come on, he wants it swept, not just scraped. You can help."

There were brooms in a shed outside the men's dressing room. Purvis handed him one, and they headed out onto the ice and began to sweep at the east end because that put the breeze behind them. It was a heads-down job. Howard wanted the ice clean as a plate. He made good ice. This wasn't a backyard rink. It belonged to the city. Howard reported to the General Foreman, but he wouldn't speak to anyone but Mayor Courtney, and him only when he opened up in the fall and closed down in the spring. Howard hardly knew who Peter Waterton was. He'd come to Long River too late. Anyone who came after 1912 was too late, although he might recognize people on the street who'd arrived as far into the century as 1925. Christopher's mother thought he was a fake: "He's all bluff, that man. He's got those two girls from a late marriage, and a dead wife, and he worships all three of them. He didn't make Dick Purvis' mistake, importing a mother for them. He knows that one mother's all you get in this world, and when she died he did what he had to, given who he was." Maureen Streeter was in grade twelve and Jane was in grade eleven. When they came to the rink, Howard treated them the same as any other kid. They were pretty. Purvis said Streeter would kill anyone who laid a hand on either of them.

"What if they wanted someone to?"

Purvis had laughed. "That's a problem. Maybe the old bugger'll drop dead before that happens."

Christopher watched Howard begin to make ice at the southeast corner of the rink. He was a demanding old man. It was better to be Purvis than Maureen or Jane. Purvis could leave, go to Greece if he wanted. It was different for girls.

"Why're you playing hookey?" Purvis had a shovel now and was scooping snow over the fence.

Christopher kept sweeping. He didn't want to tell him. Not saying was the plug that stopped up what he felt about Fielder. The others who weren't speaking to him didn't matter.

"Felt like it," he said.

Purvis leaned against the fence. "You never done it before. Goody-goody like you. Must be something gone wrong."

"No."

"Real wrong, I'd say." Purvis' eyes were wide and the smile on his face was bright. "Someone got to you. Teacher?" He put the shovel over his shoulder. "Can't be Emily, she's at another school. Fielder?"

"Fielder," he said, and turned away. "How'd you know?"

"Some kind of guess. He's a sap sometimes."

"He's supposed to be my best friend." The words came as a surprise, and they were powerful. He stood stiff and fought a sob at the back of his throat.

"Whatever it is, don't let him get at you."

"Coventry." The sob ripped free.

"What?"

"Never mind." He punched the fence hard and the tears stopped short.

"I heard you but I don't know what it means."

"No one talks to you. Silence."

"No one?"
"The whole school."
"He really got at you. Why?"
Christopher felt he could look at Purvis now. "I don't know."
"Must be some reason."
"No."
Purvis shrugged and headed back toward the dressing room. Howard had most of the rink covered with water, and it was freezing fast. In a few minutes, the ice would be as flawless as a mirror. In half an hour the gates would be opened, and the Rats would skate then to keep up their speed and stamina for hockey. Then the adults would come, mostly women out for the exercise.

Christopher didn't leave his skates here permanently, so when the Rats began carving up the clear surface of the ice, he went outside and watched. They broke off and came in one by one, Purvis first. He was tall on his skates, a man, even if he only was seventeen years old. He didn't play hockey as seriously as he did basketball, but he was good enough to make both teams.

The music stopped and, in the silence before Howard put on another record, Christopher heard the Elementary School bell ring. He thought about Emily waiting for him on the Liverpool Street corner. He could run back and meet her before she left for home, but the High School's bell would ring in ten minutes: Fielder, Blenkin, Garrett, Grandison. It was too complicated now. She'd have to walk home alone, or catch up to Dody. It only took five minutes for the school to empty and she'd see he wasn't there, or was serving a detention.

Back inside, he heard Purvis coughing at the back of the room, and went to sit beside him again. "Maybe you should see Dr. Royce. That's a bad cough."
"Yeah? Who's going to pay?"
"Your folks."
"That's a laugh. They don't call doctors ever."
"What do they do? If you're sick—that's what doctors are for."
"What do they do?" Purvis leaned his head back against the wall. "First of all, old Mary gets mad if anyone gets sick. It's not a sickness, it's a fault, you know? A fault of the country for being cold. Your fault for being out in it. And you can lie in bed and get well or not. She won't come near you except to tell you how much extra work you're causing."
"It's just you she doesn't like being sick."

"No. That's one favour she distributes even-steven around the family."

"Parents are supposed to look after you."

"I'm seventeen."

"If I was sick, I'd just go to the doctor and charge it to them."

"I'm talking to a guy whose mother probably thinks if you don't go to the bathroom every day the world stops spinning around."

Purvis was laughing at him. "I'm sorry," Christopher said, and laughed too, because that was a stupid thing to say.

Purvis leaned over and untied his skates. "You can be sorry if you want to be, but if I was you I'd be damned happy."

Christopher watched Purvis put on his boots. "Blenkin says I get everything served to me on a platter. You think so, and probably Fielder does too."

"Well, jealousy won't get us anywhere." He tied his bootlaces. "It's kind of interesting though. What about all those others who are playing Coventry with Fielder? They paying you off too for being lucky?"

"I don't know."

"Well, don't give any of them a thought. Tell 'em tough titty."

"With muscles as big as yours you can do that."

"No quarter," Purvis said. "Not a goddamn inch. Not Blenkin either. He's a servant. I had to quit school to know that. I love playing basketball against him."

"He can do what he wants in school."

"It's why I quit. It's why I don't go home much anymore." He put his skates in a cubbyhole on the opposite wall marked Purvis, and turned, grinning, "But I think I will tonight. I hear the old man's back in town, and I got to get some money off him."

"Howard pays you, doesn't he?"

"Sure. I make ice now overnight. He's giving me seven a week. Twenty-eight a month. Not bad. But I get all I can from the old man now, and pretty soon you're all going to see the last of me."

"I think your dad owes you," Christopher said.

Purvis grinned. "I hate a smart kid."

The door opened and the first of the after-school skaters ran into the room. They had nickels for Howard, and one or two of them had pennies for one-cent candies. In a few minutes there would be people from High School arriving. Fielder, Smith, Cameron, the Dobroskis. If they came and didn't speak, the silence could spread all over town. He stood up and said to Purvis, "You have to work now, or are you going home?"

"I mostly work after hours."

"Let's go then."

Purvis nodded and headed down the room toward the door. Howard came out of his office. "Come back after supper. I'm going to give Riley the night off."

"Why?" Purvis asked. "He don't have any friends to see anyway."

"I'll see you outside," Riley said.

"You'll go outside and police the rink," Howard said. "Now."

Riley got up and left. Purvis opened the door, and they went out together into a false twilight. With the clouds so thick and dark, the light from the west hardly glowed on the horizon. They walked back up London Street.

"How much money do you figure you'll need to get out of here?"

"Every morning I figure it's a dollar more than I got."

"Why?"

"Because every morning it's a new place I'm going to, and it's always farther away than the last one."

"You said a boat."

"Who's to say I can get on one? There's probably a few more than two or three lined up for that kind of job."

"You want to make certain it'll work out."

"I don't want to leave and then have to come back," Purvis said. "If you're going to go, go. No goodbyes."

He wanted to tell Purvis he'd miss him, but he was shy to say it. "What's your favourite place?"

"Greece right now."

"Those stamps."

"It's why I ordered them."

They were going to pass the school, and it reminded him. "Miss Lee's been there."

"She the new teacher?"

"She's okay."

"I've seen her a couple of times. She tried to skate. I don't think skating's up her alley."

"She's a bit sloppy. I don't think her mother taught her how to dress."

They cut across to Liverpool Street and headed up toward York. The Purvises lived on York Street too, just a couple of blocks north of him. They rented the old MacPherson place, which was one of the big ones in town, but it wasn't stylish. It was shaped like a barn, and Mary had added to that picture of it by putting a chicken run out back.

Christopher couldn't stop himself from looking to see if Blenkin was still in his room. He wasn't. The lights were out. But in the room next to his, he could see the top of Miss Lee's head. She was sitting at her desk. "There she is," he said.

"Who?"

"Miss Lee."

Purvis stood tall and craned to glimpse her. "Nice hair is all I can see."

"That's the best thing about her. Want to talk to her about Greece?"

"She'd have a bird if we walked in."

"I know her. She even likes me," Christopher said, and hoped it was true.

Purvis looked uncertain.

"Come on. I need to get my homework book anyway." He ran across the street to the south entrance and opened the door. Purvis walked across and then hesitated. Christopher went in and let the door begin to close behind him. Purvis' hand stopped it, and he stepped inside the school.

"First time in two years," he said.

"You really hate it, don't you?"

"I'm not stupid," Purvis said, "but this bunch here made it look as if I was."

"Miss Lee's pretty good."

Their voices echoed in the empty building as they climbed the stairs. Barney, the janitor, grinned at Purvis when they got to the central hallway where he was working. "Well, John, you back to pay off?"

"No payoffs, Barney. What you talking about?"

"The books you ripped up when you left."

"It wasn't books, it was attendance records. My old man gave in on that," Purvis said. "Cost him six dollars. I told him he shouldn't do it."

"Probably would've sent you to reform school," Barney said.

"They'd've had to catch me first."

Miss Lee's door was halfway open. Christopher stood so she could see him if she looked up. Barney and Purvis' voices disturbed her, and when she saw him, she smiled. "Come in if you want." She leaned back in her chair, and he could see she was happy to be interrupted.

He opened the door wide and gestured for Purvis to follow him. She looked surprised and stood up while they walked across the room toward her.

"This is John Purvis," he said. "I told him you'd been to Greece. He wants to go there."

She held out her hand to Purvis. "I've seen you, but we've never met."

Purvis moved awkwardly forward and took her hand as if he didn't quite know what to do with it. Then he pulled away abruptly. "I don't know if I want to go or not."

"To Greece?"

Purvis nodded.

"She went on a freighter like you want to." Christopher told him.

"But I was a passenger," Miss Lee said. She looked a bit embarrassed and then sat down. "I only mean that men can often work their way across by signing on as crew." She looked up at Purvis, and her smile folded back over her teeth.

Christopher sat on one of the desks in front of her. Purvis still stood, as if he needed to be told what to do. Miss Lee said, kindly, "Greece is very beautiful. I can't imagine anyone not liking it." Her hand made a small movement, as if it might be directing Purvis to sit down.

He sat on a desktop near Christopher. "When did you go?"

"In 1936."

"Three years."

"Yes. When I graduated, I felt too young to teach. I was twenty. Now I think it's almost time to go again."

"You travel all the time?"

She smiled and nodded her head. "In a way. Not always to exotic places. Coming here to Long River was travelling too."

"Was it?" The idea made Purvis laugh.

"I taught last in the prairies. Swift Current. I wanted mountains again after a year with all that flatness. It was beautiful in its own way. And the people are the nicest I've known."

"But why come here?"

"I didn't plan it. I was asked. It felt like an adventure."

"Is it?"

"No. But it's pleasant enough."

"He has a Greek stamp with a map on it." Christopher said. "Are all those islands part of it?"

"Yes," she said, "you really do need a map for Greece. Some countries are just there—all of a piece—but Greece is its mainland and all those islands too." She was being a teacher. "It's also a country whose past is part of us." She glanced a little uncertainly at Purvis.

"I don't get what you're talking about," he said.

"Greece, Rome, the Holy Land. They're the places our civilization comes from."

"That's not why I'd go to Greece."

"No?"

Purvis shrugged. "Why should I? All I know is it's warm there and you can dive for sponges."

"It's not warm in the winter."

"I bet it doesn't snow like this there."

"I don't think it snows anywhere like it has today." Miss Lee's smile was no longer as broad or as stiff as usual. "It's good to have company," she said, easily. "I sometimes get tired of sitting here marking papers."

Christopher didn't quite know what she was saying, but Purvis answered her. "Travelling makes you a loner," he said.

"Oh, I have friends." Miss Lee looked embarrassed again.

"Sure," Purvis said, and the word was like a period at the end of a paragraph. Beyond it there was a blank space. Christopher tried to think of something to say. He felt it would be his fault if these two couldn't talk to each other. But the silence wasn't bothering Miss Lee. She was looking at him now, and the expression in her eyes confused him. It was different from what he'd seen in any other teacher he'd known. She leaned forward just a little, and he thought for a moment she might be going to reach out and touch him.

"I missed you in class this afternoon, Christopher."

He could only nod his head.

Purvis looked delighted. "You got to play hookey every now and then, eh?"

"I suppose," she said.

"You really get fed up," Purvis said. "The same old junk coming at you all the time."

"Is that why you want to travel? Go to Greece?"

"Maybe. Is that why you travel too?"

"I hope not."

"You didn't always," he said, serious. "I mean, you had a home and went to school right through college. When did it start?"

"What if you suddenly don't have a home, John?"

Christopher glanced at Purvis. He had been pushing her. Now all that was left of his attack was a grin on his face. "That happened to you?" he asked.

She nodded, not unwillingly. "My father was killed. A hunting accident. My mother died the morning of his funeral."

"Christ," Purvis said. "How?"

"No one could tell me." Miss Lee's face was as hard as Christopher had seen it. She was always a teacher, and this was a lesson for Purvis. You don't just travel, become a traveller for no reason. And you don't ask questions just for the fun of it. The answers sometimes hurt.

"My mother died when I was nine," Purvis said.

"I'm sorry," Miss Lee told him.

He laughed. It was harsh. "You can't go travelling when you're nine years old."

"You're right." She was smiling again. "I was lucky to be seventeen. I was left a little money, so after a while I could make a life for myself."

"Yeah," Purvis said. He nodded. "How lucky can you get?"

Christopher saw her suddenly stop talking to Purvis and look at him. "Having something you depend on stop happening—bang, just like that—it's a terrible shock."

"I guess I'm the really lucky one here," he said.

"I think so," she said. "Remember that when other things go wrong."

"Like Fielder," Purvis said.

Miss Lee looked annoyed. "You must say no to Donald, Christopher."

"What do you mean?"

"No, in every way you can."

"How do you say no to everybody not talking?"

"In every way you can," she said again. "Nobody but you can do it. It's your problem."

"Coventry," Purvis said. "What is it?"

"A city in England."

"I mean where does Coventry come from?"

"Sent to Coventry," she said. "It comes from a time when Cromwell was in the midst of overthrowing Charles the Second. People who were on the King's side were either killed or sent to prisons. One of the big ones must have been in Coventry. So, they were sent to Coventry, for being on the wrong side. I don't think anyone knows when the first silent treatment was imposed on someone who was supposed to have behaved badly. But it must have been in a school in or near Coventry." She shook her head as if she might be angry. "It's a terrible form of violence—suddenly not belonging."

Christopher shivered involuntarily. All of this was for him, and he wished she would stop. She'd been right in the first place—this was his problem. He watched her face. It looked to him to be a foolish face now—everything in it too large—lips, eyebrows, cheeks, forehead. But her eyes were black like her hair, and those two things always made the rest of her forgivable. He glanced again at Purvis. He was watching her too.

"What're we talking about?" John asked, and sat up straight. "I belong. That's the thing that's wrong here. I belong to Long River, and I don't want to." His hands were suddenly fists, but he laughed. "The quicker I'm out the better."

After a moment, Miss Lee said, "It's good to talk. Things come clear."

"Sure," Purvis said, "but so what?"

Miss Lee got up and walked over to the windows that looked west from the school. It was dark outside now. "You're impolite," she said, turning to look at Purvis. "That's a kind of violence too."

Purvis stared back at her as if she wasn't so superior any more. "Everything is," he said, finally. "When I chew my food, even. Sometimes violence is good."

"You want it to be."

"No."

"I did, too, once."

Her voice was soft but precise, so that Christopher heard it as if it had come amplified from a long way off, like Marjorie's voice in one of the dreams he still had about her.

She leaned against the high windowsill, her skirt hung down flat over the rack of her hipbones, and the pale pink spot on her blouse was still there to be seen, even under the artificial light of the room. He heard the words in his head again: "I did, too, once," and he didn't want her to say any more, because it might be too private for him and Purvis to hear.

He stood up. "I've got to go. It's late."

"Just when it's getting interesting," Purvis said. He didn't stand up.

"You must go, too," she said.

He stood up then, and his voice was polite. "You've been other places besides Greece."

"Yes, but we can't talk right now," she said. "Come another time if you want, but I don't think you're going anywhere, John."

"Why?"

"Because you'd've gone by now."

"It's been hard to think about," Purvis told her. "In this town, who's been anywhere?"

"Dr. and Mrs. Gordon," Christopher said.

"Sure," Purvis said, and laughed. "I see them a lot, don't I?"

"All right," she said, "come back." Her voice was kind again, as it had been when they'd first arrived. "I'll bring some pictures and keep them here for you."

"Can I come too?" Christopher felt childish asking.

"Of course." She moved and came close to him.

He knew he wasn't being invited, only told that she was available, as she always was. He saw her every day in class, but he was curious about what Purvis would ask her, and even more interested in what she would answer. "I have to be able to get out of Long River too."

She smiled again, and put her hand on his shoulder. "Not right away. You're one boy I know who should never quit school."

"Maybe there'll be a war," he said, as if he believed that war would make him automatically older.

"I hope not," she said. "It's not a solution—just more violence."

"There'll be one," Purvis said.

"Maybe it will be your salvation, then."

"I'll be eighteen soon."

"Just eighteen?"

Purvis nodded and turned away toward the door. "So long," he said, not facing her. "Good to meet you."

"Thank you," she said.

He watched Purvis go through the doorway and then turned to Miss Lee again. "Did you make an assignment today?"

"Just read the rest of *Julius Caesar.*"

"I have," he lied, wanting her to think the best she could of him.

She sat down behind her desk. "It's odd being students and teachers." She smiled a little tiredly up at him. "We spend each spring ending things, while the rest of the world gives birth."

"It's not spring yet."

"Do you think it won't come on time?" Her voice was hopeful, but it was precise again. "The equinox is nearly here."

"It's going to be late." He watched her pick a paper up from a pile of them and put it in front of her. She didn't reply, and he knew she wasn't going to. "Good night," he said.

"Good night, Christopher."

In the hallway he stood still and listened to Purvis leaving the school. He wondered if Miss Lee knew about Blenkin and Garrett, and if she did, what did she think? It wasn't a question he could ask her. Blenkin and Garrett somewhere hugging and kissing. He went into the grade nine room and got his homework. He thought of facing the whole school tomorrow, especially Blenkin and Garrett. Friday: Garrett second period. He opened the downstairs door. The temperature had dropped. Purvis was waiting. They walked together up the hill toward York Street. Purvis was silent, and it occurred to him that he didn't want to talk either. This was a friend he was walking with who wasn't going to talk for no reason. He pictured Fielder—always wanting to move fast. There was a kind of flame inside of him that sometimes got blown out, and then he wasn't Fielder any more. Purvis wasn't like that. He was tough. He gave no quarter. But he didn't mind being equal—even with someone three years younger. Stamps were stamps. He didn't care which one of them had the best collection.

Then he did talk. "She's a good lady."

"Miss Lee?"

"You think she meant it?"

"Sure. Go see her. She works late most days."

"Where else has she been?"

"Mexico. She mentions lots of places. New York."

"That's good," Purvis said.

They walked in silence for another block. It was snowing gently again. The flakes in the beams of the streetlights they passed made a moving polkadot pattern, white flakes against the black night. He wanted to talk to Purvis about Blenkin and Garrett, but if he did and Purvis noised it around, they'd know who had started the gossip. They'd been stupid to meet in the lab. But teachers couldn't date like other people, especially not at their own homes. He felt sorry for them.

When they got to his place, Purvis stopped and looked down at him. "You take Fielder outside tomorrow and beat the crap out of him."

"He'd win a mad fight."

"That doesn't matter. It's doing it that counts. It'll get Coventry off his chest."

"Maybe, but I don't think so."

"You can't listen to Miss Lee about the rough stuff. She doesn't have a clue about how the world works."

"She does," Christopher said, "and she's against it." He felt as if he'd said something wise he'd not known was in him. He laughed.

Purvis stared at him and then grinned. "Well, shaking her head and going tut-tut isn't going to change it." He turned and headed up York Street toward his father's house. Over his shoulder he said, "You jumping Saturday?"

"Yeah."

"Maybe I'll go watch." His voice was muffled by distance and the falling snow.

No goodbyes. Maybe Purvis was trying to say that tomorrow and the next day were safe up there ahead of them. Christopher liked that. He went in to supper.

4

In the morning Sarah waded through the foot of new snow, insisting on leading him to school. She was a surprise. She was happy. "It will be up to the door pretty soon and we won't be able to open it. Then we can stay home. Daddy will build a fire in the fireplace and we'll all sit together on the chesterfield and tell stories. I have a good one. Last night before I went to sleep I wrote it in my head."

"All about being buried in the snow," he said, and pushed her to make her go faster.

"No, stupid. That's what's happening really. Stories are for being somewhere else."

"What do you know about being somewhere else? You were born in Long River."

"When times are better," she said, very serious, "Daddy's going to build a bridge in India—up in the mountains in the north—and he's going to take us with him."

"A bridge?"

She turned and tried to walk backward so she could face him, but she fell full length into the snow. He picked her up and faced her toward school. "A railway bridge," she said.

"Is that another one of his bedtime stories?"

"Yes it is, and it's a true one, you wait and see."

He let her plod on ahead, while he shuffled along behind. This wasn't a morning to upset her, and they were early. He didn't want to stand on the corner waiting for Emily with everyone going by, not speaking.

Sarah remained happy. She ran across the schoolgrounds to the door of the Elementary School and turned to wave at him as if they'd been friends all of her life. Maybe she was growing up. Maybe he was.

It was beginning to snow again. What he sometimes thought of as head-noises began again: "Say no in any way you can." "Take him outside and beat the crap out of him." He didn't want to try to do either. Miss Lee hadn't been able to say what she meant by saying No. And his gut twisted and pained when he thought of fighting Fielder. They'd fought ever since they'd met, careful not to let it get too serious. Fielder was Fielder. What could you do? Let whatever was going on happen, and when it was over—but the betrayal, when he thought about it, made him listless and sick. He walked slowly to the corner, squinting his eyes so that he saw only a blur as he went across familiar ground. People passed him. No one spoke, but he felt safe because he didn't know who they were. Then a hand held his arm and stopped him. "What are you doing?" Emily asked.

He opened his eyes and grinned.

"Where were you after school?"

He leaned into her and smelled the scent in her hair. "Detention."

"No," she said, and her body went limp against him. "Pat told me."

He'd forgotten about Pat, and looked away to see who was watching. Then her arms tightened around him, they were holding each other now, and she was waiting, her face and eyes serious. He couldn't talk about it, but he said, "Emily," and that was a relief.

"She thought it was funny. Was it?"

He shook his head.

"I waited a long time."

"I played hookey, and then I was with Purvis." It occurred to him then that he could've talked to her.

"Fielder's a—" She stopped.

"What?"

"No. Pat likes him. She thinks making the whole class stop talking to you is big time. I thought she'd be sick laughing."

He didn't know what to say, and he knew without looking at her that she was watching him and waiting. Then she hugged him closer and said into his ear: "Do you want to play hookey again? We could go to Gran's."

He was immediately there. The fireplace, the stove in the corner, the soft old-fashioned furniture. Fielder at school with his joke not working. Blenkin and Garrett wondering where he was and what he was doing and also what the Chairman of the School Board was doing if his son had peached on them. "You'd be in trouble," he said.

"I don't care."

"They'd never let us even meet again."

"Gran wouldn't tell. I'd get Dody to forge a note for me."

"I want to," he said. It was almost time for school. "Listen. Yesterday I walked in on Blenkin and Garrett. They were necking in the lab." He watched her eyes brighten and her lips begin to smile. "Please don't tell anyone." She shook her head. "Especially Dody," he said, so he could laugh and be himself again—someone on his way to school. Normal.

"Will they be mad at you?"

"Not if I act just the way I always do."

"They should be scared of you."

"Don't be so sure. Maybe they want me to say I caught them, so they can deny it and have me expelled for lying about them."

"Could they do that?"

"There wasn't anyone else with me. I saw them alone."

"I won't tell."

He hugged her close. "I'm glad I told you. I feel better." She looked upset. He smiled at her. "Everybody's seeing us out here again."

"They see us every day. They're used to us—*Christopher*." She spoke his name as if she needed to. "Until last Friday everything was good. Like it's been since Christmas day."

"I know."

"What's happening?"

"It doesn't have anything to do with us.'

She kissed him on the mouth and backed away, still holding his hand. The pink in her cheeks was very strong, and her eyes were very steady. "Maybe no one else wants us to be together. But I do."

"Yes."

"I love you," she said.

"Yes," he said again. There was too much happening in her eyes for him to understand all at once. "I love you too," he said. He smiled across the space between them.

She let go of his hand. "See you after school."

"Yes," he said, for the third time, and let her leave first. He watched her to the door, where she turned. Unlike Sarah, she didn't wave. She only looked across the distance betwen them, and then disappeared.

He tried to think what it was that might happen when Blenkin saw him at roll call. He might have to meet Garrett in the hallway. The first bell rang. He walked slowly up the stairs and into the grade nine room. No one spoke. Some didn't notice he was there. Others stared. Fielder wasn't here yet. Instead of going to his seat, he went to the windows and leaned against the chest-high sill. Fielder was running down the sidewalk. He'd be here close enough to time that he wouldn't be marked late.

He sensed someone arrive at the window and stand beside him. He braced himself. It could be a new phase of Coventry. But when he glanced up to see who it was, the face wasn't hostile.

Isonovich smiled. "Hello." He nodded his head. It was a kind of comic formality that was part of all his gestures. "It's over."

"Why?"

Isonovich turned around and faced the class. "I'm declaring it over."

"How?" Monica looked surprised at herself for having asked the question. She hovered near her desk.

"I speak to him. It's over."

"Since when are you in charge?" Cameron asked.

"Silence is silence. When I talk to Waterton it is over."

"For you," Bell said. "Not for us."

"Isonovich." Pat Gordon's voice was sarcastic. "You are a moron."

"No, I am Russian."

"You wouldn't do this if Fielder was here," she told him.

"It was silly anyway," Dorrie Dobroski said. "Hi, Christopher."

"Hi," he said, and knew he was standing still and looking stupid, but he could see something normal returning to the classroom.

"I'm glad you did it," Monica said to Isonovich.

He looked down on her from his six-foot-four. His haircut that left only a large tuft on top of his head, his shirt with its torn collar and his thick wrinkled pants that rode high on his rubber boots made him look like a scarecrow. Monica in her blue dress that matched her eyes didn't look as if she belonged here either. Isonovich took her hand, as his gentlemanly father might have, and bent to kiss it. For once, he got applause. Monica tried to curtsey and got a laugh.

Then Fielder came through the door. Christopher looked at him as he walked across the room in front of Blenkin's desk. He felt guilty for having spoken to Isonovich, and sorry, because he'd never know if Fielder had come intending to end his joke.

"What's going on?" Fielder said to Isonovich.

"You can see."

"It wasn't any of your business, bohunk."

There was silence again and, after a long moment, Isonovich said into it, "I think I have a little news for you. I'm not playing on your basketball team from now."

"Tell Blenkin that."

"Yes, I will."

"He'll be happy to hear it."

Isonovich shrugged.

Blenkin arrived and closed the door. Fielder went to his desk and sat down. Christopher watched Isonovich fold himself up into his desk, and then he looked over at Fielder who was leaning back and staring at the ceiling.

"Sit down," Blenkin said.

There was no one else standing. Christopher took his place in front of Smith, and Blenkin called the roll. Everyone was present. Fielder was now staring at Isonovich, and he kept doing it throughout Grandison's math lesson. He did nothing else. Just stared, and at recess when Isonovich got up and walked out of the room, Fielder followed him. So did every boy in the class. The girls went to the windows to watch what they knew was going to happen.

Christopher ran through the crowd and caught up with him on the stairway. He held his arm. "Don't do it," he said.

"Screw off," Fielder said. He ripped his arm away and headed out the door.

Isonovich was there, tall and so thin that the pale slanting sun that had just broken through the clouds made a long shadow of him that looked like a black pole on the snow. Christopher turned and saw the whole school coming down the stairs to watch the fight.

"Now, I'm going to tell you something," Isonovich said.

"No, you're not."

"I am."

There was usually talk, back and forth, words that finally became punches, but not this time. Fielder hit Isonovich with both fists, one in the stomach and the other high on the chest. Isonovich pulled back, folded over and covered up. Fielder punched again. Christopher hadn't seen a fight like this. There were usually a couple of punches and then it became a wrestling match.

"You don't know," Isonovich said. He was sixteen and behind a grade, because he'd had to learn English for a year when his family got out of Russia. His voice sounded as if it might be a grown man's, a teacher's. He took two more punches on his arms, and then he reached out to hold Fielder.

Fielder broke free and pulled back. His face was pale; he neither smiled nor frowned. His eyes were steady. "Bohunk," he said. His lips hardly moved.

Isonovich began to fight then, and anyone could see that Fielder wanted it that way. He went toward him, taking punches from the fists on the ends of Isonovich's long arms, and hitting back as hard as his balance and the snow would let him. He was small beside Isonovich, but he was very fast.

Christopher stood in the inner ring of the circle of watchers. The crowd was silent. Any noise would bring Blenkin, or worse, Grandison. He'd thought the fight was about him, but it wasn't. The anger was gone from Fielder's face. He punched and took punches back. In the silence, Isonovich grunted. He was a stickman moving to save himself, but he was also trying to make Fielder stop. Both of them were bleeding from the nose now.

Then suddenly Isonovich quit fighting. He stood up straight and put his hands at his sides. Somebody laughed, and Fielder turned his head to see who it was. Isonovich grabbed him and held on. Fielder tried to pull free, but he couldn't.

Isonovich looked unsteady on his feet and his breath came short and fast. He was using all the strength he had. Christopher wondered if he'd had any breakfast. It was a crazy thought in an insane moment. "You don't know," Isonovich said. Fielder struggled. "You don't know a damned thing about how you treat people," Isonovich shouted. He let Fielder go free. "I don't like it."

Someone laughed again. The energy from the fight was in the crowd. Everyone was grinning. Even angry and a winner, Isonovich was funny. His serious face, above a body that moved as carefully as a giraffe's, had a bloody nose in the middle of it, and now there were tears on his cheeks. "You think about it, Mr. Dictator Fielder. You think about making everybody do one thing. My father lose a country, and I have no home because of that. You think I want to be here in this terrible little town so I can be your bohunk? Everybody say we're lucky to be in a free place. This is free where we starve? I think you crazy."

"What're you talking about? Waterton deserved it," Fielder said. There wasn't tension in his voice. He was himself again. "It was a joke."

"Can't you think what things mean, Fielder?"

"You're full of crap, Isonovich."

"No."

There was no anger left in either of their voices. The crowd looked puzzled and disappointed. It was a relief when Mr. Grandison broke the circle. He didn't say anything. He took Fielder and Isonovich each by the arm and walked them quietly back into the school and, instead of going up to his office, he steered them into the boys' washroom.

The bell rang.

"Not much of a fight," Lamb said. He wanted a laugh but didn't quite get it.

Christopher held back from pushing his way through the crowd. He waited until it was nearly dispersed up the stairs before he followed, hoping that the washroom door would open so he could see what was going on in there. Muncie came out.

"What's happening?"

"Are we speaking to you again, Waterton?"

"What's Grandison doing to them in there?"

"Why'n't you go in and see?"

"Is he mad?"

"I don't think so." Muncie went on up the stairs.

Christopher followed and walked into the grade nine room again. It was a different place than it had been an hour ago, even ten minutes ago. Everyone had seen and heard Isonovich and Fielder. They sat in their desks, five rows of them, and he saw that their faces were empty, as if everything about them was going on inside their heads. Miss Garrett was at the front of the room with her back to them. She was leaning over the desk attaching wires to a piece of equipment that was black and made of metal.

He sat down and knew that his own tensions had been triggered. During the fight he remembered only watching as if it had been an accident that was happening at a distance. Now everything was close up and harshly clear. Now he knew something about Fielder and himself he hadn't known before. Coventry, the silence, was over. Nothing could bring it back. The old feeling between them was done. He wondered if they'd be friends now. Yes. If Fielder wanted. But Fielder would have to come to him, not because he was stronger now, or more of a leader, but because he'd moved on, and what had been happening between them since Christmas was some kind of struggle. Not on his part, but on Fielder's, to keep things as they'd been since they'd first met.

He saw him now, coming into the room ahead of Isonovich and Mr. Grandison. Their bloody noses were cured, their lips were thick, and both had swellings beneath an eye. They went to their seats. Miss Garrett stood straight and faced her principal. The class waited, making a silence that only Grandison could break. Christopher found he was holding his breath, because what was happening wasn't what he'd expected. Grandison was not glaring at the class. His head was not cocked toward his good eye, and his voice when he spoke was quiet and exact.

"I abhor blood and violence," he said. "They are senseless. No one ever wins, and you can see that neither Isonovich nor Fielder has emerged the victor. I am responsible for you, and for them while they are in attendance. Their parents will be informed about what happened, and a suitable punishment will be devised for them."

His glass eye stared. His good eye blinked. "I don't know what to do about the rest of you. You heard Isonovich." Mr. Grandison actually smiled. "I think it impossible for you not to have. What did he say, Bell?"

"Fielder shouldn't've given Waterton the silent treatment."

"Is that it, Miss Alpert?"

"Yes, sir."

"Cameron?"

"I think he said he wanted to go back to Russia."

"Was that it Miss Anders?"

"He said he didn't like it here."

"Smith?"

"He said he didn't want to live here and be Fielder's bohunk."

"Anything else?" Mr. Grandison looked around as he did in Math class.

Monica stood up. "He didn't *say* anything." Her face was scarlet. "He shouted it, that he'd lost his home, which is the most horrible thing that can happen, and it happened because someone got powerful and killed people who wouldn't think in a certain way. He said Fielder was like that, and that's why there was a fight. There has to be a fight when that happens."

"I see," Mr. Grandison said. "Then there are fights—wars—that should be fought?"

"I'm supposed to answer no," Monica said, "but what if someone's doing that to you?"

"Sit down, Miss Lewis," Mr. Grandison said, not unkindly.

Christopher watched her smooth her dress down behind as she sat, and then he glanced at Isonovich. He was weeping. Tears shone on his cheeks, and his mouth was half open as if he were struggling for breath. Monica saw him too, and bit her lip.

"You may be right," Mr. Grandison said to Monica. "The dilemma is not an easy one. What, in fact, if someone *is* doing that to you?"

"I wasn't doing anything to Isonovich," Fielder said, suddenly. "I was doing it to Waterton."

"Were you, Fielder? I think you were doing it to everyone. That is Mr. Isonovich's point, and it is mine. Only Waterton, who suffered the silent treatment, remains untouched by your leadership, Fielder. What have you to say to that?"

"I don't know."

"I think you do."

"I was going to talk again to Waterton this morning."

"But Isonovich beat you to it, and you called him a bohunk."

Christopher watched Fielder's face; he'd seen the expression many times before. He was being caught again. By a grownup. Once more, liquor in the punchbowl.

"I don't remember," Fielder said.

"Don't you?"

"No. Lots of people get called bohunks."

"Is that so? Bell? Smith? Your good friend Waterton?"

Christopher saw Fielder look at him for the first time. He needed now an excuse to grin. He almost laughed. "I've called Waterton worse than that."

"But not bohunk, Mr. Fielder."

The grin stopped. Grandison's voice was sharp and precise again. His good eye stared.

Fielder licked his upper lip. "Maybe not."

"Correct," Mr. Grandison said. "You have not and you will not, for the very good reason that you keep bohunk as a label for people who are not worth sending to Coventry." Mr. Grandison rocked forward on his toes and glanced around the class. Miss Garrett looked especially prim. "Think about that if you will." He surveyed the class once more, and then turned to Miss Garrett. "Please excuse the interruption."

"Not at all," Miss Garrett said, "it was a pleasure." She gestured wildly and stopped; her face crumpled toward embarrassment. "I mean," she said, but Mr. Grandison had turned away from her again.

"The two of you will please come to my office after last period." He left the room.

Garrett drew magnets and an armature on the board, explained about the magnetic field and the flow of the current of electricity that was generated when she turned the handle of the dynamo. She referred to negative and positive poles, and turned the class around to view the illustrations at the back of the room. It occurred to Christopher that Blenkin may have done them for her. They weren't store-bought. He thought about her and Blenkin in the lab, looking stupid and awkward.

He glanced back at Garrett at the front of the room. She was talking now in her enthusiastic young-girl voice that came strange out of the face of someone already practising to be an old woman. After they'd met, his mother had said, "She's too good to be true. She's everything a schoolteacher's supposed to be, and hardly ever is. When she turned away from me I expected to see a big key in the middle of her back for when she winds down." And that was true, except for when she was stroking Blenkin and kissing his closed eyes. She'd looked then as if she'd got a new face and a new person to go behind it. The false surprise when she was pleased hadn't been there, and neither had there been the prim and often angry old maid who taught science and girls' Physical Education.

Now, she stood quiet and looked down at the dynamo in front of her on the desk. She reached forward and picked up the wires that led from the poles of the generator. She held them in one hand and turned the dynamo's crank with the other.

"I can feel it," she said. "That's the electricity coursing through my fingers to make a connection, a circuit—round and round. Does anyone want to try it? Feel the current?" She continued to turn the crank and hold the wires. Here and there around the room small laughs were expelled. Chatter began. She ignored it. No one volunteered.

"Go on, Fielder," Christopher said. "Maybe it'll cure your black eye." It felt good to be talking in the old way again.

"Do it yourself, generator-mouth."

"If you want to, Waterton," Garrett said. She dropped the wires in front of the dynamo.

There wasn't much else he could do. He stood up and walked to the desk. Miss Garrett picked up the wires again, and put one in his left hand and the other in his right. She held the crank at the top of its run. "Ready?"

He nodded. Behind him there was silence.

Miss Garrett began to turn the handle. He felt the tingle of current in his fingers. He glanced up. She was looking at him, and suddenly her eyes went wide and dark, her mouth straight. She turned the crank faster. The current increased. She watched him and bit her lip. Then her arm was a piston and the electricity shocked him. His arms and hands hurt; she cranked faster, and from behind her clamped lips came a high quiet angry sound, like the tense howl of an animal attacking. His fingers wanted to let go of the wires, but they couldn't. The pulsing pain went up his arm and across his shoulders. He didn't cry out. He was too surprised, and he was caught by her fierce stare. His elbows sprang up and down, like wings. Her head bobbed as she cranked, and her expression changed so that she looked glad. From behind him there were snickers and then whoops. He fell back against Monica's desk and the wires were pulled out of his hands. Miss Garrett laughed and her eyes were opened very wide again. *There,* they said.

"Oh," she cried out, "oh, my, did I turn it too hard?" She lifted her hand from the crank as if it were something that had misbehaved and was going to be punished.

"Jeez," Callaghan said. "you electrocuted him."

"No, the lights didn't dim," Smith said. "They always do that when the switch is thrown."

"You can smell flesh burn too." Fielder was up and standing close to the dynamo.

Christopher thought, They're helping her out.

"I'm sorry, Christopher," Miss Garrett said, not kindly, and betraying herself by using his first name.

He didn't answer, and when he turned to go to his seat he felt dizzy. He forced a smile and sat down.

"Turn it," Fielder said. He had the wires in his hands.

She grinned, relieved, and cranked the handle. Fielder held on until the current and the shock came and then pulled back. Bell was behind him and grabbed the wires. Christopher watched. In the end it was Dorrie Dobroski who held on the longest, and Garrett made high squeaks of laughter every time someone pulled away. It was only a game. He looked down at his hands. They were swollen, but not badly. Isonovich leaned forward. "You are sensitive to electricity. I think I would be too."

He wanted to tell someone why Garrett had gone crazy. He imagined standing in a circle at the back of the room with Fielder, Smith and the rest, maybe even Alpert and Gordon: I caught Blenkin and Garrett necking in the lab.

Either they'd believe it and spread the news, or they wouldn't and it would be as bad as Coventry for the rest of the term. And Blenkin and Garrett would know who told on them.

The bell rang.

Fielder got up from his seat and stood in the aisle. After a moment, he said, "What's the matter, did she hurt you?"

"Not much."

Fielder grinned and then laughed. "She looked like she'd gone nuts."

He got up from his desk. The fingers that had held the wires still hurt. He looked at them again and then held them out for Smith and Fielder to see. "Do they look swollen to you?"

Fielder shrugged.

Smith said, "They look okay."

"What do you want to do, sue her?" Fielder asked.

"She'd make life really miserable for you," Smith said.

"I didn't say I was going to do anything."

"You were just too stupid to let go," Fielder said.

"I couldn't. It felt like I was paralyzed."

Smith laughed. "Three more turns and she'd've made a magnet out of you. All your molecules would've been pointing one way."

Isonovich, Bell, and Callaghan were there now looking at him too. "You do something to her?" Bell asked. "She looked like she was going to keep cranking till you fried."

"I think she's finally bonkers for real," Callaghan said. "You going to tell your old man?"

That was the right question. Christopher put his hands in his pockets. They were tender, but the hurt was nearly gone.

"What a great thing to do," Callaghan said, "get her fired."

"Who ever heard of firing a teacher?" Christopher asked.

"Okay, but it'd sure be fun to give her hell."

"Have you ever tried to tell your old man a teacher did something wrong?" Smith asked.

"The thing you have to remember," Isonovich said, "is we're here to be made good boys. Waterton will now be good about electricity." He looked sly.

"So, what will you and Fielder be good about?" Smith asked.

"Ah, that is different," Isonovich said. "We will see what Fielder will do about bohunk."

"What's so big about not calling you a bohunk?"

"I'm glad for the fight," Isonovich said to Fielder. "I didn't think I could do it, you know? Now if you call me bohunk again I'll say no with my fist on your stupid-looking nose."

Fielder didn't bother to reply, and Smith said, "Too bad nobody can do that to a teacher."

"Hit a woman?" Bell said, laughing.

"She's not a woman," Smith said.

"Yes, she is," Christopher said, and waited for the rest of it to come out for them to hear. But his throat closed over the words. "I mean she gets mad like one." He moved from his desk and down the aisle to the cloakroom. The others followed, even Fielder, and when they were outside and splitting up to go their different ways to lunch, Fielder and Smith walked with him up the sidewalk to where Emily was waiting with Dody Wentworth.

Emily came close to him and looked up into his face. He was attacked as usual by sudden emotion. "Thanks for being here," he said. He wanted Smith and Fielder to go, but they stood waiting. Dody tried to get Fielder's attention, but he didn't even push snow down her neck.

"Is it over?" Emily asked. "The silence?"

He nodded.

"Then what's the matter?"

"He got electrocuted this morning," Fielder said.

Dody laughed, and Emily smiled uncertainly. He loved Fielder now for being there and saying the right thing. "It's nothing," he said.

"Fielder exaggerates," Smith said, pompous.

"Tell you later."

"Tell me now."

"Okay, today Garrett brought a dynamo for making electricity."

"Stupid Waterton volunteered to be the guinea pig," Fielder said.

"Stupider Garrett turned the crank too fast and gave your boy a shock," Smith told her.

"I wasn't even thinking about that," Christopher said.

"Then what were you?"

He leaned forward and whispered in her ear, "You."

She kissed his cheek and pulled away, still looking serious. "Phone me after school."

Fielder and Smith were beginning to head up the sidewalk again. He let Emily go and watched her walk away. Three months ago there'd been no one outside of himself to make trouble look smaller. He turned and went after Fielder and Smith. They were with him again, but now there was what was left of a real hurt between them. Fielder wasn't ever going to say anything about Coventry. He didn't believe in saying he was sorry. It was one of the things that made him stronger than anyone else. Smith turned around to face him; Fielder glanced over his shoulder. He didn't run to join them. He'd made them wait, because of Emily. After this long time with Fielder, he felt split off from him—by Coventry, by the bohunk fight, by having caught Blenkin and Garrett and not telling anybody about them. He was in a new place, but he didn't quite know where it was.

Fielder said, "My little sister is blind."

"*What?*" Smith said, as if he were unsure about whether this was another of Fielder's jokes.

"Cataracts. Dr. Royce found out she was born with them."

"Can they do anything?" Christopher held Fielder's arm to stop him.

"If they harden." Fielder looked hurt.

It wasn't a joke. "Harden?"

"It's what Royce says. They're just like milk in her eyes now. They got to harden up before they can operate."

"There's nothing anyone can do?" Smith asked.

"Just wait," Fielder said. "And hope."

The stood now on the corner where they had to separate.

"Jesus," Smith said. "You got enough to put up with already."

"I'm sorry," Christopher said. There were no other words, and nothing anyone could do.

"Don't be," Fielder said. "I just figured I'd tell you. Maybe it's a good thing. My old man, every time he comes in he just stands by the crib and stares at her. Maybe he thinks it's his fault." Fielder began to walk away.

"Don't go," Christopher heard himself say.

"Why? It's lunchtime."

"Yeah, right," Smith said. "What the hell else can happen today?"

"Nothing," Fielder said, grinning. "That's three. Things only happen in threes. Ask your old lady."

"Your sister didn't happen today."

Fielder didn't answer. Christopher watched him and then Smith leave. There'd only been the fight and then the dynamo. He walked thinking: three has nothing to do with it; more bloody awful things happen every day.

He headed up the hill toward home, but he wasn't hungry. He felt sick. He hadn't done anything for Fielder, and the nausea came from not knowing what to do.

At his gate he paused, still thinking of Fielder, but knowing he wanted now to talk to Emily about him. On the porch, he broomed the snow off his boots and went in. His mother was in the kitchen stirring the soup.

In the nook, he picked up the phone and asked for Emily's number, so he could tell her why Fielder had had to do Coventry on someone and also had to call Isonovich a bohunk and get in a fight with him. He knew his mother was listening but he didn't care. Emily answered. He'd known she would, but he would have insisted they put her on the line if she hadn't. And afterward, when he'd finished telling her and had hung up, he put the receiver back on its hook and went past his mother's enquiring look to his room. He sat on his bed and waited. His mind kept listening again to Emily not being able to say anything real to him. He'd talked and she'd said what she could and then he'd talked again. Her family had been there.

He lay down on the bed and heard his father tramp up the back stairs and come in the kitchen door. Then he heard their voices, and Sarah's when she came running in from the living room to see her dad.

Now he didn't know why he'd phoned Emily. She'd be in trouble trying to explain. There'd be another quarrel. He'd acted as if the party had never happened and he was welcome at the Gordons'. But he felt more foolish than sorry he'd gone to her. Until he'd begun talking the words in his head had sounded important, but Emily couldn't reply, and what he said in the end hardly made sense. What did it mean that Fielder's baby sister was blind and so he put his best friend in Coventry? It occurred to him that he only wanted her to know he was okay—Coventry hadn't happened because of a fault in him. And he was embarrassed because his mother had listened. She'd heard too much because, with Emily not being able to talk, he'd had to explain everything. He felt shrivelled up. He needed Emily to be let go free by her family so she could be with him. In his head, he heard his own mother saying, "How do you feel?" "Awful." "Why?" "Because you and the Gordons and the school, the whole damned bunch of you, are in the way." "Of what?" And before he could tell her, his father knocked on the door to say it was time for lunch.

He sat up on the edge of the bed. The thing was, he'd asked Emily for some kind of comfort. And when she couldn't give it, he felt empty and lost.

"Are you coming?" his father asked.

"Yes." He got up and went out into the kitchen. They were all at the table in the nook.

Sarah had her hands over her eyes. "Is it true that Fielder's baby is blind? Like this? Black?"

"Sarah," his mother said.

"Well, is it true?" She took her hands away and pretended to blink into strong light.

"No," he said. "Maybe it's not black." He looked at his mother. "Fielder said the cataracts were like milk in her eyes."

"That poor family," his mother said.

"They'll face it," his father said. "Something tough like that happens and people straighten out."

Christopher picked up his soup spoon. His fingers weren't tender or sore now, but they felt a little numb. He watched Garrett's face again as she turned the dynamo handle. Then there was God laughing like her and blinding Fielder's sister. He felt crazy.

"Are you all right, Christopher?"

His mother's voice brought her into focus again. He had to be all right. His father was there. He nodded and ladled soup into his mouth. It tasted good.

"I'm sure it will work out," she said.

"They have to harden."

"What?"

"They have to harden so they can operate. Fielder said that."

"Then they will."

His father looked solemn. "If the optic nerve doesn't die. Things that aren't used do that."

"Opticnerve, opticnerve," Sarah said. "What a funny word. Opticnerve."

"It's two words," his father said.

Then they went on eating.

CHAPTER FIVE

1

SHE WAS AT THE BOTTOM OF THE RUN BENEATH THE BOYS' JUMP when he got there, leaning on her poles, and he could see her watching him ski toward her. She had on blue mitts, with a scarf and toque to match. Her skis were shorter than they were supposed to be; she'd grown out of them. "I'm not good at sports," she'd said. He knew what she meant was that she wasn't interested in them, even though she was built to be an athlete.

He hadn't seen her yesterday after school, and his mother had made him take Sarah to the Regent Theatre in the evening to see *Tom Sawyer.* The movie had been good and, for an hour-and-a-half, it had let him live somewhere else. Afterward, he'd been glad his mother had forced him to go. Sarah, on the way home, had talked about nothing but Injun Joe and what if—?

He stood beside Emily and shuffled his skis back and forth to feel again how fast the wax had made them. There were maybe a hundred people here already, even though the runs beneath the jumps had been roped off and only the downhill course was in use. Blenkin was at the Boys' Jump measuring it. They would cut it down or build it up to a standard height, otherwise a new record would not be accepted by the Ski Association.

He felt awkward now, because he hadn't said anything but Hi to Emily. His mind was on the jump, and their skis were keeping them apart. He didn't want to say it, but he needed a clear mind. "Look," he said, finally, "I shouldn't've phoned yesterday."

"Yes, you should have."

"What did they say?"

"Nothing. I told them it was Dody."

"You don't talk like that to Dody. I bet they knew."

"I don't care."

"It's stupid not being able to—" He stopped. The jumping was more important than the Gordons right now.

"Yes," she said. She shifted her skis closer to his and reached out to touch him. He held her hand and felt her fingers holding his through her mitt. She leaned toward him. "Gimme a kiss."

He glanced around at the people near them. Some of them were watching. "Not here," he said, even though he knew she was asking for more than a kiss, and he wanted to give it.

She nodded her head firmly. "Yes, for luck."

He pecked at her lips. "Okay. Tell me good luck."

"Good luck." She backed away. "Pat's coming in a while. I guess Fielder'll be here."

"Everyone'll be here."

"Your mum and dad?"

"And brat Sarah. Will yours?"

"I think so."

He looked up at the trestle on top of the hill. A banner with blue letters on a white background said: Long River Winter Carnival. First there was going to be the Junior Jumping, then the finish of the cross-country race, then the Senior Boys' Jump, then the Downhill Races and in the afternoon the Open Jumping from the trestle. After supper there was a playoff hockey game between Long River and Indian Falls. And, finally, the Winter Carnival Dance at the Royal Ballroom. The sky above the trestle was light grey. It was better that there was no sun. "Perfect," he said, excited now that he was here, and it was close to the time when the competitions were going to start.

"Are you going to do a practice jump?"

He nodded.

"Can I help carry your skis up?"

"Sure," he said. He looked around. "Your mother's not here yet."

She nodded and grinned at him. They climbed the switchback trail and rested halfway up. He put his arm around her as they leaned back against the slant of the hill, and the barrier he'd felt had been there between them fell away. He said her name and watched her eyes watch him. His mind did what it always did when he first touched her: it drifted quiet and content. He only needed half as much breath as usual, and where his body touched hers, he felt a deep comfortable yearning to be closer. She knew. She smiled. "That's better, *Christopher*." The emphasis again, as if it made both the name and the person hers.

She leaned against him, awkward because they were each holding a ski, and put her lips against his. They were cool, but her tongue was warm between them. He could hear someone coming up the trail below them, a fir branch let go of its load of snow and it fell onto the pathway in front of them. He began to move away from her, but she wouldn't let him. "More," she said. He kissed her short and hard, and then she let him go.

It was Lester coming up the trail. He pulled Emily onto her feet and headed on up the hill. At the jump, Blenkin said, "Are you registered?"

"No, sir."

"Do it after your practice jump." He looked at Emily. "And carry your own skis up during the competition."

"I'm going," Emily said. "I want to get a good place to see from."

He watched her leave and then looked down the hill. At the far side of the main run was a table, and behind it was Miss Garrett and George Peterson, who was president of everything Mayor Courtney wasn't. Even from this distance, he could see Miss Garrett's stupid grin. The ropes were gone from the bottom of the Boys' Jump hill and the spectators had been herded into another roped-off space from where they could watch safely.

At the top of the run and with his skis on and his toque pulled down tight around his head, he felt the first pang of real tension. Until now, there'd been only excitement, and then Emily had cancelled that out. He felt the muscles in his legs tighten. He breathed deep and then let the air fast out of his lungs.

Blenkin signalled to him. "Go if you're going," he shouted. Lester was near him, watching too.

He let himself go free down the slope. For half the way he stood straight, then he crouched and leaped easily out over the new snow. He wanted only to feel good about the jump and the hill, and especially about being watched by the people below. He landed maybe only sixty feet away from where Blenkin was standing just below the jump and drew his skis together for the run to the bottom. Style was part of it. Distance and form. He let his legs pump to keep him fluid as the hill ended and the run across the flats began. The applause surprised him, his muscles tensed once more and nearly unbalanced him. He turned, sprayed snow four feet into the air and came to a halt. Back up the hill, Lester was getting ready for his practice jump.

It was going to be a long day. He skied over to register. Garrett was busy with two jumpers from Indian Falls—men who would compete later but who wanted to wear their numbers now. Garrett, with boots and snow suit on, was fussing over them. George Peterson smiled a gold-toothed greeting and pinned number 67 on his back. Garrett, left momentarily with no one to serve, glanced at him.

"Good morning, Miss Garrett." He smiled at her, and it was good to feel she had no control over him here. "I didn't know you skied."

"I'm learning," she said, distant, but not quite able to find her schoolteacher voice. "When in Rome." She stopped and turned to help another contestant.

"Do as the Romans do," George Peterson said, heartily. "You going to win today?"

"Going to try."

"That's the stuff, young Waterton. Now skedaddle. We'll be watching."

He skied back to the foot of the hill. The rest of the competitors were doing their practice jumps now.

He stood by himself watching, until Fielder came, grinning as if nothing had happened between them, or to his little sister. "Listen, Waterton," he said, as if it were a secret he was going to tell, "I'm betting against you. I figure you can't stand up long enough to win this thing."

"Thanks a lot. Who're you betting with?"

"Purvis."

"He's picking me?"

"There's only Lester and you, and I picked Lester."

"Thanks again."

A skier came off the jump; he was short and skinny, and he was in control. He landed well, and there were times on his way down the hill when he looked for a moment stylish.

"Who's that?"

"Bell's little brother," Christopher said. "He's going to be good. How much do you have on Lester?"

"Four bits."

"Where'd you get it?"

"Played pool all morning—made eighty-five cents at Kelly, nickel a ball."

"You want me to fall."

"Me?" Fielder laughed. "Did I ask you?"

"I'll win just for that."

"Fair and square I think you won't. Next year maybe."

"Maybe? Lester'll be sixteen then."

"You could both get beat," Fielder said. "Indian Falls has Cressler. Callaghan wanted me to bet him."

Christopher began to move away toward the boys' run. "Pat's over there."

"I know."

"Go give her a thrill."

Fielder didn't say anything; he walked away toward the crowd and, up the hill, Blenkin blew his whistle to signal the start of competition. At the foot of the switchback trail, Christopher turned to look for Emily and saw her at the edge of the crowd. She waved. Beside her was his father, who was saying something to her, and she laughed up into his face. Standing with them was Sarah. His mother was there too, bundled in coat and sweaters, muffler and toque, looking red-nosed-miserable. She wasn't an outdoors person, except in the summer after the mosquito season, when she went out almost every day to sketch.

When he got to the top of the hill, Blenkin held out a box with numbers in it. He picked one: 9. "You're jumping last," Blenkin said, his voice official, his eyes ice-blue.

There was a small wind now. It spread across the breadth of the hill, occasionally picking up a tuft of snow and making a feather of it.

From below came the sudden howl of Don Watson's P.A. system. It was the only one in town. He'd made it up from spare radio parts, had bought a microphone for it and rented it out to dances, hockey games, Victoria day and July lst celebrations, Mayor Courtney's rallies and the Carnival. He'd take it to three places today. Watson tested it, and then George Peterson took over the mike to announce the names of those jumping. Waterton was the final name on the alphabetical list. Maybe being last twice was a good omen.

Bell went first. He landed smoothly and made a good run to the bottom and out across the flat. Blenkin did the measuring at the point of impact and then held up two numbered cards for the people to see. He turned the cards around for the jumpers to see. 82. The applause, especially from the rest of the Bells in the crowd, was enthusiastic.

Gilmour went 73 feet. Ellis was only eleven; he fell, but Blenkin showed the cards for him anyway: 55. Knight fell too, but not until he was well out on the flat. He jumped 85 feet. That made George Peterson very happy. "Good jump, Knight. We'll see who can beat 85 feet."

Lester stood only for a moment at the top of the run, and then he shoved himself off fast with his arms outstreched and his body crouched. When he leaped, he came up and out over his skis. Christopher saw Blenkin watching Lester with his hand shading his eyes. The landing was good and the downhill run looked perfect. The cards Blenkin held up were a 10 and 2: 102 feet. George Peterson made a speech about Lester being last year's champion.

Christopher sat down in the snow near the treeline. He'd never broken a hundred feet. Lonnie Pickett fell as he landed and rolled twice before his skis came off and ran downhill into the crowd. There were volunteers who lined the run for such emergencies. Lonnie was in pain. He was carried to the bottom. Mr. Pickett ran out of the crowd waving his skinny arms. He looked like Neville Chamberlain, and he was English too. He was telling the volunteer to be careful. Then Dr. Royce was there. He came from his car with splints in his hand, as if he'd been expecting broken legs. George Peterson joined the doctor and Mr. Pickett, and after a moment, he went back to his microphone.

"The news is not good," he said. "Lonnie's leg is broken. But he's in excellent hands. Dr. Royce thinks there's nothing to worry about." He paused. "Mr. Blenkin, may we have the next jumper please?"

Cressler, from Indian Falls, went 93 feet, and Hanna, who was also from the Falls, jumped 87. Christopher took his skis to the top of the approach and put them on. The crowd was silent. The wind blew from his left, but not hard. He had to force himself to remember that he liked doing this. It was something that had come naturally to him—the necessary balance and co-ordination. Blenkin was watching him now and it made him go stiff. He looked away. Someone in the crowd was waving. It was Emily. He had to go now, to let himself slide down toward the jump. Not easily. He must propel himself. This wasn't practice.

His skis were fast. He felt them light against the snow. He didn't have to worry about direction; the other eight contestants had made a double-grooved pathway to the jump. He saw his ski-tips clear it, and he brought his body upright, leaned forward over the skis and fought the wind for a moment for balance. The landing was good. Balance again. He stood upright, pulled his skis together, right foot behind the left. The bottom of the hill came too quickly, but he managed it without breaking his stance. The crowd flashed by, and he turned almost before he could handle the speed of it. When he looked up, Blenkin was already holding up his cards. They said 26 feet and the crowd was laughing. Blenkin got the right card: 96. A foot less than his best.

He skied along the edge of the crowd, shy suddenly of these people he'd known since he'd come to Long River. They called out to him. Purvis was there; he grinned and nodded. "What's six feet, kid, you can beat Lester." Fielder looked serious. "Ease up, you're scaring me." Pat was with him. She didn't look like the class president. She laughed at Fielder's joke and said, "Nice jump, Christopher." He couldn't remember if she'd ever before used his first name.

Emily was still standing with his family. "Great," she said, and turned to his father. "Wasn't it, Mr. Waterton?"

"Yes," his father said. "Does the wind bother you?"

Christopher shook his head. "A little, but it's not enough to blow anyone off the run."

"That was an awfully long jump Lester made," his mother said, anxious. "Don't you go trying too hard to beat it."

"Lonnie Pickett broke his thigh-bone," Sarah said. "It stuck right up through his skin."

"Sarah, please."

"It did, Mother. I saw it."

"Of course you didn't. No one did."

"Well, I did. Right between Dr. Royce and Lonnie's dad. I could see when they cut his pants right up to here."

Christopher put his mitt over Sarah's face and screwed it around. She pushed it away. "Listen, brat," he said. She backed off, but he could see that she was too proud of him to make a fuss. He said to Emily, "Where's your mom and dad?"

"They'll be here soon." She turned her head and scanned the crowd. "There they are." She waved, and they signalled back.

He had to move on up the trail again. Bell had just gone by, and Blenkin's cards showed he'd improved his jump by three feet: 85 this time. On the way up, he saw Gilmour land at the 80 foot mark. Ellis made it all the way this time and got more applause than anyone else so far, but his jump was only 52 feet. From the top, Christopher could see Emily now, with her mother and father, standing at the edge of the crowd with his own family. The sight of them together was a shock. It was embarrassing. Why was Emily doing it? Knight went 87 feet this time. He was doing better than anyone thought he could. Next year he'd be as much competition as Bell.

Now Lester was putting his skis on. He stood up, looked down the hill, pushed off, and this time Christopher thought he jumped with less power. Even his balance looked ragged. The cards came up. The crowd hardly reacted. Blenkin turned: 96 feet. George Peterson was less enthusiastic, but just as cheerful as he'd been about everyone else.

Cressler looked tense and determined. His approach was stiff, but his leap was smooth and his flight perfect. When his cards were shown they also read 96 feet. Christopher picked up his skis and headed toward the top of the run. Three jumps had measured 96 feet. Lester's 102 was a fluke. Maybe the wind had helped him. But it was the number to beat. Hanna's jump was a disaster. He landed on one ski and fought to stay upright until he was almost at the bottom of the hill, and then he fell. His distance was only 78 feet.

Christopher put on his skis and tightened his harnesses. There was no hurry. Two of the volunteers had rakes and were repairing the hill where Hanna had fallen. He stood stiff again, waiting. The wind up here was small and cruel. He shivered. Soon there would be no warmth at all in his body, and no suppleness. Blenkin turned abruptly toward him and signalled. The movement was so demanding that it forced him off the platform before he was ready. His approach was awkward; he crouched very low at the last moment to overcome it. Then his leap was late. Yet, after that everything but the distance was good. When Blenkin held up the cards they read 92 feet. There was small applause, but George Peterson was encouraging.

"Ninety-two feet, young Waterton. Not so good as ninety-six last time, but you've got another chance. Everybody has one more chance now as we go into the third and final round."

At the top, Bell was putting on his skis for his last attempt—jumping against himself for a personal best. Christopher skied along the rope that held the crowd back from the run. He had to pass Emily and her parents. The awkwardness of the moment embarrassed him, and he felt it making him angry. He stopped so that he was between Emily and her father.

"I thought that was a magnificent jump, Christopher," Mrs. Gordon said.

"No it wasn't," he told her, and he heard his voice nearly impolite.

Dr. Gordon chuckled.

Emily's eyes looked steady at him. "Give it hell this time."

"Such language," Mrs. Gordon said.

His father put out his hand as if he might want to protect him. They smiled at each other. It was a good moment. "I go with Emily," his father said.

Bell went by looking good and a cheer went up from the crowd when Blenkin showed his cards: 90 feet.

"That's it," Christopher said. "He's never gone that far before."

"See what you can do," his father said.

He looked at his mother. She was deliberately not talking. Sarah said, "Give me a hug and a kiss." He looked down at her. She'd not been to see him jump in competition before, and it had made her proud. He crouched and reached under the rope for her. She came into his arms and put her lips close to his ear. "Be careful."

"I will." He gave her a little hug and pecked at her forehead.

"Emily," she said, "you can give him a hug too. To make him lucky."

He stood up. "Brat," he said, and looked at Mrs. Gordon. She was smiling purposefully.

Emily hugged him across the rope, and he left them all half-grinning, except for Dr. Gordon who was lighting his pipe.

He climbed the switchback trail again. Cressler had nearly beaten him. Hanna had fallen and that had made him stand longer than he should have at the top of the run. He'd been too eager, been too ready to take off too soon, because it was Blenkin there below the jump, measuring and judging. He went slowly up the trail. There was something in him that was exhausted, and he didn't know what it was. Three jumps and four times up the trail wasn't enough to make him tired. But something there inside of him had gone flabby and was through. He tried to think about it, but then he was at the top again, and Knight was already putting his skis on. Bell, Gilmour, Ellis had jumped. He rested in the snow and watched Knight appear against the grey sky above. On his face there was no expression at all; it was smooth and in control. He landed well, skied the course with ease, and when Blenkin held up the cards the crowd made a noise that sounded as if it had been hit in the belly: 97 feet.

"Well," George Peterson shouted, "We got ourselves a brand new picture to look at. It's now Lester, then Knight and then Waterton tied with Cressler for distance, and it's a great race for second."

Lester already had his skis on. He looked determined. And stiff. Christopher stood up, and breathed in deep. Blenkin nodded. Lester attacked the run down to the jump, but he leaped a fraction late. Christopher forced his breath back out and watched Blenkin measure. The cards read 98 feet.

"Ninety-eight feet, and still in number one spot," George Peterson announced.

Christopher put his skis over his shoulder and walked slowly up the path toward the top of the approach run. Knight had bettered his own distance by ten feet. Everything about the jump had been perfect, like some kind of dance movement where the partners were relaxed against the beat and knew exactly what they were doing. Co-ordination, Blenkin would have said. Cressler was going good too, and they were tied for third. "There's only Lester and you," Fielder had said. When you think things are for sure, that's exactly when they're not.

Cressler's jump was good, but it was two feet short of his last: 94 feet. He stopped climbing up toward the top. Hanna was getting ready to go. He'd jumped nine feet shorter on his second jump than on his first. It can go both ways: out at the edge of what you can do, everything is fine-balanced. He watched Hanna prepare and then launch himself down the slope. He was small, but there was a lot of muscle underneath his ski clothes. In the air his flight was good, and after the measurement the cards read 90 feet. That was a personal best for him too, but both of the Indian Falls jumpers were out of it. First, second, and third were going to stay in Long River.

He climbed the final few feet and laid out his skis. Lester 102 and Knight 97. He put his feet in the harnesses and clamped them. He had moved slowly here, and now what he was doing felt distant. His hands. The harnesses they touched. The sound of his own breathing in his ears. He stood up and turned to face the jump, Blenkin, George Peterson at his microphone, the crowd behind its rope. The silence held him suspended against the slant of the hill. The other skiers were scattered across the flat, waiting. They thought he was gathering strength, preparing himself. He wasn't. There was in him still something finished. The feeling had rough edges, raw and sensitive. At the bottom of the hill, a red hat stood out among the browns and the blues and the blacks. Mrs. Gordon's. "I thought it was a magnificent jump, Christopher." Blenkin waved at him to begin. An order. He looked annoyed.

Christopher didn't move. The anger he'd felt when Emily's mother had been condescending returned. He moved back on the narrow platform as far as he could and then hit the slope fast. "Be careful," Sarah whispered. But he wasn't. This jump was final, and he wanted to do it without care or coaching or rules. He had his arms back behind him as the moment to jump arrived. They came forward as he wanted them to, like fists up into the air, and he leaped after them as hard as he could. The long sound he heard was his own voice shouting for distance, for balance. He passed the hundred foot marker as he landed, and he began to laugh. He stood up and skied the slope for the last time. There was even a moment to wave at his people in the crowd. Emily and his father, Purvis and Fielder. Amid the shouts and cheers, hands all along the edge of the crowd reached out toward him.

He didn't turn to stop until he was well past the other skiers. The temptation was to keep on going. The thought cleared his mind and made him calm again. When he looked back up the hill, Blenkin was still crouched with one of the volunteers measuring his jump. Christopher stood by himself and watched Lester and Knight and the others head back toward George Peterson's stand by Watson's truck. Blenkin got up, then crouched again and held up the measuring tape, the better to see it. Distances were only reported to the closest foot unless two jumps were very close. The crowd broke its silence and began to talk. It was obviously a tie. There'd have to be a jump-off. Christopher began heading back toward the truck.

Blenkin stood up again, hesitated once more, and then walked and slid down the hill, slanting his way east to make a straight line toward the truck. George Peterson was saying nothing, but he wanted to. He held the microphone close to his mouth and, over the small noise the crowd was making, his amplified breathing could be heard.

Blenkin arrived at George Peterson's side and the microphone picked up what he said. "You have the scoresheet?"

George Peterson nodded and put the mike down on the running-board of the truck. Christopher skied toward them while he watched Blenkin and George point and talk, shake their heads and finally nod.

"Okay," George said. "All right. We have a decision here. You probably guessed with all the measuring going on up there that Christopher Waterton came awfully close to Sonny Lester's mark. Well he did. It was as close as you can get. The two jumps measured exactly one hundred and two feet and three inches. That's a fact, by golly. It's never happened since I've been with the Ski Association, but there you have it. A tie for distance. But we don't have one for style. We—Mr. Blenkin and I—agree about that. It wasn't a tie in that department. But what a contest it was. The final jump told the tale and gave us our decision. So, the 1939 winner is SONNY LESTER."

Christopher stood numb on his skis just beyond the hood of the truck. Behind him there was applause from everyone, and Lester's friends were whistling and shouting. Lester moved forward to receive the cup, not from George Peterson but from Mayor Courtney, who climbed onto the back of the truck and motioned for George to give him the microphone. He had on boots, an ancient coonskin coat, special for the Carnival, and fur hat to match. He had what Sarah had called—in too loud a voice, at a political meeting—"a fat nose," and a face lined from smiling a great deal during his nearly sixty years. Christopher heard him only vaguely while he addressed the crowd about Long River and about the celebrations today. And then he talked about the Junior Jumping Event.

"This has been as fine a piece of competition as I've seen since this great facility was built. And you will recall how it was built. With our backs and hands. Neil Creighton's mill donated the lumber." He chuckled. "Neil couldn't sell it anyway." He waited for laughter. "Half the town took turns clearing the hills and building the trestle. And when we was finished we had ourselves a party that turned into the Carnival the next year, with George Peterson at the helm."

He waited for applause and got it. George looked pleased and waved his hands above his head.

Mayor Courtney looked pleased too, and began to speak again. "Well, we couldn't have this event if there weren't boys to jump in it, and I guess they wouldn't jump so good if someone like Clarence Blenkin wasn't around to help out. He's a good coach and a good judge too, because we got a great young champ here this year out of both of those fine qualities. It isn't easy to break a tie, except if you know as much about skiing as Clarence does." He stopped again for applause. Blenkin grinned and chewed his lip. Miss Garrett jumped up and down and clapped her hands. The applause was mild—no whistling and some booing.

"Now, I'm not going to hold up things. George tells me the cross-country race will wind up here any minute." He looked west, down the road that served the Castles. "Yep, here they come up Plymouth Street. They got about half a mile to go. So, let me get this over quick. Paul Lester, you did a good job. A hundred and two feet is a new record, George Peterson tells me. Congratulations. Come on over here and take this cup home for the second year in a row."

Lester moved forward on his skis and reached up. There was applause again from the crowd, and once more there were boos. Christopher looked around to see who was doing it. He wished they wouldn't. He had to go up and get his medal now. Lester took the cup and held it high for a moment and, as he did it, the crowd began to yell at the cross-country skiers.

"It's Henry Teffler in the lead," Mayor Courtney announced.

The noise increased. George Peterson climbed up onto the truck.

"Just a minute," the Mayor said, but then he gave up the mike to George, and handed Blenkin the two small medallions that were the prizes for second and third. "You give them to the boys," he said, and stood again to watch the finish of the race.

Blenkin was surprised. Christopher saw him look at the medals and then down the road toward the skiers. It was Teffler's race. The crowd was cheering him. Christopher looked at Blenkin standing there with the medals in his bare hand. The embarrassment and the disappointment were withering. He glanced at Knight; his face was blank. He might have been jumping his personal best over again. Courtney had spoken too long, as usual. This way Lester got all the spotlight there was. Blenkin came toward them and handed Knight his medal.

"Good jump," he said. "You can be top man next year."

Knight didn't say anything. He stood quiet and held the medal in his fingers, looked at it and then shuffled away.

Blenkin's eyes stopped looking at Knight and watched Teffler cross the line. Ten seconds later someone from Indian Falls finished. It was a long way back to third. Christopher watched Blenkin's face and knew he was staring, and that he was at the same time trying to swallow anger because it was frightening him.

Blenkin turned around and, without looking into his face, held out the medal. Christopher reached toward it. "There should've been a jump-off." He heard his voice hardly above a whisper, and it shook.

"What?"

Now it was easier. "I'm as good on the hill as Lester. My skis never even came apart. There should've been a jump-off."

"Why?" Blenkin's eyes were wide open. He looked incensed. "Your jump was a fluke."

"Maybe." The muscles in his stomach were paralyzed; he couldn't breathe. "If you'd allowed a jump-off we'd've seen."

Blenkin dropped the medal in his still outstretched hand. "No talking back to a judge. One more word and I'll bar you from competition."

Christopher shoved the medal in his pocket and put on his glove. "You don't have to. I'm not going to jump again anyway." And then he knew that he'd said what Blenkin wanted to hear. Teffler skated on his narrow cross-country skis up to the truck. Blenkin turned away.

In his belly there had been anger; now his guts were stiff and cold. Courtney was speaking again. Christopher skied away to the bottom of the switchback trail where he'd left his poles, and he spent a long time fitting the straps over his mitts and adjusting them so they'd be snug around his wrists.

The crowd had broken free from behind the rope barrier. He could see his family and Emily's still together. They were talking. No. His mother was talking. All the rest were standing there in the snow sucking in and breathing out balloons of frozen breath.

He couldn't get it straight why he felt no good, except that it had to do with Blenkin. Not just here today. It was every day that Blenkin kept saying that Christopher Waterton didn't belong—which was a kind of silence worse than Fielder's bad joke. He felt the cold in his stomach go sick.

His father signalled to him to join them, and he knew he must. It would be easier if Emily came to meet him, but she couldn't. Mrs. Gordon was also a judge. Pat and Fielder were standing beside her now. He began to push himself with his poles across the snow toward them all: people who weren't friends and didn't want to be together and wouldn't be if Emily hadn't chosen to stand with his family. Thinking about her doing that suddenly made him smile. They'd stood there for her, Dr. and Mrs. Gordon, to keep her safe from him. Yet they didn't object to Pat and Fielder, maybe because with those two everything was some kind of a game—both of them acting as if what they were doing was a competition. But they were going together, even if neither of them admitted it.

"Close only counts in horseshoes," his father said, "but that last was a fine jump."

He was agreeing with Blenkin and George Peterson that Lester should have won. Christopher looked around at the others. They were all going to congratulate him for being second. Even his mother. She hugged him. "My dear, being second is good too. You must've done some little thing wrong."

"No, I didn't."

"Well, Clarence Blenkin thought you did, and that's what counts."

"Our masters and betters," Dr. Gordon said. Everyone waited, but he said no more.

"Let me see your medal," Emily said, so she could move close to him.

He took his mitt off and got it out for her.

"Fielder and I are going to Ch'en's to get warm," Pat announced. "Are you two coming?"

Emily said quietly, "Mother says we can if they're along too." She turned to her parents, "We can come back after the Senior Jump. They always take forever."

He looked at his father. "What's the time?"

"Nearly two."

"I've got a lesson with Gabe." He glanced at Mrs. Gordon, and realized he'd said the right thing.

She smiled. "I'm really sorry about what happened, Christopher. I thought Mr. Blenkin could've handled it better."

"Thanks," he said, awkwardly. Then he saw Emily's face. It was puzzled and surprised. "I don't want to miss it," he told her.

She nodded and looked down at the medal. "I want you to come," she said, softly, and he felt her fingers poke into his side.

There was not only Gabe; now there was her mother to please. "I told Gabe I'd be there. He's missing this so we can have a lesson. We'll see each other at the dance. You're going, aren't you?"

She nodded.

"We'll all be there," Dr. Gordon said, "at least until the Queen is crowned."

"We can dance," he said.

She stood in front of him now, straddling his skis. Her eyes searched his. He smiled back and saw her give in. It hurt to watch. "Could I come and get you for the dance?"

"We'll drive the girls," Mrs. Gordon said. "Much simpler that way."

He looked at Fielder and saw him unconcerned. "You won."

Fielder shrugged. "Purvis didn't want to pay."

"Yeah, right. I didn't want to be second."

"I didn't want you to be second either," Sarah said. She pushed Emily aside and hugged him around the waist. Everybody laughed.

He could see her not liking the laughter. If you were young, things you did spontaneously on your own were either bad or funny. "Hey," he said. "Twice in one day. That's a lot of hugs from you."

Fielder and Pat were moving off. To Emily he said, "See you tonight."

"Okay," she said, and began to go with them.

He said goodbye to the Gordons, and then saw his mother and father looking at him, both uncertain and anxious. They wanted him to tell them he wasn't disappointed about being second. It felt as if the lie was too hard for him to say. He only smiled at them, poled himself away and skied fast to catch up with Emily. "I wanted to go with you," he said, and held her arm. Pat and Fielder went on ahead and stopped to wait. Emily laughed her soft laugh, as if she might be relieved. "Yes," she said.

"Your mother was happy I didn't."

"Christopher." Her eyes were suddenly darker than he'd seen them.

"I didn't mean it that way."

She nodded. "I want us to be together."

"I promised Gabe."

"It's okay. Go."

"You're mad."

She came close and gave him a hug. "You want to go to Gabe's. I'll see you tonight."

He couldn't let her go. "I need my lessons."

She smiled a little. "I'm jealous."

"Are you? Why?"

"I wish I had a Gabe," and she turned and went to catch up with Pat and Fielder.

He stood watching, feeling he'd chosen wrong.

Behind him Pete Sanderson's name was announced. He turned and couldn't help watching. From the top of the trestle and all the way down it, Pete crouched, and when he leaped it was like watching a black flower suddenly bloom in mid-air. The slow motion of his glide toward the slant of the hill was the miracle that made jumping the best physical thrill there was. How else could a man fall three hundred feet and not kill himself, but instead make something beautiful? Pete was doing it. Did it. And came across the flat, his skis making no noise at all. When Pete was able to work, he cut ties for the railway, and his skis might be the only extra thing he owned. He was thin and full of grace, and he smiled at Christopher, turned and stopped. For a moment he looked as if he might speak, but then he only nodded and moved back toward the hill.

Purvis emerged from the crowd. Christopher lifted a ski pole in answer to his raised hand, and waited for him to catch up. The effort made Purvis cough. He looked tired and cold.

"What's the matter? Up all night at the rink?"

Purvis didn't answer the question. "Look, kid, that was lousy what Blenkin did."

"What can you do?"

"I know what I'd like to. Which way are you going?"

"Home."

"I got to go to the rink."

"For the hockey game already?"

"Howard's got ideas about decorating the place."

Christopher poled himself along, and Purvis walked with his head down and his hands in the pockets of his jacket. They went along Plymouth Street toward town. "Going to the dance tonight?" he asked. They were stopped now at London Street.

"Maybe," Purvis said.

"It's the big one."

"Sure, after the game." Purvis moved off toward the rink, and then he turned again. "You don't have much luck, do you, kid? I mean, Blenkin should've made you and Lester jump again. What's he got against you?"

Christopher wanted to tell him. Purvis was across the street now and beginning to head to the rink. A car—spanking a broken chain against a fender—passed between them. "Something, I guess," he said when it was quiet once more.

Purvis came back across the road. "You know what he did last night? I'm coming in for an easy basket and he puts his elbow damn near through my gut. All night long, he elbows, trips, interferes, and the ref gives him nothing. Nothing. Scanlon teaches Sunday School with him, and Blenkin stares him down. I complained. Blenkin interfered. Scanlon just stands there and Blenkin comes over and says anyone who argues with an official gets thrown out of the game, as if because he's a teacher he's in charge everywhere."

"He can't stand losing," Christopher said.

"He's going to lose one of these days."

He watched Purvis stand in the snow and look helpless. It wasn't a sight he'd ever seen before.

"I walked in on him and Garrett in the lab at school."

Purvis wasn't impressed. "You're making it up."

"No. They were there."

"Doing what? Holding hands?"

"She was sitting up on the lab table and he had his head on her chest, and his hand—" He felt as if he were falling. It was difficult suddenly to breathe. "She was stroking his hair and kissing his forehead."

Purvis looked delighted. He might want to tell everybody. "Come on, come on. What about his hand?"

"Nothing. He just sort of had it tangled up in her sweater."

"Sure. Right." He laughed. "I don't believe it. Those two. One thing's for certain, they were made for each other. Do you think their kid would be born with a pencil up his butt and greasy curls?"

"Purvis," he said. "Look, nobody knows except you and me."

"So I guess I can't talk, eh? Sure." Purvis began to laugh and cough at the same time. "If they ever got into bed together, do you think they'd know what to do?"

"Why not? They're teachers, but they're not stupid about everything. Just don't blab it around about them."

"High-minded little twit, aren't you?" Purvis struck a pose with his hand shoved into his jacket. "I hereby declare that Blenkin and Garrett are people. Are you saying it's okay he didn't give you another chance to beat Lester?"

Christopher didn't answer; instead, he said, "I'm sorry you lost fifty cents on me."

"I am too. I don't like losing that way, or the way we lost the game last night."

"I got to go to Gabe's." He wanted to stop talking now.

Purvis put his hands back in his pockets. "You still taking lessons from him? Waste of money, isn't it?"

"Maybe. But I need them."

"I thought if you couldn't just do it right off, you're never going to be a musician anyway. Who taught Gabe?"

"He said it was hard being alone. He made a lot of mistakes."

"Sounds like what happens to everybody. That's life, eh?"

There was no answer to that. He watched Purvis shrug and turn away. It wasn't awkward that they didn't say goodbye. He skied up London toward the school, and then further up York to home. Behind him, every now and then, he could hear the crowd cheer a jumper. He knew he'd jump again next year. At school they gave you marks. Maybe the world gave you applause. And sometimes money. He put his skis away and went into the house to get his horn from the closet. He had pictures on his walls now. Gabe had given him Johnny Hodges and Coleman Hawkins. Jimmy Dorsey and Charlie Barnett he'd cut from *Downbeat* magazine. The Jimmy Dorsey one was a publicity photo; the others were action shots: Hawkins with a fedora on, playing in a jam session; Barnett in front of his band; Hodges at a microphone with Duke Ellington's band behind him. Applause every night, and not just a few times when the snow was right for it in the winter. He took his medal out and tossed it onto the top of his chest of drawers. Those things had to be presented right to mean anything. It had been a stupid day. Blenkin, yes; but the Gordons made up rules to suit themselves too. Fielder and Pat: what was happening? Maybe now it was supposed to be all right to see Emily anytime, so long as those two were chaperones, which was a laugh. Who was kidding who?

He had a peanut butter sandwich and two glasses of milk. The walk to Gabe's made him feel good again, and when Gabe answered the door, Irene was there sweeping the linoleum in the living room. It was worn badly around the woodburning heater. She smiled her unhappy smile. Her stomach was larger than he'd seen it. Maybe she was pregnant again. When they were downstairs in Gabe's room, he said, "You guys going to have another baby?"

Gabe grinned. "June. It took you a while to notice."

"I didn't think you would."

"None of your business, kid."

"Sorry."

"This one's for the town. She had to hide little Denny and try to pretend he was premature. Now she's never home. Packs that belly all over the place showing it to everybody. Her mother just beams. So does mine. They can enjoy this one. Some day I figure the old man might forgive me too."

"Is it that bad?"

"Nothing's that bad. Let's play music. What've we got this week?"
"All the scales on the flat side."
"Okay, warm up on them. What's the key of C-flat?"
"Seven flats."
"Same as?"
"Key of B. Five sharps."
"And D-flat?"
"Five flats. Same note as C-sharp, seven sharps."
"And the G-flat scale is the same as?"
"F-sharp. Six sharps."
"Good. You can name a few; now play them."
He began with F, and worked his way through all the flat keys. Gabe set up rhythmic riffs behind each scale. He liked to practise too.
"Am I pushing you too hard?" he asked after they were through.
Christopher didn't want anything at Gabe's to be just kidding around. He held his horn across his knee and thought how being with him and working at music made him feel free. No, it wasn't that. What he did was leave his old self behind and here he worked on building someone new who didn't have anything to do with family or school, or even Emily. "I don't think you could push me too hard. Is there anything wrong with what I'm doing?"
Gabe shook his head. "You've come as far in three months as I did in a year."
"It's the lessons. You didn't have any."
"No, but Jimmy Collins played in Toronto a while before he landed up here in the cement plant. He did a lot for me. The horn's easy. What's hard is the music that goes with it."
Christopher looked at Gabe. His eyes were too serious. "What's wrong?"
"Nothing. You can't teach jazz, is all. You teach scales and chords and what's possible on the horn. The rest comes from playing with guys that know more."
"I'm playing with you."
Gabe grinned. "Sure. So let's do it."
Christopher began "On the Sunny Side of the Street." He played the melody, and Gabe blew some harmony.
"More air," Gabe said, after they'd finished. "Like I told you. Open your throat and get lots of air down there for your diaphragm to push out." He blew a G. "Hear that?" It sounds skinny. Now listen." He blew the same note, and it came out big and round even though he blew it softly. "Okay. One note at a time from the bottom of your horn.

Match my tone."

He listened as he played against Gabe's big sound, and made the muscles in his throat and stomach respond the way they must.

"Now, let's do 'Moonglow,' big and slow, triple *forte*."

It was as if a third horn had been added. He thought that people three houses away would hear them. He had to struggle to keep his throat from closing and his lungs from emptying too fast.

"Make it louder," Gabe said.

He didn't think he could. Then the second time through the piece, Gabe asked for *pianissimo*, and he knew then that he had a lot more work to do to become a real horn player. The sound he was making wasn't soft, it was weak. He loved Gabe for making him understand.

"I'll play the tune, you do the triads behind me that the chords call for." Gabe put his horn back in his mouth and played the melody very slowly. He was two changes into the piece before Christopher got the first three-note chord clear enough in his mind to run it. He began to play what he hoped was right, and Gabe stopped. "You can't fake it," he said. "The notes have to fit, or don't play." His voice was harsh.

"It's too hard." He felt as if Gabe had turned against him. "You sound like someone who's—I don't know." He unhooked his horn from its neckstrap.

"A priest," Gabe said.

"What?"

"A priest is what you're trying to say."

"Maybe schoolteacher."

"Look," Gabe said. "You don't tell it, you live it. That stupid place out there with its hard times and Hitler and Franco and Chamberlain and Roosevelt screwing around is just something you have to put up with."

"I don't know what you're saying, Gabe."

"I'm saying I got a God, and I'm the priest. No faking. I'm looking for the right notes, but more than that, once I've got the right notes, I want to know how to choose them so they can mean the most they ever can."

"Are you mad at me?"

"No. Look, kid, what I'm saying is if you find something that's got a *real* mystery in it, then there's no use screwing around just making money with it, or making a big man out of yourself showing off doing it. That's what they call desecration. You got to become a priest. There isn't any other way."

Gabe could've been a priest. His skin was pale and he looked out from behind his horn as if it could be a thing he used somehow to worship with. Upstairs, little Denny began to cry, and Irene's voice, soft and sure, began to comfort him.

"What about them?" Christopher pointed to the ceiling.

Gabe smiled. "They come second. And the job at the store comes third, and everything else is fourth."

Christopher knew he was smiling too. "You didn't walk out on her."

"Second's not bad."

"It is if you're the one who's second."

Gabe was silent for a moment, and then he shrugged. "I'm doing the best I can in that department." He unhooked his horn and put it in its case. "I think I've embarrassed myself."

"Why?"

"I guess I trust you, kid. I must. I never said priest out loud to anyone before." He bent down and closed the lid of the case. "So, how's it with you and Emily?"

"I don't want to talk about it."

"Not so good eh?"

"I can't be a priest," Christopher told him.

"Maybe that's a lot of bull I said about priests, Chris. Mouthing off."

He thought now, caught short, that he either had to cry or tell him. "Look, please, Gabe, nobody talks to me the way you do. Now I'm growing up, my parents are just afraid I'm going to make a mistake, or they're asking questions to try to understand me. Fielder's supposed to be my best friend and he gets the whole school to give me the silent treatment. Today, Blenkin makes sure I come in second, even though I tied Lester." He stopped before he told him about Emily. "How the hell do you be a priest with that going on?"

Gabe stood up and put his horn over by the warmer inside wall. When he turned around again, Christopher knew he wasn't going to give him an answer. He said, "All that's part of the deal. You aren't any different from anyone else."

"Then why did you tell me about it?"

"Maybe I think you're already headed in that direction."

"Priest?"

"Sure. A priest of something."

"I want to play this horn."

"You blow on it three or four thousand hours and use your brains so you learn something every time you pick it up and you will. I guarantee it. It's not a dream. It's hard work."

Christopher put his horn away and locked the case shut. The arithmetic of the three thousand hours made an almost audible sound inside of his head: eight hours a day for a year. Grandison would be proud of how quick he figured it. Four hours a day for two years. It was too much. He put his coat on and felt in his coat pocket for lesson money. "Gabe?" He handed him the dollar.

"Thanks."

"Gabe?"

"What?"

"Could I bring my horn over to the dance tonight and play lead with you for a couple of numbers?"

"You want it all right now, don't you?"

There was no use saying no. "Maybe before the crowd gets there. I just want to be with the band."

Gabe nodded. "I'll pick a couple of numbers."

"Three. I want to play that much anyway."

"We start at nine," Gabe said, and began to climb the stairs. "You quarrelling with Emily?"

"No. Her mother."

"What'd you do?"

"We swung in a hammock at a party."

"That'll do it every time. Irene and I did that too. But it was in her back yard."

"This was on her porch."

"Hammocks are good for smooching. We moved onto the back seat of Phil Henrick's car. Never should've left the hammock."

Irene heard him. "I wish I could buy you one for your birthday," she said.

"No fun alone."

"We could leave the kids with Mother."

"Don't talk dirty in front of the boy."

"Are you a boy, Christopher?" she asked. "I don't think so."

Gabe opened the outside door. "Nine o'clock," he said. "No pay, just glory."

"I'll come early and help set up."

Gabe nodded and closed the door. It was cold outside.

2

The Carnival Ball wasn't an ordinary dance, like Labour Day or New Year's Eve. From the first time it was held, it became spontaneously a family affair. Babies, children, eleven- and twelve-year-olds were brought along or, in the case of the pre-teens, they often arrived in groups or sometimes in awkward couples trying to look as independent from their parents as possible. By the second week in March, winter was five months old, and by the time the snow was gone and the ice was melting in the river five or six weeks from now, the cold and the dark would have taken up everyone's consciousness for half a year. Such concentration needed to be broken, for fear that winter might become a habit rather than a season. The Ball was a celebration, too, not yet of the death of winter, but of the first glimpse of the light of summer. The skiing, the hockey, the curling produced champions. The Carnival produced a Queen and four Princesses. The ballroom was decorated with streamers and balloons. Gabe's quartet of musicians wore blue jackets and white pants and shoes. Mrs. Mabel Courtney, who was in charge of the Ball this—and every other—year had seen to it that paper leis were given to them to wear. Gabe had already draped his over the edge of his music stand.

Christopher had come in the rear entrance to the hall, partly because he felt shy arriving with his horn, pretending he was good enough to be a member of the band, and partly because that way he didn't have to pay. He was later than he wanted to be: his mother had insisted on pressing his pants again, and had forced him to polish his shoes and take them with him in a paper bag so he wouldn't be seen on the bandstand wearing boots. Next year, she'd said, next year you can have overshoes to wear out in the evening instead of boots. He sat in the dark behind the bandstand and changed into the shoes. When he stood up and walked in them he felt light on his feet and light, too, in his head, as if what was happening wasn't quite real. He put his horn up on the stand and waited for Gabe to notice him. The hall was cool. Management relied on the crowd to warm it up. The quartet was sorting music, and Gabe was calling numbers.

"Seventy-five; the new one: 'Tuxedo Junction,' " he said. "Is that enough?"

"Should get us to about the supper break," Marty said.

"I hate these big ones." Buster rolled his sticks across the head of his snare drum. "They always want to go to six in the morning."

"They're paying us," Gabe said.

"Five bucks apiece extra isn't gold bricks."

"I'll get you out of here by four," Gabe told him, and glanced down. "Hey, we got a new member of the band."

Jim Collins turned around from his piano. "I'm glad. I was going to start charging the kid for coming here and staring at us."

"Move over," Gabe said to Marty.

Christopher heaved himself up onto the stage and went to the back of the stand for an extra chair. He sat between Gabe and Marty and gazed out over the ballroom floor. The crowd was gathering. His throat closed and his ears rang as if he'd climbed too high too fast. These early ones were dancers. They were dancers like some people were skaters or stamp collectors. They were couples mostly, but some came alone. The women sat against the wall until they were asked to dance, or they danced with other women if they weren't chosen and thought they might miss a set. The young who were here already were the jitterbugs, and they'd be the last to go home.

Christopher tuned his horn, first with the piano and then with Gabe and Marty's horns. The quartet played from cut-down standard arrangements for thirteen piece swing bands. They used them mostly just to check out the melodies and the right chords, but now they were going to play as if they were a band and he and Gabe were a saxophone section. The lead alto part was mostly melody. The piece in front of him was "I'm Confessin'." He looked at it and then glanced up again at the gathering crowd. It was watching what was happening on the bandstand. He didn't feel nervous anymore. The breath in him was strong, and his head was clear.

"I like it," he said, out loud.

Gabe laughed. "You haven't played anything yet."

Even the jitterbugs liked to start down tempo. They always did their manoeuvres slow and easy in front of the bandstand, as if they were professional athletes warming up for a big event.

"I'll do the intro," Gabe said, "and you come in at the chorus. Give it some guts." He tramped his foot four times and the music began.

Christopher counted out four bars and then blew the first notes of the melody. The piano, the drums, Gabe's horn, all supporting that little phrase, was a shock that closed his throat again, and blinded his eyes to the music. He bobbled the interval between C and E and heard Gabe say, "You can play it, kid." Bars three and four were a repeat of the first two. He got them right. "More guts," Gabe said.

The next four bars went well, and when he began to repeat the whole eight bars again before going into the bridge, his muscles began to relax.

At the bridge, Marty's trumpet took over, and he had to read notes that weren't melody anymore. They weren't hard to read, only strange. Gabe's horn was with him playing harmony too, but he didn't know the music and he didn't know when he was making a mistake.

"Now you got the lead again," Gabe said. It felt good this time. He played the simple melody line, and listened to Gabe's harmony and Jim's piano laying down the chords. Buster's brushes were working across his snare. Marty's trumpet played legato punctuation at the end of phrases; then he put a straight mute into his horn and got up to play the melody into the microphone.

"Okay, leave it to us. I'll tell you when to come in again." Gabe played an *ad libbed* obligato to the muted melody. It was pretty. Very pretty. Christopher sat with his horn at his side ready to play, and looked out at the dancers. He felt very high up, and powerfully himself, as if who he wanted to be had suddenly happened.

Gabe went to the microphone and played the tune while Marty picked out little riffs behind him. Jim was offering up long runs of piano notes to fill in the background; Christopher was in the middle of what they were doing, and he felt himself hearing it in a way he'd not been able to from down on the dance floor.

And then down below, Fielder's face was grinning up at him. Pat was there too, and Emily in a blue dress and with a white cardigan sweater across her shoulders. He had wanted to be finished playing before they came. What he'd asked of Gabe wasn't something he wanted to have Fielder make jokes about, or even to have Emily compliment him on. He was in the band; Gabe was letting him *pretend*. And it occurred to him that he wouldn't have to face that if they'd come later. He stood up and turned to put his horn back in its case.

"Play it," Gabe said. It was an order.

He turned again.

"At the mike," Gabe said

Jim Collins was doing his chorus now, and there were only a few bars to the end of it. He looked at the mike and then back at Gabe. His eyes were serious. "It's all yours, kid. Come on, you want it, take it."

If he didn't the music might simply stop. The mike was there in front of him now, and beyond it couples were dancing. He saw Fielder's face again. The grin had faded. There were going to be no jokes if he played the tune right.

He heard Jim finish and do an *ad lib* turnaround back to the chorus. He blew the first two bar phrase. Gabe and Marty played soft behind him and filled. He blew the second phrase.

"Play to the back of the hall."

He closed his eyes and obeyed Gabe's new order. He could hear the piano better. The drumbeat helped. He was higher up than he'd ever been on skis. The first four notes of the bridge were an awkward melody and needed to be played strong to announce the tune's new key. He got them to sound right. The chords behind him moved everything through a new set of tensions and back to the original eight bar melody.

He opened his eyes again and saw the people dancing. They weren't couples; they were a crowd doing what his horn told them to do. This simple tune was making it happen. "I'm confessin' that I love you, I'm confessin' that I care." Everything was easy now, and he didn't want it to end, but the last four bars were there to play.

He was through with the melody. He wanted to play jazz. He floated through darkness, but that was all right: there would be applause to land on.

Then it was chaos, not darkness that surrounded him. The new notes he played—hoping—weren't jazz, they were only noise, and he couldn't stop now.

If he kept playing maybe they'd come out right. He played more notes, faster, searching at least for F, the keynote. He couldn't find it. It was like pissing himself in public, and not being able to stop.

Then Marty and Gabe and the piano were playing loud, running over the crazy sounds he was making so that he couldn't be heard anymore.

He opened his eyes. In the silence that followed the quartet's ending, the crowd in front of him separated and became people again. He knew them all. There was no applause. Some of them looked surprised. A couple were laughing. Fielder, Pat, Emily were looking up at him.

He sat down. Gabe was there, and he put a new arrangement onto their music stands.

"Play it," he said.

Christopher shook his head and began to take his horn off its neck-strap.

"I said play it." Gabe pointed at the music and began to beat out the time.

"I can't."

"We all make mistakes," Gabe said, and began to play "This Can't Be Love."

Christopher looked at him playing the tune and staring back.

"This can't be love because I feel so fine."

The jive dancers were doing their up-tempo routines. Fielder and Pat were gone from in front of the stand, but Emily was still there, a smile like a wound on her face, as if she knew exactly what he'd done and what it meant. But if he got up and left now the icicle in the middle of his gut wouldn't melt. The first chorus was nearly done. Eight beats more.

"Now," Gabe said.

Christopher blew. It was an easy tune, but it was fast, and he'd only played it once with Gabe at a lesson. But now he had the lead, Gabe was playing second tenor, and Marty was backing them both.

As the chorus began to end, Gabe flipped over his music; on the back was a set of riffs he'd sketched to play behind him when he soloed. "They're easy," he said, and stood so that his horn was at the mike. He fooled around with the tune and then gradually moved away from it until what he was playing was pure improvisation. Marty played the riffs softly until Christopher had the rhythm in his head. He kept playing, but he was still hurting, because, once again, he'd not believed that making music was something exact. Wishing didn't make it so.

The riffs he was playing to back Gabe's solo, the punctuations Jim and Marty were inserting, and the long lines of Gabe's choruses meshed. He was part of it, but he didn't know and understand what he was doing.

Gabe finished at the end of the fourth chorus and sat down. It was his tune. Marty and Jim didn't solo. He turned the music over again and pointed to the top of the score. They all played the piece one final time, and the crowd applauded as if the noise they made were part of the music.

"Good," Marty said. "You might blow a little in a year or two."

Gabe was laughing. "Jeez, kid, you sure know how to scare a person."

"I don't know what happened," Christopher said. The others were all looking at him; the explanation was important. "It was like being with you guys made me think I could—"

"Well, you can't," Gabe said. "But maybe you learned early, and that's a plus."

Christopher got up. It was a test. He'd asked to play three tunes. Gabe didn't stop him from going. He'd made him play the second tune for a reason. Maybe so he wouldn't have to go away a failure—and Gabe might be the only man in town who'd do a thing like that. But the lesson was over. He was going back now to the three thousand hours. Maybe four thousand. He left them while they did the first chorus of "Them There Eyes." Fast and tricky. The jitterbugs went wild.

On the far side of the bandstand, he jumped down into the dimness that was behind it. He had his horn in one hand and its case in the other. He sat on a box of electrical equipment beside where he'd left his coat and boots and began to take his horn apart. He knew Emily was going to appear in a moment, and it was like waiting for a second sound in the night. He laid the body of his horn in its case, and when she spoke he twitched.

"Hello." She crouched beside him, and he put away the neck and mouthpiece before he turned to look at her.

"Did I scare you?"

He shook his head and shut and locked the case. "Where's your mum and dad?"

"They dropped us and went on to the McLachlans'. Mother's helping with Enid's dress. She's a finalist for Queen."

"How'd that happen?"

"She got her name on the top of a lot of Carnival raffle tickets."

"Her old man bought them all."

"Not all of them."

"Well, she's not ugly."

"Or very pretty," Emily said. Her voice was not quite a whisper. They weren't talking about Enid, and they were just words to keep from talking about what happened on the bandstand. Her eyes moved quick and they searched, he knew, for a way of telling how he was feeling. He wanted her to find out and tell him, because then he'd know himself. She was in front of him now, kneeling.

"You'll get dirty," he said, and began to stand up.

She held his arms and shook her head. "Kiss," she said.

He bent forward and put his lips against hers. The ice that had been dripping cold into his gut disappeared. When the kiss was finished and he'd laid his head on her shoulder, he heard himself make a noise that might have been a groan. He was leaning on her and knew it. Her arms around him now were comfort. Her perfume was sweet. The kiss she'd asked for was a way of getting him close again. They hadn't stayed close like before. Not since the party, because he'd held off, waiting for things to become normal. He wasn't holding off any more. Not now. The mindless notes he'd played at the end of his solo were in his head again—a ball of noise that had made a fool of him.

"It was so stupid," he said.

He wanted her to answer, but she only kept on holding him and waiting. He didn't have any more words.

Finally, she said, "Do you want to dance?"

His weight was too heavy on her. He sat straight again on the box, and she stood up, lifted her dress, and brushed the dirt off her knees. He watched, but it wasn't a game of peek. They were beyond that.

"Pat's," she said, pulling and smoothing the silk above her knees and then checking the backs of her legs to see if the seams were straight. "She's a lot taller than me."

He stood up beside her. Gabe was blowing "Out of Nowhere." The beat was exactly right. It made his body shift in spite of itself. But the people out there in front of the bandstand had listened to him and heard the fool he was. "Everybody came early," he told her. "More than I expected."

She understood what he was saying. "They don't care."

"I do. I was up there and it was like I was in a goddamn movie." He laughed, embarrassed again. "You know, where the guy who's never played anything but Beethoven picks up a trumpet and all of a sudden plays like Harry James. What I did must've sounded stupid."

"It just wasn't the same music, that's all."

His muscles in his gut hardened over the fear of what had happened; it had had such power. He wondered if he could stop it if it appeared the next time he played.

He could feel her waiting again, but when she spoke it wasn't about dancing. "Let's go for a walk then. It's hours before the Queen ceremony." Already she was leaving to organize it for them. "I'll find Pat and tell her. And get my coat and boots."

She went quickly, gesturing something positive, and he followed, looking out for Pat and Fielder too. They were on the edge of the crowd at the far end of the bandstand. He watched Emily go to them, talk, turn and bring them back to him.

"They want to come too. Chaperones." She laughed.

Fielder grinned, but he didn't say anything.

"Coats," Pat said, in charge as usual. "Meet you back here."

"I'll be at the back entrance," he told them.

"What'll we do?" Fielder asked. "Go to Wei Ch'en's?"

He decided to trust him again. "I just want to get out of here for a while."

"It's cold out," Fielder said.

"No it's not, I think it's even snowing again." Then, "You got it bad for Pat, haven't you?" He couldn't help saying it. A payback.

"It's your fault," Fielder said.

"I don't think so."

Fielder grinned. "She's different when she's not in a crowd."

"I bet."

"Not like you two. I think you're bloody married." He looked as if he might say something else, but then he left for the coat room.

Christopher hid his horn under the bandstand and put his boots and coat on. When he looked back into the hall, he saw his mother and father dancing. Even that was embarrassing now. If they hadn't been there to see what he'd done, they'd hear about it. He went to the rear entrance to wait for the others. It was snowing gently. Up the alley, two men stood by the telephone pole. One of them was tall enough to be Purvis. They were drinking from a bottle. He heard a voice and then a laugh.

"Hey, John," he shouted.

"The champ," Purvis called back, and came toward him. He wasn't drunk, just high. The bottle in his hand was half full. "Style," he said. "They got you on style. Who ever heard of it? Blenkin's a crud, and George Peterson'll say Yes to anything."

"Blenkin said it was a fluke."

"Your jump? Beautiful. A goddamn bird."

It was Lamb by the pole. He came toward them, but he could hardly walk. He slipped in the snow and fell. Purvis leaned over and pulled him up. "Lamb, you got to smarten up. You know what I'm going to do?"

"No," Lamb said. It was an effort. One of his sisters was a candidate for Queen, but he'd never see the ceremony.

Purvis let him go and he fell again. "I'm going to go in there and find Blenkin and bring him out here and pound him."

Lamb managed to get up and lean against the building. "Why?"

"He hurt me. Last night he hurt me. Every game he plays he cheats. He cheated my friend here."

"That's your friend? He's only in grade nine."

"Nevertheless . . . nevertheless, my friend, he's my friend."

"He's gotta grow up some."

"Not much. He's pretty near there." Purvis put an arm around Christopher, and behind them, Fielder's voice said, "Leave him alone, Purvis."

"Don't give me none of your lip, or I'll put you off the ice for good."

"My-oh-my," Lamb said. "The pretty little Gordon girls. Where you goin'?"

"Yeah, where you going? You'll miss the fight." Purvis laughed and coughed at the same time.

"You going to fight Waterton?" Pat asked.

"He's my friend," Purvis said, and took a drink from the bottle.

"Don't drink it all," Lamb said. "That's my bottle."

"I'm just keeping you out of jail," Purvis said, and drank again.

"Right," Fielder said, "let's get out of here before the cops come." He took Pat's hand and led her down the alley toward the street.

Christopher felt Emily take his arm. "You don't have to pound Blenkin for me," he said to Purvis.

"That was the last straw." Purvis shook his head. "Were you there, Lamb? Did you see Waterton jump? Four feet longer than Lester's and he called it a tie."

"Sounds like him," Lamb said, and stood up straight. "Blenkin rules. Don't cross that—" He leaned toward Emily and smiled a loose smile. "Do you mind if I swear? You don't, do you? Bastard. Bastard Blenkin rules. You take shit from him for four years and then you graduate. I'm going to graduate in three months." He hiccoughed. "Except if Hit, Hit, Hitler makes a war and then I'm going to do it before that." He fell against the side of the building and began to be sick in the snow at his feet. Purvis went to him and held him from falling.

"Please," Emily said.

Christopher turned with her and walked to the mouth of the alley. Fielder and Pat were a block away, and even though she was wearing a skirt and stockings, she was willing to play. At a vacant lot along Manchester Street she stood watching while he made an angel. Then she fell back into the snow and made one herself. Fielder was lying looking up into the streetlight; white flakes slanted down through it. Pat rolled over on top of him and washed his face with the new snow. Then she was up and running, brushing herself with her mittened hands as she went. When he caught up with her, she screamed. Maybe the pitch of it made him hesitate. It was enough. She tripped him off balance and ran back and hid behind Emily and Christopher.

"Mother's going to kill you if that skirt's ruined," Emily shouted.

Pat laughed, and she and Fielder jogged together up the street.

Emily reached up and wiped some snow off Christopher's forehead. She kissed him and after a moment, she said, "Are you really friends with Purvis?"

He nodded.

"You never said."

"We both collect stamps is all, but he's a good guy."

"He's drunk tonight."

"Maybe, but so's everybody else in town."

They began to walk again. The street was empty except for Fielder and Pat. They were throwing snow and running up the hill toward the school. He felt awkward suddenly. He and Emily had never played. "Are we too serious?"

"Why?"

"We never play."

"You want to?"

"I guess not, or we would."

She held up her fists, but he grabbed them and put them back down by her sides. They were close again, and he kissed her. "I guess that's the reason."

"We kissed that first time on Christmas day." They liked remembering; that was a kind of play.

"I wanted to touch you before that."

"You did. My hair and my face, the first time we came home from skating."

"I didn't think about anything else after that."

"Just your skis and your saxophone."

"You said you were jealous of Gabe. Are you?"

She shook her head, and pulled away from him so they could walk again. Fielder and Pat had disappeared. They ran then, and crossed over to Liverpool Street and walked out of breath up the hill to the school. Why the school? He held Emily's hand and pulled her across the roadway to the back entrance because he could see Fielder and Pat there. Fielder was boosting her through the window next to the woodpile. She went backwards, feet-first, and disappeared until only her mitts were visible. "Oh my God," she said, and had to let go. Then: "Okay, who's next?"

"Emily," Fielder said.

"Why? What're we doing?" she asked.

"Why not? No one's going to be here tonight, that's for sure." Fielder made a stirrup of his hands. "Come on, sister will help you."

This was very sudden, and it was a different kind of play. "Sure," he said to Emily. "We can do it." He steadied her while she stepped into his hands. On the ledge, she turned as Pat had and backed through the window. Christopher climbed in, and followed. They were in the storeroom, and it was dark. Fielder lit a match and they turned to find the door only three feet away. He twisted the knob on the Yale lock, and they all walked out into the entranceway at the bottom of the south stairs.

The match died, and in the dark Pat said, "Yeah, good question."

"Which one?"

"What're we doing here?"

"Come on up. We can make a bonfire in Grandison's office."

"Oh no you don't. Gimme your matches." Pat's voice was serious.

Fielder loved it. He ran up the stairs. They could see him move against the streetlight that shone in through classroom windows above them. They went up too and found him in Blenkin's room at the desk. He pulled open its centre drawer and here in the stronger light they saw him pull the class register out.

"So, what are you doing?" Pat's voice sounded as if she were talking to someone stupid.

"I think I'll mark myself present for the rest of the year."

"Then he'll know who's been here."

"All right. I'll mark Waterton in."

"Great," Christopher said. "Who needs to deal with him until June?"

"Fielder," Pat said. She took the register from him. "This isn't fun." She shivered. "I'm getting cold."

Fielder opened the drawer again. "Sure," he said, his voice a little concerned.

She put the book back into the drawer. "I've got snow-water running down the middle of my back."

Fielder took her hand. "The furnace room," he said. "Barney keeps it real warm there." He took her hand and dragged her away.

"Do you hate Blenkin?" Emily asked.

"Yes, in a way."

"It didn't seem so bad this afternoon when it happened. Was Purvis telling the truth?"

"About the jump? He lost a bet on me with Fielder. Fifty cents."

"Four feet's a long way. Maybe he meant four inches."

"What's the difference? Four feet, four inches. Knight's old man was there with him. Blenkin couldn't—"

"Cheat?"

"Why would he?" That felt like the right question.

"I don't know."

"Neither do I. Anyway, they gave it to Lester. I guess that's legal."

After a moment, she said, "Which one's your desk?"

He showed her, and she sat in it and folded her hands on its slanted surface. He could see it was how she sat at her own desk. Her silhouette in the half-light from outside was bulky, square in her winter clothes. Her pretty face looked toward Blenkin's desk.

"Maybe next year you'll be the one he wants to win," she said.

"I might not jump next year."

"Because of today?"

"Not really. But I told him I wouldn't."

"Did you?" She got up. "What did he say?"
"Nothing. You know that grin of his."
She nodded but didn't laugh with him. "It's stupid not to like you. He doesn't have to do that to get his own way. He can do anything he wants. He's a teacher."
"It's my old man."
"The School Board?"
"And my mother's on the Parent-Teacher's," he said.
"So's mine."
"But she's not modern. My mother's modern. It's a real pain. She wants the strap banned."
"She'll never get them to do it. Why try it?"
"Why? Because Littler strapped me the third day I was in school here."
She picked up his hands in hers and looked at them as if the strap marks might still be on them. "Poor Chris."
"It's a long time ago," he told her, but it wasn't, it was as near as the stirred-up memory.
"I've never had the strap."
"The only girl I knew who got it was May Kaplik."
"She's pretty tough, though. She does it with men."
"Who says?"
"Pat."
"Did she see her?"
"Of course not, but everybody knows." She reached up and kissed him. "We're not supposed to be here," she said. "I don't want to get caught. She took his hand and led him out of the room into the hallway. "Do you have a favourite teacher?"
"Not really. Miss Lee, I guess. But she expects me to be good at English. That's a pain too."
"Which room's Miss Lee's? Maybe I'll get her for homeroom next year."
"Maybe she won't be here. She's a traveller. That's what she said."
He led her down the stairs. At the bottom, Emily stopped, and he pointed left. "The furnace room's there."
"I wonder what they're doing?"
He laughed. "Yeah, I wonder."
"She's sure different now."
"I figured all that talk was just a cover-up for wanting a boyfriend." He pushed at the door; it opened; a light was on, and inside on two chairs near the furnace were Pat's boots, stockings, and skirt. He drew

back. Emily didn't. He watched her stare into the room, past the furnace to where the end of Barney's single cot could be seen. Lamb talked about doing it with Marcie Johnson there.

He could see Pat's bare feet. Fielder still had his boots on. He reached, pulled the door closed, and turned to Emily.

"What'll we do?" she asked.

"Wait."

She nodded and looked distracted. "I can't go back without her. We're supposed to be together."

He sat down on the stairs. She sat beside him, stiff. But in a while she leaned close to him, and he put his arm around her again. When he kissed her, he could taste salt. "Are you crying?"

She nodded, and began to sob through a kind of laughter.

"What's the matter?"

"I don't know. That's my sister in there."

"He might as well be my brother."

"It's a shock." Her voice sounded like her mother's.

He wanted to touch her. "Don't worry."

"No?"

"No." He unbuttoned her coat and slid his hand inside. She shivered. "They're only lying on the bed," he told her. "They probably never even necked before."

She drew back and wiped her eyes. "Knock on the door Christopher. We're going to be late at the dance."

"Do I have to? They'll be out soon."

"Please. Do it."

He got up and banged on the door as if it might be in fun. "Okay, you guys, time to chaperone us again." There was no real answer, but he thought he heard the sound of boots hitting the cement on the far side of the furnace. He went back to the stairs and sat beside Emily. She leaned close again, and kissed his neck and cheek, and held his hand so she could squeeze it tight. In a moment, there were voices in the furnace room. Then laughter and a little scream.

The door opened, and Pat's face was illuminated by the furnace room's light. She was grinning. "Come look at me," she said to Emily. "Am I okay?" She turned and brushed the back of her skirt with her hands.

"Your hair's a mess."

"Never mind. It always is."

Emily went to her, and Christopher saw them looking at each other in a way he hadn't witnessed before.

Fielder arrived, and Pat laughed. Emily hugged her sister, and he watched as if he'd come upon a strange ceremony. He reached back inside the door and switched off the light. In the immediate blackness no one moved, then Fielder said, "We don't need to go out the window. The door'll lock behind us." He led the way, holding Pat's hand and pulling her behind him.

Christopher tested the door to see that it had locked and turned to see Pat kissing Fielder. She was holding his face between the palms of her hands as if they were a vice, and he had his arms around her waist. It was a kiss for a birthday or for Christmas, quick and firm. "Got to go," she said. "Mother'll be frantic."

They walked then, not fast—no running, no angels in the snow—two young couples going to the Carnival Ball. Christopher held Emily close, needing to do it, and listened to Fielder and Pat talk as they went down Liverpool Street and then on to Eighth Avenue.

The snow had stopped and the temperature was dropping. "God, I hope we make it," Pat said. "If we don't it'll be your fault, Fielder. At the funeral, they won't even bring your coffin into the church."

"You're sick," Fielder said. "Why don't you wear more clothes?"

"Women can't. Not to parties."

"Jazz pants," Emily said suddenly. "Mother wears them out at night."

"Jazz pants?" Fielder was laughing.

"She knits them, big wool on big needles," Pat said. "They come down to her knees, and when she gets to a party she whips them off and puts them in her coat pocket."

"I think you should get some," Fielder said.

"Why?"

"One more thing to see."

"You've seen enough already, big boy."

"Hush," Emily said, as if she hadn't meant to.

"Hush yourself."

"Does everything you do have to get a gold star?"

"Oh, God, I hope so," Pat said. "I'm cold. Let's run." She jogged a few paces, then turned and ran backwards along the sidewalk.

A car came toward them, the beams of its headlights swaying as it bounced through the ruts of the unploughed street. It veered over and pulled as close to the sidewalk as the snowdrift there would let it. The sign on the door said Bush Taxi.

"Teddy Bush," Fielder said. "I bet he's been busy tonight."

The porch lights went on at the house where the cab had parked.

"That's where Lee lives, isn't it?" Fielder said. "Where's *she* going?"

It was a tiny house, with a veranda that ran along two sides of it, and with a roof whose slant was so steep that it had very little snow on it.

Its door opened and Miss Lee appeared there without a coat on. She waved her hand as if it were a gesture she was unsure of, and then called out, "Mr. Bush, Mr. Bush, please, could you come in?"

But Teddy had his window closed against the cold and thought she was only gesturing to wait.

Christopher stopped at her gate and faced her down the length of her short walkway.

"Is that you, Christopher?"

"Yes."

"Could you get Mr. Bush to come in. I need help."

He turned and knocked on the window. "She needs help." Teddy looked annoyed, and began to get out of his big old Terraplane.

Miss Lee called again: "Christopher."

He turned around. Fielder and Pat were near the corner of her fence. Pat was jogging on the spot. They both waved at her. Emily hadn't moved.

"Christopher, it's your friend Purvis." She stopped.

"What's wrong?"

"I don't know. He's sick."

Teddy was passing him on the way to the porch. "Do you want me to help too?"

"Please, would you?" Again she hesitated, and even in her dim porch light she looked both concerned and fearful. "Just you," she said. "He doesn't need a crowd right now."

"What's going on?" Fielder asked, in a low voice. "He was drunk last time we saw him."

"No, he wasn't," Christopher said.

Emily held his arm. "I'll wait."

"You'll freeze."

'I'm with you, Christopher. Aren't I?"

"Yes. Look, it's just getting Purvis to the taxi. I'll catch up."

"Miss Lee can help," Emily said, almost harsh.

"Please? Purvis might be really sick." He squeezed her arm and saw her face trying to give in to this new event. She nodded and turned to go with Fielder and Pat. He ran after Teddy to the house.

Purvis wasn't in the front room. Neither was Miss Lee. He and Teddy waited, and in a moment she came out of another room and gestured for them to go into it. Purvis was lying on a bed that had a ruffled spread on it. He lay on his side, and his head was resting on one of the two pillows. On the other pillow there was blood.

"What's the matter with him?" Teddy asked.

Miss Lee stood by Purvis and bent over him. "John," she said, and took his hand away from his mouth. It held a handkerchief that also had blood on it. She kneeled on the bed.

"What's going on here?" Teddy's small voice was querulous.

"He's sick."

"I can see that. He's been in a fight."

"He needs a doctor. The blood's not from fighting, I don't think."

"Can he walk?"

"He walked here," she said.

"Why?" Teddy's voice was sharp.

Miss Lee stood up. "I don't know. We had a talk once." She gestured. "Christopher was there. He brought him." She bent over the bed again. "Your friend Christopher's here, John. I want you to get up now."

Purvis shook his head slightly. "Stay," he said, and coughed again.

She stood by the bed once more. Teddy moved to grab Purvis' arm, but she stopped him. "Christopher," she said, as if they were in a classroom. "I think he's sick. I've phoned Dr. Royce, at the hospital. Mrs. Shaw's just had her baby. He said he'd wait."

"I haven't got all night," Teddy said. "I think he's drunk and somebody beat him up." He looked at her. "What's a schoolteacher doing mixed up in a thing like this?"

"Nothing, Mr. Bush. He came here for help."

"Whyn't he go home?"

"I don't think he feels welcome there." Miss Lee's voice was strung out now, thin and desperate. She held Teddy from leaving. "Christopher, talk to him."

He went to the bed. "Purvis, what's going on?"

Purvis gave him a weak smile. His lips and teeth had blood on them. "I don't know."

"Fight?"

"Yeah, that too."

"You didn't—?"

"Sure, I told you I was. And then this started."

"You're getting blood all over the place."

He coughed for a long time, and pulled his knees up to his chest, as if he were trying to relieve pain. "Yeah," he said, when it was over, "like you said, I should've looked after this thing."

"Miss Lee can't do anything for you."

"It's a nice bed." Purvis rolled over onto his back. "That goddamn bench at Howard's was killing me."

"You drunk?" Teddy asked, loud.

"I had a couple, Teddy. What's it to you?"

"Who's paying for this trip?"

"How much is it?" Miss Lee asked.

"Two dollars."

"That's far too much."

"Not tonight it isn't. Why don't you call his dad?"

"He should go to the hospital."

"Two dollars. Take it or leave it."

Purvis sat up. "Who you talking to, Bush?"

"Not you, Rink Rat. Are you coming or not?"

Christopher steadied Purvis. "Take it easy. Let's just go."

"Not with him."

"You got to."

"I'll break his driving arm."

"Tomorrow," Christopher told him. He could smell rye on his breath now.

Miss Lee was taking money out of her purse. She separated two dollar bills and came across the room to Purvis. She handed him the money. He looked at it and then at her. She stared back at him. "That's all I can do for you, John. The help you need's at the hospital."

"Will you visit if they keep me?"

"You go now and I will."

"Do I have to ride with Bush?"

"I'd phone and get my dad, but everyone's at the dance," Christopher said.

"Are you coming with me, Waterton?"

"If you want me to."

"It's hot in here."

"I think you may have a fever," Miss Lee said. She had his jacket in her hands now and helped him on with it. "Do you feel very weak?"

"Just a little." He turned and looked down at her. "You got pretty hair," he said. He raised his arms as if he were going to hug her, but the coughing began again.

Teddy was gone. Christopher held Purvis' arm and steered him, still hacking, to the door.

"Thank you, Christopher," Miss Lee said. "I'm glad you happened along."

Teddy gunned the Terraplane's motor, threatening to leave.

"Okay," Christopher said to both of them. Miss Lee smiled, and he moved Purvis out along the walkway. He coughed some more, and when he got to the taxi he spat onto its dirty windshield. Teddy didn't bother to notice the long thin line of frozen blood streaking it from top to bottom.

When they were in the back seat and Bush had the Terraplane in motion, he said, "Rink Rat, loverboy," and laughed. "You can never tell about those old-maid schoolteachers."

"Shut up," Purvis told him. "You don't know a damned thing. She's not old."

"I bet she ain't a maiden either. If I was spitting blood I wouldn't be talking so damned tough."

"Don't talk at all," Christopher said to Purvis, under the sound of the motor and the tire-chains. He felt afraid and didn't know why. He was also excited and knew that was the wrong thing to be. He sat by the frosted window in the dim light and watched Purvis—thinking, I knew you were sick. I told you to watch it. You're a damned fool for not going home. They'd have to look after you.

"Why'd you have to fight him?"

"Best thing I ever did."

He had to ask, "Did you tell him it was because you lost the bet on me?" He felt ashamed for asking.

Purvis shook his head. "I was having too much fun." Laughter made him cough again, and then he lay back down against the seat. "I did it," he said, quietly, and then he blew his nose into the bloody handkerchief.

"How?" Christopher asked, needing to know.

"I just walked up to him and looked worried and important. You know, like you got a message from God. He wasn't dancing. He never dances. He just stands there chewing his lip and shoving his thumb up his ass. He thinks it's his duty to go everywhere and look stupid."

After a while, Christopher asked, "He just followed you out?"

"No. When I got his attention, I put an elbow in his gut and called him a couple of names. Then when we got to the alley I hit him so goddamn hard I thought I'd killed him." Purvis laughed, and liquid gurgled in his throat. "I was afraid it was all over, but it wasn't, because then the fight started for real, and it went on until there was nothing left. He was crawling around in the snow, and so was I."

"He'll have you arrested."

"No he won't. He went the distance. If he was going to call the cops he would've run first hit. And anyway, I kept saying Garrett's name: I hear you been doing experiments in the lab. It made him wild. Me too. Best thing I ever did."

"Front entrance," Teddy said. "Two dollars."

Purvis tossed the money into the front seat. "I'd have you wait, but the hospital don't want this stinking rattletrap of yours in its yard any more than it can help."

"Thanks. Rat."

"Rink Rat to you, Bush."

Teddy laughed. It was sudden. He picked up the money and looked at it. "Two dollars is two dollars."

"Especially for a thirty-five cent ride."

"Okay, whatever it is, get well and get out."

Christopher opened the door. Teddy swung around in his seat and stared at him. "Does she also go for boys your age? Or is it anything in pants? Maybe I should drop around too."

Dr. Royce's face appeared at the opened door. "Does he need help?"

"I don't feel so pretty good," Purvis said.

"Can you get out? What are you doing here, Christopher?"

"Yeah, I can get out." Purvis leaned on the front seat. And as he did so, he grabbed Bush's ear and twisted it. "You talk about her around town and I'll know who did it, Teddy. I'll kill you."

Teddy pulled away. Dr. Royce's voice was commanding. "Get out, John Purvis. Are you drunk or sick?"

Christopher pulled Purvis out of the car and let him lean against it.

"Drunk, I think," Dr. Royce said.

"No." Christopher wondered if his voice carried the four feet between him and the doctor. "He's coughing blood."

Purvis slid down onto the cement slab that served the entranceway. He looked up puzzled into Dr. Royce's face. "Weak," he said.

"There was a fight. It's what maybe brought it on," Christopher said, and bent with the doctor to help Purvis up.

"I see."

"He's had the cough for months."

They got Purvis through the door. Miss Baker, the night supervisor, was there. Her wooden leg bumped and creaked down the five stairs from the main floor level. She'd been a front line nurse in the war. She said nothing. Never did. His mother said the war had taken her fiancé, and her need to make small talk. She'd been known to slap women who cried during childbirth. She didn't mind screams, but crying was weak. Christopher gave Purvis' arm to her and followed them up the stairs to the lobby. Miss Baker had brought a gurney.

"Up," Dr. Royce said.

Purvis leaned across it while the other two held it steady. He bent farther down and put his face on its pillow. In another moment, he rolled slowly onto its white surface. A little blood trickled out of his mouth.

"Now," Dr. Royce said, "what *are* you doing here, Christopher?"

"We were walking along Eighth," he began, and wished he hadn't said the street name. "Emily Gordon and me and her sister and Fielder."

"Going to the dance."

"Yes. I'm his friend. I wanted to help get him here."

Purvis was lying on the gurney, smiling. "Damned good friend too. We collect stamps."

"Do you?" Dr. Royce said. "Well, we'll be a while here. Why don't you go back to the dance?"

"I'd like to stay."

"What about Emily?" The doctor was smiling. He knew about them too.

He thought about her, but the answer was simple. "She's with Pat and her parents. She was going home with them anyhow. I'd like to know what's the matter with John."

"So would I," Purvis said.

"Do as you please." The doctor signalled Miss Baker to wheel Purvis away through swinging doors that were on the right of the nursing station. "What kind of friends are you with John Purvis, Christopher?"

"Good," he said, puzzled by the question. "Why?"

"He doesn't ask you to do—peculiar things?"

He'd never been embarrassed by Dr. Royce before. "Purvis isn't a homo."

Dr. Royce nodded his head once, and his voice made a soft Aaah-sound. "I just thought I should ask."

"Why?"

"What happened tonight? Do you know?" Dr. Royce asked.

"I didn't see anything. Purvis tells the truth. You ask him."

"All right. I will."

Christopher sat on a bench down the hallway from the desk and waited. Purvis was sick. There was no doubt of that, but he'd also told Blenkin that he knew about Garrett in the lab. He sat trying not to think what might happen and felt sick himself.

He watched the nurse working on files. Or maybe they were bills. Everyone was terrified of going to the hospital because of how much it cost. A baby, he knew, cost thirty-five dollars for the doctor and two dollars a day for ten days in the ward upstairs in maternity. Five dollars a day for a private room. Mrs. Shaw had a baby every year and stayed two weeks. She said it was her holiday. The Shaws had a maid, a girl from the country they paid ten dollars a month and room and board. Along with the worry about Blenkin, there was also the problem of Purvis' parents having to pay for John's being here.

Miss Baker had come out of the examining room and had picked up the phone. He watched her talk into it and then wait a long time. The nurse at the desk spoke to her, and she leaned down to see the paper that was being held out to her. In a moment, she spoke again into the phone and then hung up. He sat and stared at the opposite wall. The thing he didn't want to think about kept returning. Maybe Blenkin was badly enough hurt that he wouldn't bother to think about what Purvis had said about him and Garrett—which was nonsense. He wouldn't think of anything else, and he'd know who had told Purvis: Christopher Boker Waterton.

It was cold in the hallway. A small draft came down it from the old men's ward at one end and flowed to the old women's at the other. He got up and walked down toward the women's end. When he turned, he saw Miss Baker go into the old men's ward. In a moment, the doors swung open and Miss Baker and a nurse named Clotier, who was from Montreal, came through pushing a gurney with a basket on it. They walked together, and Miss Clotier wheeled the gurney through the doors where Purvis had disappeared. Miss Baker stayed by the desk.

"What's that?" he asked her.

She looked at him, her grey eyes solid like plates. "It isn't the laundry," she said, and turned again to the nurse on duty.

"A body?" he asked, but she didn't reply.

He felt suddenly crazy, as if he were watching accidents. And Emily. She was alone, waiting. He'd told her he'd catch up. He said her name out loud. The nurse at the desk looked at him. Miss Baker was no longer there. He closed his eyes and breathed in deeply. He'd said I Love You, and his mother had said he looked noble. He wondered if he looked insane now. He wanted to get past the accidents and go to Emily, but he didn't know yet what was wrong with Purvis. He went toward the desk.

The doors swung open again and Dr. Royce appeared. He looked as if he might just now be getting over a surprise. He took Christopher's arm and walked him to the door.

"That basket," Christopher said. "Did someone die?"

He had to know.

"Yes. Old Tom Mulligan."

"You just put him in a basket—because he's poor?"

"No. Not that, Christopher. It's just until morning when Mr. Dunphy will pick the body up."

"Why did he die?"

Dr. Royce smiled. "Old Tom? Boredom, I think. His heartbeat was still under sixty."

"Did he have a small heart?"

"You remember that, do you? I expect he did. Prospectors could be the biggest dreamers of us all."

"Purvis?" Christopher asked. "Is he—?"

"No, his heart's a big floppy one—"

"I meant, what's wrong?"

"T.B. Tuberculosis. There'll have to be a test, but it looks pretty straightforward."

"It's bad?"

"Hard to tell."

"But he's coughing blood. That's bad, isn't it?"

"Let's look on the bright side, Christopher. It may be only one part of a lung that's damaged. It doesn't have to be more than that to bleed a fair amount."

"He played basketball last night, and had a fight tonight."

"Short of breath, too, he tells me. But coughing up blood isn't necessarily a result of the fight. He would've done it anyway."

"Can you get him better?"

Dr. Royce put his hands in his pockets. He was over fifty and grey now, and he looked tired. It was nearly midnight. "I don't know. We've got a lot of hocus-pocus we prescribe. Bedrest, high and dry climate. I'm not sure it does any good. I've seen X-rays of lungs with scars big enough to prove to me that some very serious T.B. has just got better with no help at all."

"But why is he so weak all of a sudden?"

"Half a bottle of rye is certainly a part of it."

Outside, Teddy Bush's taxi pulled up alongside the entrance. The door opened and Dick Purvis got out, and a moment later Mary Purvis stood with him. She took his arm, not to be escorted by him but to help him up the stairs and into the lobby. He was trying very hard not to stagger and held himself so stiff that his chin rested on his adam's apple and his chest stuck out like a pouter-pigeon's. His wife had a handkerchief in her left hand, and she was weeping. Christopher watched them wrestle with the door. The struggle made Mr. Purvis angry. He flung himself away from his wife. "Where is he? Where is that boy of mine?"

"I'm sure Dr. Royce has him safe, Dick. Good evening, Dr. Royce."

"Is he bad off? I mean, what happened?"

Dr. Royce held up a hand to stop them talking. "He's resting. I had Miss Baker page you at the dance because it seemed the best thing to do. We should move him to a private room. He must be isolated."

"I don't understand," Dick Purvis said. "I thought he was just beat up. Is he sick?"

"A private room," his wife said, in a weak voice.

"He's sick. He coughs blood. We'll do tests to make sure, but I think there's little doubt it's T.B."

"T—who? That boy's as healthy as they come."

"When was the last time you saw John?" Dr. Royce's voice was abrupt and demanded attention.

Dick Purvis leaned against the nursing station desk and looked bewildered.

"He was always so independent—just wouldn't come home no matter how a person pleaded," Mary Purvis said. She looked distressed, and wiped her eyes with her handkerchief. "This is so sudden. What are we to do?" Her southern American accent was very strong.

"We'll do everything that needs to be done." Dr. Royce turned to the nursing desk. "Miss Cline will give you a form to sign. He tells me he's seventeen. We'll need your consent for medical procedures."

"Sure," Dick Purvis said. "It's like Mary said, we've had a hard time keeping tabs on John."

"A private room's out of the question," Mary said, suddenly. "A public ward will be sufficient."

"Isolation is necessary."

"For how long, may I ask?"

"Until we can get him a bed at Tranquille."

"Tranquille, what's that?"

"The T.B. hospital at Kamloops."

"We simply can't afford it."

"It's free, Mrs. Purvis. And perhaps Dick can drive him down when we're ready to send him."

Dick waved his hand on the end of a limp wrist. "Sure, it's *only* two hundred miles."

"Christopher, I think you should go back to the dance now. Your friends will be waiting."

"Can I see John?"
"No, that would be dangerous."
"Can't see him?" Dick asked.
"Of course you and Mrs. Purvis can. We'll take special precautions."
Christopher went to the door and looked back when he opened it. He'd never seen Dr. Royce's face disturbed before. "John will have a private room," he said. "He needs it. He may be as big as any man in town, but he's young, legally an infant, and he's your responsibility. Now, I want no fuss about this, Dick. He may be here a few days, and as for the money—" Christopher saw the doctor's eyes blink and then stare at the Purvises—"you can give up a few quarts of rye."
"Now, just a darn minute, there," Dick said.
"Christopher," Dr. Royce said, pointing.
"We don't have to take that from you," Mary Purvis said. "We can pull John out of here this minute if we want."
"I'm afraid you can't. He's got T.B. It's not a private matter anymore."
"Then let them who're making it a public matter do the paying. He's a bad boy, an evil boy, Dr. Royce, and he brought it on himself."
"Now, Mary, honey, he's not *evil*."
"I tried to love that boy. I did. You know I did."
Dr. Royce came to the door. "Christopher, you do as I say."
"Will he die?"
"He may."
Stiff in a coffin: it was a useless, hopeless, withering image over which Mary Purvis' face was suspended.
"I hope you'll be happy," he said, loud.
Dr. Royce was holding the door wide open for him to go.
Mrs. Purvis' face was pale. "Is that the Waterton boy? What are you doing here?"
"He came with John," Dr. Royce said. He looked more tired than ever now.
"I suppose this'll be all over town soon," she said. "Not one word, you hear? I'll do the telling when the time comes."
He felt Dr. Royce's hand push him onto the outside stairs. "He's slept on a bench at the rink all winter."
Dr. Royce's nod was curt, and he let the door close behind him. "Stay out of family matters."
"He could die. You said so."
The doctor sighed. "All right, Christopher. Come see me, perhaps Monday, and we can talk this out."

"No."

"Suit yourself."

"They should be—"

"What?"

"Arrested." He wanted them to hear.

The doctor smiled. "It would be good, wouldn't it, if it were that simple?"

Christopher wanted to go now, but he heard himself ask, "Why are they so stupid? Purvis is the best guy in town."

"He's going to be all right."

"If he's going to be treated like that, why bother?"

"I'm sorry about this," Dr. Royce said. "It was wrong of me not to ask you to go the moment they arrived."

"I'm glad you were with Mrs. Shaw so you could wait for John."

"So am I. Now, let this be among ourselves."

Christopher nodded and turned away. On the sidewalk down Doncaster Road he looked up into the sky. The weather had cleared. The stars were faint and there was no moon. It was colder now than he'd felt it in weeks. March 11th. The days were nearly equal light and dark, and still there were no signs of spring. Two hundred inches of snow. Purvis might've made it if he'd had a better winter. He thought how it hurt not to belong, to find out suddenly one day that you didn't. Never in so many words, though. An elbow sharp in your gut: a shoulder pushing. *When we got to the alley, I hit him so goddamn hard I thought I'd killed him*. Why not do that? You don't belong at home. You don't belong at school. Not even downtown. How did he hit him? Where? One blow with everything in it. And then the blood from your lungs is a protection from them doing anything more to you. At least you're doing it to yourself. Your own body is saying, No matter what, you can't beat them.

"But Jesus, Purvis," he said out loud, "how does a good guy like you get crapped on like this?" He was deliberately going along Eighth Avenue to pass Miss Lee's house. There was a light on inside. He didn't care if it was only a night light. He pounded on the door and waited for her to come and let him in as if there were no doubt that she would, and would welcome him too. Her eyes were swollen, and the hair that Purvis had called pretty was tangled and mussed.

"How is he?" she asked, and held his sleeve to pull him in beyond the door.

He stood in front of her and saw how upset she was. He couldn't stop it, he began to cry. His tears and sobs were suddenly there between them. Through the blur he saw her face, and her hands in front of it fending him off. How could a teacher look so young?

"Is he dead?"

He could hear what she was thinking. Of course she knew about the fight: Blenkin. Purvis would've been delighted to tell her. She was a teacher too. He had to reach out for her, and he touched the fists in front of her face. He was shivering now, and he answered her through clenched teeth. "No, he's okay."

"All that blood. He's very sick."

"Yes, but Dr. Royce says he might have a chance."

She took her hands away from his and went into her kitchen. When she spoke again, her voice was composed. "Thank you for coming back to tell me. I needed to know that much at least. Do you want coffee?"

"Yes."

"Come in here then, Christopher."

He went to her, still with tears running down his nose, but the sobs were under control. She'd been drinking coffee. The pot was half full and warm on the kitchen range. He still felt as if he were pounding on her door and wanting to disturb her. "Did you—?" But the rest of the words wouldn't come.

She poured coffee. "Don't think anything more about this than you absolutely must, Christopher." The English teacher had surfaced in her once more.

"Why?"

"Because there isn't much about it that makes sense."

"You cried too," he said, and realized he was wiping his nose with the back of his hand. "You cried because of *something*, didn't you?" Then he knew what he wanted to say. "I hope you liked him?"

"Yes."

He waited for more, but that was all. The one word answered both questions.

"It's a shock," she said, and handed him his coffee. "I only saw him a couple of times."

"He didn't come other times? He would, you know. Purvis was like that if he wanted something."

She sat at her tiny kitchen table and gestured for him to sit too. "You know I could be in trouble for this. Teddy Bush will tell what he saw—John Purvis in my house. On my bed."

"He came to your house for help."

She drank her coffee down in three harsh swallows. "I shouldn't have told you that." Then she smiled, as if to reassure him. "This has been a terrible night for you, hasn't it? Some kind of accident that began happening when you walked by here at the right moment." She leaned forward on her elbows. "It isn't over. It won't be until it finishes in its own good time. Try to remember, you're only a witness."

She knew about accidents too. He leaned on the table.

"He's my friend. Better than Fielder, in a way."

She smoothed back her hair, combed it with the fingers of both hands. "Christopher," she said, "you're a good student. I believe you already know how to think. Some of us are cursed too early with that ability. Try to use it to make life easier for yourself if you can. John Purvis is not a tragedy. He's somehow helpless. And so am I. We're weeping now, and I don't think we only weep at tragedies. At least, I don't think we do." She got up from the table. "If you knew how pathetic it really is."

"Tell me."

"The more it is, the less it's worth worrying about."

"He might die."

"That's pathetic too, not having the strength to choose when to do it."

The tears were gone, and the anger he'd been afraid of arrived. "That's rotten. You don't like him, and everybody wants to wreck things. What'd he do to Mary, or his dad? Or Blenkin and Mr. Grandison? All he did is ask—I don't know, something. But everybody judges. You do. His stepmother said he was *evil*. Where'd she get that from? You say he's pathetic, whatever the hell that means. Coming down here I figured what Blenkin was saying every day to him: You're nobody. But he's Purvis. A guy." He stopped. Her face had no expression on it. She wasn't listening.

"It's very late, way after midnight," she said.

"That's the other thing you do."

"What?"

"All of you. After you've judged, or you get in a corner. It's too late, you say, or, we won't talk about that any more right now—which means never."

"I'm not all the adults in the world, Christopher. I'm just a guy, too."

"Why did you say that about him? What's it supposed to mean?"

"We all look for ways out."

"You just don't want to be—caught?"

"I could've told him to go, but I called the cab, and by doing it I might've given him my job." Her voice was quiet, but it yelled at him.

He didn't want her to be angry. "Okay," he said, and walked away into the other room. He felt weak, but it was the only thing he could do.

"Emily will be waiting for you." Her voice had lost its edge.

He turned. She was smiling.

"You two," she said. "Lucky boy." She held out her hand. He took it, and she leaned forward and pecked him on the cheek. "Thanks for coming back to tell me about John."

He went to the door. "Will you really be in trouble?"

"This is a very small town."

"If you tell the whole story, just as it happened?"

"Oh, I'll do that, all right."

"They'll understand then."

She laughed, and reached around him to open the door. "Now, when I open it, you run out. It's below zero. Be careful."

She pulled on the knob. The door cracked and its hinges squealed from the cold. He went quickly out onto the porch and stood there alone. The air was dry and frigid. When he breathed, it hurt. All around him, as he walked, smoke from chimneys rose rigid, straight up toward the small hard stars in the sky. He thought about Purvis lying in a bed in a room alone, and about the empty bench at the rink. Is that what she meant by pathetic? Something that made you smile sadly? When people are in trouble, you are angry for a moment, and then you smile sadly.

He turned onto London Street and headed toward the dance. Because he wasn't there, Emily's mother would be pleased. Then he remembered he'd left his horn under the bandstand. It could be stolen. More trouble. He began to run, and when he got to the Royal, he searched for the saxophone first and found it safe. Then he looked for Emily, but she was gone, and so were Pat and Fielder.

He walked around the hall again to make sure, refusing to talk to anyone and seeing in his head a picture of Emily standing alone and waiting. It hurt. How had Purvis and then Miss Lee taken over the whole night? Emily had come to him behind the bandstand after he'd played and had let him lean on her until it must have hurt. Now she would have to be asked to say okay to the rest of her bad day. It was unfair. He didn't want that. The sharp edge of the craziness he'd felt at the hospital cut at his ability to think straight.

He stood near the bandstand and forced himself to listen to Gabe blow "My Funny Valentine."

The crowd shuffled easy around the dancefloor. He thought about

"I'm Confessin'." The hard ball of notes was still in his head. His stomach felt weightless, as if there was a hole beneath his ribcage.

His parents weren't dancing, and they weren't in the sparse group along the wall. He was glad they'd gone home and might even be asleep by the time he got there. Explaining might bring on real nausea. He headed out the back entrance to the alley.

He walked fast and hoped his cheeks and nose wouldn't freeze. Halfway home he began to feel sleepy. It was funny. It made him laugh. This was what happened to people when they started to freeze to death. He thought about lying in a snowdrift and floating away into sleep and then into black nothing forever. It was probably not much different from bleeding to death. But he wasn't either bleeding or freezing.

CHAPTER SIX

1

WHEN HE WOKE HE KNEW HE WAS SICK AND THAT HIS ROOM wasn't as cold as it usually was. From outside, he could hear a wind in the jack pines, and when he got out of bed to go to the bathroom he could see their branches swaying and snow falling from them. He stood in front of the mirror and shivered. His face was pale, and it was wrinkled on one cheek where he'd lain on the folds of a blanket. He didn't have a sore throat, or pains in his chest, or a headache and fever, but he was sick. He leaned with both hands on the basin and felt as if there were pieces of heavy metal grinding sharp against his muscles. It was difficult to move, not because he couldn't, but because he didn't want to. In his head was a picture of Purvis lying on the gurney, blood on his lips. *I tried to love that boy. You know I did.*

Out loud, he said, "It would be awful if you really did and couldn't show him."

"Christopher, who are you talking to?"

"Myself," he said. He opened the door and his mother was there, a bit pale, too, but smiling.

"Is there something the matter?"

"I don't feel so good," he said, and moved past her into his room again.

She followed him. "What is it?"

He got into bed and pulled the covers up around him. "I don't know."

He lay feeling safe, while she felt his forehead and asked him all the questions he'd already asked himself.

"I think you were drinking last night."

"No."

She sat on the bed, and his father appeared at the door. "Christopher, you weren't at the dance."

"Yes, I was." The nausea was returning. "I'm sick to my stomach."

"We saw Emily there," his mother said.

"She went with her parents." He didn't want to talk about Purvis. He got out of bed again. "I think I'm going to be sick." They let him go, and he closed the bathroom door behind him. The sickness didn't make sense. He kneeled in front of the toilet and waited. All that was wrong with him was that he hadn't slept well. There'd been dreams he couldn't remember, except they'd been sharp-edged. Crisp. Like fever dreams, or ones that came because there'd been pain in his body. He'd turned and tossed.

His stomach wasn't going to heave. The sickness had an edge on it too, but it also had weight. He felt heavier than he'd ever been, as if the earth's gravity had doubled during the night. He got to his feet and leaned against the window. It had pebbled glass halfway up it, and a clear pane the rest of the way. The frost was gone from it. The weather had broken. The wind out there was a Chinook, coming in over the mountains to the west and all the way from the warm southern sea. In a while the icicles that had formed during the last melt would begin to drop, and the drift against the white picket fence would shrink. Maybe after that, spring would start to come.

He wanted to be well.

"Are you all right, Christopher?"

He told them Yes. The bathroom was the one place in the house where no one could pursue him.

Except Sarah.

"I have to go," she said, not sounding at all as if she really did.

"Wait," he said.

"I have to."

"No, you don't."

"I'll do it in my pants."

"Stop it," his mother said. "Christopher, I have breakfast—well, brunch, really—all ready. Maybe you could try a little. It may settle your stomach."

She didn't believe he was sick. Sarah began to cry. He jerked himself away from the window and yanked open the door. His father wasn't there, but Sarah stopped crying, and her eyes got very round. So did his mother's. He picked Sarah up, set her on the toilet and closed the door behind him. She shouted and cried again, and ran out of the bathroom and threw her arms around her mother's waist.

"Are you satisfied now?" his mother asked.

"No. I want you to kill her." He hoped his father hadn't heard, and he felt suddenly dizzy. When he got to his bed he sat down and rested his head in his hands. "Just leave me alone."

Sarah was still wailing.

"Sarah, stop it. Why don't you talk about it, Christopher?"

"Because I don't want to. Right now."

"You'd better tell me." She was standing at the door with Sarah by her side.

He decided to get it over with. "Purvis is in the hospital. That's where I was last night. He's probably dying."

"Dying? Don't be silly. What of, for heaven's sake?"

"Tuberculosis."

"And you were with him?"

"Yes."

"How? Why? It's contagious."

He watched her face go fearful. She turned and called out, "Did you hear that Peter?"

He got back into bed and rolled over to face the wall. There were sobs in his gut that he didn't want to have break loose. He lay stiff and waited, hardly breathing. They were talking in the living room. He could hear, but he didn't want to listen. Then his father came and sat on his bed. His voice was flat and demanding.

"Tell me what happened."

"I already told Mother." She was in the room again, and so was Sarah.

"Tell me."

"I was with Purvis. He's got T.B., probably."

"What did you do? I mean, how did it happen that an adult didn't take him to the hospital? His father or mother—they were at the dance."

"She's not his mother." He wished he hadn't said it. "I saw him in the alley out back after I'd finished playing with Gabe." That was the truth. "He was coughing blood. I think he'd been in a fight, but it could've been something inside that was broken. We went to the hospital to see. I waited and waited for Dr. Royce. He said it was T.B. After a while his dad and Mary came."

"You mean Mrs. Purvis."

"Mrs. Purvis came, and I went back to the dance and got my horn. You were gone, so I walked home." It felt good to end with the truth.

"Is he really going to die?" Sarah asked.

"I don't want to think about it," he said, too loud, but that was the truth too. Sarah didn't ask again.

His father got up from the bed. "I think I might call Dr. Royce."

"It's terrible if it's true," his mother said. She sat on the bed. "Is that what's making you ill?"

"Please leave me alone. I hardly got any sleep at all last night."

"I don't wonder." She got up again and said no more. He heard the door close.

Outside, his father said, "Should we call Royce?"

"You know what Dr. Royce will say."

"No."

"That Christopher's healthy and not to worry."

"So was young Purvis healthy."

"He wasn't well looked after."

"No, I suppose not."

He stopped listening and closed his eyes. He didn't want to keep seeing Purvis lying there with blood on his lips. He tried for another picture. Blenkin appeared. *One more word and I'll bar you from competition.* He watched Blenkin look angry, and then he forced Purvis to stand in front of him and hit him in the solar plexus. Blenkin doubled over and vomited onto the snow.

He lay in his bed, going on fifteen years old, not fully grown. When Blenkin stood straight again, he was very tall.

Purvis was there once more, standing in the snow. Blood came out of his mouth in a very long thick red gush. It froze, and Purvis struggled to break it off and pull it out of his mouth, but it was a pole now, a red pole. One end was stuck in Purvis' throat and the other was buried in the snow. His mouth was forced wide, and his lips were shoved back. His cheeks split. The noise he made was a high dying scream, like a train whistle.

It was dusk in his room. The train's whistle was real, and it sounded again across the town as it passed the mile-board east of the bridge, which meant it was ten minutes after five in the afternoon. The insane image of Purvis fighting his frozen blood was strong. His own skin tightened, and he shivered, even though it wasn't cold in his room. He was warm, but the shivers didn't stop. The thought that kept them coming was that he had to get up. If not now, then sometime. The train whistled at the crossing west of the bridge and began to slow for the station. He watched it in his head run the last thousand yards, past the cranberry swamp and Mrs. Kaplik's house, down the long straight mainline tracks, running through switch-frogs, and going slower until the big fifty-five percent hog that pulled the train through the mountains—the biggest steam engine there was—halted and sat making noises that were its own: the bell ringing free, steam valves blowing a kind of exhaustion out into the still air between it and the station. On the other side of the yards, there was the shunt of the new engine coming out of the roundhouse and heading over to the train to relieve the big one still standing there, its great barrel black above its drivewheels, and smoke pushing up into the sky from its stack. The train was connected to the dream: Purvis struggling like a mechanical animal, wailing; and what was going on around him in the house was still buffered by sleep. He drifted again into its darkness and woke once more when the phone rang.

He listened to his mother answer, "Of course," she said. "No bother at all, Mr. Courtney." And then his father said hello, and that was all he said for a long time, until finally: "The Board has its regular meeting tomorrow. We can hear the case then, I suppose. You've phoned Grandison—? Yes, we will, but I'd rather not do this on the phone. Could we meet at your office over the noonhour tomorrow? Yes, but twelve-fifteen would be better."

It didn't surprise him when his father said Miss Lee's name. They were in the kitchen now, and their voices were loud. "Courtney wants the Board to fire Miss Lee."

"Why, for heaven's sake?"

"Something about her and John Purvis."

"Purvis? I don't believe it."

"Bush took him to the hospital from her place."

"I thought Christopher—"

"Yes. Is he awake?"

There was a pause. Christopher sat up on the edge of his bed.

"Don't be hasty, Peter. What did Courtney say?"

"Just that. He got sick there. I suppose she had to call Bush for fear it was something serious."

"It was."

"Yes."

His father's voice was at his door, and he couldn't think whether to lie down again, or stand up. The moment was not long enough to make the decision, or to begin to think what to say about Purvis and Miss Lee. His father turned the light on and stood with his mother in the room.

"Why do they want to fire Miss Lee?" It was the right thing to do: speak first.

His father looked surprised. "Perhaps you know better than anyone."

"No."

"You were there with Purvis."

"No. No, I wasn't. I went with him in the taxi, because we were walking by Miss Lee's—"

"Walking? Why?"

"Emily and I, Pat and Fielder, too. Ask them."

"I'm asking you."

The nausea was back. It was stronger than the demand in his father's voice. "Miss Lee," he said, and stopped to think about the sickness, and suddenly knew he wasn't going to throw up. "Miss Lee is the best teacher I ever had. She was good to Purvis."

"You said this morning that he was in a fight, and you then went with him to the hospital."

"Yes."

"But that isn't true."

"Yes, it is. He was in a fight. That's why he was at Miss Lee's. He didn't have anywhere else to go." He wished he hadn't said that. It was stupid, but it made him want to cry. He looked at his father's face. It was serious, grim.

But it was his mother who spoke. "There's been some neglect in that family, Peter."

"You keep harping on that. He's eighteen years old."

"Seventeen," Christopher said.

"What happened? From the beginning," his father said.

"All right. We were going back to the dance. Bush's taxi stopped in front of Miss Lee's house. She came out and said she needed help. I told the others I'd see them at the dance and went in. Bush did too. Purvis was coughing blood bad. He could hardly walk. We got him out and took him to the hospital."

"Why was he there?"

"I told you."

"Peter," his mother said, "how could Christopher know? Only Dorothy Lee can answer that."

His father didn't reply right away. He stood in the middle of the room and put his hands in his pockets. "She'll lie," he said. "She'll have to."

"If she'd had something to lie about, she wouldn't've called Bush," his mother said.

"She said she wouldn't lie," he told them.

"When did she say that?" His father's voice demanded again.

"I went back to her place after. She said she knew she'd be in trouble. I said if she told the whole story you'd understand. She said she would." He was able to meet his father's eyes directly now, and he saw the expression in them change.

"She knew she'd be in trouble?"
"Yes."
"She said that to *you*?"
"Yes. I said it isn't fair, and she said, Who said anything's fair?"
"Oh, I like her," his mother said.
"It will be fair."
"What?" Christopher asked.
But his father turned away and headed out the door.
His mother followed after him. "Why can we be so sure there's no justice? Because of the Courtneys of the world. They have a lot to answer for."
"The Courtneys of the world make justice happen too."
"Are you sure?"
"It's out in the open now."
"For what reasons?"
"Teachers can't have secret lives."
"With John Purvis? He's just a boy."
"Miss Lee is not so old."
"But she is single and alone and overworked and underpaid."
The phone began to ring again.
"If it's Courtney, tell him I'm not here." He picked up Sarah at the door and hugged her.
"I didn't think I should come in," she said to him.
"Why?"
"I thought there was going to be a spanking."
"He's a bit old for that. I might give him a biff on the chin, but not a spanking."
"It's for you, Christopher," his mother said, and when he arrived to answer it, she mouthed, "Emily."
He held the phone against his chest and waited until she and his father and Sarah had gone into the living room. He felt weak. Purvis and Miss Lee were still strong presences in his mind, and for a moment he struggled to picture Emily. He didn't see her clearly until he heard her voice.
"I'm at Dody's," she said. "You weren't at the rink this afternoon."
"I don't feel so pretty good."
"Are you sick?"
"Maybe. I don't know."
After a moment, she said, "You sound different."
"No. It's okay."
"What happened last night?"

"I'll tell you when I see you."
"Tomorrow?"
"Yes."
"Before or after school?"
"After."
"Okay. Look, in a way last night was good. My parents—"
"I know," he said. "They liked it that I wasn't there."
"They think it's cooling off."
He didn't answer.
"I don't think it is," she said.
"No, it isn't."
"That's good."
They were both talking with other people listening. "I'll try to be there after school," he said.
"We can go skating."
"Isn't the rink melting?"
"It's still good. It might turn cold again anyway."
"I guess." He tried to think how to say goodbye without it sounding too abrupt.
Very quietly, she said, "Are you kissing me? I'm kissing you."
"Yes," he said, and then there was a comfortable silence. The sickness in his stomach receded. He closed his eyes and felt his mother come close and put his robe over his shoulders. She dropped his slippers at his feet. "The floors are very cold," she said, and he nodded at her.
"I've got to go," Emily said. "Dody's mother wants the phone."
He didn't want to say goodbye now. "You kiss good," he said, softly.
"So do you."
"See you tomorrow."
"Okay."
"You hang up first."
"If you want."
"I don't want, but you have to."
"I'll count three and we'll do it together. One, two, three."
He listened to the silence again.
"You didn't do it," she said.
"I didn't want to." He heard her soft laugh, and told her, "Thanks for phoning."
He didn't put the receiver back on the hook until she was gone. Then he shuffled through the warmth of the kitchen to his room and lay on the bed. It felt good to have gone back to Emily. She was the same all the time. Calm. Together they were a space where everything

inside it was still, like a quietly held breath. He caught the sweet smell of her and rolled over against the wall away from his family and Purvis and Miss Lee and Mayor Courtney. The train's engine whistled twice and in a moment he heard its first heavy grunt, and after that its sounds were gradually lost until nothing was left of it but its whistle as it passed the crossing a mile west of town.

He held his pillow and pressed his face into it, but he couldn't keep her perfume from fading, or the pit at the bottom of his gut from going empty and filling with something sick and cold. Purvis had gone to Miss Lee. She had done her best, but she was going to be fired in front of the whole town, and nothing was going to help Purvis now.

I was there, Courtney, and he was coughing blood up onto her bed. There was no secret life. How the hell do you have a secret life with someone who's dying? If you're the Mayor, aren't you supposed to help people?

The door to the hallway opened. Sarah stood there with her thumb in her mouth. He smiled at that, and she took it as an invitation to come to him.

She whispered, "Turn on your light."

While he did it, she went back to the door and closed it. "Are you sick, really?'

"Maybe."

She sat on the bed. "Because of everything that happened yesterday?"

"What happened?"

"You know. The ski jump, and then Purvis is going to die."

He thought about playing with Gabe: nothing was sure; there wasn't much control. "Does Dad say that's why I'm sick?"

She nodded. "Mother says you've had to do a lot of growing up lately."

He looked at her serious little face. Her clenched fists were on either side of her mouth, and her hair was straight as it always was at the end of the day. He thought of Fielder's little sister lying blind in her crib, and about Fielder not ever saying anything more about it. Sarah was funny. So was his mother.

"Are you in love with Emily?"

He sat up. "Are they talking about that too?"

"Mummy just said there was nothing *wrong* with being in love."

"That's nice."

"Yes," Sarah nodded her head as she talked. "But how can you be in real love if you're only a boy?"

"Who said that?"

"I can say things for myself." She put her fists in her lap and looked straight at him. "I'm worried about John Purvis."

This was why she'd come, and he didn't want to talk about Purvis with her.

"I don't want him to die," she said.

"Well, that's very different. You used to be quite interested in dying."

She shook her head. "I've been doing some growing up too."

He tried not to laugh, but her face looked for a moment perfectly adult. "He's not going to," he said, as if it were the answer to a joke. He picked up his pillow and hit her a weak one on the arm. It was what he needed to do. Or maybe he wanted to hug her for coming to be her own kind of grown-up-little-girl company for him. He let her bash him with the pillow and then he held her and rolled with her down the length of the bed. She was laughing now. He tickled her and let her tickle him back. He lay on the bed and she grabbed the pillow to hit him. It stung more than he'd thought it would. She giggled when he fended her off and she rolled to the other end of the bed. He went after her and rose up on his knees, a dragon that made noises like a big cat hissing. She stood up and pointed her finger and shouted "Blam, blam," and he fell writhing at her feet.

"Don't die," she said. "I only wanted to wound you a little so I could take you home for a pet."

"Would you call me Arthur?" It was a joke Smith would love. "Arthur Petdragon?"

She stopped playing. "I don't know what that means."

"Neither do I."

"Yes, you do."

"Stupid joke."

She still looked miffed. "That's what adults always say when they don't want to tell me anything."

"I'm not an adult." He didn't want to stop being seven with her. He tickled her ribs and tripped her up so that she landed hard on her butt on the bed.

"Don't," she said.

He pushed her back, and her head hit the wall. She began to cry. "I'm sorry," he said, and picked her up in his arms. She was too big to do it comfortably, and he felt foolish, but she held onto him when he sat again on the bed.

"Winter is awful," she said, not quite crying now. "People die of the cold. I wish it was over."

"It almost is. It has to be. It's the middle of March."

"Purvis is going to die. You just aren't saying, because I'm too little to know."

He looked at her. She had only the tip of her thumb in her mouth, as if she were trying to break the habit. His parents weren't here; she was, and in a new odd way she was a comfort. In the other room they were talking about Courtney, or maybe they were talking about him as some kind of riddle instead of as someone growing up to be his own person. He hugged her close. "Okay," he said, "I'll go and see him and Dr. Royce, and I'll let you know for sure whether he'll die."

"Yes," she said. "Tell John I'll talk to God about him."

"Will you?" He didn't know whether it was funny or not.

"God listens to little children. The Bible says."

Her eyes were wide and fearful. She wanted him to say Yes, God listens to little children. "Jesus loves me, this I know, for the Bible tells me so."

"And Jesus is God, and when somebody loves you they listen," she said.

"Sure." He tried not to grin at her. "You're a real little thinker, aren't you?"

"Mother says I think too much."

"You do, you do, that's for sure. I'll tell Purvis you're praying for him."

"I don't think I can pray," she said. "You have to know a lot of different kind of words. I just talk."

"Okay, talk is good enough." He felt tired, and sorry she'd brought up God. "Listen, I think it's time for supper."

She got up off the bed. "Are you coming?"

"Maybe," he said, but in the end he didn't and later, after the dishes were done, his mother brought him a piece of lemon pie and a glass of milk. "You'll be fine in the morning," she said.

"Maybe I won't."

"Yesterday was a bad day."

"You think I'm acting nuts, don't you?"

She sat on the edge of the bed and tried to take his hand. He didn't let her. "I think you're someone who's been through a lot lately."

"You mean Emily."

"Well, that's been pretty intense, but it isn't everything. That saxophone started it, I think."

"Now you're being crazy."

"It's a very adult toy."

He didn't know what to say. She was always full of messages. But he wanted to tell her, to see what she'd say. "I made an ass of myself on it last night."

"Did you?"

He felt the nausea again. "I wanted to play jazz but I couldn't."

"Was it awful?"

"Yes."

"I'm sorry. Did Gabe—? What did Gabe do?"

"He made me play another tune."

She nodded. "That's good. I heard you'd played."

"Not very well."

"They didn't say that."

"There's nothing *wrong* with being in love," he said, mimicking Sarah's voice. "There's nothing wrong with wanting to play jazz, or ski jump, or be Purvis' friend even if he is damned near grown up, but don't walk by Miss Lee's house or be her friend. That's where nasty things go on that you get fired for."

He expected her to be angry, but she said nothing for a long moment, and then she reached out deliberately with her hand to feel his forehead. "I think you should know that your father will fight for Miss Lee, Christopher."

"Do you think so?"

She nodded. "When the facts are all in. He's a good man." She got up and stood by the bed. "You don't have to stay here, you know. Why don't you come into the living room with us?"

"Maybe I will." But again he didn't leave the bed. He heard his father switch on the radio at ten to hear the world news. There was a new pope in Rome, elected March 2nd, and today he talked peace when he appeared on his balcony overlooking St. Peter's Square. The Spanish Civil War had come one step closer to being over: General Franco was in Madrid. He'd captured it on the day Prime Minister Chamberlain of Britain said that if France were threatened by Germany, he would send two divisions there as an expeditionary force. British garrisons in Malta, Cyprus, and Hong Kong were to be strengthened. A new military station was to be built at Aden. The rearmament budget in Britain was to total over six billion Canadian dollars. The news reader didn't say how many British pounds that was. Italy was demanding French territory near its border. The people of Slovakia wanted the right of self-determination. Hitler wanted protection for the Germans in Bohemia and Moravia.

Between news stories, he heard his mother say, "Where *are* all these places that are threatening us?"

He didn't hear his father's reply.

Deep in the night, he woke frightened by an explosion. His window was clear of frost; outside it was raining. The noise came again. It wasn't an explosion; snow and ice slid and fell off the roof. His heartbeat slowed and calmed. He pulled his blankets tighter around himself.

At school, Blenkin stared out the window. Garrett grinned beside him. He woke again sick. This time when he went to the bathroom, he vomited.

"Flush it," his mother said, suddenly in the room.

He reached up and turned the handle. She knelt beside him, her face already wide awake, and he put his head against her shoulder.

"Poor Chris," she said. "What's happening to you?"

"I think it's okay now."

"Do you want to go back to bed?"

When he thought about it, the answer was no. "I'd like to sit awhile in the living room." He heard his voice come out high and weak.

"Okay," she said, and stood up.

He got to his feet. "I feel kind of stupid."

She looked at him but didn't say anything, and went with him into the living room. He saw her sit on the chesterfield. She was wearing her blue nightgown with the ruffles at the wrist and neck. For a moment, the smell of her milk was in his nostrils. He thought of her sitting there feeding Sarah. He'd been seven, almost eight. Sarah was fussing, making noises as quick as her breathing, and reaching with her hands while her mother leaned forward and freed her breast. The nipple was a bright brown, as big as Sarah's mouth, and the breast was long and white with one blue-green vein down its side. It hung free of her nightgown as she bent over the child. He often saw that scene when his mother sat on the chesterfield. But the smell of her milk came from farther back. He sat by her and then, almost too quickly, put his head in her lap. She said, "Oh," a sound that was both a surprise and a question, but he didn't move. He closed his eyes. Her hand smoothed the hair at the back of his head. There was nothing to say. In his head there were pictures of a blue sky seen through trees at the edge of a lake. He lay quiet for a long comfortable time.

"Was it terrible?" she asked softly. "Purvis?"

He didn't want to reply and disturb this pleasure. "No."

After a while, she said, "That's a real reason for staying with your own group, people your own age."

He didn't know what she was trying to say, and thought of Purvis with no mother. He sat up. Her face was serious when he looked at her, but then she leaned back and smiled at him.

"That was nice. It's been years, hasn't it? I'm sorry it's such a tough time for you."

"It isn't," he said, annoyed. "Don't push, eh? I've just got a bug."

"That wasn't pleasant what happened to you at the jumps."

"Blenkin's stupid."

"He's angry. At everybody."

"Not Miss Garrett." He felt as if he'd run hard into a door.

She grinned. "Well, that's news."

He held his hands up. "I didn't mean that. She's just the only one he smiles at. Why can't he be fired?"

She got up. "You know the answer."

He stood beside her, three inches taller. "No."

"Go to bed now, Christopher." She hugged him. "Rest tomorrow. I'll talk to your dad about it."

"What?"

"Not going to school."

"Thanks." He watched her go back to her room and close the door. She was peculiar but often sane. He shivered. The fire in the furnace was burning low. He went to the bathroom again and looked into the mirror. Pretty soon he was going to have to begin shaving. His eyes were jittery, but his stomach felt calm. He didn't want to go to sleep and dream again, but when he went back to bed it was warm under the blankets, and with the pillow held tight in his arms, he kept repeating that he wouldn't dream.

2

"I'll be back and forth. Maybe three trips," she said, and left with a load of paintings for the library, wearing a pair of slacks and a bandana around her head. Her eyes were clear and bright, and her mouth smiled even when she spoke seriously about him possibly having to look after Sarah when she came home from school. Her show was set to open tomorrow evening.

He lay in bed and listened to her start the car again. She'd driven Sarah to school and his father to work through the slush caused by the warm weather.

It felt good to be alone in the house. When he thought about it, he knew he was apart in every sense of the word. Emily, his friends, were at school; Purvis was in the hospital. Where was Miss Lee? There was silence in the house, and from outside there came only a few sounds: an engine in the yards west of the station shunting boxcars; a car going by the house. But there was no wind or rain. He looked out of the window and judged the temperature to be just above freezing.

When he stood up, he felt only a little weak. Too much sleep. His stomach was empty. It didn't feel bad, except it was full of gas. He tried not to think about where Miss Lee was. Mayor Courtney had phoned just before his father had gone to work. He'd wanted Miss Lee suspended. "She's not guilty yet," his father had said, and he'd refused. The mayor spoke again. And finally his father had said, "You are not a member of the School Board. The Board will handle this tonight. The charge against her is yours. I assume you'll speak to it." When he'd hung up, his mother had asked, "How angry is he?"

"Angry enough. He thinks the town is his private domain, and he's never been challenged by Robert's Rules of Order before."

"I suppose you could've been more diplomatic."

"I've got other things to do today. The river's in rotten shape with all that wet snow on top of the ice."

"I mean, Miss Lee might not *want* to teach today."

"And make a circus out of what should be a confidential enquiry?"

Miss Lee could've phoned in sick. He pictured her still sitting in her kitchen drinking coffee, and he wanted to go see her. He'd cried in front of her, and it hadn't been embarrassing. She'd been crying, too, before he'd come back from the hospital.

He lay down again on his bed and watched the ceiling, but what he saw was her sitting in her tiny living room. She looked good, because her maroon robe was covering her awkward body. She wasn't crying any more, and Purvis was there, not just because he had no other place to go, but because he wanted to know if she liked him. Maybe he was glad he was hurt and coughing blood and drunk. If he'd been well, going there would never have been as easy as when he was in pain.

They must've seen each other again, right after they'd met at the school. Purvis could've gone back and offered to shovel her walk and carry wood in for her stove. That would be easy. No one ever knew where he was going to be next. And Miss Lee was a loner everyone thought stayed home and marked papers. They'd have coffee after he'd shovelled the snow and brought in the wood. And then he'd sense he could come back again. There'd be signals. Emily had made some when she'd wanted to start being more than friends.

He remembered standing outside of the Gordons' house with Emily. The signal was there: how quiet she was, her eyes steady, watching him watch her. He'd been allowed to reach out and touch.

What had Miss Lee done to show Purvis it was all right? To do what? She was a teacher, as Garrett and Blenkin were: things had to happen quickly and be done wherever they could. She was lucky Purvis, who shovelled snow for money, could shovel hers and then visit. It'd have to be fast—the decision. Purvis would know what she was offering, because he liked to get what he wanted. He wouldn't have been shy. They were on her couch, and it was too small for them, because they were both big people. Purvis hadn't bled on the couch, but on the bed. He'd known where that was. And she'd put him on it when he'd come in hurting and coughing blood. He watched them and saw them loving in that small space. They struggled. It was what he thought he knew about that final moment of making love. Purvis was breathing hard. Her mouth was open and her eyes were wide.

In the clench of his hand, he held himself stiff and closed his eyes. Deep inside of him his own convulsions also began, sensations still so new that their strength and wildness surprised him again, and when they were over he became both sleepy and sad.

Miss Lee and Purvis were on her bed now. They rested safe there, because no one knew where either of them was. Unless they were caught, no one cared either. It was perfect for them both.

And then Purvis got mad at Blenkin—or did he feel he could beat up on him because he had a place to go and Miss Lee to love him? Either way, the fight and his cough had stopped what was happening between them. No matter how quick it had begun, the end came so soon that it could hardly be counted as having happened at all.

He pulled the blankets up around him once more and knew that he was going to go to sleep again. Miss Lee's image, seen close to Purvis, began to fade, and when he woke at noon, his mother was in the kitchen preparing to go out again. He didn't move now, because the sickness in him was gone—or he'd become used to it—and he still didn't want to get up from this safe place. She came to the door and asked him how he was. He rolled over and shoved his face into the pillow.

"I'll be gone most of the afternoon. Be good to Sarah."

He sat up and watched her through the window. The paintings she carried were wrapped in newspapers. He saw her get into the car, as excited about her show as he'd been about playing with Gabe's band. His father probably felt the same way about being Chairman of the School Board and would feel as good about building a bridge if he ever got the chance. Sometimes at night, his father sketched houses on a pad of paper he kept by his chair in the living room, and his mother would sit beside him and dream with him about living in a three thousand square foot house that they'd never have. They were both good with their hands. Christopher looked at his own. They were the image of his father's if you just glanced at them, but they were useless for drawing, measuring, shaping. They weren't hands to think with. They were for touching and feeling. He really wasn't like either of them, and they knew it. They'd be able to control him better if he were like them. Or maybe the word was Influence; make him more a Waterton and less himself.

He got up. There was an energy in him now that wouldn't let him stay in bed. In the kitchen he ate cornflakes and toast with honey on it. They settled easily on his stomach. He wasn't sleepy anymore, and now the sadness was gone. The small guilt he always had when he was well and not in school made him think what he should do. The answer was easy. He put on his outdoor clothes and walked toward the hospital to see Purvis.

The sky was clearing in the west. The band of blue there above the hills was brighter than he'd seen it since well before Christmas, but there was no smell or feel of spring in the air yet. It was still raw, despite the temperature being above freezing. The hospital in daylight was not the set of lights and an entranceway it had been on Saturday night. It was a very large house, with gables, screened porches, a peaked roof, and dripping eaves. It was surrounded by pine trees, and the sidewalk curved around them and ended at the door. This was the extreme edge of Long River; beyond was only wilderness. There was a car in the roadway and several others in the parking lot beyond.

Miss Baker was not on duty. Miss Thompson stood in front of the nursing station desk. She was a bony woman with a frizz of orange and white hair that stuck out from under her cap like the needles on the pines outside the building.

"What are you doing here, Christopher?" she asked. Her voice was smoke and whiskey, habits that she supported, at least in part, by being the only woman veteran who played poker at the Legion Hall.

"How's John Purvis?"

She pulled her face out of shape. Perhaps it was a smile. "Every Rink Rat in town's been here all day trying to get in to see him. You're not one of those, are you?"

"No. I was with him when he was brought in. May I see him now, please?"

"Only his mum and his dad are allowed in. He's a pretty sick boy."

"Could I just say hello at the door?"

"He's in isolation. There's only a window."

"Can I see him?"

She sighed, nodded, and led the way down the corridor and through the swinging doors near the nursing station. He saw Purvis through a narrow window. He was lying on the bed. He looked as if the person he'd once been had walked away and left an imitation behind. In a chair beside him, Mary sat with her hands in her lap. She wore a green smock over her street clothes, and a white mask hid her face except for her blue eyes. They stared at Purvis and blinked as if they were trying to hold back tears.

"Don't excite him," Miss Thompson said. "He's stopped bleeding. It'd be a pity to have him start up again." She turned away toward the nursing station.

Christopher waved his hands back and forth across the glass. Mary looked up. Her head jerked, and her eyes were amazed that anyone but a nurse was at the window. Then Purvis saw him. His face stopped being a mask, and he pushed the covers away. Christopher watched him stand up and come toward him. Mary's voice was high and annoyed, but he couldn't make out the words that she said.

Purvis' face came very close to the thin glass. "I'm a goddamn prisoner," he said.

"I know. How are you? What does the doctor say?"

"Good. Everything's good."

"You look fine." He didn't. He was pale, with round spots of colour over his cheekbones. He looked as if Mary had put rouge on him. "When will you be out?"

"I got to get out of isolation first."

Christopher nodded. It was awkward having to speak so loudly, and embarrassing that the nurses at their station could probably hear.

"How's it in school?" Purvis' face grinned. "Blenkin come back today?"

"I didn't go."

"Why?"

"I said I was sick. I wanted to see you."

"You scared of him?"

He looked at Purvis' eyes. They were scornful. He didn't answer.

Purvis laughed, and he coughed hard. Mary got up from her chair and began to pound him on the back. Not very hard, but he twisted around. "Hey, don't do that."

"It's helpful for the coughing. I want to be helpful."

He turned back to the window. "Blenkin," he said, as if he needed to remind himself about what it was he'd been saying. "You got him cold. You go tell Grandison on them and they're dead."

"You come with me and I'll do it." It was Rink Rat talk, and he knew that, but it was already making Purvis look more alive.

Miss Thompson was back. She stood beside him and put her hand on his arm. "I think that's enough. Too much excitement's not good. You, too, Mrs. Purvis."

Mary came out into the hall. "Goodbye, John. You rest now, y'hear?"

Purvis looked at her but didn't say anything. She waited a moment and then walked toward the nursing station, still with her mask and smock on.

Christopher went to the opened door. "I'll come back if they let me."

Miss Thompson said, "We probably won't. Don't you cough on him, John. Close the door." She reached out, grabbed the knob, and pulled it shut.

When he looked through the glass again, Purvis was sitting on the bed. He glanced up, but that was all. Christopher waved, and Dr. Royce came down the hall. "You weren't in there, were you?"

"No."

"Don't. At this stage, he's dangerous."

"Is he going to get well?"

"I don't know."

"When's he going to Tranquille?"

"Soon. Just as fast as we can get an okay to send him."

"It's that bad?"

"It's better that they look after him." Dr. Royce took his arm and led him out beyond the swinging doors and down the corridor to the reception desk. "It's going to be a long time before we know if he's going to make it. Some people do, even though they've got it bad."

"How long?"

"A year. Two years."

"That's a long time."

The doctor smiled. "Only when you're young. Look, now, we want him quiet, and friends only excite him. The best thing you can do is stay away." He left then, hurrying as he always did.

Christopher went down the steps to the front door and out into the afternoon sunlight. The sky was patched with broken clouds. And then he saw Mary leaning against the car in the roadway. He could see her hands resting on the car's roofline, and her head was slumped forward against her arm. She had a little round hat on now, and she turned. Her face was wet, and for a moment he thought she might be crying for Purvis, but she wasn't. Her mouth was a straight line, pinched at its ends.

"Come here," she said. "I want to talk to you. What's he doing being friends with a boy your age? Is *that* wrong with him too? Is he not a real man?"

"He's sick," Christopher said. "Please don't talk that way about him."

"I have a right to a life of my own," she said, angry. "You listen to him say things, and you tell them around this little town. They're not the truth about me, not the truth at all." She sounded calmer now. "If the truth be known, I'm a giver. There's some of us born that way. I'm one of them, but even so, I have a right to a life of my own."

She came toward him. "I left Alexandria to have a life of my own: I thought that anyway. Alexandria is north of New Orleans and east of Baton Rouge, but you wouldn't know that. I went on a trip around the continent. It was adventuresome of me, just buying the ticket on the train that allowed me to travel for a month anywhere on the continent. My daddy always said I was adventuresome. That was one of the things he said about me, and he was right. I could be sometimes adventuresome. I met Dick on the train. I don't think I even knew where I was. He took advantage of me. People always take advantage of givers."

Her voice had become high and slow, and its accent was very strong.

Christopher said, "Is John going to die?"

"Dick's like my father. They look somewhat as if they're kin, too, and there's a little weakness in both of them that keeps them away from real success. What did you ask me—?"

"I asked about John. Is he—?"

"That boy is like my little brother. He takes and takes. You have to believe that. It's a stain on some people's characters. Oh, it don't look like it, but just being there in the room is enough for some people to be sucking up every bit of life there is around and about. No, he's not going to die. What's going to die is my reputation. They're all blaming me. I come every day and sit with him, to the neglect of my children and my husband."

"I have to go, Mrs. Purvis." She wasn't crazy. He could see that. She was angry.

"You remember what I said. You've heard the other side of the story now, the side where the truth is."

He began to leave.

He looked back at her when he got again to the sidewalk. She stood straight and still, then she went to the car and got into it. The lettering on the side of it said, Pearl Soap. The car started and jerked into motion along the snow-crusted street. When it passed, she didn't look at him. The little pillbox hat on top of her head had a veil on it, and she'd pulled it down over her eyes.

Her voice stayed in his head, high and stunted, as if it had never had a chance to grow up. He'd only heard her yelling at her children from her back porch, or talking downtown in a store. Neither of those voices had been the one he'd heard today. He'd never been spoken to like that by an adult before—as if he were a real danger and not just someone to scold or teach or ask stupid questions of. "If the truth be known, I'm a giver." She believed that, and Purvis was a taker.

The melt had made it hard walking, but he didn't think about it. He slipped and slid across town, and eventually came to where he knew he was going. He went up on the porch and looked in the window. The door to her bedroom was open. The bed was unmade. A skirt and sweater lay on the couch in the living room. She hadn't grown up, but only in this one way. "Christopher, I'm just a guy, too." He'd made her say that, admit she wasn't all adult, a god. Gabe and Irene had made a mistake. Maybe it was admitting it that made them human. Blenkin was the opposite; he wouldn't admit anything. Put him with Mary in a locked room: a nice Hell for those two, and half the trouble in town would be locked away with them.

It was getting late. He couldn't see Miss Lee's kitchen clock, but it couldn't be too long before Sarah's class got out. He left the porch and ran a block and walked a block until he was outside the school. The bell rang and he waited on the sidewalk for the junior grades to appear. Down the hill at the High School, Blenkin was looking out his homeroom window. Junior Business class. He had a bandage on his forehead. Purvis hadn't lied. The sight of Blenkin hurt and staring at him, unable to do anything now about Christopher the truant, made him want to laugh. He could also see into Miss Lee's room. She had not phoned in sick. She was there, sitting on her desk, talking seriously to the class. This late in the day, very few would be listening. There was no way to tell her that Purvis was still alive and was being sent to the sanitarium. Maybe she'd phoned the hospital herself. Sarah was coming across the schoolyard. He'd promised her he'd see Purvis.

But now Emily was at the doorway to the school, and he went to her.

She had her skates over her shoulder. Sarah came with him and stood looking happy that she was going to have her brother to herself. Emily said, "You don't have your skates."

"I have to look after Sarah. My mom's got a show at the library tomorrow. She's there." He felt his voice go lame. "I'm sorry."

"We haven't seen each other since Saturday."

"I know."

"When?"

"Tomorrow for sure." He watched her eyes trying to believe that. "For sure," he said again, and reached forward and pecked her on the cheek.

"Be early for school," she said.

"Okay." He backed off. She smiled then and ran across the yard to be with Dody.

He walked with Sarah up the sidewalk toward home. She held his hand. "I think it's getting chillier," she said. She loved to be formal, as if being grown up was a matter of the right words and saying them in the correct tone of voice.

"Maybe it is. Maybe winter'll stay all summer."

"No, but it might stay all spring. Do you know, the first thing I'm going to do when I grow up is leave this awful town."

"What a lovely idea." He wished he was with Emily, alone, not skating. The rink wasn't anywhere he wanted to go today, either, not with the Rats there talking nothing but Purvis.

"And how is John Purvis?" Sarah asked, still formal. "Did you go see him like you promised?"

"Yes. He's fine."

"Is he con—con—?"

"Contagious."

She repeated it. "That means germy."

"I talked to him through a window so I wouldn't catch his germs. He's going to another hospital soon."

"Where they know more."

"Just about T.B."

"I think they know more everywhere else."

He didn't answer. Sarah's brain was a swamp full of weird creatures that just kept talking as long as you let them. T.B. would lead to lungs and lungs to breathing, breathing to choking and dying. His mother said it was how she learned. But he wanted to think about Emily. Her grandmother's house was across the road, and the old lady was at the door chopping with a shovel at some ice on the stoop. If Sarah weren't with him, he could go help her. Instead, he walked up the York Street hill taking small slow steps, keeping pace with his sister.

When anything happened to him—the jumps, lessons, playing at the dance—Emily got cut out of his life. When Purvis got sick, or he'd been with Miss Lee, or was himself sick, she was excluded. Now he was looking after Sarah. Emily had been there, ready to skate. She would go with Dody, and maybe she'd skate with someone else. Probably not. But if things kept getting in the way, someday she would. Smith. Maybe Callaghan, or one of the Bells. It hurt. It was like being in another room, as Purvis was, behind glass, a prisoner of having to do what he had to do. Gabe and Irene lived in the same house and everything there happened to both of them. He looked at Sarah. She was watching her feet, head down, and thinking whatever she wanted to. There was something free in that. People liked it when she retreated to a corner to play. It was a relief not to have her wanting something or asking questions. He couldn't remember doing that, but maybe he had, until Fielder had come along and they'd made a kind of game of being always together. Not a serious one. He'd loved Fielder, right up until Emily. Or Coventry. Without Emily to think about, and Isonovich to fight Fielder, he might hate him. They were still close, but it was different from what it had been. Not close so much anymore, just familiar. If there'd been no Emily, Fielder would never have hooked up with Pat. Everything was easy for those two. It was as if they were walking along and suddenly there was a fence. They didn't ask what was on the other side. Up and over, laughing all the way to the bed in the janitor's room.

"Mommy's going to be famous," Sarah said.

"That's stupid." The thought of anyone expecting that embarrassed him.

She looked up at him. "Can't a mother be famous?"

He tried to think if they could.

"Well, can they?"

"Sure."

"Then she's going to be, and so am I."

"What are you going to be famous for?"

"Drawing, or building bridges, I'm not sure which yet."

He went ahead of her along the walkway and opened the door. She didn't need help with her outdoor clothes now that she was seven. He went into his room and got out his horn. The noises he'd blown through it on Saturday night were still in his head, except now he wondered how they could have been so wrong. Gabe said, "Know where you're going. It's just that some notes sound better than others, so you learn to pick 'em good." The mathematics of it made it safe. No accidents, if you knew the rules and could get the music in your head. He adjusted the reed and blew a few notes, noises. He blew the blues scale. Flat 3, flat 5, flat 7. It was a set of right notes. Who'd picked them? When? Gabe said nobody. "Those notes come from pure experience. If all you've got for an instrument is a piece of wire nailed to the wall of your shack and tied to a broomstick you use to tighten and loosen it with, you're going to make sounds that are your very own. What we got here is a scale that comes close—but only close—to putting down the notes those old-time blacks chose for their songs. A bunch of pretty good accidents."

On Saturday, Miss Lee had said, "This has been a terrible night for you. Some kind of accident. . . . It won't be over till it finishes in its own good time. Try to remember you're only a witness."

Emily was an accident. He hadn't planned for her. He hadn't run down the hill to the fire in F-sharp minor and plunged through B-seventh to E for Emily. Maybe what Gabe and Miss Lee were saying was that you had to use your own accidents to help make a life for yourself. Purvis and Miss Lee had lives first, and then they'd happened to each other, and he wasn't part of that. Emily had happened to him. He'd happened to his parents. He blew on his horn. This saxophone was something he'd planned for. The idea of it had grown in his mind, and everybody had said yes to it, all the way out to Aunt Ethel who'd sent fifty cents glued between two pieces of thin cardboard.

He held the saxophone between his knees and started very slowly to play "I Can't Get Started." He blew the first few notes and then waited, listened. Gabe's voice said, "You want to do everything too quick, kid. Slow it down. It'll be maybe two years before you can hear fast enough to get it right." Bunny Berrigan's recording of the song used hardly anything but the melody. He began it again and played the first phrase. "I've been around the world in a plane." His tone was thin. He stood up and blew the way Gabe had taught him. "Settled revolutions in Spain. But I'm brokenhearted 'cause I can't get started with you."

He backed off and thought about which notes could be bent, which ones could be played against the beat, which ones were long enough that a couple of notes from their chords could be added until the next note was ready to be played. The notes he filled with sounded wrong. He tried to hear different ones in his head and imitate them on the horn. They sounded better. What he was doing was simple, but the notes and the way he played them were at least his own. Maybe the music was hokey and square, but it was better than the straight melody. He went over it again. His little finger slipped off one note onto another. The new note sounded good. When he played the phrase again, he kept it and carefully ran a scale off it up to the next note. Nothing like this had ever happened to him before. He could feel a pulse in his neck begin to pound, and he wanted to let loose and play a lot of notes. But when he did, they sounded no better than the ones he'd played on Saturday night.

Gabe said, "I'd rather play one piece fifty times than fifty pieces once."

He closed his eyes and blew the first phrase again. He listened for new notes to play at the end of it, but when he used them they sounded wrong. It made him angry. He sat for a long time without being able to think what was wrong. Then he put his horn down and went to the phone and asked central for Mr. English's music store. Gabe answered. He knew he would. "It's Christopher," he said. "It was awful what happened on Saturday night."

"Then don't blow that way again."

"No. Look, I've been playing. The same piece over and over. I find some extra notes, and some of them are right but, I don't know—"

"What's your point, kid?"

"When are we going to study *music*? I'm sick of tunes."

"Tunes are your business right now."

Christopher held the phone tight to his ear, as if Gabe might be saying something more that he couldn't hear. "Just tunes?"

"What's the matter, Chris? You sound like you're fussed about something more than the horn. Your mother on your back?"

"No. I want to play. You got the music in your head. You can give it to me."

"Just like that?"

"Somehow. Where'd you get it?"

"Practice, off records, theory books."

"Get me a book."

After a moment, he heard Gabe's quiet laugh. "Sure kid, why not? Who am I to hold up progress?"

"Can I rehearse with the band?"

"No, we don't rehearse."

"Why?"

"Because we woodshed material on our own and play new numbers over at a dance before the crowd gets there."

"I have to get my own band?"

Gabe laughed again. "Jeez, what is it, three months you've had the horn? It's not ski jumping, you know. It's a whole life."

"Not if all you can do is play good enough to stay in Long River."

"It's a start, a little place where you can pay some dues."

"You're going to leave, aren't you? When?"

"Maybe soon."

"How? You guys don't even have bus fare."

"Don't get cocky, kid. If there's a war, I'm going to try for the navy band."

"A band to march to?"

"You come over to the house. I'll play you a couple of records. British bands. Best musicians you can find in some of them."

He felt deserted already. "I'm too young to join up."

"It hasn't happened yet. Maybe if it does, you can own the band in town. Something to work for."

"It better not happen till next year then."

"I'll get you a book. Got to go. Miracle's happened. We have a customer."

The phone went dead, and he put the receiver back on its hook. He glanced into the living room and saw that Sarah was cutting pictures out of an old catalogue. He wondered if he should stop her making a mess, and then he didn't care.

When he went into his bedroom again it felt cold, and he shivered as he stood over his horn lying there on the bed. Its curves and the intricacies of its mechanism were beautiful, and it came to him that he could feel for it in a way he couldn't for anything else in his life. He picked it up, but he didn't play it. The case was on the bed too. He opened it and put the saxophone away. Shards of sickness moved in his gut. He lay on the bed with the horn beside him and listened to Sarah's voice in the other room talk to her paper cutouts, telling them who they were and what she was going to make them do.

He closed his eyes and chose the key of A so he could run its scales and chords. Moving up, he ran the key of B-flat. Then he knew he was going to go to sleep. Sarah was safe. His mother was coming home soon.

No one wakened him for dinner. Fielder's voice brought him to consciousness. He was sitting on the bed in the dark, and he said, "Turn on the light, eh?"

Christopher reached up and pulled the chain on his lamp. "What're you doing here? What time is it?"

"Eight-thirty. Your mother says you're sick."

"Maybe."

"You should've been at school today. Blenkin had a black eye and a bandage on his head. Fell on it."

"I saw him."

"How?"

"I went down to pick up Sarah. He was at the window." He watched Fielder's face and saw that he wasn't holding anything back, but how could Blenkin and Purvis have a fight without anyone else knowing?

"He walked stiff and he was really cranky. He also asked me twice where you were."

"Maybe he wanted to say he was sorry for screwing me out of winning on Saturday."

"Sure sure. Right. He's famous for that. So, what's wrong? You don't look sick to me."

"I just didn't want to go to school."

"Neither did I, but I went."

Christopher stared again at Fielder's face. He looked upset. A couple of things had happened in his life, too. Pat, his blind sister. He decided to tell him about Blenkin, but Fielder said, "It's Purvis, right?"

"I wanted to visit him."

"Nobody's allowed. I heard that."

"They let me in. Not all the way. He's in isolation."

"Is he on his way out?"

He watched Fielder's face again. Maybe this was why he'd come. "I don't know."

"Christ, he's only seventeen."

"Eighteen next month."

"It's crap to throw a guy out of his house these days. There aren't any jobs."

"His stepmother said he was evil." At the back of his throat there was something that burned. He couldn't swallow it.

Fielder looked surprised. "Her? She said he was evil? When?"

"Saturday when she came from the dance to see him at the hospital."

"Drunk."

"Maybe. But I saw her today, and she didn't let up on him." He sat up and leaned against the wall. "Outside the hospital she came at me and started telling her life story."

"I bet. All about how she came here from the Deep South. Why, is the question."

"She met Dick Purvis on a train and he did it to her."

"She said that?"

He nodded. Now, he had to talk about John again, and he wasn't sure he could. Already his breathing was shaky. "I don't want to talk about it."

"She's nuts now, and she was bananas to start with."

"There isn't any law that says she had to look after Purvis."

"Why not? Jesus, you got people like her and Blenkin running around. . . . Leave her on the trail. It's what the Eskimoes do."

"They're going to ship Purvis to the sanitarium."

Fielder didn't say anything for a moment. The look on his face was strained. "For how long?"

"Dr. Royce said two years, if he doesn't die."

"He's going to die, isn't he?"

"Nobody knows."

"Nobody knows bloody anything. Maybe we'll all get it." Fielder stood up. "Now they're talking five years my little sister will be blind."

"But there's an operation for her. Purvis just has to lie in bed and hope."

"The operation's no good if the big nerve to the brain doesn't work. It might not, you know, not if it isn't used." Fielder sat down again. His eyes were glassy with tears. "I just found that out."

"I know," Christopher said. "My dad told me."

Fielder looked as if he hadn't heard. "I take her into my room. She's so goddamn pretty. And I get out my flashlight and shine it in her eyes. Maybe there's light gets through if it's bright enough and it'll make the nerve work. I put her in the sun too in case that'll help. My mother doesn't do anything. She just sits there when I yell at her and says stupid things like, The Lord giveth and the Lord taketh away. My old man comes home from the Legion and when he sees her most of the time he cries. What the hell good does that do, a goddamn adult who sits around and blubbers? Then he calls Dan Foster and they talk about war, both of them bombed out of their minds. Tonight he said, I want out, Dan. Let 'em fight. I'll be there. They'll need us, by God. We know the Jerries. Forty-two isn't old."

"Do you want him to?"

"What?"

"Go."

"Why not? He keeps telling me that's what he's good at. He got the Military Medal when he was a sergeant and Mentioned in Dispatches when he was an officer. He's got drawers full of pictures he thinks I haven't seen. In every one of them he's grinning or laughing with his arms around friends or a girl in a café. He looked like a goddamn movie star."

"Can he be an officer again?"
"What do you mean?"
"Well, he doesn't—"
"Look like one."
"Is that the way they act?"
"It's different being drunk in the army. It's for fun."
"Will you guys go with him?"
"To war?"
"They have camps, don't they?"
"He doesn't talk about that. It upsets my old lady, too. I think he just wants to send money home. That'd do it for him. The money'd keep us safe, and the war'd make him happy."
"What about your little sister?"
"We'd probably be able to afford to go south to a specialist. Royce told us we should. He's just a G.P."
"He wants Purvis to go away quick, too."
"How's Dick Purvis going to pay?"
"The government pays if you've got T.B."
Fielder got up and went to the window, even though there wasn't anything to see on the other side of it. "That figures," he said. "If you're going to die, they pay. But if you might be cured, to hell with you."
"I'm glad they're going to pay for Purvis."
Fielder turned toward him again. "What do you do? I mean what single thing can you do to make it better? She lies there with those eyes. They don't even look like eyes. What the hell did she do to deserve that? I walked around the house blindfolded from before dinner. My old lady yelled at me but I did it anyway. I ate blind, and I burned myself and walked into things I never look at when I've got eyes. It's not just black when you're blind. It's different. Everything's different. There's no balance in your head, you know? You start for somewhere and your head stays where you were."
"I hope your dad gets to go, Fielder. Maybe it won't be so bad as you think."
"It feels lonely," he said. There was no strength in his voice.
The words were painful, and they were true. "I wish you wouldn't," Christopher said.
"What?"
"Say things like that. You're not supposed to." He sat up on the edge of the bed and grinned as if that might help Fielder be himself again. "You're supposed to be the guy who makes jokes about everything. You

were all right on Saturday. What happened?"

"Purvis, I guess. No. I told you, I put on the blindfold."

"You want to be blind for her?"

"Yes. No, who wants to be blind? What it is, Waterton: everybody's so goddamn weak. You know? Nobody *does* anything. They just sit around and take it."

"Not Purvis," Christopher said. He had to tell the story now, and it felt good.

"You mean at the rink? That's nothing."

"No. He was the one who beat up Blenkin."

Fielder's face cleared. "*No.*"

"Saturday at the dance."

"Jesus, I'd like to've seen that."

"Purvis said he hit him so hard he thought he might've killed him."

"I guess he knew he was on his way out."

"Purvis never knew a thing until after it was over."

"You don't hit a teacher," Fielder said.

"Unless you're Purvis."

"Tell me about it. Jesus."

"Purvis said they went the distance. He said it went on until there was nothing left. Purvis said Blenkin was crawling around in the snow. They both were."

"That goddamn Purvis, eh? I want to go to school now, just to look at Blenkin. Today he was trying to be normal, but he was hurting, that's for sure."

"One of the reasons I didn't go to school is I was scared."

"Why? What's it got to do with you?"

"The reason Blenkin got mad enough to go the distance was Purvis kept saying he'd heard he'd been doing it with Garrett in the lab room. I'm the one who caught them, and I told Purvis. Blenkin knows it has to be me."

"You caught them? Where? Up on the table?"

"They were just kissing and petting."

"Shit, that's enough. Why didn't you go to Grandison?"

"Sure sure, Fielder. My word against theirs. Who's going to win? That's a big thing, accusing teachers. But it's all different now."

"Why?"

"Because Purvis went to Miss Lee's house after the fight and that turd Bush told the mayor and he wants Lee fired."

"Purvis and Lee? How, for God's sake? He's seventeen."

"I don't know. I went back there after the hospital, and she was really upset."

"Because Purvis was found there?"

"No, maybe, I don't know. Because of everything, I guess."

"She's the only human being in that whole Jeezly school."

"Keep it down, Fielder. My mother hates swearing."

"Jeezly? That's swearing?" He looked like the old Fielder again. "Purvis and Miss Lee. It must be neat doing it to an older woman."

"Who says they were doing it?"

"He didn't go there because she was good-looking."

"She's a traveller." Christopher stood up.

"What's that mean?"

"Purvis wanted to go to Greece. You can dive for sponges there. I got Miss Lee to talk to him." He held Fielder's arm. "Look. This is private. I could get my neck in a sling from Blenkin."

"Not if he knows you could tell on him."

"Are you going to blab this all over town?"

"Maybe." His eyes grinned.

"You're a prick, Fielder."

"I thought your mother didn't like swearing."

"That isn't swearing, it's the truth. I'll tell about you and Pat."

"Go ahead."

"That she's scared she's going to have a baby."

Fielder's head jerked, and he was embarrassed that it had betrayed him. "I'll kill you, Waterton."

"Maybe."

"It's not been long enough."

"Then she *is* scared."

"Emily told you."

"No, I just guessed."

"Double prick."

"Sure, but don't tell about Purvis, except he's going to the sanitarium. Are you my friend or not?"

"How could anyone be friends with you, Waterton?"

"What about Pat?"

"She was supposed to get her monthlies today."

"But she didn't. I thought you had a safe?"

"I did." He looked away, and then wiped his nose against the back of his hand. "Jesus, who wants to have a safe on the first time and lose all the feeling?" He put his hand in his pocket and brought out a small packet. "I got some new ones at Kroll's, but she doesn't want to do it anymore."

"What if she's going to have a baby?"

"I don't know, Chris. Do you get married when you're fifteen? Jesus, I'm not even quite fifteen yet."

"Dan Foster's girl married Will Orrin."

"They were sixteen."

"Maybe he was."

"I talked to Howard Streeter," Fielder said.

"Really?"

Fielder nodded. "Kelly told me to. I didn't say who it was."

"What'd Howard say?

"He said if he had a dime for every girl who was late around there, he'd be a millionaire."

"That all?"

"He said when they're young they aren't reliable. They can be early or late or stop for a couple of months. Then he kicked my ass right there in the dressing room and said that's why you wait till you're old enough and they are too. Sending me to Howard was Kelly's idea of some kind of joke."

Christopher took the package and showed it to Fielder. One of the three safes was missing.

"I wore one in bed last night."

Christopher laughed. "So, what happened was, in the furnace room you tried to get the one from your wallet on and couldn't do it."

"It's not that easy, you know. You got to be quick, especially when they might change their minds any minute. She was saying no all the time we were in there."

"I think we heard."

"And she chewed my ear at the same time."

"I heard giggling."

"That too: no, chew, giggle. What happened was, the safe tore. I felt stupid—so, I just did it."

"Now you know how to put one on." They were a long way away from Purvis, Miss Lee, Blenkin, Saturday night. It felt good. "And you blew off into it."

"They stretch and go wrinkly when you try to wash them."

Christopher sat down on the bed and collapsed back onto the pillow. He couldn't hold back laughing any longer. Fielder came over and lay beside him.

"The big French Safe Caper."

They didn't stop saying the words or quit laughing until after what was funny was used up. It was like it had been three or four years ago when one of them farted in church—not on purpose, but a surprise. He reached up and turned out the light.

"What was it like doing it with Pat?"

"Soft," he said, as if he'd been thinking about it too. "The kind you can't ever imagine."

"Emily's soft to kiss."

"Not that kind. Christ, Pat's not soft to kiss at all. But I'm going to remember just being there for the rest of my life. From the moment she grabbed my dong and put it in—"

"She knew to do that?"

"I wasn't getting anywhere. Jesus, I didn't know the first thing. I was missing by a mile. I just knew I was there. Three cheers. Her pants were off and her knees were up and I was in between." His laughter overran his words. "You play basketball, you got a coach and a rule book."

They lay in the dark and laughed and quit and laughed again. They didn't talk. The next subject was going to be Emily and Christopher didn't want that. Emily wasn't Pat. She was young, and she'd hurt easy. Holding and kissing were a way of looking after her.

"Nothing there with Emily?"

"No." He heard footsteps in the kitchen and sat up. "That you, Mom?"

"Yes."

He turned on the light and gave Fielder a shove off the bed. His mother tapped on the door. "How are you? What are you two doing in there?"

"Nothing. I'm okay."

She opened the door. "Hungry?"

He hadn't thought about it. "What is there?"

"You know. Cold veal, potatoes, peas. I'll warm them up if you want." She glanced at the clock. "Your father should be home shortly."

"Okay, I'll have some."

She smiled at Fielder. "How about you?"

"No, thanks." He stood awkward, as he always did when he was doing something that was only polite. "I got homework to do." The lie moved him out into the kitchen. He put on his boots.

Christopher watched him go down the steps and across the back yard to the trail that led to the school. Fielder never turned to wave or say goodbye. That wasn't his way of going. Everything was on or off for him, like alternating current, but always driving forward. Straightforward, even with Pat.

Christopher closed the door. His mother was warming the potatoes and peas in a frying pan. "It's getting colder out there again," she said and smiled at him. "Are you about over this now, Christopher?"

"Being sick? I don't know. I always feel okay after I've slept."

"Do you want to see Dr Royce?"

He did. But not about himself. "No, it's okay." He sat at the kitchen counter and got out a knife and fork from the drawer. "What did he say when you phoned him about T.B.?"

"Not to worry. Sometimes a little contact with it is good. Makes you immune."

He watched her turn the potatoes over. There was a lovely brown butter crust on them. It made him hungry for the first time since Saturday. "What about Miss Lee?"

"Your father will handle it. He's good at that sort of thing."

"But will it be okay for her? I mean, fair?"

"Board meetings are democratic. We live under a parliamentary system. And your dad is chairman. She's about as safe as she can get."

He ate slowly and knew that he was waiting for his father now, hardly tasting what was in his mouth. He rinsed the plate and put it in the rack by the sink to drain. Sarah was asleep. He went into the living room and turned the radio on. Tommy Dorsey was at the Palladium in Los Angeles, but the program was almost over. Tommy was playing his theme song, and the announcer was calling him The Sentimental Gentleman of Swing. The time was 9:59.

When the news came on at ten, there was another name in it that was new to him. As the situation got worse in Europe, men he'd never heard of before were quoted as if they were world figures. The new name was Eden. Anthony Eden. Not long ago, Winston Churchill's name had caught his attention for the first time. Now he was in the news nearly every night. Eden said Chamberlain was wrong. We were closer to war than most people realized. But then the news reader quoted Mr. Chamberlain as saying the Munich Accord of September 29, 1938, could be trusted, and that we should be calm and determined in the face of present difficulties.

He thought about Fielder's father listening in his living room, or down at the Legion. The hall would be quiet now, and when the European news was finished everybody would begin talking at once about when the war was going to start again. Fielder said his father believed the war this time would be in the air and not just in the trenches. He'd written army H.Q. in Ottawa asking that he be allowed to form a Searchlight Company and that the army supply a searchlight to practise with. Fielder said that he only had his puttees left from his old army uniform, because he'd worn the rest of it until it was tatters after he'd come home. On Saturdays, he took his puttees and his rifle to the Legion. Others who wanted out did too. They marched, and he was never so drunk or so cheerful as when he came home after making the final inspection and dismissing his veterans and young men from around town to the singalong conducted by Doug Jerrold's wife, Cynthia, at the piano in the bar. Gabe said the place was spotless, and the piano was the best one in town. Regimental colours and plaques were on the walls. It was like magic, Gabe said. You walked in there and it was another world. There was no Depression. The old ways were worshipped, and men were allowed to cry when they put their arms around each other and swayed and sang to the music Cynthia played. Always the same songs, mostly about war, but some were from musicals: *Chu Chin Chow*, or maybe the comic or happy-sad tunes sung by The Dumbbells who'd entertained them overseas, and just a few coming-home songs, pieces they remembered dancing to in the first months after they returned to Canada. Only a few spoke against the war now, Gabe said. They called war bad, but this one was maybe necessary.

The back door opened. His father came through it quickly and walked into the living room, obviously looking for his wife, and expecting her to be alone. "Chris," he said, as if the name were an exclamation. Then he shrugged and sat down.

His mother spoke first. "What happened, Peter? Is Dorothy Lee safe?"

"No."

"She's fired?" Christopher asked.

His father looked at him and he could see that he wasn't happy to have him here for this conversation. "Suspended," he said. There was no way to speak around what had happened. "But in fact she has been fired. The vote was unanimous among the members. I asked the secretary to record my disagreement with the verdict."

"Is that allowed? For the Chairman to do that?"

"I don't suppose so, Laura, but I did it anyway. Miss Lee left after the vote to suspend and came back a few moments later with her resignation and gave it to me. I'm sure she meant for it to be the end of the year, but there was no date on it. I pointed that out and, clear as day, Courtney signalled, and Paulson moved we accept with regret. It was seconded and there was a call for the vote. I had to call it. It was all over so quickly."

"Is it all allowed?"

"It was in order. The system worked."

"It's just that at that moment it was a little sick."

"She had her time in court. Grandison even appeared as her advocate, but in fact he was on side. Everybody was. It was beautifully orchestrated. Motions were made, seconded, discussed, voted upon, and never once did anyone move, or for that matter want to move toward finding out what happened on Saturday night. Resignation or dismissal were the only alternatives. That was seen to before the meeting. A few phone calls, and the strategy was fixed."

"It was you, wasn't it, Peter? Courtney wanted to show you who is boss. Dorothy Lee was a chance to do it. He just knew you'd stand up for her."

"There was no animosity until I turned the chair over to Butterworth and spoke as an ordinary Board member. From there on in it was grim warfare, a show of power. Afterward, in the hallway, Courtney bumped me on purpose as he went by."

"What can he do now?"

"I'm Chairman. All he can do is bump me."

"You have no protection anywhere else. None."

"Yes, I do. I'm good at my job. Everyone knows that."

Christopher suddenly realized that he hadn't breathed for a long time. He let the air out of his lungs. "That's it?"

"Yes."

"They didn't listen to her?"

"No. Or maybe they did. The truth sometimes prosecutes."

"What about Bush?"

"They listened to him."

"I was there at her place. So was Purvis."

"Purvis is in isolation in hospital, and in any case you're both infants under the law."

"Poor Peter, you must've been livid."

"I said that what we were doing was hasty, certainly unkind and probably unjust. I was not in the chair so Butterfield recognized Courtney, who said morals had nothing to do with justice, that Miss Lee, as a teacher, must be clean living, but more than that must be seen to be clean living, and this was not the case. It's an old judicial argument, but it works perfectly well on most occasions to say one must do and also be seen to be doing. Courtney said School Boards do not deal with the law. They represent the community and act in accordance with what the people think, feel, and want, which is as it should be. The Chairman had been here only a few years, and perhaps was not yet a fully-integrated member of the society that lives in Long River. I've never heard that semi-literate be so eloquent."

After a moment's silence, his mother said, "We've all had our quarrels with teachers, haven't we?"

"Meaning what?"

"Well, I suppose they're easiest to be angry at. They're powerful people. Whatever is making the world the mess it's in is powerful too. We feel helpless in the face of it. Miss Lee certainly makes it easy for us to get a little of it off our chests. Will nobody protest her going?"

"She resigned."

"That's it then?"

"Certainly. Resignation in this instance is an admission of guilt."

"How cosy. I don't think much of your system."

"The system is good."

"A good union is what's needed."

"The teachers have an association."

"Will it protest?"

"Why? She resigned."

"She was made to feel so unwelcome by how she was attacked, Peter. It was all she could do. How hurt she must be. Can we see her?"

"See her if you want."

"I will." She stood up. "And I still wish you had a union."

"My Bolshevik wife." He stood up too.

That was all. It was as if a curtain had dropped. The two of them walked single file out of the living room into their bedroom. His mother turned and smiled her good night, and shut the door.

His mind ground down hard on what his father had said. He got up and walked out into the kitchen, ran the water cold, filled a glass and drank it. The muscles in his throat pained each time he swallowed. The hurt felt as if he might be somehow sharing with Dorothy Lee the accident she'd said had begun to happen on Saturday.

But he wanted to do more than just hurt. He closed the door between the breakfast nook and the living room and lifted the phone's receiver off its hook. He asked for Miss Lee's number. It rang five times before she answered it. "It's Christopher," he said.

"Oh," she said, distant. "What is it?"

"My dad told me."

"Of course. Your father."

He hadn't expected her to be formal, adult. He'd been at her house when what was finishing now had just begun. "They didn't ask Purvis," he said. "They didn't ask me."

"No, they didn't. I don't suppose they felt the need."

He saw his father following the rules for meetings. "Purvis wouldn't've let them get away with it."

"I don't want to talk about it."

"But I do." He knew his voice was too demanding. He waited.

In a moment, she said, "What do you want, Christopher?"

"Tell me how you feel."

"Right this moment?"

"About what they did to you."

"I told you I might be in trouble."

"It's unfair."

"Yes."

"You didn't do anything. I mean—" He stopped, not able now to match Purvis' name with hers.

"No."

"So my dad's right. He stood up for you."

Then she broke. He could hear the intake of breath and the choke that tried to hold back tears. "God help him, he's a good man."

"He thinks that kind of meeting—what happens at them—is good. But people can use them to be unjust."

"You're too young to know, Christopher."

"What?"

"*I'm* too young to know." She was getting control again. "The system's not about justice. It's about order."

"I don't understand."

"Yes, you do. You've sat in classrooms for nine years." She stopped on a sharp intake of breath once more. "Now, look, this is enough. You shouldn't have phoned, and I shouldn't have answered. One always longs for a last minute reprieve." She laughed. "It hurts to know there's no such thing." She laughed again. "Which may be why we invented hope. Would you tell John Purvis something for me?"

"Yes, what?"

"That he's right about travel, and when he's well he must do it, often."

"Why?"

"Because it stops us living our same old stories over and over. Same old stories never end until—"

"You die," he said, as if he'd got the right answer first in class.

"No. There's more to tell him than that." She drew in her breath and sighed. "I'm glad you phoned, Christopher. I didn't know I needed to talk to somebody besides myself. Good night. Goodbye."

"Yes, thank you," he said, not knowing what he was thanking her for. "See you at school in the morning."

Her voice was distant again. "Of course."

3

In the morning, the wind swirled very fine snow across the town. He got up and looked out his window and saw it being blown nearly horizontal to the ground, as if it were salt thrown downwind. A car moved along York Street, and he thought it might be Grandison's; it was early, too early even for him to be going to the school, but after last night maybe all the teachers were meeting before work. Garrett and Blenkin would be there.

He sat on the edge of his bed and tried to think about them, and Miss Lee. Would they shake her hand and make those kinds of noises people make when they're sorry? Or would they do nothing; just stare and shrug: "If you shake hands with the Devil—" The Devil was Purvis. The Devil to them, evil to Mary. When he thought about that, he saw again Miss Lee smiling her awkward smile and shaking her head: "Not quite, Christopher; get beyond the easy answer." Purvis wasn't the Devil. Making love was: with him on her bed, and the maroon folds of her housecoat under them, but she'd said that wasn't true. His father had said: "She'll lie, she'll have to."

He lay back on his bed and covered himself with the blanket again. Down the hall Sarah was crying. Living, he thought, her same old story over and over again. She had years to go before she could travel. Would they send Purvis to the sanitarium today and lock him up because there was no medicine to cure T.B.? The disease was a crime. So was being friends with Purvis. Miss Lee had resigned. And Christopher B. Waterton was in trouble because he'd told Purvis, who'd told Blenkin what he'd been doing with Garrett in the lab room.

Sarah wasn't crying anymore. His mother knocked, and he told her to come in. She turned on the overhead light and looked at him. "School this morning?"

It sounded as if she were giving him a choice, and he wished she hadn't. "No. I feel lousy."

"Again?" She looked at him. "I heard you on the phone last night. To Fielder?"

He shook his head.

"Who?" Her voice was more insistent than usual.

"Miss Lee." It felt good to tell her.

"That was awful gall, Christopher."

He watched her wait for him to say something, but he didn't feel like arguing that point.

"Was she all right?"

"No. How could she be?"

"Of course. I hope you didn't pry."

"No."

"It's a very adult problem."

"Meaning what?"

"Her having anything to do with John Purvis."

"She didn't." He sat up. "What are you saying?"

"That she wasn't very wise. She's a teacher. She should've sent him packing."

"Coughing blood? Don't be stupid, Mother."

"That *was* awkward. I meant, she should have sent him away other times."

"There weren't other times."

"How do you know that?"

"She told me." It occurred to him that he hadn't asked Purvis about other times—not in the taxi, because of the way Bush had talked, and not at the hospital, because Mary had been there.

"Why did she tell you?" His mother's face was red and her eyes blinked.

"I asked."

"You did pry." She sat on the bed, and when she spoke again he knew she wasn't talking about Miss Lee. "You mustn't."

He stood up to escape her. "Mustn't what?"

"It's come too suddenly, all this. Emily . . . Gabe and his blue music. Is that why you were friends with Purvis, to feel older? Can't you stay back with Fielder and Smith and the others? Just do it a little at a time so there's some control possible." She stood beside him. "Dorothy Lee may be put-upon by all this. I believe she is. But she shouldn't be talking to someone who's—"

"What?"

"Not got all that much experience in life."

"You didn't talk this way last night."

"I hadn't thought about it—not all the way through."

Sarah was at the door and her face was anxious. "Are we going to have breakfast?"

"Of course, dear." His mother looked at him uncertainly. Then she went with Sarah and closed the door, presumably so he could get dressed and go to school. He heard his father down in the basement shovelling coal into the furnace. Outside, the snow was still being driven across the yard as if it were white rain. He went back to bed and pulled the covers up around his shoulders. A deep comfort relaxed his muscles and warmed his bones. Then his head filled with bits of images—Mary Purvis leaning against the side of her high old car; Purvis on Miss Lee's bed coughing blood; Miss Lee's eyes beneath the mess of her beautiful hair. But not as beautiful as Emily's, who appeared close to him, her mouth ready to be touched by his. This was the fourth day since he'd last seen her. Blenkin was at school calling the roll, but it was his father's voice.

"Christopher."

He woke up and turned over.

"Why aren't you up?"

"I don't know. I don't feel well, I guess."

"You guess?"

"Is it late?"

"Not if you hurry."

"What are you doing home?"

"I had some Board business to do on the phone."

"What kind?"

"Never mind. Get yourself up."

"I'm still not really well."

"Christopher, did you do something to Mr. Blenkin? Is that why you don't want to go to school? Were you impolite to him Saturday after the jumping?"

"No."

"You sure?"

"Yes."

"Purvis has nothing to do with school?"

"No."

"You're not sick."

"I don't feel good, that's all. I don't want to go."

"You have to."

"Why?"

"Because it's what you do for a living."

"For a living?"

"If you didn't do that, you'd be out working, or spending all day every day looking for a job."

The threat was softly said, but there was a fist in it. "I don't understand. I'm your kid."

"Yes, you are, and my kid earns his keep, one way or the other."

"Like Purvis. You'll kick me out."

"No, not like Purvis. This is your home, but it's not a place you can lie around and pretend to be sick. Even if you are a little under the weather, you get up and go. It's training for later on. The world demands excellence. Anything less and there's a danger you'll wind up standing on street corners. Or worse, trying to tear down the system along with Tim Buck and his Commie pals."

Anger made him say it: "A Bolshie wife and a Commie son," and he saw a hand coming toward him. He rolled and ducked beneath it, and then stood up beside the bed.

"Peter," his mother said. She was suddenly there.

"Close the door, Laura, go out and close it. Goddamn it, you're making a slacker out of this boy and I won't have it."

She didn't close the door. Christopher watched her come toward them with her chin down and her eyes wide. "You're not to," she said. "Please. Let him be." Then there were tears in her eyes that overflowed down her cheeks. "Things get blown out of proportion," she said. "We're all so upset."

"He must go to school," his father said, his voice still loud. He looked at his watch. "Late or not."

"Yes, Peter, all right. Christopher will go to school."

His father was looking at her now. Christopher had never seen him look so uncertain. "Laura," he said.

She shook her head. "No violence, Peter. We can't have it here when it's all around us. Go to work," she told him in a normal voice.

In the kitchen, he said, "What time do you want to go to the library?"

"You've known for weeks what time the show will open."

"Five," he said. "The show opens at five and the reception's at 7:30. Okay, five."

"Take Sarah to school," she said. "She's late too."

There was nothing left for any of them to say. Christopher stared back at his father and wished there were words. He stood and waited so that when he closed the door to his room it wouldn't be seen as an insolent gesture. Then he took his pajamas off and dressed. What had happened had created a vacuum in his head. He walked through the kitchen to the nook. The toast and cereal there were cold. He picked up a piece of toast and held it between his teeth while he put on his jacket and boots. He only sensed that his mother was in her bedroom, and he didn't disturb her.

On his way down to the school, he ate the toast, and felt that every time he swallowed, something hard in his belly was squeezed more solid. He walked slowly, and the snow needled at the right side of his face as he went. All of the bells in both schools had rung, and after those bells there was always a silence all over town, as if everyone must listen for truants, whose footsteps in the hard snow would betray them. But now the wind was high and the temperature was falling. He was safe, at least until he got to school.

He'd promised he'd come early to school so he could meet with Emily, and now she was already at work in the class Mr. Littler taught in the room at the southwest corner of the square clapboard Elementary School building. Its windows looked west across the playground. He stood there and looked up at the room where Emily was. He shivered, not from the cold, but because he'd not known how much he wanted to be with her. The longing came hard and sudden.

He moved closer and stood on the sidewalk. Someone was at the pencil sharpener by the window. He couldn't see who it was, but he waved and the face pressed closer to the pane to look down at him before it disappeared. It might have been Dody. Almost immediately there was another face at the sharpener. He didn't have to guess who it was. He waved again, and she pointed down toward the entrance to the school before she disappeared.

He walked around the building and already Emily was there waiting for him, standing in the cold, wearing a skirt and blouse, with a light cardigan over it. He pushed her back into the space between the outer and inner doors. She put her arms around him, not caring if anyone could see. He put his lips down onto hers and felt her relax against him. Everyone else in Long River had their heads down doing what they should. They were safe. He felt well.

"Are you okay?" she whispered.

"Yes."

"You weren't here—"

"I slept in." He kissed her again. "Did you just walk out?"

"I asked to be excused." She pushed her face in close to his neck and breathed in deeply. It was as if they had all day to do this.

"What are you doing?"

"I like your smell." She looked up at him again. "Chris, what's happening? One phone call since Saturday."

He could say it to her now, and before he couldn't say it even to himself. "Purvis. Miss Lee's been fired. Blenkin and Garrett. I think it's made me sick." He felt her shiver.

"Miss Lee's been fired?"

"They think she did it with Purvis."

"Did she? She couldn't have. Did they prove it?"

"No. They just made it so tough on her that she resigned."

"It's not right."

"It's what they do." He laughed. "It's to protect us."

"Is it? I don't care. I didn't come down here to talk about stupid teachers. See me after school. Promise?"

"Yes."

She held herself very close to him and stopped shivering. "Kiss," she said.

Between them, it was the harshest order possible. "Kiss," he said back to her, and when their tongues met, he heard himself make a noise as if he'd been surprised by his best wish coming true. When they were together everything was simple, and he didn't like having to leave her. She moved away. He watched her climb the stairs. When she was halfway up Mr. Littler appeared. She stopped. Christopher stepped back into the shadow of the entranceway. She was a girl, Littler could only ask her if she was all right.

"Yes sir," she said.

"Then don't dawdle."

She moved on up the stairs. He waited to give Mr. Littler time to go back into his classroom, then he went outside again and headed toward the High School.

Behind him, Mr. Littler's voice said, "Just a minute, Waterton."

He stopped and turned.

"Come here, boy."

He walked back to Mr. Littler and stood waiting.

"Why aren't you in school?"

"I'm late."

"I can see that. Were you in my school?"

"No."

"But you were talking to Emily Gordon. She lied about having to leave the room, and she came down to see you."

"She didn't lie."

"Are you contradicting me?"

"I'm telling you the truth."

"You're a liar too. I'll speak to Mr. Grandison about this."

Christopher waited for a moment, but Littler didn't say anything, so he felt free to turn away and start once more to go toward his school.

"You are insolent as well."

"Yes, sir," he said, without turning back. He expected more—an order to stop. But it didn't come. It was cold outside, and the wind made it colder. He went down the hill, opened the south door and stood at the bottom of the stairs. He'd forgotten to ask his mother for a note and would have to see Grandison, even if Littler didn't call him.

It wasn't warm here, but it was inside out of the wind. He leaned against the wall and waited. Upstairs someone made a joke and a whole class laughed. They were working. This was what children did for a living. He hadn't known. Isonovich loved it. Monica Lewis. Pat Gordon, and maybe Smith, who wouldn't dare admit it. For Lamb and McDonald it was a place to hang out. If there'd been jobs to go to, they'd've quit when they were fifteen.

The bell rang. He went slowly up the stairs and into the grade nine cloakroom. The central hallway filled up for recess. Very few would go outside. Blenkin saw him alone hanging up his coat. There was a scabbed cut on his forehead but no bandage.

"Are you late, Waterton?"

"Yes."

"I marked you absent."

"I'm just late."

"You have a note?"

"No. I forgot to ask."

Miss Garrett was suddenly there at Blenkin's side. She was white-faced. Her curls were tight around her head, as if she'd made them in anger. Blenkin looked uncomfortable.

"*Why* were you late?" she asked.

He decided to tell them the truth. "I didn't want to come at all."

Then she was by his side, tense and hunched forward.

"Lillian," Blenkin said, before she could speak.

Her eyes narrowed, and she looked as if she were a little girl who was about to be disobedient. "Don't," she said, through tight lips.

"What?" Another time this might be funny.

"Miss Garrett." Blenkin hadn't moved, but his voice crackled with reigned-in power.

She turned away, her eyes wide again, and went to Blenkin. He looked at her with no expression on his face; she smiled stiffly, hesitated, and then went out once more into the main hall.

"You'll bring two notes tomorrow," Blenkin said. "One for your absence yesterday, and one for your lateness today."

There was a temptation to argue, to see if he could. "Two?"

"Yes." Blenkin turned away and paused, hesitating too, as Garrett had, before he looked around again. His face was red with anger. "I suppose one will do."

Christopher watched him begin to retreat from the cloakroom entrance. "What was she saying to me?" His heart was beating fast. "Don't what?" he said after Blenkin.

"She must've thought you knew." Blenkin said, and left.

"She meant don't tell on you," he said, but Blenkin didn't show he'd heard.

Christopher walked out into the hallway and went into Miss Lee's room. She was not there. Mrs. Conklin was. Married women weren't allowed to teach—another broken rule.

"Yes?" she said, looking up at him from her desk.

"Miss Lee?"

Mrs. Conklin smiled. "You of all people must know where Miss Lee is."

He didn't want to answer that. "Excuse me," he said, and backed away out of the door. Now, he heard what everybody in the hall was talking about. Muncie was laughing. "Well, Jesus, she resigned, didn't she?" He held Christopher's arm. "I hear your old man tried to tell the meeting last night that it's okay for teachers to screw Rink Rats."

"As if you'd care, Muncie."

Muncie slammed him against the wall, but he was laughing. "That goddamn Purvis, eh? What a guy. Humpin' her and coughin' his lungs out at the same time."

"Don't be a prick," Lamb said. "Purvis could die."

"That was yesterday. I hear he's all right now."

Christopher kept on moving. In the cloakroom he picked his jacket off of its hook and went back down the stairs. There was not now even any sense of adventure: he couldn't stay. Muncie was everybody, and he was laughing. Fielder would be delighted. Callaghan and Smith too. His father was no hero for defending Miss Lee, and the accident she said had started Saturday night was still happening. He went back out through the south door again, out of everybody's sight, and headed for Eighth Avenue.

His sense of what was happening to him was vague. He felt there was a horror he couldn't identify trailing him, and he couldn't understand why. Purvis and Blenkin had fought. Purvis and Lee had been together at her house. Who cares? The question hardly made sense. Both Purvis and Miss Lee were disappearing, and what was happening to him was tied to the reason they were going. Stupid reasons made by men and women who were supposed to be grown up. Garrett's face was like a balloon suspended in his mind: her eyes glinting, her teeth tight together, her voice at the same time angry and afraid. She could go crazy at any moment and try to do something worse than electrocute him.

Blenkin was always the one out front, never back in the pack. Now he was connected with Garrett. Purvis had done it to him two ways: beaten him up and then gotten Miss Lee fired. Teachers *could* be fired. He and Garrett could be asked to go if people found out about them. Probably the whole thing should be a joke, except that some people would be laughing out of the other sides of their faces.

As he turned in at Miss Lee's gate and ran the length of the walk to the porch, the hard ball in his gut got bigger. He knocked. There was no answer, and he had his hand on the knob before he saw a white envelope stuck between the door and its frame. He picked it out and held it in his hand. It meant she was gone, and she was the only person he might have been able to talk to. *For John Purvis,* it said in her handwriting, *Personal and Private. Please Forward.* Silly. Why not mail it? And why a message to Purvis only? Who came back and told her Purvis was all right, and phoned her after she'd been fired?"

He shoved the envelope into his pocket and went down off the porch again. Where was she? He went back to the door and looked through its window. The light was dim, but he could see the bed had been stripped. None of her clothes or her dirty dishes were lying around. She was gone. How? There was no train until five o'clock. But there was a bus.

He began to run, not caring who saw him out of school, and headed down London, past the Royal and beyond until he got to First Avenue. There he turned the corner in time to see the bus, long and low and encrusted with churned-up snow, close its doors. He ran faster then, and when the bus began to pull out he was beside it and banged on the door with his fist. The driver braked and stopped. "Come on, come on," he said. "Where're you going?"

"No," Christopher said. "Miss Lee. Is she here?"

"Why?"

"I want to see her."

The driver turned in his seat and looked back down the length of the bus. Christopher climbed aboard. Halfway back was Miss Lee. She was shaking her head, and he thought he could see tears. He took out Purvis' envelope and held it up. She nodded, and her awkward mouth formed, "Thank you," and something else he didn't get.

"What?"

She stood up. "Leave it be, Christopher. Leave it be. I told you, it's no tragedy." Her voice was a hoarse loud whisper, as if she hoped no one else on the bus would hear. She sat down again and looked into her lap.

"I guess you're out of luck," the driver said. "Off you get."

He stood for a long time on the sidewalk wondering what he'd have said to her if she'd come forward from her seat. "Did you? You and Purvis. Did you?" If they had, then the injustice of her going would have been real. She should be with him. And if they hadn't, then it was only a game between his father and Mayor Courtney that made her the loser. He thought of her staying in Long River and fighting for her job. She should have. It was as if she'd only needed a small excuse to make her resign and go. But the idea of fighting people who had all the power made him feel sick again. He went back up London Street, knowing he was in trouble. His father had ordered him to school. Blenkin, Garrett, and Conklin knew he'd been there.

Coming toward him, more than a block away, was his mother. He ducked into Wei Ch'en's and watched her walk by. He wasn't afraid of her. He never had been, but there wasn't any way he could explain what was happening to him right now. He only hoped it wasn't a pattern in his life he was going to have to live over and over again. She walked with her head down, the tassle of her grey toque dangling over her shoulder, with her hands in the pockets of her winter coat, toward the market. For her, things were fine. Her paintings were going to make her add up to more than she'd been before.

He heard May's voice say hello, and he turned to look at her. She was smiling. "You quit school? Not Christopher Waterton."

"No." He looked around. There were plenty of coffee drinkers, and a few who were eating a late breakfast. He sat on a stool at the end of the counter by the cash register.

"Going to the dentist, or what?"

"I just got bored and walked out."

She rang up a ten cent coffee and donut. "You look sad."

"You look happy," he said.

"Sure, why not?"

"Winter's almost over."

"Ha ha. Come on, what's the matter?"

"Miss Lee got fired."

May nodded. "Bush was in here this morning. What's it to you?"

"I was there Saturday night when Bush came to get Purvis from her house. He was coughing blood, and besides they hadn't known each other a week."

"I've seen it take less than a week to go from hello to all the way." She was laughing at him as she always did.

"I guess you're supposed to be the expert," he said.

She wiped the counter in front of him and then leaned against it so her face was close to his. "Listen." She grinned. "Ch'en and I are going to get married."

"Really?" The shock made him sit back and look at her. Maybe this was another joke.

"He kept at me. I said, you want it, marry me. You know what happened? I'm like the crown jewels now. He hasn't put a hand on me since. Not once. It's like I'm a goddess—a white girl going to marry a Chinese. He's having the place upstairs re-done, and his tong brothers are putting on a party for us. He asked me what I wanted for a wedding present. It was too sudden. I didn't know. I just laughed and said the Studebaker that's been sitting all winter in Lorimer's showroom. I'm getting it."

"You're not even old enough to drive."

"See? I knew I could cheer you up."

"So, it's a joke."

She shook her head. He looked at her left hand, and she said, "Don't worry, there'll be a ring. I'm just having a plain gold wedding band, like my mother's. There's still a lot of the Old Country in me." Her voice was almost prissy.

"Do you love him?"

"Yes. Who wouldn't?" She stood back from the counter and smiled. "On my sixteenth birthday. April 21st."

"I didn't know you were sixteen."

"They failed me in grade three, so I've always been older than you guys."

"It's crazy."

She shook her head again. "Ch'en said, 'You get what you need all the time.' That doesn't sound very crazy to me."

"If it happens, it isn't."

"I'm not Miss Lee."

"I know."

"She's got two cents worth of books in her head and ten dollars worth of trouble because of it." She smiled. "Taking on Purvis is *real* crazy. You want a coffee?"

He felt in his pocket. He had Purvis' letter and fifteen cents. "Hot chocolate," he said.

"That's a dime."

"I know." He still had his hand on the letter. "She was lonely—Miss Lee."

"You liked her a lot."

"I didn't know until a while ago."

"You got Emily."

He nodded and watched her face. It had stopped smiling.

"When I get happy I say, Piss on the world and everybody in it. I shouldn't do that." She smiled again. "But it feels so good." She got busy then and it was ten minutes before she brought him his chocolate. She touched his hand, still smiling. "So, wish me luck, eh?"

"Yes. I do. Good luck."

"I always sort of fancied you," she said, and laughed. "You're a nice guy."

"But I couldn't buy gas for your Studebaker."

She leaned again on the counter, close to him. "I'm going to be so bloody high class. You know what I want? A horse. And riding pants and one of those hats that looks like an upside-down pot."

"There's lots of horses around."

"I mean a real horse, not a cayuse."

She went to the cash register, and he sucked down the hot chocolate she'd brought him. It was sweet, and the whipped cream on top of it gave him a moustache. He watched himself wipe it off in the mirror behind the counter. Nothing in his face had changed. He wondered why? He felt older. May looked older. She had her hair braided across the top of her head. Wei Ch'en came out of the kitchen. He was taller than May by about three inches, but there was no way of telling how much older he was. Twenty years, maybe. When he was sixty, she'd be forty, four years older than his mother was now. The circles his mind made surprised him. Ch'en had come to work behind the counter. He stood watching May make change for a customer, and when she turned around, he looked a little as if he'd been caught doing something he shouldn't.

"Ch'en," she said, because he was staring, but her voice was different than Christopher had heard it. The edge wasn't there.

He stood up and smiled at May.

Ch'en said, "She tell you?"

"Yes. You're a lucky guy." He put his dime on the counter.

"Good. I know." He picked up the dime and held it out. "On the house."

Christopher didn't know what to do.

"Come on, you take it for celebration."

"Thank you."

"First and last time," May said. "That's a gallon of gas."

"She tell you that too about the car?" Ch'en laughed. "Being Canadian husband going to be headache, eh?"

"I don't think so." He didn't know what else to say. The door opened behind him. It was easy to go then, saying thank you twice more and goodbye as if he'd been at a party. Outside, he stood on the sidewalk and felt good. Good for May. Everybody liked Ch'en. Maybe she was a gold-digger. No. May was straight. He walked away down the street and around the corner.

At the library he paused and looked in the window. One of his mother's paintings was there. He'd first seen it when it'd been a quick pencil sketch of a lake with a small island in the middle of it. The birches on the island now were lace against the evergreen, and near the shore was a long-billed bird that looked down into the water. Maybe it saw something there. Maybe it just looked down into the water because that's what it did for a living. The painting was neat and pretty. There was no need to think about the bird, but it was there. That was the way his mother was; she always put something extra in. The bird: he wondered if one like that even lived in this part of the world. The things she did didn't always make sense, but that was the difference between her and everyone else he knew. There was what she did, and then there were the echoes afterward to think about.

Right now, he didn't want to be caught out of school by her. Elmo Kidner came jerking up the street toward him. "Can't talk," he said, importantly. "I'm on my way to see Jeff Harris."

"You going to be his mechanic?" It wasn't a good joke.

"Going to pump gas noonhours so he can go to lunch. He never been to lunch before. Always had it at the garage."

"Maybe times are getting better."

"For me if the deal goes through," Elmo said. He began to cross the street and then came back. "You know what I heard today? The army's coming to guard the bridge."

"That right?"

"If there's a war, I'm going to buy a gun and get Hitler by myself."

At the end of the avenue behind the City Hall was the Works Yard. He walked along the pathway on the east side of the building to the old board fence that surrounded the depot where Long River's mechanical equipment and engineering supplies were stored. Behind it, one of the Castle Hills rose up from the edge of town. When he was younger and they'd first moved here, he used to come and sit on the high stool at the drafting table his father had built in the the shack he called his office. Harrison Dodd, the City Engineer, didn't like the shack to be called an office and, once a year at least, he asked when the drafting table was going to be removed. In his view the general foreman should be out on the job eight hours a day and not going over drawings and blueprints as if he were practising to be somebody he wasn't. But Dodd seldom visited the yard. His office was across the hall from the mayor's. He was more to Mayor Courtney than just the City Engineer.

The old fence leaned and, after three months of heavy snowfalls, it was only about half as tall as it was in the summer. Near the gate, there was a gap in the fence. He looked through it and saw no one. Smoke rose from the shack's chimney. The gate was almost closed. He squeezed through and ran across the compound to the shack. This was a game. He couldn't see his father, because he was supposed to be in school, but he wanted to talk to him. He stood by the door for a moment, listening, and then he shoved it open.

Inside it was warm. The drafting table slanted up from its stool to the shelves above it. The tin stove was clean and black. The floor was swept and the walls were neatly covered with cardboard. There was a mat at the door.

He sat on the stool and picked up a pencil and wrote on a piece of scrap paper: "Dad, I went to school, but I didn't stay. Miss Lee was gone. I didn't expect that so soon. Blenkin and Garrett know I told Purvis about them necking in the lab."

He looked out of the shack's one small window to where an old tractor sat rusting against the fence. Then he turned and wrote again. "Why do you believe it's okay to have meetings where people can vote to say you're not good and you don't have a job anymore? I've been to Coventry."

He crumpled up his note and threw it into the wastepaper basket. The ball of paper bounced and settled at the bottom: there was writing on the other side of it. He picked it up again and smoothed it out on the table in front of him.

"Laura," it said.

"Oh, Jesus." His stomach went hard and cold.

"I'm sorry about this morning. I shouldn't have said you'd made Chris a slacker. You haven't, and he isn't. He's a person now. It's difficult to know," and that was the end of it. His father had stopped, too, when he'd gotten to the hard part.

He read it again, and then again, seeing that strong man saying Sorry. He never said he was sorry. The cold in his gut made him shiver.

If his father was writing notes to himself, practising to say he was sorry, what chance did his son have to get tough enough to handle people like Littler, Grandison, Blenkin? He crumpled the paper up again and put it in his pocket. Out of the window he saw movement. His father was at the gate with Harrison Dodd.

Carefully, as if they might hear, he got down off the stool and went to the door. It didn't squeak; the sound would offend his father. He closed it on its oiled hinges and walked, one pace at a time, choosing icy snow to step on that held his weight and made no noise. He hid behind the rusting tractor. Beyond it was a truck and then the upturned deck of an old horse-drawn sleigh near the fence.

He crouched and watched the two men. Harrison Dodd was tall, with a perfectly round pot-belly. He wore high boots and a canvas engineer's jacket under an open parka. Something important had brought him out of his office. They walked together to a shed marked DANGER in red foot-high letters. His father unlocked the door, and they stood counting the boxes of dynamite inside it. Christopher ran stooped over on the other side of the sleigh to the gate. He glanced as he went through it. Neither man had seen him.

The pathway took him out onto Manchester Street, and he walked up it toward the schoolgrounds again. The ball of paper in his pocket felt enormous, dangerous; but he couldn't throw it away.

It was important for him to know that they'd both written—he and his father—and he didn't know whether writing instead of saying was an act of cowardice or whether it was a need in both of them to get things right. *Precise* was Grandison's word. *Correct* was Blenkin-the-bully's word. Follow orders and you'll be correct. He took out Miss Lee's letter to Purvis and put it in his shirt pocket.

As he passed Fourth Avenue, the twelve o'clock whistle blew at the roundhouse on the far side of the railway yards, and when he got to the Liverpool Street corner, Emily was there with Dody and some grade eights.

"You weren't at school."

"No."

"Why?"

"I want a lawyer before I answer that." He wanted her to smile, but she didn't. She looked at Dody and said, "I'm going to walk with Chris."

"You'll miss lunch," he said.

"We can go to Gran's. I want to talk to you. What's happening?" She gave Dody a friendly push. "See you later."

"You two," Dody said. "When're you going to get married?" But she left and ran to catch up with the gang they'd been walking with.

Emily put her arm around him and they walked. He knew she was waiting for him to talk, but he couldn't begin to tell her what she wanted to know. They'd been apart for a long time, and too much had happened since Saturday. He held her close, feeling desperate for something good to tell her. "I love you," he said. It was true, but the words stuck to his tongue like winter steel, because it wasn't what he was thinking. He felt her arm squeeze him tighter, as if she were comforting him and saying, Yes, I know, but what's the matter?

Her grandmother wasn't home. Emily got out her key and opened the door. He watched her take off her coat and boots, and he took off his. Then she went to the bedroom and came back wearing her grandmother's slippers and an old sweater and skirt she kept here for visits in the winter.

In the kitchen, she asked what he wanted for lunch. Soup? A sandwich? There were eggs. Gran had some cheese. He chose tomato soup and a cheese sandwich, and then watched Emily become someone he'd not known before. She moved from cupboard to stove, to sink to counter as competently as his mother. Her face was smooth and serious. He stood watching her for a while, and then he went into the living room and phoned home to tell them there where he was. His mother sounded distracted. "That's nice, dear," she said. "Tell Mrs. McLeod hello for me." He said he would and put the receiver back on its hook.

He sat at the kitchen table. Emily stirred the soup and said everything was ready. The time to talk had come.

"When I first got there," he said, as if he were answering her first question, "Blenkin and Garrett were on to me. Garrett was stupider than I've ever seen her. She came right into the cloakroom with me and I could smell her rotten breath when she said Don't."

"Don't? That all, just don't?" She put the soup on the table.

"Look," he said, "they made Miss Lee quit last night. That's how fast things happen. Garrett knows what's going on. They could be fired tomorrow if what they're doing gets around. Lee's gone. They couldn't make an exception and say it's okay for them to be doing it. The mayor doesn't like the way my dad's running the School Board so he makes it fire Miss Lee to show him who's boss. He hates people going against him. You know what he did after my dad defended Miss Lee? He bumped him in the hallway after, crashed right into him on purpose."

"It sounds like school. Are they grownups?"

"Who? My dad?"

"No. The Mayor, Garrett. I don't know. The School Board."

"Who knows? I guess so." He laughed. "They're all we got." That was funny and it made him laugh again. He watched her begin to smile, but it wasn't genuine. "I shouldn't have told you," he said, and ate some of his sandwich. "They had their fun. Miss Lee's gone. I saw her on the bus this morning."

"Already?"

"Would you stay?" He knew he was beginning to talk too loud. He took Purvis' letter out of his pocket. "She left this behind."

Emily glanced at it, and then looked back at him. "You went to see her?"

"She wasn't at school. Mrs.Conklin was. And that's another thing: she had to quit when she got married, but now suddenly it's okay for her to teach again. They can't even keep the goddamn rules they make up themselves. At the meeting they didn't need me and Purvis there to tell them the truth. Just Bush to lie. If the mayor had the truth how'd he be able to fix my old man? That's the question." He watched Emily get up and come around the table to him; there were tears in her eyes. "Why are you upset?" he asked.

"I'm not," she said. "You are."

He stood up and saw only what he wanted and needed in her. He shivered, and didn't know why, because it was warm in the kitchen. She turned away and walked into the living room. The fireplace had embers from when her grandmother had sat in front of it, maybe to drink her morning tea. He followed her, crouched down and tore some of the birch bark off the wood stacked on the hearth. It crackled and flamed on the embers, and he put a small stick of wood on top. It lay there smoking for a while, then it began to burn, and he put more birch into the flames. He watched it catch fire and begin to throw heat out toward the hearth rug.

He turned his head to look at Emily. She had brought pillows from the sofa and was lying down on the rug against them. She held out a hand, and he took it. She was smiling. He let her pull him down beside her. Still she was quiet. "You're not saying much."

She shook her head and glanced toward the fire. "It's like it's ours."

"Your gran's place is tiny." He kissed her lightly. "But it's nice." He kissed her again. Her lips were softer than he'd ever felt them, and they tasted faintly of salt.

She held his face in her hands and kissed his eyes and cheeks and neck. "It's like a doll's house," she whispered in his ear. "Hug me really tight."

The privacy here, the fire, the hearthrug, the pillows made a place he'd never been until now.

"Miss Lee's just a teacher," she said, and her mouth sealed his before he could answer. "I want us to be like this every time we can," she said. Her head rolled on the pillow so that she was looking into the fire. "Gran will let us. She knew Grampa McLeod when they were maybe our age on the Isle of Lewis up north of Scotland. Each girl made a tent. They were allowed to do it. It was a kind of ceremony that said they were growing up and could choose somebody to marry."

He waited and tried to picture old Mrs. McLeod being Emily's age in a tent, maybe on a beach. Emily was waiting too. He could feel her hardly breathing and lying very close. Her breasts were soft. He let his hand touch them, slide across them and down around her back again, and down farther to where her skirt covered her hip and the top of her leg. He kissed her very gently. It made him feel good and he wanted this to be a game: how lightly could he touch her? He did it, and wondered how she felt—if she were flying as high as he was. He touched where her skirt had parted from her blouse, and watched her lying separate but close. The warm room and the cold snow outside held them away from the other parts of their lives. This was what being with Emily did. He was caught up in it, unthinking. Only watching and feeling light at his extremities and heavy in the middle where all of his blood suddenly was. Pleasure was there too, and he wanted her hand to hold him.

"Chris," she said, softly, and pulled him closer to her. Her eyes watched him. The perfume that had been Emily turned to musk. He breathed it in. It was sudden, it was not her, and it made him think she had changed. He wanted her sweet smell back.

He saw that she knew what had happened, and was only lying there now, waiting. Her lips formed another word. He thought it was Please. She still held his hand; then she let it go, and waited. She was not afraid; her eyes were fresh and clear, and they trusted him.

He leaned even closer because he was supposed to. And waited. It was strong, what she was offering. His mind was empty of words. He needed words to tell her.

Something.

She lay there, close, not moving, offering.

He took his hand away, not touching anymore. What she was offering was immense. And he was the one who was afraid. He had stopped feeling. It hurt. Inside his head, he forced the words: I love you. He said them. She moved her head, saying yes. She was open, she could be hurt. She was so open that she was beyond confusion. But he wasn't.

He moved away from her and pulled his legs up underneath him so that he was kneeling beside her. It was what he was supposed to do. First. He could see her breathing shallow and quick. She lay straight on the rug, her legs a little apart. What had to be done was his to do, and he felt himself draw in a deep breath, while he looked around the room that was a second home to her and a strange place to him. He couldn't think here, or understand.

Still she didn't move. Make a move. Do what her sister did. Say no. Chew. Giggle. But then she drew her knees up too and lifted her hips a little way off the rug. The grey skirt slid along her legs, and the musk was stronger. Gently, still as if he were touching, he pushed her down against the rug, and then he looked at her again. "I've got to go," he said, and stood up and knew he wasn't being loving any more. What he had to do was leave. He went to the pegs near the front door and took down his jacket. He saw Emily's face only for a moment. It didn't stop him. His boots were on the floor. He picked them up and fled outside. Something had been building, but he didn't know this was going to happen, and there was no way of saying why. He dropped his boots on the porch, stuffed his feet into them and walked hard away. He got his arms into his jacket and buttoned it, found his mitts and put them on. The horror that had been following him since morning was with him, and he began to run, not up York Street toward home, but west. He ran with his head down and saw only the blank white snow and his own breath frozen and whipped away by the speed of his going.

He kept on running, walking, not being able to just walk. And he was in many places at once. In Lee's bedroom, in her living room with his hands holding her fists, in her kitchen crying, the lab at school and Blenkin groaning, at the counter with May, and that was different because she was able to say yes safely to Ch'en. Ch'en could take responsibility for what she wanted. He sat with Emily on the stairs at the school. Outside the furnace room. Fun for Pat and Fielder on the janitor's cot. But they weren't in love. He stopped running. They'd only wanted to know what it was like. Fielder wanted her to do it, just as he wanted every basketball to go through the hoop, and Pat wanted to be the first across the line again like she was in everything else. They didn't need to be in love. Loving wasn't what they were doing, and it wasn't Gabe's music, or goddamn Grandison's math. There wasn't any equation and no answer.

He stopped walking. He could go back, there was time. Except going back meant just that. The cold was in his gut again and it was uncomfortable, but it deadened nausea. Emily was still lying there on the hearthrug. A body lying quiet, hair back off its forehead, mouth a little open, hands down its sides. Fielder said, "I'm going to remember just being there for the rest of my life." For him, there was Emily at her grandmother's, and there was the hurt he'd done.

He turned, wanting to go back, but in the distance, the bell at the school began to ring. Calling people back to their job. It was a peculiar kind of relief to know that she wasn't at Mrs. McLeod's now. He stood listening to the final bell. The class was assembling; his seat was empty and Blenkin's afternoon roll call was beginning. It mattered that he wasn't there. That was where his life was—with Fielder and Smith and the Bells and Isonovich and Callaghan, Marie, Monica, the Dobroskis, Jenny Alpert. Everything now was turned over, scrambled—the finish of more than just the accident Miss Lee said started on Saturday night. He took her letter out of his shirt pocket and held it in his hand. He was a long way west. The hospital wasn't far. He began to walk again.

The sidewalk at the entranceway was always swept clear as summer. Inside, to the left of the nursing station, was a gurney. Purvis was lying on it. He had his eyes closed. The shock of leaving Emily was overridden by this dead face. No one was near, and if he was alive they should be. No nurse, no Dr. Royce. He touched Purvis' arm, afraid to speak in case he was discovered and made to go away. Then Purvis turned his head and opened his eyes.

"Waterton," he said. "Is that you for sure?"

"Yes."

"I've been having dreams. They're like, I don't know, so real I can't figure if I'm asleep."

"Why're you on this thing?"

"Hospital rules. Not allowed to walk."

They were taking him away. "Purvis," he said, "Did you know Miss Lee resigned?"

"Because of me?" His voice wasn't strong.

"In a way, but it was Bush. He made up a story and the mayor got the School Board to—"

"Don't tell me. I don't want to hear. Where is she?"

"Gone. On the bus this morning."

After a moment, Purvis stopped staring and laughed. "That was bloody quick. Same for me. I'm going too."

"On the train?"

"No. There's a Norseman flying south with a heart case for Vancouver. They're going to drop me off at Kamloops."

"I guess it's better than driving."

"They don't want me here. I scare hell out of them."

"Why?"

"There's no medicine for T.B."

"But there's stuff for you to do at the sanitarium."

"That's hokey-pokey, kid. It's a place to die, except some fool 'em and live."

"You'll live."

"Yes, I will."

"Feels like everybody's going."

"You got Emily."

He didn't want to tell him about Emily. "Miss Lee left you a letter."

"Yeah? Let's see." Purvis took the letter and carefully unsealed the envelope with a long thumbnail.

Christopher watched him read it, stare at the ceiling for a moment, and then read it again before he folded it up and put it back in its envelope. He smiled, not because of the letter, but because Miss Baker was coming.

"Are you two going steady?" she asked. "Come on, young Waterton, this is a hospital."

Purvis said, "I'll cough in your face."

She pulled a mask over her mouth and nose. "Go ahead."

"Where's the ambulance?"

"Out back." She began to push the gurney down the corridor.

Christopher walked with it. "I'll write."

"Okay," Purvis said. Then suddenly, he held the letter up. "Here, you keep this."

"It's yours. You'll want it."

"I got it memorized." He twisted his head on the pillow. "Go on, take it. It's for you too."

Christopher held the letter in his hand and glanced at Miss Baker. Her eyes were bright with watching. They were at the back door. She paused. "So long," he said to Purvis.

"Yeah," Purvis said. "They said they'd send me my stamps."

"Sure. We'll trade by letter."

"I'll do the ordering," Purvis said.

Christopher watched his eyes. They were as young as Sarah's, and they hurt to look at.

Miss Baker took him away. The doors closed, and he was left standing at one end of the long corridor that bisected the hospital. In his head was Miss Baker's voice saying, "It ain't the laundry." No, it wasn't. He held Miss Lee's letter tight in his hand and began to walk. No, it wasn't the laundry. He wanted Purvis safe now and back soon. Miracles happened. But he couldn't hold him in his head. He thought of Emily on the hearthrug. Nothing Purvis had said or done was an answer to that. Gabe had already given his answer: Irene and the child. Fielder mostly made jokes. The sidewalk beneath his feet and the houses he was passing made it clear that he was headed home.

When he opened the door, he knew there was no one there. The furnace needed coal and he shook the grates to get the morning's ashes away from the fire, then he went back upstairs and sat at his homework desk. Miss Lee's letter had to be read. He wanted to, but it was Purvis', and he should've kept it. It wasn't possible for him to remember it all, how it looked on the page. The envelope lay open in his hand. He took out the letter. Miss Lee's handwriting was full of edges, but it wasn't hard to decipher.

John,

You're going to hear that I was fired. It wasn't quite that. I accommodated them by resigning. Don't feel guilty. Looking back, I can see there was nothing either of us did that we wouldn't do again. I didn't know how to refuse you. There are not a lot of lovers in the world—not many of us for whom that is the business of life, and so we are often lonely. Or feel that way. What a sudden surprise you were, after meeting so many men who could only loosen up and dance at a funeral. In a better time and in a more charitable place we might have continued to find each other.

You are someone who is like a wild horse shut up in a corral. And you've managed to make your heart continue to beat by thinking you were keeping it ready for anger. That's a safe thing to do: what any of us can count on in people is their anger, which is another word for fear, and we have both been transported out of Long River by that double-faced monster.

I promise I will find the address of your sanitarium and will write you there. I think I never have enough people to talk to, to give me a sense that my universe has permanent centres. Besides, I may be pregnant, who knows? I have rebellious moments already when I hope so. So, you see? I will have much news for you in in my first letter.

Make yourself live, Purvis. Do that. It will be the best revenge you can have. Don't worry about me. It appears I was just passing through. We will keep in touch, and when I am living somewhere and you are passing through, we will meet again.

I didn't go to see you. I wanted to. You may think me cowardly, but I am sick with what has happened. I didn't want to see you through a glass partition. That would've been too much.

Love,
D.L.

P.S. *I find now that I have no stamp for this, and it's both too early and too late to go to the post office for one. I feel wild too, and I'm going to leave its delivery—romantically—to fate, or maybe to those dirty minds who having punished will feel it's all right to indulge in a moment's charity.*

However and whenever this gets to you, you may show it to our mutual friend, if you want. I wouldn't see him die of curiosity, would you? He may be growing up to be a lover too, and so the world must not be put in even a little danger of being deprived of him.

The story, Christopher, the whole story and nothing but the story. You deserve it. Without you it wouldn't have happened.

The postscript made him cry. He was not a lover, and didn't know how to be. Even in an empty house where he could let go, the sobs choked him. He went to his bed and lay on it. Pictures, scenes, words pummeled his mind: Purvis on Lee's bed bleeding, Bush's voice, the hospital. Afterward, Miss Lee crying and his own tears, and her face on the bus: her face on the bus and Purvis' dead face as he lay on the gurney.

And then Emily's face, calm, believing—what?—something, as she lay waiting. Miss Lee saying, "Besides, I may be pregnant, who knows?" And now she was caring for herself in a way only grown people could who knew the world and could get a job somewhere and be whoever they wanted to be.

His mother saying, "Can't you stay back with Fielder and Smith and the others?" I guess not, Mom, but I didn't know I wasn't. If I'm not, I'm not. Are they staying back? Fielder and Pat? Isonovich and Lewis? And how about May? You got to see all that to believe it.

He lay on his bed for a long time with the letter still in his hand and a hole in his body where his gut had been. That was good. He wanted no feelings about anything. Miss Lee had nothing to do with him. Purvis had T.B. He'd done it with Miss Lee and she might be pregnant—and have T.B., too. They were both gone now. Her bus was a hundred and fifty miles away. The Norseman was heading for take-off along the ploughed runway out at the airplane grounds south of the

Castle Hills. That also had nothing to do with him.

Emily had had nothing to do with him. He'd gotten up and walked out. One moment he'd been kneeling beside her, and he knew now what he'd been feeling—the connection between her lying there and the things going on in his body, and in Emily's. For her it meant saying Yes. The smell of it returned. For him there was only No. She had something to say Yes to. Everything was good. He'd said that too: everything's good. Over and over. Then at the moment when everything was perfect— the house, the fire, the hearthrug, the pillows—it wasn't a game of finding out. It was the thing that being in love was doing to them, and there was no control at all. Emily had known that her moment had come, and that her Gran's house was her tent on the beach, and that he was here and the ceremony would be complete when he said Yes too. But the next time he'd become conscious was when he was outside going down the sidewalk toward Purvis. He was alone in the house, inside a silence that was marred only by the roar of the new fire he'd made in the furnace.

He got up and shifted his horn down from its shelf in the closet. The case was worn. Someone had carried it for a long time, maybe playing one-night stands across the country. It was a hard-worked horn that a professional had blown until he could afford a better one. He held it in his hands and felt connected to the owner who had bought it new and had played it until it had been time to pass it on to Christopher Waterton in Long River. Another kind of accident, not unlike birth, because it had been the beginning of a new life for him.

Miss Lee's kind of accident didn't feel new; it felt as if it had been going on for a long time and kept on happening, like ocean waves, coming in and dropping on the shore, one and one and one, different waves but the same ocean. Different people all ending at the same accident, the one that was supposed to run down, stop in its own good time.

Miss Lee had told him to try to remember that he was just a witness. But he'd been made part of it, and he was afraid. Some of what he'd been witness to was his because of her; and Blenkin and Garrett, his father, the Board, Courtney—everybody was being sucked in. So, there was Miss Lee's accident, and one that had happened in his new life: what he'd done to Emily wouldn't end.

He took his horn out into the living room and walked with it, blowing notes and hearing them slam back off the walls in that big room. "Chinatown, my Chinatown, when the lights are low." He'd never played the tune before. It came automatically, as if he'd been thinking of Ch'en and May. Maybe what Ch'en was offering her was some kind of dream she'd have to wake up from. Whatever it was, Ch'en had stopped her old life and was giving her a new one. There had to be magic in that. At least the *feel* of magic.

"Blue moon, you see me standing alone." The notes came out more hollow than blue. "Without a song in my heart, without a love of my own." The words didn't march with the tune. He blew louder and tried to run the scales that sounded as if they might go with the long whole notes—moon; alone; own. It was a relief to think about music. His mind broke loose from Purvis and Miss Lee, but after a while, tricked by this new concentration, it suddenly convulsed and threw up what it had done at Mrs. McLeod's. He saw Emily's face watching and waiting and trusting, and he imagined it later on when she knew he was gone. There were no tears. He was back by his bed. He put his horn down; there was still a sound in the room and he was making it. Emily wouldn't cry. She would swallow it. The quiet Gordon. He sat on the bed and put his horn away in its case, his hands moving fast and nervous; he didn't want to think of Emily. Beneath the dryness in his throat and the pain in his chest, there was a sense that he'd escaped again to here—his room—a safe place.

He looked out the window. The sky was a clear blue and had gone cold, as if winter was refusing to give up. His mother and Sarah were walking up the laneway toward the house. He put his horn in the closet, took his jacket from the bed, and headed out the front door as his mother and sister were tramping their feet on the back porch.

At the Elementary School he watched the senior grades leave. Dody Wentworth was alone. Emily had not been at school. He doubled back and walked to Mrs. McLeod's house. At her door he listened, but there was no movement inside that he could hear, and when he knocked the silence continued. He stood exposed on the porch for a long while, not caring who might see him there. The bell at the High School had rung. He could go home now without any questions being asked. Emily wasn't here, and it felt as if she weren't anywhere—as if the decision he'd made in front of her grandmother's fireplace couldn't be reversed. Or maybe he shouldn't try to reverse it: let it happen.

He walked back up the hill and swept his boots off on the porch. It was definitely colder. The storm door creaked on frosted hinges when he opened it.

His mother was in the kitchen. Sarah was in the living room doing more cutouts.

"Emily phoned just a moment ago," his mother said. "I told her I thought you'd be home any minute. She said to call."

"Thanks." He gave her a kiss on the cheek to keep things normal.

"Good day at school?"

"Sure," he watched her face. Grandison could have phoned, and her question might not be innocent. She may even have seen him downtown and would in a moment mention it casually, as if there was some logical explanation he could give for being there. She never made assumptions when it was more interesting not to.

"I'm making macaroni and cheese for you and Sarah. Your father and I will have a snack later on when we get home."

"Do I have to put her to bed?"

"She'll go when she's ready."

"That'll be after you get home then."

"Don't be bossy with her."

He didn't answer. The phone was sitting on the breakfast nook counter underneath the cupboard where the everyday dishes were kept. He lifted the receiver and asked central for Emily's number. "I'm sorry, Christopher," Caitlin Rourke said, "Emily's line is busy."

He thanked her and hung up. Everybody in town knew about them. Maybe it had been a kind of boasting to walk around town with their arms around each other: Look, we can be in love, too. And the adults thought it was cute. He and Emily had passed Caitlin's window at the telephone office dozens of times.

He went to his room. His mother was running water for a bath. It embarrassed him that she was taking her little show at the gallery seriously, as if this were New York or San Francisco.

He lay on the bed and thought about Emily's not being at school. She hadn't stayed at her Gran's, and now her line was busy. He couldn't understand how quickly he'd tried to phone her, except that his mother had been there and might have asked questions if he'd not done it immediately. What would he have said? "Hello, this is Christopher, I didn't want to do it." And she'd say, "That's okay, we don't have to if you don't want to." He picked up his pillow from the bed and threw it across the room at the far wall. That's not fair to Emily, goddamnit. You'd been waiting, hadn't you? At your gran's, and at the school with Fielder and Pat in the furnace room. And you talked with her after, didn't you? You know how it happened and what she did. Maybe Pat liked it. Fielder does everything good the first time. Jesus, you know she could be having a baby. And you didn't care. You just lay there and waited, no words, just the smell. It was okay for Pat and Fielder; they were just fooling around.

He rolled over so that his face was against the edge of the bed and he was staring at the floor. Emily lay on the hearthrug and her head on her grandmother's pillows. He tried to make her move, do what Pat had done, but she didn't, couldn't, because she was Emily in his mind and not real. She might lie there like that forever.

Something was happening, and when it happened over and over he knew in his sleep that it was a dream. He saw her behind a curtain undressed. When he pulled it aside, it was Sarah. Each time he pulled it aside, it was Sarah's fat little belly, and then she peed from the bottom of it onto the floor. The puddle widened and was cold to stand in. When his mother wakened him, his feet were cold.

"Still a little shaky from your flu?"

It was flu now, his sickness, given a familiar name. "Yes," he said, and focused his eyes on her. She was wearing her black dress, whose skirt was like velvet and whose top was silk with a few rhinestones scattered across it. Her stockings were black too, and her hair was loose around her shoulders.

"You're staring," she said. "Do I look all right?"

"Mothers aren't supposed to be so good looking."

She bent and kissed him. "That's exactly the right thing to say." She stood up and smiled at him. "Be nice to Sarah. The macaroni's ready any time you want it, and there's lemon custard for dessert."

"Okay," he said, and got up. His father was at the door waiting for her. Under his coat he was wearing his good blue suit. He looked nothing like the foreman he'd seen at the yard earlier in the afternoon. Christopher told them to have a good time. His father raised his hand and nodded. He looked nervous, because this wasn't his party, but he was smiling as he shut the door. Sarah hadn't said anything. She had her head down and was cutting out a girl in a blue dress from a picture book.

"What're you mad at?" he asked.

She shrugged her shoulders and her lower lip stuck out.

"It's her party," he told her.

"But I could go. I'm not a nuisance."

"Next time maybe you'll go."

"What are you, a grownup?"

"No."

He sat down and turned on the radio. It warmed up slowly and the program that faded in was *Little Orphan Annie.* She was talking to Sandy about how far it was to town and how hungry she was. Sandy said Arf. There was an actor at a microphone somewhere in the United States who did nothing but say Arf when Annie was alone and had no one else to talk to, and he got paid for it. Now on the program someone else spoke to Annie. He surprised her. It was a hobo, and he had a can of possum stew he was willing to share. Christopher hadn't heard the program since he was ten.

"You listen to this every day?"

"No," Sarah said.

"Why not?"

"Because."

"Come on, why?"

"Everybody's too nice on it. If I was a little girl and only had a dog, I'd starve, or freeze."

"It's just a story."

"Well, it's not very true."

"What about the stories you tell with your cutouts?"

Sarah didn't answer. She smiled to herself and trimmed smooth the edges of the girl in blue. "This is Marilee. She's got pneumonia. A snake bit her."

"You don't get pneumonia from snakes."

"This was a pneumonia snake."

"That doesn't sound very true to me."

"Yes it is, because her mother wouldn't let her go to the movie."

"What movie?"

"*The Lives of the Bengal Lancers,* starring Gary Cooper."

"It's on at the Regent."

"I know, and it's a true story. Nancy Singleton at school went, and she said they shoved slivers of wood up under the soldier's fingernails and then lit them with a match." She sighed. "Marilee sneaked out the back window to go see the show and the snake bit her, right in the throat."

The announcer on the radio was telling everybody to send in the aluminum seal from the top of a can of Ovaltine, together with your name and address, to get a free scroll suitable for framing with Daddy Warbuck's ten rules for being a good American on it. He turned off the radio and stood up. "I think you're a crazy spoiled kid."

"The snake gave her pneumonia. I didn't."

"You think everybody's a snake. If you'd been beat up all the time around here, the world out there would look like fairyland. We're too nice to you."

"I don't know what you mean."

"Yes, you do."

"No, I don't."

"Yes. Do you want macaroni and cheese, and lemon custard for dessert?" he asked, heading for the kitchen.

"Is it poisoned?'

He turned toward her. She was grinning and going yuk-yuk-yuk into her fists. He went back and held out a hand to her. She hesitated, then took it, and he pulled her up. She jumped into his arms, and he walked with her into the kitchen. She was a bundle of bones, but hugging her to his body made him think of Emily again. Sarah was lying in his arms with her head back, playing dead. The opposite of Emily, who'd lain there on the hearthrug silent—doing what, exactly? It occurred to him that she'd been holding in everything she'd been feeling. If he'd really touched her, there would have been some kind of explosion. The dead cold in his gut that had been there ever since he'd left Mrs. McLeod's felt as if it were part of him now, something he'd begun to live with; or maybe he'd have to live around it.

He sat Sarah on the counter by the sink and let her supervise while he got the macaroni out of the warming oven and put everything they'd need to eat with onto the table in the nook.

Sarah wasn't a talkative child at mealtimes. She played with her food as she did with everything else that was put in front of her. She built a castle out of the macaroni and used the tomatoes in it for decoration. He liked macaroni and cheese, and ate two platesful and four pieces of bread. The custard was good too. Sarah hadn't got to hers yet, but she'd begun to eat the macaroni. Outside it was dark: March 14th; nearly the equinox, when there'd be equal day and night. He wondered if it being so cold at this late date was a record. The house creaked—boards contracted as the temperature continued to drop under the clear sky.

"Do you really hate Mr. Blenkin?"

He laughed, surprised. "Am I supposed to?"

"I bet you would've beat Lester."

"Maybe. I don't think so."

"He's not supposed to change the rules."

"He did, and he didn't."

"I'd hate him," she said. "I'd make a snowman out of him and put the nose-carrot up his bum." Her face managed to stay serious.

"That's easy to say," he said, also refusing the joke. "He's six-foot five tall."

The need to laugh disappeared from her face. "I was talking magic." Her voice was very prim, as if she were her mother making an important point.

The phone rang.

He listened to it again, as if the first double ring might have been a mistake, and glanced at Sarah. He couldn't talk on the phone with her in the room. The third ring sounded more demanding than the first two.

He reached for it and picked up the receiver, suddenly unconscious. He could hardly picture what she looked like, and her name was hidden in his memory. The loss was terrifying, and the struggle to retrieve it felt as if it used real muscles inside of his head.

"Emily," he said, finding her name at last. Sarah started to laugh, and he began to hang up.

"Everybody's not Emily," Fielder said.

"I thought it was going to be her. What's up?"

"Just a friendly call. I'm baby-sitting."

"So am I."

"Have to tell someone."

"What?"

"The red flag's up."

The words didn't mean anything. "What?"

"Pat phoned. It's okay."

"Then it was hardly a scare at all."

"Three days is three days."

"Well okay. Good."

"She says you walked out on Emily. Is that true?"

"She talks too much." He couldn't say anything else. It was going to be news now, all over town.

"It's not worth it," Fielder said.

"What?"

"Screwing around with women."

"Look, I don't want to talk about it, okay?"

Fielder didn't reply. In a moment, he said, "When are your folks coming home?"

"I don't know. Eight maybe."

"Come on over after they get back."

Fielder wanted it like old times, and why not? They were back before Christmas again. "I might, but it's getting bloody cold outside."

"We're down past our last ton of coal. It's supposed to be spring." Fielder's voice was serious.

"Not for seven days."

"Whoever heard of thirty below on March 14th?"

"Is it?"

"By our thermometer. You can come, it's only five blocks."

Christopher hung up. Sarah was eating her custard, stirring it until enough stuck to the spoon to make a mouthful. He got up and went into the living room and picked up the newspaper from his father's chair. It was two days old. That's how long it took to come from Vancouver and be delivered. He opened it to the funnies and read The Gumps and Jiggs and Gasoline Alley, but the words ran together in his head.

Sarah came into the living room. He watched her bend down and say something to a teddy bear. The words were said too softly for him to hear, but he knew she felt safe still. She understood that what she had her cutouts and dolls and bears do and say were made-up things. When she was four, Janice-Louise-Mary, her imaginary playmate, had been real.

He went into his bedroom, closed the door and picked up his pillow. "Emily," he said, and knew he should be laughing at himself. The real Emily lay on the hearthrug and she wasn't going to move.

He lay back on the bed, flat out like a dead body. It was the way he felt. Beyond that there were only echoes at a distance. Nothing to touch, feel, smell. I love you. "Nights are long since you went away." Nothing flowed in his mind: it was a gallery of pictures that were old now. Blenkin's fist bunching up Garrett's sweater. Purvis and Lee somehow together. Emily. I may be pregnant, who knows? Gabe and Irene had an accident. Fielder and Pat hadn't. Maybe Purvis and Lee will. And Emily still hadn't moved.

There was a tap on the door. "Christopher? Can we play something?"

"What?"

Sarah came into the room. "Snakes and Ladders."

"Isn't it time for you to go to bed?"

She gave him a pitying look. "You heard Mother say I could go when I wanted."

"You get into your nightie and we'll play."

She opened the board and got out the counters and dice. "Roll for who goes first."

"You get undressed."

"No. Don't spoil it. I want to play first."

He picked up the dice and rolled an eight. She rolled an eleven.

The front door opened and closed. It was not quite slammed. Sarah turned her head, but she didn't run to greet her parents. Christopher put the board aside and began to pick her up and take her into the other room to show them what a good babysitter he was.

Then his father spoke, as if he'd asked the question before and was repeating it more forcefully this time. "Laura, what did you do to make Courtney think he could act that way?"

"Would I have come to you?" There were tears in her voice. "Would I have told you—"

"Unconsciously, Laura, unconsciously."

"That old goat?"

"Is he?"

"Yes, he is." Her voice had changed. "And you'd better think about this straight, Peter Waterton."

Christopher held Sarah close and stopped her from running to the living room. "Don't," he whispered in her ear. "Listen." She relaxed against him.

"What do you mean, straight?"

"Some things are all or nothing. We're one of them."

"All of a sudden he feels able—"

"Nonsense. There's nothing sudden about this at all. There's no protection from him. Wives, as far as he's concerned, are city property, and they do what he wants or he fires their husbands."

"He really said that he wanted—"

"Your wife to come and have coffee with him at the hotel tomorrow. It's happened to me. You're upset. Were you upset when Yvonne Lester gave in?"

"That was just a rumour."

But Lester has his job. He's going to be City Clerk when Butterworth retires. And why, Peter, why did Stan Kaplik leave town a dozen years ago? Who knows the true story? And why did his wife become a madam?"

"She's not. She's—"

"What, then?"

"Loose, wanton, drinks."

"Some people lose themselves when they're abandoned."

"Kaplik was the one abandoned. It's why he left."

"No, he was Stanislaus Kaplik, and I bet he was proud. Maybe he could hardly speak English, but he had the job he needed to provide for a wife and three daughters. Think what it was for him to be twisted by Courtney. Or was he a man who thought his wife had vamped the mayor? Do you think that might be what happened, Peter? And he got angry and left. She was alone and naive and thought Courtney could help her. There were the girls to feed, but after Courtney'd had her, he chucked her out. Then he told her what she should do for a living, and he still protects her while she does it. Now he wants to humiliate me, Peter, so he can humiliate you. Give him your manhood, or be fired."

"I'm not Kaplik or Lester."

"That's right."

"I'll kill him."

"No you won't. Think what there is to do."

"What?"

"Don't ask what I did to lead him on. Come with me."

"Where?"

"To his hotel. Both of us."

"And be fired."

"Yes."

"You don't care?"

"All or nothing, Peter. I can't care. And you mustn't either."

"But he wins."

"Yes."

"I don't want that."

"And I don't want to give myself to James Courtney. I want to win for us."

"I don't like it."

"It's the way things are. We can't change them before tomorrow morning. But you know what I think. You said you were married to a Bolshevik, Peter."

"Being for a union doesn't make you a Commie."

"Kind of you to say that now, my darling, but you called me a Bolshie."

"Not in anger."

"There was no trouble to be angry about."

"A union wouldn't stop this."

"Yes it would. There'd be rules for firing—"

"And no one would ever be fired."

"You're a boss at heart."

"Aren't we all?"

"No. I'm a painter."

Sarah broke away from him, and he had to run after her to the living room door. His parents were standing with their arms around each other. His mother saw them. "You heard," she said. She looked alive, electric; her eyes were wide and black.

Christopher nodded.

"I'm glad."

He looked at his father's blank face. It was strange to see him not in charge, and he wanted to go to him and shake him awake. But he only asked him, "What does it mean?"

His mother answered. "That we're going back to Victoria." She laughed and gestured toward the porch where the thermometer was. "Thirty-five below, and this is the middle of March. In Victoria it's forty above."

"Stop it, Laura," His father said. "This can't be a celebration."

"Why not?"

He didn't say anything, but went to the door and looked out. Facts were important to him.

"Is she right?" Christopher asked.

"No. It's forty-five below."

"In the morning we can drop you at school when we're on our way to see the mayor," his mother said. She was almost laughing.

"If the car starts," his father said. "I've never seen it like this. Two hundred inches of snow, melting yesterday and now this. What's going on?"

"Change, Peter. It's coming. The last of these terrible years is digging its heels in, that's all. It's going to be fine soon."

They were leaving.

"I don't want to go to Victoria," Christopher told them.

"You like it here?" his mother asked.

He saw her beginning to laugh. "Goddamn it," he said, and they stared at him. "I don't want to be laughed at. You brought me here. I got friends." He stopped. That was all. Just friends.

"Don't swear," his mother said, but her voice had no threat in it.

Sarah said, "Are we going tomorrow? I want to bring my dolls."

"Not tomorrow, darling. Come, I'll put you to bed and tell you how many paintings I sold."

"How many?"

"Guess."

"Three."

"How ever did you know?"

He turned away from his father and went to his room again. Once more his window was crystalled over with ice, but he had the sense that outside there was a clear blue sky, and he knew that at forty-five below it was dead calm.

Courtney. Jesus. Courtney wanted to— He couldn't force his mind to deliver the words. Kill him, his father had said. Why not? He began to shake. His father was in the basement putting more coal in the furnace. It wasn't cold in his room, but the shaking got worse, and he lay down on his bed to try to stop it. He closed his eyes and watched himself go, leave. Climb on a train. Hide somewhere on it. Get off somewhere else so that he could have his own life. Courtney and Blenkin ruled the world. And not just them, either. The whole town hadn't done a thing for Purvis, and now his parents were going to do nothing about Courtney. After a few years rotting in warm wet Victoria, he'd become one of them. A goddamn adult. Then a sudden picture in his head of his mother being kissed by Courtney made him groan.

He sat up again. His nose dripped. He blew it on a kleenex he found in his jacket as he put it on to go to Fielder's house so he wouldn't have to sit in the living room watching two people named Peter and Laura tell each other it was all right to be fired and go live in Victoria at Grandfather Waterton's as they'd done before when his father'd had no job. It was the truth now—what he'd told Blenkin—that he'd never jump again. Victoria had no snow, let alone a hill and a trestle to jump from.

He put his boots on, his wool cap and leather helmet over the top of it, his long blue scarf over his nose, and went out the door without saying goodbye. Nobody came after him to ask where he thought he was going in forty-five below weather. His mother was still answering Sarah's questions, and his father was in the basement. He might stay there, because when he had a problem that's where he went until it was time to go to bed.

The calm was absolute and sound travelled toward him from every direction. He walked hard, knowing that the squeak of his boots in the packed snow could be heard blocks away. He was out alone. Only a couple of cars and a truck or two were moving along the streets somewhere downtown. He turned up Fielder's street and felt the cold begin to penetrate his clothes to his skin. The scarf across his nose was frozen stiff, because his warm breath was not enough to keep it thawed. Fielder's house was on Sheffield, a street of older small houses that had been built after the war when people thought Long River was going to be a real city. The driveway to Fielder's house slanted up a rise that gave his house a view of sorts.

He knocked on the door and tried the knob. It was unlocked. He pushed on through quickly and leaned with his back against it, feeling the heat in the house like a caring hand. Fielder shouted, "That you, Waterton?"

He didn't bother to answer. Fielder knew it was him.

There were no rugs or carpets on the floors and, in the living room, there was one overstuffed chair, a wrecked chesterfield, and a big old RCA Victor radio dialed to San Francisco. A sweet tenor band was playing a Latin tune. Not even an end table. The drape on the window was hung crooked, and the floor had dust balls on it that had drifted out from under the couch. The fireplace was not used; it was blocked off by a piece of plywood to help keep the cold out of the room. The hallway led to the Fielders' large kitchen, where there was a table big enough to sit six in matched chairs that had at one time been expensive. The stove was hot and the kettle was boiling. The linoleum had a track worn in it from the hallway to the back door. Fielder was at the sink washing a bottle for his sister. Blind Julia. "You're nuts for coming," he said.

"I know, but I needed to get out." He thought about telling Fielder why. Maybe he would.

"They bugging you?"

"No. Courtney—" He stopped. The picture of the mayor and his mother sickened him again.

"What about him?"

"My dad's going to be fired tomorrow."

Fielder turned from the sink to face him. "You're kidding. You mean that?"

"Yes."

"The Watertons don't get fired."

"Anyone can be fired."

"What for?"

"He was on Lee's side." That was true, and his mother was dragged in on it as an extra hurt.

Fielder came over to him and sat down. His eyes were as serious as he'd ever seen them. "What's going to happen?"

"Victoria. My grandfather's, I guess."

"Then I'll see you in the summers."

"Sure."

Fielder went to the icebox where the baby's formula was. "When she hollers you got to be ready," he said.

"Cissie's in bed?"

"She goes early when they're out." He laughed. "Doesn't want to be awake when they come in."

"Not Sarah, she'd stay up till midnight if you'd let her."

Fielder put the bottle on the table and poured it full. "You know what's stupid?"

"What?"

"You get married, and even if you like each other—wham—you're unhappy."

"It comes from outside."

"Being unhappy?"

"They got you coming and going. Like they fire you when they please."

Fielder was silent a moment, then he said, "When you and Emily got unhappy, did that come from outside?"

"If they'd just let us alone."

"The Gordons?"

"Sure, who else?"

"They were scared for her. You guys were really serious."

"They should've been scared for Pat."

Fielder grinned. "We're still friends."

"Do you think you'll do it with her again?"

"She said it was fun at first, but in the end she really didn't like it."

"How blunt can you get?"

"That's Pat, eh?"

"It doesn't bother you?"

"It might've if I'd been you, and Emily had said no. You put a lot of time in on her. Is that what happened? Pat said you were at her grandmother's."

Christopher sucked in a breath. "I think I was the one that said no." He watched Fielder's eyes. They made no judgment.

"Emily's pretty young."

"Not really," Christopher said.

"What do you mean? She's thirteen."

"I don't want to talk about Emily."

"Okay. How about school? You're going to catch hell when you go back."

"Who says?"

"Everybody knows you walked out."

"Do they know why?"

"Tell me."

"It doesn't matter." He got up from the table and went into the living room. The music on the radio ended. Fifteen hundred miles southwest, an announcer said, "KPO San Francisco." A tone sounded. Christopher turned the volume up. "Ten o'clock, Pacific Standard Time," another voice said, and began to read the news.

"The German invasion of Czechoslovakia, which began late last night Pacific Standard Time, has resulted in the complete collapse of the Czech nation. German army divisions have swept through Bohemia and Moravia, and Adolph Hitler, the German Chancellor, has accepted President Hacha's capitulation. Tonight, he has put all of Czechoslovakia under German protection. The operation, he said, was undertaken to protect German nationals living in the Czech states of Bohemia and Moravia. The German government has stated that the country, under President Hacha, will be given a guarantee of autonomy."

Fielder was standing at the doorway with the full bottle of formula for his baby sister in his hand. "That's it," he said. "It's started."

Christopher felt excited. "They're not saying it's war. They'd say that first, wouldn't they?"

"The state of Ruthenia," the announcer said, "has been put under Hungarian protection. Meanwhile, Hungary has begun its own military operation against Carpatho-Ukraine."

"Where the hell's that?"

"My dad would know," Fielder said.

"British Prime Minister Neville Chamberlain has called the German action 'a breach of the spirit of the Munich Accord.' However, it's believed that Britain will not go to the aid of Czechoslovakia. Mr. Chamberlain stated earlier that when the province of Slovakia under Joseph Tiso declared its independence last week, and had therefore disrupted the Czech state, Britain no longer regarded herself as bound by any guarantee to maintain Czechoslovakia against unprovoked aggression."

"What does that mean?" Fielder wanted to know.

"Winston Churchill, Britain's new Minister of War, is quoted as saying, 'All is over. Silent, mournful, abandoned and broken, Czechoslovakia recedes into darkness.'"

"It all just means they aren't going to do anything about it." Fielder reached down and switched off the radio.

"Hey, I want to hear that."

"Why?"

"Because." Christopher switched on the news again. "A year ago Vienna," the announcer was saying, "six months ago the Sudetenland, and now Czechoslovakia."

Upstairs the baby yelled as if someone had stuck a pin in her. "Julia," Fielder said, and moved from the doorway.

"Is something wrong?"

"She always screams." He poured hot water from the kettle into a pan on the stove. Julia stopped yelling and settled into ordinary crying. Fielder put the cold bottle into the water and went upstairs. Julia stopped crying, and Christopher could hear Fielder talking to her. He didn't sound like Fielder. His voice came back down the staircase soft and low. He stayed up in her room for a long time, and when he appeared again, the baby had a dry diaper on, as well as socks and a stained sweater that had once been blue.

"Here," he said, "you hold her."

Christopher sat down at the table and took Julia from him.

"Three months and a couple of days," Fielder said.

Her eyes were wide open and blank, blind. He looked away from them. She was chunky, and her face was round, and the hair on top of her head was growing long enough to curl. "She's pretty."

"I know." Fielder was testing how hot the milk was by squirting it onto the inside of his wrist.

"You're bloody expert, aren't you?"

"Why not? She's a great kid." He sat down. "Here. Gimme."

Christopher handed him Julia and watched. She immediately turned her head so that her face was buried in the folds of his sweater.

"She can't see, so she smells. Her nose works, you can almost feel it." He put the nipple down close to her and she put her lips around it. The noise of her feeding was loud sucks and soft grunts. "Cissie doesn't have curly hair. This one's going to be a beaut."

"You're not supposed to have favourites."

"I'm not a mom. I can like who I please."

"You look like a mom to me." The teasing sounded stupid. "Can't she see at all?"

"Wait."

The bottle was already half empty. Fielder took it away and put her over his shoulder. He patted her back and rubbed it. She burped loudly. He opened a drawer at his side of the table and took out a flashlight. It was a three-cell torch. He put Julia on his lap and flicked on the light. It shone in her eyes, and in a moment her lips curled up into a grin, and she waved her arms and kicked her legs. He did it again, and she made a noise like a giggle.

"She can see," Fielder said. "I've proved that. Light gets through, so the big nerve is okay." He shut off the light, and Julia yelled. It was almost as if she'd said, "Hey." Fielder laughed and put the nipple in her mouth. She remembered it and began to suck again. Fielder looked across the table. "When we first found out, I wished she wasn't born."

"But not any more," Christopher said.

"No."

The radio was still talking, but not about Czechoslovakia.

Christopher got up and went into the living room to turn it off. Fielder's place was familiar to him, but not quite another home. He walked back into the kitchen and pulled a chair close to Julia and her brother. He must have been close enough that his smell reached her. She turned her head to get a better whiff of him and opened her eyes. The milky discs stared blindly. He glanced up at Fielder.

"What a kid, eh?"

"She's blind," Christopher said.

"But that's all, and maybe soon we'll have enough money to see a doctor."

It was funny. They both began to laugh. "Maybe Hitler'll take another country," Fielder said. "Maybe that'll do it."

"If that's what you want."

"Do you know how much a captain gets paid?"

"Is your old man going to be a captain?"

"At least." Julia sucked at the last of the bottle, and Fielder took it away from her. She was getting sleepy again. "Just a minute and I'll put her away for the night. Maybe we can get some more news on the radio."

Christopher nodded, and sat waiting at the table, suddenly exhausted.

CHAPTER SEVEN

1

In the morning, he didn't want to wake up. Even inside his dream he felt tired, and something else: full of sadness. Emily was there in a room where he'd never been, and she kept saying, in an amplified voice, "What are you doing here?" She knew where she was. Maybe she'd invented the place. When he came to consciousness, his own room was full of a strong but pale light that he knew came out of a clear sky outside. The cold was still there. March 16th. He shivered under the blankets and stretched out full length. His mother knocked at the door.

"Christopher." Her voice was settled, sure. She was going to tell him something already decided upon. "I think it's too cold for Sarah to go to school. We'll want you to look after her while we go downtown, so you can lie in a few more minutes if you want."

"You're going to do it, are you?"

"Yes."

"See the mayor."

"I can hardly wait."

"You're crazy."

"Don't talk to your mother that way."

"I'm sorry."

She laughed, came to his bedside, and leaned over to kiss him. He held his breath so she wouldn't smell it and felt her lips brush his cheek. She sat beside him, always willing to interrupt chores, like breakfast. "You know," she said, smiling, "I never expected to like you coming up to fifteen. Most of the boys that age I've known have been such horrors."

"They seem okay to me."

"That's because you don't have to live with them." She paused. "Have you quarreled with Emily?"

The question both hurt and surprised. He could only shake his head.

"Her parents were there last night. I hardly expected Elizabeth Gordon to come. She bought a painting." Another pause. "Emily sounded upset on the phone. Did you get in touch with her last night?"

"No, I went to Fielder's." He left it at that.

"I was hoping what I guessed was the truth."

"What?"

"That you two had broken up, because we'll be leaving."

He sat up and rubbed his eyes. "When?"

"Soon." She laughed again. "Very goddamn soon."

He watched her blush. He'd never heard her swear, and it was a shock.

"We don't belong here. We never did. Things are getting better, and if they really are going to start that insane war with the Germans again, they'll need engineers to build things."

He wanted to see his father and pushed at the blankets she was sitting on to make her get up. When she spoke again, her voice was sympathetic. "It'll be hard at first, but you'll go to a better school and have more friends."

He kicked the covers back and stood stiffly while she retreated from the room. Whatever was happening was out of his control. There was no way to stop it. He sat again on the edge of the bed and pulled on heavy socks and went to the closet for his housecoat. His saxophone was there. If he could play it well, there might be freedom. Lester Young began playing before he was twelve. Harry James, Bix Beiderbecke, Louis Armstrong started early. Right now, there'd be hundreds more playing in little bands and making enough to live, maybe bunking down in club dressing rooms, or hardly sleeping at all, dozing after jam sessions at people's places, waking up with someone cooking breakfast in another room at two o'clock in the afternoon, and in everybody's head there was what they'd learned the night before, new ways of playing against the chords, better chops and faster fingers, more things that the brain made automatic. The exhaustion in him was gone. If it weren't early morning, he'd practise, because he'd only touched the horn once since Saturday. He forced himself to hear again what he'd done at the Royal. The people moved down in front of him. They watched. He looked at them and shivered at the sounds that made some of the crowd laugh. But it wasn't true that anyone had laughed at him. They'd looked surprised. Gabe was the one who knew what to do: not back off, but get in close and insist that something be done right to take away as much as possible the feeling he'd been a fool.

In the kitchen, his mother was talking to Sarah; then she called, asking if he were coming to eat. It was a shock to see his father sitting at the breakfast nook table. He was pale, his face square and wooden, as if it had been reshaped overnight by disaster. Christopher looked at his mother. Did she know? Was her cheerfulness part of her knowing? She did that; when things went bad she always began to float, as if what was rotten was something that held her up instead of drowning her. He took his plate and went to sit at the table, but the urge to talk to his father was gone.

"Will your truck start, do you think?" she asked.

"I think so." With some visible effort, his father's voice sounded as sure and certain as it always did. "I suppose we can walk if we have to."

"I don't understand," Christopher said. "What's going to happen?"

"They're going to visit the mayor," Sarah said. She got up from the table and took her dishes into the kitchen.

"I was invited to visit him at the hotel. I'm going to go—with my husband."

"But then what happens?"

"We'll see," his father said, and got up from the table too. He went downstairs and shovelled more coal on the furnace.

"There's more to it than what you're saying."

"Maybe," his mother said. "As long as you're staying home, why don't you have a bath? There's plenty of hot water in the tank."

"Am I dirty?"

"I really do look forward to your grandfather's electric hot water heater so I can have a shower any time I want again."

He ate the last of his cereal and stood up. "Is everybody finished with the bathroom?"

She looked up at him and nodded. He could see she wanted to talk now that Sarah was in her room. "Of course there's more to it."

"Dad doesn't want to quit."

"No."

He waited but she only looked as if she were trying to think what to say. Finally, she said, "It's a terrible world we live in."

"He doesn't want to quit and he doesn't want to be fired and you're making him."

"That's a funny way to look at it. Would you want a job that asked that your wife be savaged by—"

"No," he said, too loud.

"Then think clearly. What else is there to do?"

"Let him do it himself. It's between him and the mayor."

"What is?"

"It's Miss Lee, isn't it?"

"No."

"Yes it is; he defended her."

"It's not even that Courtney wants to run the town," she said. "He does run it. But he has to have more. Me. Your father's most precious possession." She stood up as tall as she could. "That's what I've become. I'm not who I am in this, Christopher. I'm not a human being. I want to be one again, and that's why I'm going to see Courtney this morning. It's why your father is coming with me, too."

He went to the sink with his dishes and she followed him. "It's okay for me to say this, I think. Last night was my night. Maybe that's funny—two dozen paintings hung as best they could be in a village library. Hardly Paris or New York. But it was my little time, and it felt good. You want to be a performer, Chris, somebody who works in the spotlight. I know now that spotlights are arranged moments. There's nothing real about them, except for one thing: you leave your defences and protections at home, and all of you is naked for the audience to ogle. My poor little paintings made me that way, but I found out there's magic in it too. The people somehow sense what's going on and treat you for the moment like the person you want to be. I was open to Courtney. I smiled. I laughed. I talked with him. And he said this. Listen: 'You're a good-looking woman, Laura. I've had some differences with your husband, but I think they can be fixed. You come on down to the hotel where there's not such a crowd.'

" 'When?' I asked, because I was astounded and wanted to know, and he chuckled. Men who have paunches do that, they chuckle; and he said, 'Tomorrow morning.' And after I got my breath, I said, 'What if I don't?' And he said, 'Well, those differences are pretty big ones.'

"I know what I should've done. Now I know," she said.

"What?"

"Scream as loud as the thing he'd done to me hurt, and point to him and yell what he'd said. It's a great picture in my mind now, him standing there with his face red, and all the people he's walked on gathered around yelling at him too. We always think of these things too late, don't we?"

"It's stupid," he said, and she laughed, and he had to laugh with her. Then she simply stood and looked at him, but he didn't feel convinced. "Okay," he said, "but it's still between him and Dad."

After a moment, she nodded and sat down to her coffee again. "If I went alone, I'd take a gun."

He'd never thought before that a gun could be a sign of weakness. "Why not a policeman?"

"Tina Cotter called the police when Len beat her up. They listened to Len and said that maybe she deserved it and left. Len beat her up again for calling the police."

"I don't want to hear all this," he told her. "There's nothing I can do."

"I've said it all for a reason. Sarah will leave Long River and hardly look back." Her voice was weary. "But you. I want you to know so much about everything that's gone on that even while you hate me for making you move, you'll know it's right and has to be done. It's like declaring war. It's got to be so right that the war is better than saying yes to whatever the other thing is."

"And the other thing here is doing it with Courtney."

Her head jerked as if he'd hit her, and it occurred to him that she'd never even considered that as a possibility. "That's the most important part of it, isn't it?"

She nodded, and the surprise in her face turned to tears. He wondered if she'd cried about this before, in the bedroom with his father comforting her. It didn't feel like it. What was bursting out of her had been held in a long time, and he looked away because he didn't want to see her face. It was young, like a child's when it was hurt, and it reminded him of Sarah who might come out of her bedroom now, because she always knew when things were going wrong. But it was the basement door that opened, and his father was there. He glanced and moved across the kitchen toward them as if he'd been released from a cage. Christopher saw his hand grab at him, and felt the pain in his arm.

"What have you done, boy? What's going on?"

"Nothing—"

"Laura—?"

"Stop it, Peter." Her voice was quiet; she bit her lip.

His father stood over her then, more awkward than Christopher had ever seen him.

"Tell him you're sorry," his mother said.

"Why?"

"Because he was just listening is all." She stood up. "And I told him too much."

"Were you badgering her with questions?"

"No." He shook his head. "I didn't make her cry."

"I just wanted to. Can't a girl have a little cry? I'm the one Courtney wants to get into bed with."

"Don't talk like that." He was caged again.

"You're right, I shouldn't, but I've been thinking all along that he'd only insulted me. But it's more than that, isn't it? First of all I thought this had to do with you, and then I thought it had to do with Courtney. It only just a moment ago got really through that it's me it has to do with."

"Of course it has to do with you, Laura. Look, we don't have to go through with this."

"Yes we do. What time is it?"

"Just after nine."

"Good. They'll be phoning for you. An hour late. I'm surprised Dodd hasn't already. Get your coat."

"He never comes till nine," his father said. Then he turned and said, "I'm sorry, Christopher. You shouldn't've been dragged into this."

"It's okay."

"Is it?"

"Yes."

"We'll be back soon and you can go to school."

"I don't want to go."

"Why?"

He thought of telling them, but Blenkin and Garrett were his own problem, and the notes to excuse his absences could wait—forever, if he was leaving Long River soon. "It's too cold."

"It's up to forty-two below and climbing."

"Then maybe I'll go." He smiled at them both and went to sit in the living room. He heard his father go out and begin to start the truck. It turned over. Then again. It began to whine and catch, whine again, and finally hack and cough until its noise settled down to a powerful hum. His mother left then, walking as if she were on stilts through the living room, kitchen, and out the back door without saying goodbye even to Sarah.

He waited and wondered how long his little sister would play in her room before the silence would bring her out to see what was going on. He thought then of Fielder holding Julia in his arms. Three months ago a diaper would've been a stink and a joke. He'd've been embarrassed to be seen holding a baby. But he was still the same Fielder at school. Julia was added, and that was all. He wasn't changed, except that she was there, and maybe if she weren't blind he might hardly notice. Not in the same way. Maybe rotten things made you think in a way good things didn't. Good things made you scared you were going to lose them. Like Emily. He thought about her as clearly as he could, as far back as the fire, and beyond that to where she didn't exist. He had a hard time remembering what it was like to be alive then. It was somebody else's time: family, school, rink, jumping, the river. Emily had made another kind of time. It was like that with Gabe, right up to the moment when he'd tried to make jazz on the bandstand. Emily lay on the hearthrug. She hadn't moved.

Sarah came into the room with her checkerboard. She put it on the fender stool his father had made with the jackknife he'd told Emily about. "That was a terrible winter," his mother had said. "We were so badly off that making this and doing over the kitchen was all that kept him sane."

Sarah didn't say anything. She put the checkers on the board and turned it so that he had the reds and therefore first move. She was good at the game, and he always had to play hard to beat her. This morning he didn't care, and in the end when her three kings slaughtered his two men, she complained that it was no fun winning so easy. He set the game up again and began to concentrate. But the phone rang, and he thought it might be his mother. It was Pat Gordon.

"What are you doing home?" he asked her.

"Same as you, keeping out of the cold. Look, Waterton, you're killing my sister. Who the hell are you to walk out on her?"

"I didn't," he said, without thinking. It was what he wanted to believe. "What do you mean, killing her?" Nothing inside of him was alive. His breathing had stopped.

"You heard me. Are you coming back?"

He made his gut muscles move and help him take a breath, and he tried to think. "I don't know." Until now he'd only thought of this as his problem. Emily was there again on the hearthrug. "It's none of your business."

"Yes it is. She's my sister and she's in her room crying."

Why was Pat doing this? Whatever was happening had to keep on until it worked itself out. "You can't be part of . . ." he said, and then there was a loud electrical noise in his ear, and Caitlin at the telephone office said, "I'm sorry you two, but there's an emergency and Mr. Dodd must speak to Mr. Waterton."

"He's not here," Christopher said.

Pat was cut off. Mr. Dodd's voice came on the line.

"Where is he?"

"He's with the mayor."

"The mayor's not here." Mr. Dodd's voice sounded anxious, not angry.

"No, at the hotel. He'll be home soon. I'll tell him you called."

"He's supposed to be at work."
"He took my mother down with him."
There was a pause. Mr. Dodd always breathed through his mouth as if both nostrils were permanently blocked, and when he spoke, it was with a funny English country accent. "Zommerzet," his father had said, imitating it. "He must come at once. The river's frozen itself to the bottom—" He stopped. "You tell him, lad."
"Yes sir. Is there a flood?"
"Such as you've never seen before. Now you tell him to get down here quick." He cut the connection, and Christopher turned to see Sarah standing by the table. Her eyes were wide and fearful.
"A flood," she said. "How can there be a flood in winter?"
"I don't know."
"Is it coming here?"
"No, we're high up, Sarah." He gave her a hug, fearful of hysterics. "For Pete's sake don't have a fit, okay? Mom and Dad will be home soon."
"I'm not going to have a fit." She began to cry. "They'll freeze."
"Who?"
"Mom and Dad. People in the flood."
"Nobody's going to be in a flood. It's the water that's going to freeze, not the people."
"It never froze in the river," she said. "It's there under the ice."
"Hush. Never mind."
"They're downtown. The flood will go there."
"No."
"How do you know?"
"Because I hear them coming now."
They both went to the kitchen window. The truck was there in the laneway. So soon. "See? They're safe."
They came in quickly through a cloud of condensation, as if they were strangers who'd come to the door on serious business.
"There's a flood," Sarah said.
"Where? Did the pipes burst?" His father began to head for the basement.
"No," Christopher said. "The river. Mr. Dodd phoned and said you had to get down there right away."
"The river?"
"He said it's frozen to the bottom."
"Is it?" his father said, calmly. "Dodd will have his hands full for a change." He began to take off his boots.

"We were just downtown. Why didn't we know?" his mother asked.

"Mr. Dodd only called a minute ago."

"Is it bad?"

"Yes."

"What part of the river?"

"He didn't say." He watched his father leave the kitchen without having asked a question. He turned back to his mother again. "That was quick. What happened?"

She smiled with her lips. "We're free to go any time we want."

"We're fired?" Sarah asked.

His mother didn't answer her. "You were right, Chris. It was between them. Courtney didn't even acknowledge my presence in the room."

"What did he say?"

"He said—and without so much as a hestitation—'I'm glad you're here, Waterton. It's time to get it straight about you and Long River. I said when you came you was over-educated. On top of that, I didn't like you then, and I still don't. A man doesn't want to admit his mistakes, and I'm no different from anybody else in that respect, but I don't mind saying it's time for you to go. Now.'

"There was a bit more abuse and then your father said, 'What about my holidays. I'll want pay in lieu of those.'

"And Courtney said, 'Get a lawyer and try to collect, if you can. As far as I'm concerned, you've been on holiday since you bulled your way into being Chairman of the Board.' And then he told us to get out."

Christopher said, "Is that all?" He felt weak and angry.

She smiled again. "Perhaps not. I left out the part where he said he'd see to it that any lawyer in this town would charge ten dollars an hour, and since your father's holiday pay might come to twenty dollars he'd have to hope like hell there was a lawyer in town who could handle the case in two hours or he wouldn't break even."

"The mayor can do that?"

"He just did."

"What's going to happen?"

His mother sat down on a kitchen chair and took Sarah onto her knee. "Things are going to be just fine." She gave Sarah a kiss and looked up at him. "Are you going to school? Sarah and I are going to go see what needs to be done so we can start packing."

"Is that all?"

She laughed. "Perhaps not. This may have opened your father's eyes a bit."

"What does *that* mean?"

"Well, he might not become a radical—" She left it at that and stood up.

"I don't think I want to go to school."

"You should. You can tell everyone about the flood."

"They'll know." He walked into the living room. His father was sitting in his chair, and he might have been made out of wax, except his hands were moving while they stretched and then made fists.

He wanted there to be another side to tell. "What happened?"

"You heard what your mother said."

"There's nothing you can do?"

"No." He got up. "The mayor owns the marbles."

"Don't they have laws?"

"No."

"Just because he doesn't like you, we can starve?"

"Yes. But we won't. Please don't worry." For the first time his face held an expression. It looked as if he were pleading.

"I'm not worried."

The phone rang and his mother answered. It was Harrison Dodd again. His father said, "Hello Dodd," and then made only small sounds that might have been either yes or no, then, finally: "Harrison, I'm sure you know I don't work for you any longer." Dodd spoke for some time, but his father only said, "You can handle it." He hung up and began to head for the basement.

"No," his mother said, and took him by the arm. "Please don't just disappear."

He turned and looked at her. Christopher had not seen him absolutely dead-eyed before; he wasn't even sad, just blank. "I think you wanted this," he said.

"No. But once it started happening, I wasn't going to stop it. Would you work now for Courtney?"

He shook his head. "And I won't help him, either."

"What did Dodd want?"

"He wants to try dynamiting the ice."

She nodded. "I thought so. Is it bad?"

"That's a thirteen-mile-an-hour river. It can't flood east because of the cutbanks there. It's come west." He gestured. "With all the ice that was in the channel."

"I don't understand."

"It snowed. Then it thawed. Then it went to fifty below. The wet snow bunched up and went to the bottom and froze. Dodd says it's a dam that's made the water back up and run through the cranberry swamp, over the tracks and the flats, even beyond the station. It's made a new channel for itself this side of the bridge."

"Still going as fast as ever?"

"No, it's a mile wide now. But when it burst its banks it must've been a bit like a tidal wave."

"What's Dodd doing?"

"Dodd hasn't got it straight that he's just hired on as foreman. A day's work'll do him good."

"A day?"

His father laughed. "There'll be ice in town till July. The river's piling up more every minute."

Sarah went to him and reached up; he put his hands under her arms and raised her to eye-level. "What're we going to do?" she asked.

"Stay in. Be safe."

"Some people will die."

"I don't think so. Dodd would've said."

"Is he mad at you?"

"Yes."

"Don't you care?"

"Not any more."

She twisted around and made him hold her like a baby. "Can we go to Grampa's today?"

"Do you want to?"

"This is a horrible place."

Christopher watched his father's face relax into a smile as he looked at her. He didn't answer; instead, he hugged her and set her down beside her mother again. "You two should be in school," he said.

"Do I have to?" Sarah asked. "Mr. Littler doesn't like people being late."

"Will you play in your room then?"

"Yes." She went, looking as if it were a special treat.

"You've never talked in front of us before," Christopher told him.

"Maybe it's time," his father said. "Nothing secret about it. It's just life."

"Everything happens at once."

"That's life too," his mother said. "Maybe you *are* too young to know that."

"I've been finding out," he said. "I want to know what can be done."

"Do you think I know?" his father asked. "Do you?"

"You're the father. You're supposed to."

His mother looked at him sharply. "Don't try to grow up thinking that."

"What am I supposed to think?"

"That you can cope. Because you can."

"That's stupid. I can't even handle school."

"I think so," she said. "You will. What you need to do will come to you. Wait and see."

"What about Purvis and Miss Lee? Will they cope too?"

"Miss Lee has done what she had to. And Purvis' sickness is like being run down by a truck."

"I don't want to be run down by any truck."

"We have," she said, quietly, "and we'll get well or we won't." She stopped looking at him and turned to his father. "That's right, isn't it, Peter?"

"Go to school, Chris." His face was sad. At least it was that. Asking to be left alone. Christopher turned away from them both and went to the door of his room.

"Aren't you going to do anything?" he asked.

"The whole town'll be down there doing whatever they have to."

He felt himself nodding and heard them leave the kitchen to go to the living room. His jacket was on the bed. He picked it up and put it on, got his scarf and mitts, and left the house without saying goodbye.

2

He didn't think of the cold. It was only one more sensation. He knew he could get rid of it by walking into the school, which he didn't do, or into the rink where, as he passed, he saw nothing was happening, or into Ch'en's, but there was no one there either; the lights inside yellowed the frost on the windows. He kept going.

His mind was a turning wheel pasted up with pictures that wouldn't come alive. Emily had moved. She was in her room now, lying on her bed, crying. She lay still and stared at him as he bent over her. Her eyes were distorted with tears. Then there was Courtney, rotten, powerful, pointing like God in a picture he remembered from Sunday School: God telling Adam and Eve to get out of the Garden.

Emily crying.

Fielder holding baby Julia in his arms.

Hitler's soldiers on motorcycles; they were always on motorcycles, except those in the newsreels who goose-stepped without ever getting tired. Maybe more Hell up ahead.

Emily crying because of him; for her he was a runaway truck. Miss Lee on the bus; Purvis on the gurney in the hospital.

"You're killing my sister," Pat said.

And ahead of him, a wonderful distraction, was Billy MacLean in his police uniform standing at First Avenue's intersection with London Street. He was holding back the crowd, and beyond was the station, the ice and the running water.

He pushed himself down the sidewalk along the window and the wall of Robinson's Grocery until he was able to look across the long shallow slope of the land to the tracks and the swamp beyond. The land opened up as a small meadow, with houses here, shacks there, the junkyard that belonged to the Gypsies who called themselves Tyler. There was Howden's barn that had become over the years a place where trucks went to be welded and repaired by Chuff Howden, whose collection of a hundred or more old vehicles was what he called his Parts Department.

The water was invisible. It was the ice that moved beyond the railway tracks, and it froze and broke off and flowed again, pressed against a shack and made it lean, then swamped it and took it along, boards, nails and all. The houses were still standing. Perrault's was built on a high basement and looked like it might be a three-storey building. It had ice piled up over its first floor. At this distance, it looked as if it might be pushed over soon, but the ice there wasn't moving. A mile away, at the shore of the river near the bridge, a slab of ice twenty feet high rose up and broke off. It was like watching a moving picture that was all shot in slow motion.

The only place where the water was visible from this distance was on the tracks, and he could see the reason. Engine number 1410 rolled slowly into the station and went a hundred yards beyond. Then it stopped, blew three short blasts on its whistle, and started back up the tracks toward the bridge. It broke a shell of ice as it went, but so long as it kept moving the tracks were only covered with water and the main line was open to the river.

The crowd was silent. It watched the disaster creep forward through forty-below cold, ice block by churning ice block, a machine propelled by the unseen river that flowed in whatever direction the ice and the land forced it. Not allowed its natural course, it had gone insane. No one was moving. Even in this cold, the fascination was enough to hold the crowd, still as a cornered animal.

He looked around. There were very few people here he didn't know, at least by face if not by name. There were no tramps or hoboes going through in this weather. In winter, everyone had a place to hole up. Or they died.

He saw Gabe and pushed his way through the crowd to him. "It can't get up this far, can it?"

Gabe shook his head. "School closed?"

"I just didn't go. Haven't been all week."

"Sick?"

"I don't think so."

Gabe moved, turned away to go through the crowd and back to his job. Christopher followed him. In the distance, dynamite blasted. The sound was high and it ripped the cold clear air as if it were silk. They were on the sidewalk going up London Street toward Mr. English's store. "Sounds funny," Gabe said.

"Why?"

"When dynamite's under something it makes a whump."

There was another crackling explosion.

"See? Sounds like they're just throwing the stuff at the river and hoping."

"Gabe?"

"Yeah?"

"We're leaving. My dad's lost his job."

Gabe stopped walking. "Him?"

"Yes."

"What're you going to do?"

"Go to Victoria."

"When?"

"I don't know. Soon." It was a relief to tell someone.

"Jesus. Everything's suddenly so sudden." He laughed as if he hadn't expected to.

"Purvis is gone to Tranquille."

"Well, that's good."

"And Miss Lee—"

"I know about Miss Lee. What a load of crap that is."

"It's Courtney."

"I know. Did he fire your dad?"

"Yes."

"Because of Miss Lee?"

"Partly." He didn't want to say the rest to anyone.

"Kid, I'm really sorry to see you go. You're going to be a hell of a horn player."

"Am I?"

"I had to learn by myself," Gabe said, and he laughed again. "Figure how good I'd be if I'd had a teacher like me."

"I know." He laughed too. Gabe might never have told him he was going to be good if he weren't leaving town. "You'll be going into the navy band."

Gabe moved off again toward the store. "Maybe. When it happens."

"You think it's going to?"

"He can't get away with gobbling up countries much longer."

"You think somebody's going to do something about it?"

"I hope so."

"Nobody does anything about anything."

"Like what?"

"They just gripe about bad times. Courtney is mayor and nobody does anything about him. Miss Lee. The whole town knew about Purvis' old lady. Purvis was the only one who ever did anything. He beat up on Blenkin. Somebody should've done that years ago."

"You're really peed off."

"Aren't you?"

"I just want to play my horn with guys better than me for a while." Gabe said.

"You're going to."

"So will you. In Victoria."

"Do you know a teacher there?"

"No, but I might find someone who does." Gabe stopped in front of the store and turned to go in. "How's it with you and Emily?" He grinned. "Haven't seen you two lovebirds downtown for a while."

"Okay," Christopher said, too quick.

"You being a good boy?"

"Too good." It was the closest he could come to a joke, and stop the talk about Emily at the same time.

"I hear Fielder wasn't."

"*What?*"

Gabe nodded. "He should never've talked to Howard about it. That rink is no place for secrets."

"It's all over town?"

"Well, I know."

"What does that mean?"

"Don't worry. I heard from Howard himself. He was in buying a secondhand phonograph for his kid. He figured Fielder was the youngest he'd heard from on that score. Scared him about his daughters."

"Fielder's okay now," Christopher said. "I just hope it doesn't get back to Pat's mother."

"Pat Gordon? That who it was?"

"Gabe, please. I thought you knew. Don't tell anyone."

"Of course not, why should I? But things are looking up for all of us if the youngest class act in town's starting to do it."

Gabe left him then, and Christopher felt as if he'd betrayed Pat and Fielder, but only because he'd trusted Gabe as he would a father. Gabe wasn't his father, any more than Purvis had been. Even his father wasn't his father anymore, not since he'd seen him without his job and saying, Do you think I know what to do? He was just a guy, too, and it hurt to think of him now, because he was so much more than Gabe or Purvis. He wanted suddenly to be at home again; the cold was getting to him.

He shivered as he walked, but by the time he was going up York Street he was warm once more. And when he was back in the house he expected to see his mother moving fast. After every major family decision, she was suddenly in a hurry. But she wasn't. He took off his boots and walked through the silent house to the living room. They were sitting there, not talking. His father was in his chair, and Sarah and his mother were sitting on the chesterfield. He sat down by the radio. His mother's smile was faint. In the distance, more dynamite exploded. His father's face had gone pale and stiff again. Christopher couldn't make out whether they were just being quiet, or whether they were waiting for something—the answer to a question maybe, or for the phone to ring.

Then Sarah said, "What if this is a dream someone is having and I'm just in it?"

He watched his father's face come alive and begin to move toward laughter. "Sarah," he said, and got up and went across the room to pick her up off the chesterfield. She wrapped her legs around his waist and lay back in his arms. "They could wake up and we'd be gone out of the dream. We could be in another one then," she said, delighted with herself.

"Sarah," he said again, and swung her around so that she had to cling to him and be close. He kissed her cheek and then blew hard into the side of her neck so that she shivered and held on harder. "How'd you get to be such a philosopher, and only seven years old?"

"I think a lot about dreams."

Christopher looked over at his mother. She smiled, but he thought it might be hurting her that it was Sarah who'd got her husband up out of his chair. "What's going on?" he asked.

She shook her head. "We can't start to leave until—" She stopped and shrugged.

"Until what?"

"Until we're finished here, I guess. I thought it was going to be easier than this."

Sarah was back down on her feet again, and his father said, "I had no chance, Laura. He won without me lifting a finger."

"Can't you see? Look at it right, and we're going to start to win if we—"

"Go back home to my parents to live? I'm thirty-nine years old."

She didn't reply right away. Her hand looked for a handkerchief between her breasts. Then she said, "Maybe you should listen very hard to your daughter."

"I'd like to."

"Courtney's stopped dreaming us," she said.

"So now we can go be someone else's dream." His voice was bitter.

"I don't have to tell you that's wrong."

"The goddamn world isn't ready to let us have our own."

She looked defeated. She got up and went into the bedroom and closed the door. His father stared after her, his expression both confused and annoyed. Then he turned toward Christopher. "Why aren't you at school?"

"I wanted to see what was going on downtown."

"I told you to go to school."

"I'm not going to go to school. I'm in trouble there."

"Why?"

"I skipped to go see Miss Lee when she was fired." That was the easiest thing to admit.

His father suddenly looked interested. "She left in an awful hurry. Did you see her?"

"On the bus."

"That all?"

"Yes. It was just pulling out."

"She could've phoned."

"Why?"

His father shrugged. "I don't know. Maybe just to say thanks."

"Dad, what if she was guilty?"

"It doesn't matter. It's how she was fired."

"And how you were fired too?"

"Yes." He turned away again and held out his hand to Sarah. "Show me the pictures you've done today."

"Don't you want to hear about the flood?"

"Is it bad?"

"Up over the tracks. They've got an engine running from the station to the bridge and back to keep the main line open."

"Come on, Daddy," Sarah said, dragging on his hand.

"That was quick thinking. Callaghan's a good man."

"The river's pushed the ice right up across the swamp to the flats and the yards."

The phone rang. His father looked uncertain for a moment and then went to answer it. Sarah stamped her foot. "*Daddy*." She ran into her room and slammed the door.

It was Harrison Dodd. Christopher could tell, because his father began to grin almost immediately.

"He what?" his father asked. "I don't believe it." And in a moment he put the phone's receiver back on the hook, without saying goodbye. "Laura," he shouted, "Courtney's going to have me arrested for theft."

She opened the door and came out into the living room again. "The truck," she said.

He nodded. "Absconded with city property."

"Take it back," she said, her voice cold. "Don't play games."

"I think I'd rather embarrass him."

"I'm sure you would. School Board Chairman jailed. Big laugh."

"Laura. Be serious."

"I am. Do you want to play the fool with him and Dodd? Will that make you feel better?"

After a moment, he said, "Yes, maybe."

"Then go and get it out of your system."

"Courtney's the fool."

"Is he? Or is it just people who play his game who wind up foolish?"

He went to her and tried to give her a hug, but she pulled away. "What do you want, Laura?"

"Stop being a stupid male."

"Am I?"

"Of course you are. Have you forgotten already what Courtney wanted?"

"No, I haven't."

"Then take the truck back to him and come home and—"

"What?"

"Leave, damn you. Start leaving."

He turned away, stiff and remote again.

"It's been a shock," she said, her voice kinder now.

He nodded. "Yesterday I had a job."

"And you were Chairman. Now you're an engineer again, and not a foreman. You want to fight? Fight for yourself, and us. We've been long enough crouching in this hole. It must be safe out there again. Surely by now—" She broke off talking and went into the kitchen. "By the time you get back I'll have lunch ready."

Christopher watched him nod and start for the door. He wanted to be with him. "Can I go?"

"Why?"

"Just for the ride."

"I don't think so."

"One last time in the truck."

"No," his father said. "I might see Courtney. Or Dodd."

"Will there be a fight?" The words were strange: this was his father he was talking to.

"What good would a fight do?" He began putting on his boots and coat.

3

He left the house soon after his father did, choosing to leave when his mother was out of the kitchen. He wondered if his own feelings were also his father's: a sense of failing, of no longer belonging to Long River. The whole family had been fired by Courtney, and now having to leave town made him feel in some basic way that they'd already gone. If he were again at the top of the jump on Castle Hill, he could imagine that the town's colours might already have faded, and even if its shapes hadn't crumbled, they might be less meaningful. The rink was there, but both the fun and the struggle to be part of it were alone. The school was there, but even it was no threat. It occurred to him that there was something about leaving that gave him power, the kind he'd always imagined, until today, that growing up would give him.

He was walking again toward the school, the place where his father wanted him to be. His job: to be a student and a boy, as his mother was a mother and a painter and his father a father and a foreman. But, still, he felt that going to school now was giving in and trying to belong again. Miss Lee had gone twelve hours after she'd been fired. Packed her bags and climbed on a bus. He saw her face again; it had already said goodbye and was pained to see him running after her. For what? To ask questions. His father had said that you grow up physically by just eating and sleeping, but you grow up in the head by asking questions—and by getting the answers right for yourself. He didn't want to belong again. Maybe he was following along after Purvis and was joining the Rink Rats. Maybe he'd quit school. This one, anyway. But Fielder was there, and Smith and Callaghan and Isonovich. It hurt to be cut off from them. And Emily. He looked up and she was shockingly there on the sidewalk in front of her grandmother's house. She wasn't looking at him, but was turning into the walkway that led to Mrs. McLeod's door. The sight of her stopped his breathing. For a moment he wanted to run away, and then he wanted to see her as much as he ever had.

He shouted. EM-I-LEE. The three syllables were his way of calling her: she would hear, know, look around. But she didn't. He began to run and wave. At the door she turned, and he ran down the sidewalk and up onto the porch. He stopped beside her and saw her watching him as if he were still at a distance. Then he realized that if she were only staring, he also had nothing to say, and it hurt. Her eyes were hard to look at. They didn't move or come alive just because they were seeing him. He had thought she would want to look at him as she had before. The pain forced words out of him.

"I didn't know what else to do."

After a while, she said, "Didn't you?"

He shook his head. "No." He couldn't say what he knew was right: that she wanted them to make love. Now, she might say, "Did you really think I wanted us to do it?" And he would be a fool.

But she had a question. "Did I do something wrong?" Her voice had tears in it.

"No," he said again.

"I want to know what happened."

Now his breathing was normal, after having run to see her. He thought: What happened was. After that there were no right words. He remembered getting up from beside her, but the reason he'd left was something he couldn't say. "You were lying so still."

"We were here by ourselves."

"It was a different feeling," he said.

"Yes."

"I know."

"But that was all that was happening." The tears were in her eyes now.

"Don't," he said, and tried to put his arms around her.

She moved fast, like a cat away from danger. "Don't yourself."

"Why?" The word got out before he could stop it.

"I cried," she said. "For you." He'd never heard her sound harsh before.

"I didn't," he said, helpless. "I felt—"

"I don't care what you felt."

"Dead inside." It was no relief to say the truth.

"All the way over here," she said, "I thought of how I'd kill you if I saw you."

"I didn't want to do that to you. Goddamn it, Emily—"

"It hurt," she said, and the crying caught up with her.

His mind slipped and held on to what it could. "Fielder could've got Pat in trouble."

"He didn't. She never knows when she's going to get the curse, and anyway they had nothing to do with us."

"She had Fielder wondering."

"She scared him."

"Why?"

"I don't know." She wiped at her tears. "They always looked as if they were going to have a fight any minute. She was smart. Mom and Dad thought it was okay. A couple of kids being normal."

"They only did it once."

"It was just scary fun. She got so tense about it that she laughed and giggled for the whole day after she found out she wasn't in trouble."

"We wouldn't have done it just once," he told her.

The door opened, first a crack, and then all the way. "Oh," Mrs. McLeod said. "I thought you two—" Then she saw Emily's tears. "Are you crying, Em?" She looked at him. "Come in, the both of you. It's cold out there."

"No." He tried to back away.

"Yes, you too. You'll have to learn some manners, Christopher Waterton." The Gaelic guttural that was usually soft in her voice had become suddenly strong.

"I was just going to school."

"At this hour? It's noon."

Emily said, "Gran, please, we don't—"

"We'll see." She smiled.

He couldn't walk away.

In the living room, she turned and stood in front of her chair by the fire. "Sit on the sofa," she said.

"I'd rather be by you," Emily told her.

"All right, but both of you be over here. Don't make the boy a stranger, Em. It's not anyone's fault, and don't blame him." She sat in her chair.

"I'm not," Emily said, uncertainly, and squatted on the hearthrug and then put her head against her grandmother's knees.

Christopher sat on the fenderstool and saw again how square and solid Mrs. McLeod was. The shadow of her lurked in Emily's build, in the way she stood and walked. The eyes, too, and probably the hair. "A McLeod of Lewis," his mother had said about the old lady. "They're as much like the rest of the Scotch as the moon is to a prickly pear. Shipwrecked Norsemen, probably."

She knew the old Gaelic tongue, but there was no one in Long River who used it. Her speech was not Canadian, but wasn't foreign either. There was no put-on elegance in her. The life she'd had to live from the time she was born until she was nearly forty hadn't made her gentle or mannered, but the last thirty years had been easy. Emily had said that one of the stories she liked to tell was about how she had been sent at six to the mainland, to a Presbyterian minister's manse, where she was to wash up, clean the house, and run for the Reverend's invalid wife. In return, she was to be taught to read. She wasn't. She came back home nearly a grown woman without having had a lesson. All three of her children went to university.

"You two were here when I was out the other day."

"How did you know?" Emily asked.

"Things were a little askew in the kitchen. I didn't think you'd stay for lunch alone."

"I didn't care if you knew."

"But that's when this thing happened between you."

"Yes."

She smiled. Her false teeth had gold fillings in one or two of them to make them look natural. She was still a little vain. "Em," she said. "A man will do strange things—"

"Just get up and leave?"

"Is that what you did, Christopher?"

"Yes." He couldn't look at either of them when he said it.

"Emily," she said, "could you say what would've happened if he hadn't?"

"Gone?"

"Yes."

"Nothing."

"Do you believe that, Chris Waterton?"

"No. It was different."

"How?"
"I don't know."
"Yes, you do."
"I don't want to say."
"Then we'll take it as said."
"I told her," he said. "I went dead inside. I couldn't hold onto the feelings anymore."
"He was scared," Emily said, not kind.
"Why?"
"A friend of his did it with a girl and they thought she might be in trouble."
"Weren't you scared, Em?"
She shook her head slowly, as if the question didn't mean much to her, and looked up at her grandmother. "No. It was something nice that was happening. New."
"A step along the way," her grandmother said.
"Maybe, but I don't think it was like what happened to you, if that's what you're driving at."
"Not in every way, that's for certain."
"Pat and I know about you," Emily told her.
"Yes."
"Nobody else has a grandmother who—" She stopped as if she'd come up against something solid.
"Who had a sod hut away from the village and entertained young men to see which one she'd marry?"
"Young men?" Emily grinned. "I didn't know there was more than Grampa came to visit you there."
"Your mother always wants the edges smoothed off life. I was surprised that you got to know at all."
"Daddy told us. Mother tried to say it was just a story."
He watched Mrs. McLeod glance away from Emily. "See this house?" she asked.
They looked with her.
"It's tiny," Emily said.
"The house Robert and I finally built was always too big," she said, "This one suits me fine. It reminds me of where I was born because it's small, but it also keeps away the bad pictures of where I grew up by being neat and clean and having cupboards always full of food."
"You starved," Emily said.
"Yes." The word was drawn out, as if she might be starting to keen. "At the manse there was the bottoms of bowls and scraps. I was six, I

was seven, I was eight. So small and helpless. But even so I might've been better off than some of the girls I left behind me." She straightened up. "Never mind, that's over, although it's always present in my head as a place with no light at all. You see? I'd rather talk about that than the other. But it was important, that starving. Girls who don't eat enough all their lives don't always have an easy time getting babies. So you can see one of the reasons we had sod huts where girls held court. When they were with child and could give a family sons they were married."

"I wouldn't want just anyone coming to my hut," Emily said.

"We invited the men we wanted. We chose. When almost every girl can have children, it gives the man the choice. Your mother had to wait for your father. She is his creature. I never was Robert's. I could've learned to read years before, when he did, but I wanted it to be in my own time when I felt right about doing it."

"You just stayed in the huts?" Christopher asked. "Like nuns?"

"There was work to do. I think if where our parents lived had been blessed with more than one room, we'd've courted there."

"But everybody would know," Emily said. "Wouldn't they tease?"

"They teased my cousin. She was an enthusiast; she never did know who the first baby belonged to."

"And you did?"

"I'd been eight years in the manse, and the fear of God was in me. I chose Ian first, and tried to think that was what God wanted of me."

"You didn't get his baby?"

"No. I asked him to go, and it was a year before my father could force me back to my hut. He was easy on me because I'd been cheated out of a mothering as well as reading by the Reverend. Then I chose David, and nothing happened. After a long time trying we were still without child. But by then I knew something of a man and of myself. That's not what your mother'd want me to say to you, is it?"

"She wants to send me to a private girls' school," Emily said. "The opposite of you."

"She's prim inside, that mother of yours, under all that rouge and high heels and silk stockings."

"You'll tell her I don't want to go?"

"I've never been able to tell her anything in my life, and your father was only somebody to be friends with if I could. But they're family, and so are you and Patty. I always thought that someday you'd find your old gran had a few things up her sleeve worth knowing."

"We've always been able to talk," Emily said.

"Yes, even when you've been busy with this young man."

"Later, Gran," Emily whispered. "Was Grampa next?"

"He came back from away because his sister died from trying to have her baby. He was eighteen and not married. I was nearly sixteen and the same. It wasn't love. We were leftovers. Peg's funeral was long gone when he got there, and he didn't quite know why he'd come home, except he loved his mother and hated the man he'd been working for."

"So, you didn't choose him."

"You could say that. Or you could say I did more than choose. I listened to him say there was a way out. I saw him and knew that he wasn't just another Ian or Davey who'd do what his father and all his grandfathers had done—work and drink and wait for their sons to grow up to look after them. It wasn't just a choice I made."

"But he went to the hut with you."

"Yes, my Em, that's true. He had infused in him by our people the need for the hut and a woman and the babies that would be his."

"Did you get his baby?"

"After."

"Why? You couldn't with Ian and David."

"It just happened."

"Uncle Matthew?"

"No, Matthew came years later. I lost our first one, a painful thing no bigger than my two thumbs. Matthew was born nearly twelve years after we were married and then Alan and then your mother came along when I was thirty-four years old." She sat back in her chair and clasped her hands over her stomach.

Christopher watched her face and tried to see in it why she was telling her story. A sod hut. No windows. Maybe straw on the ground inside of it, and somebody who looked like Emily doing it with Ian and David and Robert. It was crazy to think about. He wouldn't dare tell it to his parents. He thought about telling it to Fielder, but he knew he wouldn't. Whatever it was, it wasn't a joke, and it wasn't gossip.

"Now," she said, and sat up straight again, "that was just to tell you, in case your mother told you different—that your old gran wasn't a scarlet woman. The human race will do anything to keep itself in children, including going against the silly church. If there are no babies, there is no world."

"Why keep a place like Lewis going, if it was so poor?" he asked.

"The head will never give you the right answer to that."

"Just the heart," Emily said, as if she'd got the right answer to an examination question.

Mrs. McLeod laughed. "The heart's dumb. It works with sign language. Robert walked away too."

"After you'd been to the hut?"

"We were the odd ones. We knew that, but I didn't know him well enough to be sure I wanted to choose him. We saw each other— never mind, it's too long to tell. I chose him, and we were in the hut. He stayed a while. He kept his distance, and then he tried to come close, and I wanted him to. But then he walked away. I thought I was wrong in something I'd done, but I knew that wasn't true. I thought about it some more: Ian had hurt me once and had laughed. Davey cared only for himself; I might have been a sheep for all he knew what was happening to me. Robert hadn't gone after we'd tried for the baby. He'd gone before. I saw him the next day. He had the face of a man still puzzled by a conundrum. I could have told him then that the answer to why he'd left was that he truly liked me."

"Just liked you?"

"That was the best thing. We loved soon enough. He said he had things to do that weren't just babies and a dogtrot for the rest of his life toward the cemetery. We got married without me being with child. It made us free, and the boat we took was more than a month at sea before it got to Halifax. We were pretty well fixed by the time Matthew happened, and he was born in a bed Robert made specially for himself—long, because he was gangly like your mother, Em." She looked at her granddaughter. "Sometimes walking away is a good thing. It's hard to have grown-up feelings if you've got no way to be grown up. Your grandfather walked away, and he was only a long boat-ride away from being a man.

"Christopher could've said."

"Did you have the words?" Mrs. McLeod asked him.

He shook his head and tried to think of what he could say now to Emily. She was refusing to look at him.

"Em," her grandmother said, "going away wasn't telling you a lie."

"We weren't living on the Isle of Lewis, Gran, and I wasn't put out to work when I was six—"

"But you still have to marry when you get pregnant."

"Em," he said.

She stood and shouted, "Don't you call me Em."

"I've said too much," Mrs. McLeod said. Christopher got up from the fenderstool. Emily said, "You shouldn't've heard all this."

"I didn't want to come in," he said, and the truth of that made him feel he could look at her. She turned back to her grandmother once more, and there was nothing he could do but leave.

"It's all right, Em," Mrs. McLeod said. "There's nothing in that story I want secret."

At the door he found his jacket, toque, scarf, and mitts again and, when he turned to be polite to Mrs. McLeod, she was standing close. Her face was old and concerned. "What?" he asked, because she looked as if she wanted to say something.

"You got it half right." Her eyes were bright and kind.

"Half?"

"But you're not to mind. It's all even grown men ever do."

She didn't smile, so he knew she wasn't making fun of him. He looked over her head to see Emily, but she was gone from the room. Her shadow moved in the kitchen. There was nothing more to say, but he said Thanks anyway and opened the door. The cold that rushed in was less bitter than it had been an hour before. He told her goodbye and walked out to the street before he turned around and looked at the little cottage again. Mrs. McLeod was only just now closing the door. He felt a gentleness in that, and wondered why he was surprised by it. She hadn't taken sides, even though Emily had wanted her to. She'd told a story that had no sides to it either. There was something for Emily in it, and something for him: more gift than story. Emily didn't understand. She was angry at him, disappointed that her grandmother had treated him for a moment as if he were family, and she'd yelled at him for calling her Em.

"I love you, Emily," he said, out loud. The shock was electric, and it lit up kissing her, touching her, pictures with feelings he wasn't allowed to have anymore. He wanted to stop them, and to stop thinking of Emily. He couldn't. She appeared once more on the hearthrug with her head resting against her grandmother's knees. He sat on the fenderstool again and looked at her. "All the way over here I thought about ways to kill you." It was a terrible thing he'd done, to love her and to let her love him back.

The school bell rang, and it was an excuse to run and clear his head. The stairs at the south entrance were deserted when he got there, and so was the main hallway. He wondered if everyone had gone downtown to see the flood, or to help with it. He headed for the grade nine room and opened the door. Most everyone was there. Miss Garrett was standing behind Blenkin's desk. He hesitated, remembered that he hadn't been home for lunch and turned away toward the principal's office. He should phone and say where he was.

"Where are you going?" Miss Garrett called after him.

He glanced around at her. "I have to see Mr. Grandison," he said, because he didn't want to say he had to phone his mother. Miss Garrett looked annoyed and then, as if she'd had a second thought, fearful.

"Come back here," she said.

"As soon as I see Mr. Grandison."

She came toward him, one arm pointing at him, the other toward his desk. "Go to your seat, Waterton."

He thought only that she was being stupid. If she'd ask calmly, he would tell her he was going to Grandison's office to phone home.

And then the three of them were in the hallway together. He saw Grandison's glass eye glitter and heard Garrett's voice shout, "Christopher Waterton." Neither the eye nor the shout intimidated him now. He turned away from Garrett and said to Evil-eye, "Could I please use your phone to call home?"

"Miss Garrett has not given you permission."

"I came late. I wasn't in her class when I remembered I had to phone."

It occurred to him that Grandison looked weary. "Son, you go back now and—"

"What sir?"

"Deal with your request properly."

"I don't have to now." He didn't want her yelling at him. She stood by the door, hunched over her fists.

"What do you mean you don't have to now? You do, or you'll find yourself in dire trouble."

"Not any more." He stood, wondering what to say next.

"Young man, am I hearing you correctly?"

"Yes, sir. My dad's been fired and we're leaving."

"What did you say?"

"Mr. Courtney fired him and we're going to Victoria to live with my grandfather." He said it too fast; he was babbling, and he didn't want that.

"Because of Miss Lee? Miss Garrett, go back to your room."

She turned but didn't leave.

"Not just Miss Lee, other things too."

"He did the right thing about her," Mr. Grandison said.

Still Miss Garrett didn't leave; but she looked surprised at Grandison, and the hunch in her shoulders became more pronounced. Grandison watched a moment and then said, "All right, Waterton, you may use the phone."

Christopher crossed the hall and went into the office. It had a desk, two filing cabinets, and a first-aid box. That was all. He picked up the phone and asked central for his number.

"I'm at school," he said, when his mother answered.

"Well, you certainly aren't home."

"I'm sorry about lunch."

"So am I. Your father hasn't come home either."

"He hasn't?"

"He'll be along," she said. "Aren't you hungry?"

"No. I'm using Mr. Grandison's phone. I better go."

He hung up and turned to leave the office, but Grandison was there. "What does your father think about the flood? Is it as bad as it appears?"

"He doesn't want to have anything to do with it, or the town, anymore." He heard the anger in his voice. For himself, and for his father.

"That doesn't sound like him." Mr. Grandison looked away. Christopher had never seen him do that before. "The mayor may have been a little hasty—" He stopped and put a hand on Christopher's shoulder, and when he spoke, his voice was different too. The power was gone out of it. "I don't think your father will be long out of a job, Christopher. No healthy person over eighteen will be. The Czechs are overrun." His glass eye blinked and his good eye watered. "Hitler's on the march again. We're going to have to stop him." Christopher could see that he turned away without meaning to, distracted. He followed him out into the hall. Over his shoulder, Mr. Grandison told him, "Go on, boy, back to your room. You must learn to obey orders now." And the principal went down the stairs, perhaps to check the boys' basement for smokers, and to look in the girls' basement to see whether it was as neat and tidy as he expected young women must be if they were later on to be good wives and mothers.

The grade nine door was still open. He could see that there were empty seats: Pat's, the Dobroskis', Isonovich's, Fielder's, his own. Miss Garrett wasn't talking. The class was drawing an experiment in their notebooks. She came quickly to the door and closed it carefully behind her. Her eyes were stretched wide open, and her mouth was pinched at the sides. He wondered if she would speak at all. But she did.

"I lost my head, Christopher."

He knew he was nodding, agreeing, while he watched her begin to look helpless. "Yes," he said. "It hurt."

"What hurt?" Her voice was sharper again.

"My hands swelled up."

"Oh, the dynamo? Must I be sorry for that too?"

He saw the fear of what she was saying, to a student only fourteen years old, make her face look like a ruined doll's. "Yes," he said again, and this time the anger he felt was his own. It made him equal with her to show it in front of her, instead of being fearful of the power Grandison gave her. It was good to be going away. Already he was out of reach. But so was she. And Blenkin. Like Grandison, they'd stopped being teachers and were just people. He saw her slack lips kiss at Blenkin's forehead, her hand stroke his hair, and him looking as if she were hurting him, a child needing something and being afraid of it at the same time.

"Do you love him?" he asked, because now he could.

"Who?" she asked, on an intake of breath.

"Blenkin."

"Mr. Blenkin."

He waited.

"Yes."

"Are you going to marry him?"

She nodded. "If he has a job. You didn't tell Mr. Grandison?"

After Miss Lee being fired, she was terrified. He wanted suddenly to help. She was ugly. They both were. Who else would love them? But he couldn't let her go absolutely free. He wanted her to owe him. "No," he said. "I lied."

He saw her confused. Her body contorted. The little girl in it that he'd seen so often in class stirred, but when she spoke, her small bright voice deserted her. "Thank you." But she couldn't leave it at that. He tried not to smile when she primly told him, "After you're grown up you'll understand." Her eyes knew it was wrong to have said that, but she was able to go now, back off a step and then to walk quickly into the classroom, gesturing and crying out for quiet.

He stood at the door, not wanting to go in and looking for an excuse to leave. Maybe it would be better if he went away so she could be herself again. His seat was empty—had been empty since last Friday—and he wasn't being ordered back to it. Gradually there was silence, because everyone began to look at him, and so they all heard the explosion as if they'd been listening for it.

It crackled and then made a very big thump in the near distance and echoed, reverberated. It had authority. Very quickly he knew it was why his father had not gone home to lunch.

Mr. Grandison was behind him again. "Are you still out here?"

Christopher turned and looked up at Evil-eye. "That sounded like my dad is—" He stopped and began to walk away, trying to picture in his head where he'd be, and if he were safe.

The principal held his arm and turned him around. His expression was severe, but not unfriendly. "You're concerned, aren't you? Don't be. Don't worry about your father being a good and valuable man. He is."

"I have to see him now," Christopher told him.

"All right, go," Mr. Grandison said, and smiled around his fixed eye. "That's an order."

CHAPTER EIGHT

1

THE STATION WAS BUILT OF BUFF-COLOURED BRICK AND IT HAD a new black duroid roof. At the east end of its wooden platform was a fenced garden and, preserved in the middle of it, was old number 51, a narrow-gauge steam engine and coal car, used thirty years ago to help construct the railway. It was a miniature of 1410, the engine that was coming down the mainline track from the bridge. The engineer was ringing his bell and blowing the whistle at the same time. The water was receding from between the tracks in front of the station.

Christopher had run from the school, and now he stood breathing hard, with gouts of steam puffing out of his mouth twice as fast as the white clouds rising up around the whistle as it blew. The engine coasted to a stop.

There were maybe a hundred people waiting, mostly men dressed in heavy work-clothes. But some were in overcoats: merchants from stores up town, who had known too that the explosion was momentous enough to make them leave work and come here to watch the unfrozen water drain away down the slant of the track toward the river.

He'd thought there'd only be the crew and Mr. Callaghan and maybe his father on board the engine, but the cab was crowded. The Engineer, Tom Warden, set the brakes and blew the whistle one last time, and then he leaned on his elbows out the side of his engine and watched his passengers climb down the three long steps from the cab to the platform.

Last to get off were Mr. Callaghan and his father. It wasn't a surprise, but Christopher stood tall at the edge of the crowd and knew that he was smiling as he saw them get off and stand together as if they didn't want just yet to part company. His father was smiling, in a way he hadn't seen before.

The others who had come back on the engine waited near them. Roadmaster Callaghan turned to his Section Foreman. "Get the switches working. Chop them free, and then we'll try to use a plough to get the ice off the tracks in the yard."

"Lots of luck," his father said.

"We'll need it," Mr. Callaghan told him.

The nine-man section crew walked around the engine and disappeared from sight. The Yardmaster, the Locomotive Foreman, the Freight Agent, and the Dispatcher were all there now. Mr. Callaghan looked around at them. "Peter gets the thanks," he said. "That was one sweet shot he gave it."

Mr. Craig, the Yardmaster, said, "Hear hear," and the crowd applauded. Christopher could see that none of them knew his father was fired. Then Mayor Courtney arrived, and somebody shouted, "You're late, Court, what happened?"

The mayor joined the laughter. He had on his fur hat and coonskin coat and looked as if he was still at the Carnival. His nose was redder than usual, but his blue eyes had less colour in them than Christopher had seen before. Maybe that was because he could see who was at the centre of the crowd. His laugh faded to a grin, and he went forward to shake Mr. Callaghan's hand.

"Don't thank me, Peter did it."

Mayor Courtney didn't hesitate. "Since when has our General Foreman been working for the railway?"

"Since our powder man, Mendoza, went to the hospital with a burst appendix. Besides, the flood's as much yours as it is ours. You can shake Peter's hand."

"I don't think he's going to want to." Christopher watched his father's face close down around the words. "He fired me five hours ago."

"For Christ's sake why?"

"I'm not sure. For being over-educated is what he said, but I wonder if he isn't too old a politician to ever say the truth." He looked around at the crowd. It expected more. "Maybe it was for defending Miss Lee." He stared then at the mayor, and Courtney only put his hand to his hat as if to get it out of the way. "Or maybe—and I think this the most likely—it was because my wife didn't show up alone when he invited her to visit him privately at his hotel room this morning."

Christopher didn't know what the opposite of an explosion was, but his father had produced one, and it was as powerful as the shot that had cleared the river. Kroll, Sparks, Butterworth were there together. He recognized Brant and Sanderson, the contractors, standing with Mr. Creighton from the mill. None of them said anything, but Mr. Kroll's face flushed and he turned away. He started to leave.

"Just a minute, Kroll," the mayor said to him. "I want to talk to you."

Mr. Kroll faced him again. "I think you'll have to talk to a lot of people, Court."

"Peter and I had an honest disagreement. He resigned."

"Nobody resigns," Mr. Kroll said. "Not these days."

"Well, he did."

"His wife," Kroll said, his voice only a little astonished. "You never just beat anybody, do you?"

"I told you, he resigned."

"It's an idea you might consider yourself," Kroll said, and walked away.

Brant said, "Is it true? About Mrs. Waterton?"

The mayor hardly paused. "Paulson," he said. Christopher watched him put an arm over his shoulder "Sparks. Where's Sparks? I got a little project to discuss. Let's go back to the hotel." He broke away from Paulson and went on ahead, wallowing in important hurry.

Both Paulson and Sparks shook his father's hand, and then turned and left the platform. There was only one way back to the town. It was the same one the mayor was taking.

His father nodded, and Christopher watched the crowd stand stiff and then begin awkwardly to disperse. Mr. Callaghan shook his head and looked toward the mayor. "Pretty damned slick: how to advance while retreating in one easy lesson." But there was no need to laugh now at what Courtney was doing. Tom Warden blew the whistle—two blasts to signal that he was going to run west to where the switch frogs weren't frozen so he could try to make his way back to the roundhouse.

By the time 1410 was gone, the crowd was heading back up town. Christopher went to his father and, without thinking and as if he were five years old again, took his hand. It embarrassed them both for a moment, but then his father said, "Hi, Chris," and hugged him quick.

"I heard the shot at school, and I knew it was you."

"Come on up to my office," Mr. Callaghan said. "I've got a bit of the right medicine in my first-aid box."

"Yes," his father said, as if it were a decision a General Foreman would make.

"You don't drink," Christopher said.

"Only on occasions. This looks like one to me."

They walked around the station and up the stairs to the Roadmaster's office. It looked out across the yards toward the roundhouse and beyond to where the flood had come from. The ice was there. It looked settled, permanent, and scattered among the floes were the shacks and houses of the people who lived near the marsh and on the flats. Mrs. Kaplik's house was hidden in the trees at the edge of the swamp. He wondered if she'd got out on time.

"Christopher's getting big enough, but I wonder if he's old enough?" Mr. Callaghan was opening a bottle.

"Soon. Too damned soon," his father said.

They both smiled as if they wanted to let him into the space they inhabited, but if it was an invitation it was one he still didn't know how to accept.

"None for you, then, young man," Mr. Callaghan said. He raised his shotglass. "I don't know what you want to drink to, Peter. The future?"

"I think it's already here," his father said.

"I'm not going to drink to the war," Mr. Callaghan said, "but it's nearly here for certain, and we'll be in it. We're always spoiling for somebody else's fight."

They drank down their shots of rye, and Mr. Callaghan filled the glasses again.

"Is he in trouble?" Christopher asked.

"Courtney?" his father asked.

"Yes."

"Only if the people can keep remembering who he really is until next November. That's a long time."

Mr. Callaghan said, "Did you quit or were you fired?"

"Fired."

"The statement about your wife. You could have him arrested."

"In Long River?"

Mr. Callaghan nodded. "I'm glad I work for the railway. Maybe Kroll will stay mad enough to run against him. You could, too, you'd be a walkover."

"Nice of you to say."

"How did you do it?" Christopher asked. "The river."

His father didn't answer right away, and Mr. Callaghan said, "I love a pretty shot like that. I doubt Mendoza could've done it better than your old man."

"Then tell me, how'd you do it?"

"It wasn't just ice," his father said, "it was debris that had built up against the pier under the centre span. What you have to do is find the key log and blow it."

"He went down by rope," Mr Callaghan said, "with a pike pole and a nice charge of dynamite—about twice as big as I'd want to use alone—and he had a few kitchen matches in his pocket."

"You can't blow the key log by guess," his father said, his voice deliberate. "You have to feel for it, find out where it is by touch and get the dynamite under it. That's the kind of explosive we used—the kind that lifts rather than shatters."

"He found it," Mr. Callaghan said, "and jammed the charge under it with the pole, and I think I'll remember for a while watching you put the match to that damned fuse. It wasn't a foot longer than the pole. He had only about twenty seconds to get up and away."

"But you got up," Christopher said. The stupidity of the remark made him laugh.

"Hand over hand," Mr. Callaghan said. "He came up like a monkey and we headed across the roadway and the tracks to the other side of the bridge. When she blew, I thought, Holy Mother, the damned bridge'll go, but it didn't, and the next sound we heard was ice splitting under the water's pressure. and the flood began to be over. It was pretty just standing there and watching the channel widen north of the bridge and the jammed logs and old slash float in splinters south of it."

"I had thirty seconds," his father said, "and there were knots in the rope for climbing."

Christopher laughed. He couldn't help it. Everything his father did made sense before, not after, he did it. Then he thought of him coming home from the opening, and again in the morning after he'd been fired. There'd been no control; no sense then.

"We'll let you get back to work." His father held out his hand. "Thanks for the drinks."

They shook hands. "Sorry I can't offer you a job."

"No need. Things may open up down south."

"Hope so."

They were at the door now, and the awkward moment of leaving was nearly over. "We'll get together before you go."

"Yes, of course," his father said. "My regards to Mrs. Callaghan."

"And to your good wife."

They went down the stairs and out into the street. His father said, "I think this is it."

"What?"

"It's warming. The sky's clouded."

"It'll just snow again."

"I suppose. But it's time for this crazy weather to stop."

They walked up London Street. "Why'd you do it?" Christopher asked. "This morning—"

"This morning." He stopped walking, and they stood facing each other at the place where a few hours earlier Billy MacLean had kept the crowd back from the flood. He looked for a moment as if he was going to be serious, then he smiled. "If the bridge had gone out, how would we have gotten out of here?"

"You want to go?"

"Yes, I think it'll be easier now."

"I guess so," Christopher said, not knowing what that meant. He wanted to tell him about Garrett, but he wasn't sure he could explain it. "Are you going to do anything about the mayor?"

"No."

"Why?"

"The town's bigger than I am. Let it do the job."

"It wasn't bigger last week."

His father laughed. "I hate smart-ass kids."

"I'm serious. Ten minutes ago you said it was a long time till November."

"It is, but maybe by then the idea of opposing him will feel right."

He stood and looked up into his father's face. It was calm again, in charge. "Is it the same with Hitler? It's all right to fight him now?"

"You want that, don't you?"

"No. Except I do. It feels good when somebody does something about—"

"What?"

"Anything." He began to laugh. "Hey, you know, you just saved the town."

"Did I?"

"It would've been bigger time if it'd been in a movie, but you did okay."

"Thanks, Chris."

"If it'd been in a movie I would've seen you do it, and when the engine pulled into the station your girl would've been there and the sun would've been going down. It means something when the sun's going down in a movie. The end will be right after the hero and heroine have a long kiss. You should go home now and get yours, except you missed lunch and you might get bawled out instead."

"I don't think I'll go yet. I want to see Tindale about trucking our furniture to the coast."

"I'm going to the rink to see what's going on there."

"All right. But back to school tomorrow."

"Sure, if you write a note to excuse me."

"What is it now, three days?"

"Four."

They were going to walk in different directions. His father hestitated. "It's been a big four days."

"More like a week," Christopher said. "When are we going?"

"We'll take our time. Couple of weeks maybe."

"Not like Miss Lee."

"No, not like that." He turned up Third Avenue and Christopher watched him go. He guessed that at the end of one thing there was a halt before another began. For a moment they'd been close in a new way. But already there were other motions happening—in both of them. That might be how it was between men—coming together for endings, and emergencies.

Christopher walked away, not really wanting to go to the rink, and he was in front of Ch'en's when he heard Fielder's voice shout his name. Pat was with him, and Emily. He tried not to run to meet them.

"If I hear the story once more, I'll throw up," Pat said.

"What story?"

"About your father saving the town."

"How many times have you heard it?"

"She's heard it once," Emily said.

"And that's enough."

Fielder ignored her and looked serious. "Is he fired? Are you going?"

"Yes."

"When?"

"Two weeks."

Even Pat didn't say anything.

"I'm cold," Christopher said. "Can we go to Ch'en's for coffee?"

"We're broke," Fielder said. He had his arm around Pat.

"I've got a quarter," Emily said. She looked at him straight-on for the first time. "I didn't know you drank coffee."

"Only on big occasions," he said, "and this looks like one." He touched her hand, and then she let him hold it.

They walked back to Ch'en's, but before they got there a new white Studebaker rounded the corner and rolled down the street. May was driving, her face pale, her hands tight on the steering wheel. He couldn't believe it and ran out into the middle of the roadway and waved his hands. She jammed on the brakes. The car skidded, but it was stopped by its chains in the snow. When she saw who it was, she laughed and leaned across to open the door.

He bent down to lean in. It was beautiful: white leather and black carpets. "You weren't kidding."

"I love it. My God, it's better than money."

"Giving rides?"

"Sure. Get in."

"Fielder and the Gordons are with me."

"You might all die. The garage only gave me one lesson and now Ch'en's hiding in the kitchen."

He went back to the sidewalk for Emily. She looked unsure. "Come on," he said, high suddenly on everything that had happened today. He took her arm and pulled her toward the car. Fielder and Pat had climbed in the front seat. He didn't mind. "Get in," he said, "we're holding up traffic." He sat beside Emily on the back seat, and May let out the clutch and put her foot down on the accelerator. The rear end fishtailed once before the chains grabbed enough snow to move them off down the street, too fast.

Fielder laughed. "You mean it's yours?" He shouted as if May were a block away.

"All mine," she said, and made the corner onto Liverpool Street by using both sides of the road.

"When did you turn sixteen?"

"Soon. Don't bother me with details."

"The cops might not think it's a detail," Pat said.

"Let's go out to the airplane grounds and see what it'll do," Fielder said. "The goddamn speedo says it'll go a hundred and ten."

May headed west, doing forty past the police station. Fielder whistled and applauded, and Pat began to laugh. She slouched down in her seat.

"Jesus, a new car," Fielder shouted. He looked around at Christopher and Emily. "Climb in this thing and the bad times are over."

"Right," May said.

He watched the back of May's head, and then thought of Mrs. Kaplik. "May, did your mother get out all right?"

She nodded and, for a moment he thought that was all the reply she was going to give. Then she said, "You want to know?"

"Sure," Pat said.

"The house is a wreck. Gone. She was uptown, pissed out of her mind when the flood started. She wants to take Marie and go be with my sisters in Vancouver. Tomorrow on the bus. I can hardly wait."

"For good?"

"People who live in this place hate it, but they come back. I bet she will too." She grinned over her shoulder.

"Fifty," Fielder said. "Watch the damned road."

Christopher sat near to Emily and looked at the back of May's head. She couldn't drive. Not really. As long as nothing strange happened, they'd be all right, but if she had to get out of a jam, they'd wind up dead. Pat was laughing and fighting off Fielder. He was laughing too. The airplane grounds were around the long loop at the end of Plymouth Street, and then there was nearly a mile of straight road.

Emily sat very still beside him. Not tense. Just still, as if what she was thinking about were more important than the Studebaker ride. He turned to her and put his lips close to her ear. "We can't help it if—"

She put her fingers over his mouth and cut off his whisper.

"What happened?" she asked in his ear. "I mean, just before you left?"

He thought for a moment before he said, "Do you know?"

She nodded. "Maybe. I wanted us to do it so bad."

"Here we go," Fielder said.

"Oh, God," Pat pretended to cover her eyes.

"Sixty." May was laughing too. He'd never heard her laugh free before.

"I didn't know my body was going to do that."

He didn't want to talk about it. "That wasn't it."

"Yes it was."

"Seventy," Fielder said. His voice sounded as if he were cheering a winner.

Christopher heard Emily whisper, "I talked to Gran. She said that smell shouldn't be embarrassing. It just meant I was grown up."

"I'd grown up a long time before you."

"But, Christopher."

He could hear her struggling. "Say it. It's okay now."

"I wasn't supposed to," she said.

"What?"

"Grow up. I was supposed to be—Gran said—like a teddy bear for you." She laughed her soft laugh. "Something to dream with. Is that true?"

"Jesus, seventy-five," Pat said, awed. "That's enough. I've never been this fast before."

Fielder was laughing like a machine gun.

May gave it more power. Everybody but Emily knew she'd put her foot to the floor. He put his arms around her and didn't look outside the car anymore. She was stiff against him still. He whispered in her ear.

"It must be really fine to have someone like your gran to talk to."

"It wasn't my fault then?"

"You want it to be mine?"

"No."

"Eighty," Fielder said, tense now. "That's it, no more straight road."

May kept going. He looked up. Emily was paying attention now, and she was grinning as if this were a roller coaster and safe. The long gravelled curve at the south end of the grounds was easy to drive at fifty in the summer. He lunged forward. "May," he shouted. "Stop it. I don't want to die." He hit the side of her head with his open hand, and felt the power quit and the engine begin to slow the car.

"Easy," Fielder said. "No brakes."

He saw Pat shudder. Maybe she was laughing. The snow was banked high on each side of them. May was driving straight-armed, her head high, and he could see that she was grinning, even though he'd hit her. The corner came when the car was going fifty. It drifted out of the curve toward the snowbank on the left. May froze, the car slowed, ran along the bank, and May put her foot down on the gas again. The Studebaker leapt out into the middle of the road; she hit the brakes and the car went clockwise for a full turn and settled almost quietly in the snowbank nearest to the end of the ploughed runway. He felt Emily relax against him. The engine had stalled, and there was silence in the car because no one was breathing.

"Great," May said. She turned and looked at them one by one. "Jesus. Thanks, it wouldn't've been any fun by myself."

"Did you have to?" Pat asked. "That was plenty crazy. I loved it."

"That engine," May said, laughing again. "It can really make it go, hey?"

"And kill you too," Pat said.

"Sure." May pressed the starter and the motor fired again.

"I didn't even know what was happening till the end," Emily said.

"You two at it again?" Pat looked around.

"Always and forever, nosey big sister."

"For the next two weeks anyway."

"Hush up," Emily told her.

May put her foot on the gas and let out the clutch pedal. The Studebaker bucked, settled, the wheels spun and the chains sounded like bolts in a cement-mixer. Then it moved, caught hold of the ploughed part of the road, and surged forward. She slowed to change gears and kept it in second around the corner and onto the straightaway. Finally she changed to high gear and floated along at thirty. "I want to see where we been," she said. They all relaxed.

Christopher sat with Emily and watched Fielder hold Pat and kiss the lobe of her ear.

"Just friends," Pat said. She looked at him and smiled. Then she kissed him on the mouth. "Is that friendly enough?"

"Just about."

Christopher turned and looked at Emily. She smiled in the way he'd first seen her do it. He kissed her.

"Two weeks," she whispered. "I'm going to miss you."

There wasn't anything to say.

"Do you think we'll love each other in some way for a long time after?" She was admitting it was nearly over.

"Yes, I think so." He kissed her. "We don't have to split up now, do we? I mean we don't have to have it be us. After I'm gone we can say it wasn't just us. It was them too."

He wanted to look at her smile for a long time. This was near the end of something else. The quiet in him and around him was sad. He had to talk. "We have to do it, don't we?"

"What?"

"Go. . . . My dad says the future's already here." She hugged him and didn't answer. It was different between men and women. They stayed together, spared of endings. He didn't know about emergencies, but he remembered his mother and father last night and today: until it came down to dynamite, his mother had handled the crisis best.

He began to kiss Emily and then stopped. "Going makes this—"

"Precious," she said, quick. "What we're doing now is like we're already being a memory." Instead of being tearful, she laughed her small laugh.

"That's great," he said, and then he told her, "I love you."

She nodded. "I bet—in a way—we always will."

He felt released and sat easy against the backseat cushions. May was driving better now; her turns weren't skids. She was using the brakes with a lighter foot. They cruised through town. From Seventh Avenue, he looked across a vacant lot and saw Miss Lee's house. He said her name out loud, and May laughed. "Jesus, I heard about her and Purvis. Poor lady, she just didn't know how to live." She braked at London Street before turning down it toward Wei Ch'en's.

"Maybe she didn't," he said, "but how do you know until you've tried it?"

May parked in front of the cafe. Her cafe. None of them wanted to get out. On the sidewalk, going by, was Gabe Sommerville. He did a double take and then leaned down to make sure of who it was. Christopher opened the window.

"Some car," Gabe said.

"Thank you." May was awkward and pleased.

Gabe looked at him. "There's a benefit dance tomorrow night for the flood victims. You want to play a few sets with us?" He grinned big. "Give the band some class."

"Sure."

"No. I mean it. Okay? Come to the store and I'll give you some music to practise."

"Now?" He looked at Emily.

"Go on," she said, sounding as if they'd been together as long as Gabe and Irene.

He got out of the car and looked back at her.

"Phone me," she said.

"Can I?"

"They won't care now you're going."

"Then I will."

"I like what you said." she smiled.

"What?"

"You know. It was them too."

"What the hell are you talking about?" Fielder asked. He still wasn't moving to get out of the car.

"I'll phone you too," Christopher said.

"You better."

"Do you want a farewell party, Waterton?" Pat asked.

He thought about it. "You give good parties, Pat."

But this already felt like a kind of farewell. He thanked May and reached through the window to touch Emily's hand. Then he walked with Gabe toward the music store.

THE END

Sally Ireland

ROBERT HARLOW WAS BORN IN PRINCE RUPERT, B.C., BUT WAS brought up in Prince George where his father was Roadmaster on the Canadian National Railway. He flew as a bomber pilot during World War II, graduated from UBC with an Arts Degree in 1948 and then attended the University of Iowa's Writers' Program. In 1951 he joined the CBC, first as a producer and later as Director of Radio for the B.C. Region. Since 1965 he has worked with young writers as a member of the Department of Creative Writing at UBC. *The Saxophone Winter* is his seventh novel.

DOUGLAS & McINTYRE FICTION

SERIES EDITOR: RON SMITH

Fire Eyes by D. F. Bailey

The Watery Part of the World by Gladys Hindmarch

Hear Us O Lord from Heaven Thy Dwelling Place by Malcolm Lowry

October Ferry to Gabriola by Malcolm Lowry

North of the Battle by Merna Summers